“Shawn!” Jackie yelled. “Don’t give up!”

He blinked, as if coming out of a nightmare. Pain like he’d never experienced rushed through all his muscles. He fought to focus. Jackie lay flat on her stomach on the lake’s treacherous ice. She could plunge through right next to Shawn at any second.

“Put both hands on my pack and don’t let go,” she ordered. She twisted slightly away from him. The momentum pulled Shawn up enough to get his elbows on top of the ice. Jackie’s back arched, and she stabbed the ice with a stick end to anchor them. “Try to climb!”

He reached six inches past his first grasp. Jackie pulled on the stick and slid farther away. The strain it had to be causing her gave Shawn newfound strength. He would not let her die for him. Coming out of a frozen lake, threatening to pull him back in, proved to be the hardest pull-up he’d ever endured. His chest hit the ice.

Crack...

EDGE OF THE STORM

HEATHER WOODHAVEN

&

TANYA STOWE

2 Thrilling Stories

Wilderness Sabotage and *Vanished in the Mountains*

LOVE INSPIRED SUSPENSE

INSPIRATIONAL ROMANCE

Recycling programs for this product may not exist in your area.

ISBN-13: 978-1-335-43051-9

Edge of the Storm

Wilderness Sabotage
First published in 2020. This edition published in 2023.

Vanished in the Mountains
First published in 2021. This edition published in 2023.

For questions and comments about the quality of this book, please contact us at CustomerService@Harlequin.com.

Love Inspired
22 Adelaide St. West, 41st Floor
Toronto, Ontario M5H 4E3, Canada
www.LoveInspired.com

Printed in U.S.A.

CONTENTS

Heather Woodhaven earned her pilot's license, rode a hot-air balloon over the safari lands of Kenya, parasailed over Caribbean seas, lived through an accidental detour onto a black-diamond ski trail in Aspen, and snorkeled among stingrays before becoming a mother of three and wife of one. She channels her love for adventure into writing characters who find themselves in extraordinary circumstances.

Books by Heather Woodhaven

Love Inspired Suspense

Calculated Risk
Surviving the Storm
Code of Silence
Countdown
Texas Takedown
Tracking Secrets
Credible Threat
Protected Secrets
Wilderness Sabotage
Deadly River Pursuit
Search and Defend

Alaska K-9 Unit

Arctic Witness

Visit the Author Profile page at LoveInspired.com for more titles.

WILDERNESS SABOTAGE

Heather Woodhaven

As the Father hath loved me, so have I loved you:
continue ye in my love.

—*John* 15:9

To my husband: Thank you for being
my research partner and first reader. Your reactions
make writing all the more enjoyable. Love you.

ONE

Jackie Dutton flipped up the back collar of her navy peacoat to brace against the bitter wind. Her boots crunched over the thick snow, hours away from Boise—hours away from *any* city—in the middle of the mountainous desert terrain of southern Idaho. She would do almost anything to get a story. Unfortunately, her editor used the knowledge to his advantage.

She walked alongside Hank Swain, an older foreman whose face displayed the evidence of many years spent squinting into the sun. He led her around green and red shipping containers that unintentionally looked like Christmas decorations for the mountains. "We're talking about a two-hundred-acre project," Hank said, stopping next to a snowmobile. "So it's hard to give you a proper tour, but I think I've shown you the basics. We finished building that control structure, but as you can see, we've only started on the air-cooling assembly."

She glanced up at what looked like fans the size of airplane engines on top of fifty-foot-high poles with metallic ladders at every corner. "These acts of sabotage must be extremely upsetting for you and your crew," Jackie said.

"That's an understatement." The foreman gestured with his hand at the damaged crane. "We specialize in building at remote sites no matter the season. It's why we win most of our bids from government contracts, but winter weather makes the challenges harder."

"Isn't this a private contract?"

"No." He shook his head. "We're on federal land. Everything the McDowell Geothermal Company does is by permit and lease. Even the bid for construction had to be approved by the Bureau of Land Management."

From her rudimentary understanding, the geothermal plant was designed to drill down to the hot water underneath the ground and use the steam to produce electricity, making it a valuable renewable energy source—assuming the sabotage stopped long enough for them to finish building.

Swain spun around and pointed north. "We finished the access road you drove up on before the first snow, at least, but we can't afford to let sabotage slow us down."

The sun hovered low against the horizon of the surrounding foothills. Days ended even earlier up in the mountains, which meant she'd be driving in the dark if she didn't wrap up the interview fast. "So far, your equipment and tools have been targeted. Any ideas on who wants to sabotage your efforts here?"

He shrugged. "Off the record?"

How was she ever supposed to get a promotion-worthy story if everything was off the record? Jackie forced a pleasant smile.

He folded his arms against his chest. “Environmental groups get riled up every time anything is constructed. Some bird nest gets disturbed…”

No news there. The CEO and plant manager had given her the same answer on the phone. The foreman rounded the corner of the control building and led her back to her car. Except, she couldn’t go yet. She had no story.

“Would any of your crew be willing to talk to me?”

He shook his head. “Even if they were, they’re on the opposite edge of the site and should have wrapped up for the day.” He gestured at his snowmobile, sitting alone. “The closest place my guys can stay is a motel thirty miles away as the crow flies past that line of trees Would take them a couple hours if they drove it, though they get to go home to their families this weekend. Won’t be back until after Christmas.” The wind blew an extra hard gust. He glanced at the mountains to the west. “Speaking of which, I better go. They’re waiting for me. You should get, too. Radar says storms are coming.”

“Well, thank you and merry Christmas.” She felt his eyes on her until she got in her car and turned on the ignition. He moved to the snowmobile and took off in the direction of the in-progress drill sites.

She glanced at her phone. One bar of service flickered on and off. She quickly typed a message to her editor.

I think I could find a story here with more time. I'll need more interviews after the holiday. Don't expect check-in until Monday night.

The bar slid slowly across the screen, but she was unsure it would send until she returned to civilization. It was only Tuesday, but her cousin's wedding festivities started tonight and Friday was Christmas. She was overdue to catch up on family life. Afterward, she would have to return to interview the crew. The real story was never found by talking to supervisors.

Movement entered her peripheral vision. A man with a clipboard strapped to the front of his coat snowmobiled between tall columns she assumed were pipes. In her research, photos of similar geothermal power plants reminded her of a giant circuit board. Instead of capacitors and transistors, there were giant tanks of water and pipes. So if she could remember that her car was at the end of the long red pipe, she'd be able to find her way back safely.

She shoved her phone back in her coat, hustled out of the car and followed the trail of the man with the clipboard. Maybe she could wrap up the story and wouldn't have to come back to this desolate place after all.

"I told you it would bring more attention." A man raised his voice. Jackie couldn't see the speaker, though, as they were past the corner of the control building.

"This is what you pay me for." A second voice, deeper in tone and louder in volume, snapped back. "No one else had any better ideas."

"Well, you went too far. That detect—"

"That's enough. I told you I'd take care of it."

Jackie tensed and strained her ears. Was the first man trying to indicate a detective had been around? She didn't want her presence known quite yet.

"No. You're done," the softer-spoken man said. "Take your stuff and leave."

"I don't think so."

The wind carried a muffled groan and what sounded like a physical struggle.

"Fighting will only make it worse," the deep voice said, eerily calm. "You're dying either way."

The muscles in her stomach tensed at the threat until she could barely breathe. She pulled out her phone. Police would take too long to arrive if the closest city was an hour's drive, but maybe the foreman of the construction crew could turn around on his snowmobile fast enough. No signal. She didn't know if her text message from earlier had even sent.

She peeked around the corner. The man with the clipboard collapsed to the ground, his face devoid of life. The other man pulled something that looked like a syringe out from the man's shoulder—he had injected him right through his coat. He lifted his head.

She pulled back before he could see her. Her left foot missed the sidewalk and sank into the snow with a crunch. Nearby birds stopped singing, and the air grew heavy with silence. Even the wind halted. Had he heard her?

The crunching of his boots on the snow grew louder. The wind picked back up and made it hard to tell if the sound was coming her way, though. Should she bolt for it and risk being seen or hide? She pressed her back up against the building and sidestepped around the corner, taking care to stay on the shoveled sidewalk.

"A little tip," the deep voice announced, though she couldn't see him. "If you're going to hide, next time, don't leave footprints behind."

She glanced down at the cement. Like a wet stamp, the tread of her boots had left their prints on the sidewalk. And the only way back to her car would be to run past him. Of all the times to not have a cell signal.

She couldn't hear his steps anymore. Maybe he was on the sidewalk, too.

She continued to round the building. Her reflection, out of the corner of her eye, gave her pause. She peered into the windows of the building. No light, no sign of life, but the reflection revealed something else. The snowmobile that the man with the clipboard had ridden still had the key hanging from the ignition. She spun around. Her heart beat faster with indecision.

Another crunch of the snow convinced her. She launched off her back heel and ran for it.

"Hey! Come back here!" he yelled. "I just want to talk."

For a split second, she almost slowed down, but the dead body she ran past encouraged her to go faster. She flung her leg over the side of the vehicle and cranked the key. The snowmobile revved to life. Her bare hands covered the handles and twisted.

The vehicle launched forward, jolting her backward slightly, but she clung to the handles and leaned toward them. The man was too close to her car, so she guided the snowmobile around the monstrous construction area and pointed the nose of the vehicle in the direction the construction foreman had traveled. There were tracks in the snow and ice indicating where he'd gone. If she could find him, he would accompany her safely to her car.

A revving engine, twice as loud as hers, growled to life. She dared a look over her shoulder. A four-wheel ATV with giant wheels barreled her way. She focused on the tracks ahead, twisting the throttle of the snowmobile as far as it would go.

The tracks twisted around the construction equipment that bordered the cement pads and drilling equipment that had yet to be installed. They were harder to follow here. She turned into a clearing in between two sections of forest. The man on the ATV would overtake her before she reached the forest, and the foreman wouldn't be able to see her until she rode past the line of trees.

On the left side, next to the drilling pads, a rock wall a hundred feet tall rose up from the ground, a natural fence of the property. The foothills and forest stood in front of her. The murderer continued chase, leaving her only one choice.

She needed to outmaneuver him and get back on the road to her vehicle. His ATV may be fast, but the snowmobile handled sharp curves more gracefully. If she could get to her car with time to spare, surely she could drive away before his ATV overtook her.

She twisted her handle hard to the left. Except, he

swung wide and blocked her path. She revved the handles harder and headed for one of the foothills at full throttle. He'd taken away her options, and she'd completely lost sight of where the construction crew tracks had been.

She vaulted up and over the foothill. A thin crevice was ten feet away, running diagonal from southeast to northwest, hidden from her view until now. She gasped, all her breath suddenly gone. She twisted the steering as far as it would go so she wouldn't dive over the cliff. The crevice grew wider into more of a gorge. She rode parallel to it, straining her vision to see if the crevice had an end. Otherwise, how did the crew ever cross?

Ahead, another hundred feet or so, the deep vault disappeared and was replaced by more rolling snowy hills. She'd soon be able to cross over to the forest sections. The ATV quad motor behind her grew louder.

She glanced over her shoulder to gauge how close it was. A solid force punched her in the chest. Her head volleyed backward and forward before her body flew off the snowmobile.

She hit the snow hard and started sliding. Her fingers, stinging from the cold, tried to dig into the snow like grappling hooks. Instead, she slipped downward on an unstoppable path to the edge. Her eyes caught sight of the snow-covered boulder that had crumpled the front nose of the snowmobile.

A whoosh of air swept underneath her coat as gravity took her over the edge into nothingness. A scream tore from her throat. Her hands reached and grabbed blindly. Wood slapped her palms. She wasn't fast enough to grab the branch, though. Another slam of impact hit her, this time right in her stomach.

She couldn't breathe. As she slipped off the branch or root remains that'd caught her, her fingers gripped the knots. Tears clouded her vision as she swung, holding tightly. *Please let me breathe.* Lightning flashes of pain at her temples stung before she sucked in a huge breath and cried out. Never before had getting the air knocked out of her hurt so much. Still, she clung to the branch, gulping in air. The tips of her boots searched to find a foothold to help carry some of her weight, but she was too far away from the cliff.

The rev of an engine grew closer. Snow clumps tumbled over the cliff's edge. The cold hit the top of her head. She shivered and almost lost her grasp. "Please, God," she whispered. "Not again."

What was the use of trying? She was trapped, and the murderer had just arrived to finish her off.

Shawn Burkett jumped out of his truck. There was no time to lose.

He'd been on his way to check that Pete Wooledge, the field archaeologist, had left before shutting down for the night when he'd spotted a reckless ATV bouncing near the crevice.

Just past the land designated for the geothermal plant was a dangerous area without trails. Only the construction crew had special permission to motor in this direction, but they had strict instructions to follow the approved GPS and stay on the specified route until they reached the safer, groomed trails a few miles away.

Shawn had been ready to chase the driver down to write a ticket before he'd noticed the ATV was following a snowmobile. The moment the driver of the ATV spotted Shawn's approach he'd turned toward the trees, no doubt to hide. Maybe the man had been actually chasing the snowmobile, then.

There was no time to make a report to the field office. Whoever had fallen off the snowmobile had only seconds to spare before that branch gave way and they plummeted hundreds of feet. He grabbed his rescue pack and slapped it on his back. Normally, he took the time to examine the terrain and choose the best anchor before he rappelled off a cliff, but every second counted now. His movements were almost on autopilot, which could get him killed, so he fought to be fast but also mindful.

The rope slipped easily through the hubs of the back wheels on his truck, and within sixty seconds he had the harness, tether and backup extensions set. "Hold on. Bureau of Land Management law enforcement ranger coming to get you." He threw the rope over the edge. "Rope," he called out as a warning.

"I... I'm trying to hold on." A woman's soft voice drifted through the wind.

He pushed down the surge of anger. That driver definitely had been chasing the woman, then. But at the moment, the reasons why weren't important. He checked his carabiner and hitch before testing the rope slack and his grip. "I'll be there in a second. Stay with me. It's hard, but you can do it."

His morning and evening workout routine paid off

at times like these. Fitness proved the best defense against such a physically demanding job. He leaned back into nothingness and kicked off. The moment his feet first met air always provided a burst of fear and adrenaline, but growing up in the northwest, he'd spent so many hours rappelling that the motion was almost like second nature. The bottom of his boots reached and gently pushed off the face of the cliff. The sides of the rocky crevice held only the slightest bit of snow in the cracks with only a hint of ice on the parts that got the most shade.

The crack of a branch and a scream from below made his blood run colder than the frigid temperatures. "I'm coming. Hang on!" He slid the rope through his fingers. Too fast and he could lose control, but the woman might not last long enough for a careful descent.

He shoved his soles off the rock face harder than normal and soared down, his gloved fingers loose around the braking rope. His feet dropped right below hers as one of her hands slid off the branch. He gripped the rope tight and let go with his left hand as the branch snapped clean.

His left arm wrapped tightly around her waist and he pitched forward with the sudden weight. The branch narrowly missed them, and he thrust his right foot out to keep their heads from smashing against the rock face.

She gasped and reached for the sharp edges.

"I've got you," he said. "We're going to get out of this together." He shifted his head away from the thick brown hair that was currently in his face. "Grab on to my rope. Stick your legs out and let's balance on the rock. I'll hook us together."

"You sure you got me?" Her voice was steadier, a good sign, and somehow familiar.

"Yes, ma'am. Lean sideways into me, against me." He spoke in soothing tones in hopes she didn't panic or go into shock. "Good. Don't let go of the rope. When you feel safe, I'm going to remove my arm from your waist and fashion an emergency harness."

She turned her head to look at the ropes dangling from his harness and snapped her head up. Their eyes met. "Shawn?" Her voice rose an octave. "What? Why—"

His throat tightened with the same degree of shock in her voice. He studied her features as she stared at him, frozen in the awkward position. The same vibrant blue eyes that never missed a thing, the same mouth that could flash a smile to brighten the darkest of days and the same forehead creased in concentration. The Jackie Dutton he knew felt she had to understand literally everything that crossed her path. Why had someone been chasing her? "I'd like to ask what you're doing here, but—"

She nodded rapidly. "But we should probably focus on getting down safely first. I think it'll be easier if you let me help but continue to make sure I don't fall to my death. May I?" She reached across him and grabbed the section of free rope he had been about to unclip from his harness. She made quick work of wrapping the rope around her chest and looping it over her shoulders with a final knot in the center.

He examined her work, though she'd always been better than him. The daughter of famed reality wilderness star Wolfe Dutton, she'd grown up learning all the techniques her dad demonstrated in his *Surviving with Wolfe* TV series.

Shawn double-checked to make sure her knots were tight enough. "Is rappelling like riding a bike?"

"Hardly. Though when you get trained on knots and rappelling safety from the time you can tie your own shoes, it's hard to forget." She blew out a breath and pointed to the extra carabiner hanging from his tether.

He handed the item over and within a minute she'd adequately latched the rudimentary harness into his system. Snow began falling more heartily from above. An engine—no, multiple engines—revved loudly from above.

"Oh, that's not good..."

"Maybe the driver realized what had happened and recruited help."

"Trust me, Shawn. If it's the driver of that ATV, we don't want his help."

His forehead tightened. He really needed to know how she was forced into this predicament. Jackie would've never been careless enough to snowmobile without knowing the terrain unless it was an emergency. He adjusted his stance. "I'm going to let go of you now. Ready?"

She nodded rapidly, testing the grip, though he noticed she had bare hands and her knuckles were bright red. "Jackie, let me see your palms."

"I can do this."

Jackie had always bristled against help, but her determination could prove deadly if splinters hindered her ability to hold on. "Your palms are probably full of splinters."

Now at his side, she clenched her teeth. "We don't have time to argue."

More chunks of snow fell from above. Her eyes flicked upward. "Shawn, please tell me you didn't use your truck as an anchor."

"Do you have any idea how much that truck weighs? And there are chains on the tires. It's perfectly safe." He whipped his head around to follow her gaze. Hard chunks of frozen snow careened over the edge, barely missing their location. His truck slid forward. How? He'd put the parking brake on, he was sure of it.

"I knew it." Her voice shook. "They're coming to finish the job. Is there enough rope to get us all the way down?"

"Without making a new anchor?" The rope was four hundred feet long, but this particular spot in the crevice might be more than five hundred feet deep. The truck moved again, this time faster, as if being pushed to the edge. He didn't understand what was happening except for what would be the result.

His gaze searched the rock face wildly. Twenty feet to the left, he found what looked like their only chance. He pointed. "There. Can you get to that ledge?"

Her eyes widened in horror but she nodded. Shawn looked over his shoulder once more and understood her raw fear. The side of his truck hung precariously over the edge. "Now!"

He twisted and pressed off the rock face with his right foot. He reared back as far as possible. The momentum swung him forward like a pendulum. He grabbed the back of Jackie's coat with his left hand, pulling her farther out from the cliffs in case he misjudged the trajectory, to prevent her from slamming against the sharp rock wall.

She reached forward to the ledge with her arm and right leg outstretched. The moment her feet touched it, he also extended his feet, but more to serve as brakes. The soles of his boots hit against the ledge and stopped his trajectory. Except, a pendulum always swings backward. Jackie spun around as he fought against the pull. She grabbed the front of his harness and dropped her weight in a squat so he wouldn't pull them both off.

The way she tugged at his jacket forced his satellite phone up and out of its holder. The phone soared down just as he found his equilibrium. He never heard it hit the ground.

They both panted, clinging to each other on the small outcropping. "We made it," she whispered. The echo in between the two rock walls amplified her words. But that wasn't the only sound the echo magnified. The creaking of his truck reverberated once more as it was completely pushed over the edge.

"The rope!" Jackie searched him over. "Shawn! The knots!"

Every muscle in his body tensed. He'd knotted both ends of the rope for safety so even if he let go or fell, the knots in the ropes would save him. Those same knots would make sure they were dragged down with the truck. They would be snapped right down to the bottom and slammed into his favorite hunk of metal.

"Unhook yourself from me." If he was going down, he wasn't taking her with him.

"Don't be ridiculous." Their hands fumbled, both searching for the same thing on the rope. The ATC device prevented the rope from twisting or tangling when someone rappelled but also kept their harnesses attached to the rope. They had to get it detached. His thumb reached the carabiner and spun the lock with more force than he'd ever used.

Her hands grabbed the clip before he could and she squeezed. The device released and shot away from them like a rocket, carrying the rope down to the ground without them.

The truck spun in the air and hit the bottom of the canyon floor with a sickening crunch. As if to ensure Shawn understood the severity of his truck's demise, it continued to creak and groan. It could have been them, broken and mangled at the bottom, if they hadn't unhooked in time. "My truck," he said. "We've been through a lot together."

"Well, it looks like *we're* about to be through a lot together. Namely, how are we going to get down from here without getting killed?"

His gut twisted at her words. He was trapped on the side of a cliff with the woman he'd once loved and, judging by the way she looked at him, she still hated him.

TWO

The last time Jackie had been trapped in the wilderness was as a headstrong sixteen-year-old, ready to prove to her father that she was just as capable as her fraternal twin, Eddie. So she'd set out on her dad's trademarked wilderness survival test without telling anyone.

Everything was fine until she'd come across a mountain lion that scared her, ironically, right off the edge of another cliff. She'd found an outcropping, complete with a cave, and tried not to spook the nesting bats as she'd waited, with a broken arm and twisted ankle, for twenty-two painful and terrifying hours until search and rescue found her. Waiting to be rescued while injured had been the last straw.

Never again, she'd told her parents. Never again would she go camping or backpacking or hiking. It didn't matter that the test had been her idea. She wouldn't so much as participate in a campfire in the backyard with s'mores.

She'd experienced her fill of survival training her

entire childhood, and it took waiting with a broken bone to realize she never wanted anything to do with experiencing the wild again, even if it was the family business. Besides, she'd grown tired of trying to earn her dad's approval. She wasn't good enough, so why bother trying?

And now she found herself on another impossible ledge, in front of a man who had broken her heart. Was this God's way of making sure she didn't hold bitterness in her heart? *If I forgive him, Lord, can we speed things up and get me out of here?*

She'd *thought* she'd already forgiven him, though. He still looked like the young man she'd once known so well. His golden hair was cropped close to his forehead instead of thick and wild, and the hazel eyes still held the same mysterious intensity. She never could guess what he was thinking.

How many years had it been since he'd betrayed her family? But he'd rescued her today and put himself in danger. When he'd realized the knots would drag them both down, he'd wanted her to save herself. He wasn't supposed to be here, either. Idaho wasn't part of his life plan. There had to be a story there.

The static of a speaker caught her attention and Jackie held a warning finger to her lips. The acoustics in the canyon were amazing, and she didn't want to risk giving their location away. She shifted, pressing her back against the rock wall. Shawn followed her example, though his right eyebrow seemed to be frozen in a questioning arch. The cliff above their heads jutted out like a roof. She hoped, given the angles, that they were shielded from view.

"Update?" a voice asked through the phone.

"What should I tell him? Think we got them?" The man's deep voice carried. Jackie had a hard time telling with the wind, but she was fairly certain that was the murderer.

"I can't see that far down with the sun setting, and I'm not willing to get any closer to the edge," another man remarked. "Tell him we're done."

The static returned. "All clear here," the deep voice said. "Over."

"Over," came the reply.

"If they aren't dead, they will be once the storms hit," the other man said.

"Let's finish the job and then I'll make sure of it later. Come on."

The ATV engines roared again. Only after the noise faded into an eerie silence did Jackie feel safe enough to speak again in a whisper. "How are we going to get out of this, Shawn? Did you hear them? They're going to check back to make sure they finished the job."

"I don't understand anything yet." Shawn turned to face her. "Who are they?"

"All I know is I witnessed a murder at the geothermal plant site. I don't think they want me to be able to tell the police." She waited a beat for some kind of response, but he seemed deep in thought. "They want me dead, Shawn."

"What?" His eyes widened. "Is that why he was chasing you?" He exhaled. His expression changed as if he'd suddenly put on a law enforcement hat. "Start from the beginning. What exactly happened?"

"I heard one of those men—I think the one with the deeper voice—arguing with an employee. At least he drove a snowmobile and carried a clipboard, so I'm assuming he's staff. The employee was upset with the man about a detective." She pointed to her shoulder. "The guy killed the employee then. Injected him with something."

Shawn paled and his gaze flickered to her hands. He took off his gloves. "Put these on."

She hesitantly accepted. Her fingers felt like icicles, freezing and brittle, as if any impact could break them. "Thank you. As soon as my hands warm up a bit I'll give them back." She closed her eyes in relief, even though the pain of splinters still begged for attention.

"The good news is that what you've described hasn't included a gun."

She opened her eyes and realized the significance of Shawn's words. "He wants to make the murders look like they're accidents."

"Well, we don't know that, but the injection and pushing a truck off the cliff seems to lean that way. We can hope they aren't armed." He lifted the hem of his jacket and checked the belt at his waist. "We may have lost my satellite phone, but at least my gun holster is made of sturdier stuff."

"Was that what I knocked out when I grabbed you?" She cringed. "I'm so sorry."

"I can't complain. You were saving my life," he said.

"Which was only necessary because you were saving mine." The setting sun cast a shadow on his strong jawline. She gestured at his holster. "Is it loaded?"

"At all times." He leaned forward, ever so slightly. "They were right about one thing. If we don't find a way out of here, the blizzard heading our way will hit us."

"Blizzard?" To reach that classification, temperatures had to drop below ten degrees and sustained wind gusts would be over thirty-five miles an hour, at minimum. Not to mention the massive amounts of snow usually involved. In other words, they were facing the possibility of death either way they looked at it. "I don't know if my boss ever got my text, but I'd told him not to expect to hear from me until Monday night at the earliest." Six nights in winter conditions… They wouldn't be able to survive.

"What about friends?" Shawn asked. "Relatives? Anyone expecting you or know where you've gone?"

She opened her mouth to reply and stopped. She stayed busy, with a full work calendar at most times, but she rarely committed to social events. If she attended, it was always as a last-minute decision. That way she didn't disappoint anyone if it didn't work out. "I want to come, but don't count on me," she'd often say. In the early days of her career, she'd made the excuse because she didn't know when a story would demand her attention. Now she didn't work under such short deadlines, but she'd grown accustomed to the benefit of no expectations.

In fact, she'd asked her cousin if it was okay to be flexible about her coming to the wedding. Since it was a family-style dinner reception, her cousin was fine with it. Even her parents didn't know she was coming. Jackie thought it'd be a fun surprise and then she could join them for Christmas.

Now the plan seemed more foolish than fun. No one would miss her presence for days. And in front of Shawn, admitting that proved hard to do. "No," she said softly. "No one will be expecting me until Monday night. What about you?"

Shawn blew out a long breath, the air producing a giant cloud of fog in front of him. "I've already put notices on the exits to the land. We close in the event of severe weather. The radars said multiple winter storms will hit before the blizzard camps out here a few days."

She shivered and her teeth chattered, not so much from the cold, but from despair. The thought of having to survive in a blizzard on a ledge in the mountains with her ex-boyfriend was too much. "Wait. Won't they be worried and look for your truck if you don't call in?" She pointed at the logo on his jacket. "Surely the Bureau has a helicopter. They'd spot the vehicle immediately."

"Jackie, I'm responsible for four million acres. Spotting my broken truck hundreds of feet below—in a relatively thin canyon—is not as easy as you might think. Especially if it starts snowing." His shoulders slumped. "Besides, I already told the field office I would make sure the field archaeologist was done taking samples for the day and escort him out of the park before heading home." He spotted the question in her eyes before she could ask. "But I didn't let the archaeologist know. He's probably gone for the day by now."

He leaned his head back and sighed. "I was also keeping a lookout for a missing hiker, but his brother claims he's in a different region than mine. The point is that I've signed off for the day."

"Anyone in—" She hesitated for a second. "Is there someone in your life who will send out the dogs if you don't get home?"

He cleared his throat. "No."

So he was single, too. Not important given the circumstances, but she had so many questions. She told herself it was the nature of her job rather than interest in him, but she should still slow down. "Thank you again for saving my life." Her throat tightened. "And I'm sorry I got you into this."

"It's my *job* to save people," he answered.

The message seemed loud and clear. She shouldn't attach any feelings to the fact he'd saved her life. It was business as usual, for him. "Ranger Saves Reporter," she muttered.

Both his eyebrows jumped.

"That's what the headline will probably say. When we get out of here," she added. Positive thinking was the first step to survival. "Any food or water in your pack?"

He shook his head solemnly. "Everything in my survival kit was in the truck."

Her heart still pounded at an uncomfortable speed. She knew what needed to be done but wanted time to gather her wits. Out-of-the-box solutions often came with a little reflection. Except she could feel Shawn's gaze, studying her. "I really didn't expect to see you here," she said.

He barked a laugh. "You and me both. Possibly the understatement of the year." He offered her a kind smile. "BLM law enforcement rangers usually get stationed in California to start. It's a competitive field, but I'd been waiting for a spot in Idaho for a few years."

"My dad was under the impression you had no intention of ever coming back." She closed her mouth in a tight line. She shouldn't have even said that much. Shawn had been their neighbor and probably spent more time at her house than his own. He had been best friends with her brother, and they'd all grown up together. Her parents had practically treated him like an adopted son until graduation night, the last night they'd seen him.

His neck reddened and the little muscle in his jaw flexed. He avoided looking in her direction. "My mom remarried and moved to Sun Valley. I thought it'd be nice to be in the same state again."

"Sun Valley? Wow. A resort town." The beautiful and expensive vacation area was roughly four hours away in her estimate.

"She's living the life she always wanted. I'm happy for her." This time a small, genuine smile appeared, but it vanished the moment another breeze whistled past. "We can't afford to wait here until help arrives, Jackie."

"I know." She sagged, not fully recovered from the trauma of believing she was about to fall to her death. And when Shawn said her name, he exposed an internal vulnerability she didn't realize she still had. He knew her, and while she'd changed a lot over the years, her weaknesses were still there. "I haven't done this type of thing in ages, and my arms…"

He looked over her face. "Are you hurt?"

"No. Forget it." She didn't want to whine, and his close attention wasn't helping her heart rate normalize. She worked out every other day, but she never pushed herself to the extent needed for survival skills. Her muscles hadn't felt this depleted since she was a teenager.

A shadow moved over the crevice. The sun began its disappearing act behind the foothills at an alarming rate. Soon, they'd have no choice at all. "Okay, let's say we figure out a way down. Then what?"

The creases in his forehead deepened for a moment. "There's an extra satellite phone kept in the archaeologist trailer. If we can make it to the trailer tonight, I'm sure we can get picked up before the storm hits. If not, at least we'd have some shelter for the night."

"Yeah, that sounds wonderful, but how do we go about that? Looks like we have at least a five-hundred-foot drop to go, and the rocks look too slick to climb down by hand."

"It's too bad that man didn't run your snowmobile off on the other side of the canyon."

She couldn't stop from rolling her eyes this time. "Oh, well, I'll try to make my imminent death more convenient next time."

He laughed and pointed directly across from them. "There's a closed trail on that side that leads up and out into the forest—dangerous to the novice but still usable."

Hope surged. If there was a trail, then maybe they really had a chance of getting out and calling for help. "Okay, so all we have to do is get five hundred feet down as darkness closes in on us. Without dying first."

Shawn recognized the frustration in her tone. She blew her dark hair out of her face once more. He had a feeling she did it without thinking, but it gave him an excuse to really study her features. She turned and he averted his eyes from her face. Her navy peacoat had scuffs and bits of bark stuck to it, as well as a white stain on the hem edging that looked fresh.

She sighed. "We have to do something I haven't done in over a decade." She put her hands on her hips. "We have to ask the question we were trained to ask during every survival training."

He almost groaned aloud. His memories of Jackie brought him regret, but they weren't unpleasant. Her dad, a man he'd once considered his greatest role model, had erased every good memory when he'd shoved a finger into Shawn's chest and told him he never wanted to see his face again.

But now he was a trained law enforcement ranger, although he'd not been without his satellite phone as backup for ages. Still, he didn't need to go back to basics. "I really don't think that's necess—"

"Here goes." Jackie straightened with a nod. "What would Wolfe Dutton do?"

The name alone caused the back of his shoulders

to tense. "He's *your* dad. I think you can answer that question better than I can."

She studied the rock wall as if she'd suddenly gained new perspective. "You have more rope in the bag with you?"

He twisted and pulled the bag off his back. "A two-hundred footer, but we have no way of using it to rappel down without a way to link the harness to the rope. We're also without installed anchors for climbing." He unzipped the bag to show her his measly backup gear.

She pulled his gloves off and opened her palm. "Didn't Dad or Eddie ever teach you how to rappel when you only have a rudimentary rope and two carabiners?"

He gaped. She couldn't be serious. Off a twenty-foot hill, sure, but jumping down a canyon? "No," he finally answered. "But your brother always said Wolfe taught you more than he ever taught Eddie."

"I don't believe that for a minute." She took the rope from him and didn't waste a minute tying knots in strategic locations. "I suppose he treated us differently, but I can see plenty of benefits that Eddie had that I didn't. I also watched the television show. I think I was the only one in the family that actually did. It was easy to get my dad talking about everything behind the scenes. Eddie was just too busy with his video games." She gave Shawn a side-glance. "With you."

He shrugged. "We had galaxies to save."

"Well, I'm sure Eddie was with me when he taught us this." Her hands moved fluidly, wrapping and pulling, despite the redness evident on her knuckles. She always talked rapidly when she wanted to avoid something that stressed her out. At least some things never changed.

She tied the last knot and beamed. "If I could figure out the reasoning behind why he did things a certain way, then I could remember the technique. I suppose that's why I'm a journalist. I can't stop asking questions."

Any warmth left in his body seemed to drain away. "You're a reporter? For a TV station?"

She tilted her head and eyeballed him with suspicion. "No, I mean I used to be. But now I write for the *Idaho Gazette*, based in Boise."

"Oh." Maybe her coming here was a coincidence, but he had to be sure. "Then why are you here?"

She moved to tie the rope concoction into her makeshift harness. "My editor sent me to cover a story about sabotage at the geothermal plant being built. Surely you know about that. It's just a mile or so north of here. Probably part of your four million acres?"

Of course *he* knew about it. "But how'd your editor hear about that?" He tried and failed to keep his voice light.

She squinted at him. "Why? I never knew you had an investigative streak in you."

"You like to talk when you're stressed about something. I'm just making conversation."

"It's been years since we've known each other, Shawn," she said quietly. "You don't know if I still do that. People change. And this seems too pointed for conversation."

"Fair enough. The sabotage wasn't public knowledge. Please just tell me, Jackie."

She handed him an end of the rope and indicated he should tie it to his harness as she answered. "A former coworker is the news director at Channel 7. He sometimes passes along nibbles they won't be using. This was an anonymous tip they didn't have space to pursue." She pursed her lips for a second. "Why? Was the sabotage confidential?"

His gut churned and threatened to cause problems. He shook his head. He had to come clean. "You're here because of me."

"What are you talking about?" She stared at him, her eyes wider than he'd ever seen. She dropped the rope and held up a finger. "If you think *I* followed you here as some ridiculous ploy to get your attention, you are sorely mistaken. And if you think I've been keeping tabs on you all these years, you're also wrong. I was genuinely surprised to find you here. In fact, you can rest assured that I've gotten over you, utterly and completely. I haven't given you a thought since—"

He held up his hands. If there were more room on the ledge he would've taken a giant step back. "Jackie, that's not what I meant." His eyebrow rose, replaying her words. "Not a *single* thought?" He couldn't say the same about her, but that wasn't fair. "No, don't answer that. I meant that it's my fault that you're here. Is this off the record?"

Her shoulders sagged. "I get so tired of that question. If we are talking about personal matters, you don't even need to worry."

"But I think this is about your story. Off the record," he said again, despite her exasperated sigh. "I called in a tip about the sabotage at the geothermal site."

"You did *what*?" Her eyes softened. "To get me to come out here?"

"No." He blew out a breath of frustration. He was handling this poorly. "A few days ago, I called the TV news station. I didn't know it would end up in your hands, and honestly, I didn't think they would send someone out all this way to report on it. I thought they might call the BLM Idaho communication director, get some phone interviews, slap a stock image of the area on the screen and give it a ten-second sound bite. Once the issue became public, more resources would be sent."

She stared at him, her eyes widening. "First, that's not how this works. Public lands are a hot topic in Idaho. Many think they should be returned to the state."

Shawn shook his head and gestured past the thick patch of evergreen trees to the south of the gorgeous mountain backdrop. "Much of this is considered uninhabitable. The fact of the matter is the state couldn't afford to take care of it. We lease the resources and the state gets half the proceeds. It's a nonissue."

"That's not the point. If there's potential for a hot breaking story, they send a journalist." She tapped her index finger to her chest, and then tilted her head as if to study his reaction for a second. "Why were you so worried about the sabotage? Surely you took it to your supervisors first?"

"Still off the record?"

She rolled her eyes. “Yes.”

His face stung, likely more from embarrassment than the cold. “I wondered if the saboteurs knew something that the impact and feasibility report didn’t cover.” He suddenly felt very awake, having said it aloud.

“Like?”

He grimaced at the dimming light. They still needed to get all the way down and then climb all the way back on the other side’s trail. “Let’s get moving and I’ll tell you on the way down.”

She bit her lip with a nod. “I suppose I might be procrastinating.” She took a deep breath. “Okay. We take the center of the rope and wrap around this boulder that juts out. We tie eight gathering knots. One of us goes down first and finds a suitable anchor before we stop. The other person starts working their way down, pulling on the left side of the rope until one half of the knot pops, then the right half of the rope until it pops. You’re essentially untying each knot until you’re out of rope.”

His gut flipped at the thought.

“It’s imperative you keep the ropes balanced until you reach me,” she added.

“No wiggling,” he said, trying to keep his voice light.

“And remember it’s important that you count correctly.”

“Or the knots will all come loose and we’ll plummet to our deaths. Got it.”

Her grave expression left nothing to imagination. “I’m sorry. That’s the only way I can think of to get the rope back down to us so we can retie and start again." She shook her head. "How about you go first? I'll do the untying of the knots on the way down."

"Absolutely not." He wouldn't give her the riskiest part of the job. As he'd just told her, it was his job to rescue, not the other way around.

"Shawn, I've never done this technique on my own, and I'm not even sure I remember it right."

He sneaked a peek over the ledge once more. Five hundred feet was a low estimate. Even if her technique worked, they would have to find rocks or branches that weren't slippery from the snow and could hold their weight at least four more times. He grimaced. "I'd rather die trying than wait for a blizzard and a murderer to finish us off."

She removed her cross-body purse and handed it to him. "Could you put that in your pack?"

He did so as she removed her navy peacoat, revealing a gray ribbed sweater and tan dress pants that appeared way too thin to be out in the elements for long. Even her suede boots looked like they were more for fashion than function. She tossed the coat over the ledge.

"What'd you do that for?" His voice rose louder than he intended. Hopefully the wind carried his outburst the opposite direction of wherever those men went.

Her teeth began to chatter, but she threw the end of the rope over her shoulder and around the inside of her left leg. "It would be too easy for the coat to catch on the rope, and it's too big to fit in your small pack. I'm hoping it'll be waiting for me at the bottom. Your coat is short enough that it should be fine, but—"

"Take mine, then." He went to unzip but she held her hand out.

"No. Your arms are too long and it would impede my ability to handle the rope. But now that I think about it, you should put your gun and—is that a Taser?—in your pack."

"Standard issue," he simply replied. He did as she asked without argument in hopes they could get her down and warm again as fast as possible. The temperature hovered in the low thirties, but the wind made it feel colder. "At least put my gloves back on."

She accepted with a sheepish smile and replaced her holds on the rope. "Guide my descent slowly." Her head vibrated with shivers. "But not too slowly. I'll yell out when I find the next place to anchor." She closed her eyes as if lifting up a prayer, then flashed him a quick smile and leaned back until she fell off the ledge.

THREE

The work of going down a cliff without proper equipment made the descent tedious and grueling. They worked together without dialogue, communicating only what they needed to. Shawn counted aloud each time a side of the rope lost its tension, meaning it'd given up half a knot.

Thus far, their plan had worked. She'd found another foothold to balance on while he descended to join her. The muscles in between her shoulder blades were screaming, though.

On the fifth time repeating the descent—since the drop turned out to be a lot deeper than she'd estimated—his foot slipped off a rock hold. She could feel the popping of the knots within the rope as it vibrated from above. He was descending too fast. And there was nothing she could do about it.

He tapped his feet against the wall as he tried to catch onto something, attempting to slow down, but he dropped down past her.

"No!" She reached for him, letting go of the rope

with her right hand, a disastrous decision. She no longer had anything to hold her steady. She dropped like a stone.

Right onto his stomach.

He groaned and rolled to the side.

She fell to her knees on the snow-covered ground and spun around. “I’m so sorry.” She studied him for broken bones in the dim light. “Are you okay?”

His frown shifted into a beaming smile, and he patted his jacket. “Padding.” He laughed. “Good thing we were so close to the ground.” His smile was contagious.

She leaned back onto her heels. “I can’t believe we did it.” The physical effort had caused a sweat, despite her lack of a coat, but she was ready to find it before hypothermia became a risk. And now that the sun had almost disappeared, the temperatures would plummet well below freezing. Only, she didn’t see her coat anywhere.

Shawn caught her gaze and rose to his feet. “I was afraid of that. The wind might’ve caught it like a kite in the canyon.” He removed his coat. “I insist this time.”

Underneath, he wore a long-sleeve button-up shirt the same shade of khaki as his official jacket, with dark brown pants and trail shoes. She’d never imagined he’d gained so much muscle after high school, but all evidence of childhood had left his face. His broad shoulders strained against the seams.

He draped his coat over her shoulders before she could object. Even more than the gloves he’d loaned her, the coat radiated with his warmth. Except the sudden heat served to inform her internal thermostat what she'd been through. Her teeth chattered. She couldn't seem to get warm enough.

Shawn put his holster back on, complete with gun on one side and Taser on the other. He pulled out his cell phone and grimaced. "Still no signal. I'm going to turn it to airplane mode and so should you. The battery drains faster if it's constantly searching. We'll try again once we reach the top."

She checked. Sure enough, no signal.

He stuffed the rope into his backpack before he straightened. "Come on. The light is almost completely gone. The trail should be somewhere nearby." He stopped at a set of boulders on the other side of the canyon. "Found it."

Her eyes followed the steep incline of the trail that barely made an indentation in the side of the dirt and rock wall. No wonder they'd closed it off.

"I think we should stay close. The light is dim and I don't want any missteps." He reached out his hand for her to hold. "Just in case."

"If I fall off, I don't want to take you with me. You broke my fall last time, but if it'd been far—"

"I'm the law of the land around here." He winked and she knew he wasn't serious, but the edge to his voice made it clear he wasn't in a mood to argue. "Let's get to safety."

She placed her left hand in his and followed him. He had a giant sweat stain in the middle of his back, evidence of the physical strain he'd endured. "Think I can use my phone light to—"

"If we're dealing with a murderer, I don't think we

can risk drawing any attention to our location, especially down here without any camouflage." As if to highlight his point, the sound of engines carried with the wind. Above, somewhere on the top of the cliff, two beams of light bounced around, shining into the darkening skies. The lights seemed to be from a bigger vehicle than an ATV or snowmobile, though.

"Do you think they're friend or foe?" he asked.

"Well, either way, we should get up and find out. Right?"

He turned around to face her and reached for her other hand. "Hang on. There are some iffy spots, and with the snow..." His voice trailed off as he helped her up and over a boulder until they were standing side by side again. He dropped her other hand and turned back to the trail. His pace was fast enough that she struggled a little to keep up.

"You should take the gloves back, at least," she said. "I've got your coat."

"I'm fine." His foot pushed through the snow a little too forcefully and she could feel his balance shake. She squeezed his hand tighter and pulled back as hard as she could. He found his footing but still she didn't let go. The way his fingers trembled revealed just how close he'd been to falling.

"Snow bridge," he finally said. "Looked like part of the ledge but really was just air. I'll take it a little slower now." He took a bigger step, this time testing for firmness before he pulled her over the hole.

They walked in silence for a few minutes. She hated to admit she hadn't changed, but he'd been right earlier. She needed to talk. If her mind and mouth stayed busy, the physical reactions to stress were kept to a minimum. "You said you were worried the saboteurs knew something that the impact and feasibility report didn't cover. Why?"

"More a precautionary action than a concern. There's been a problem or two in other states. Not ours. In every organization there is a bad apple, and sometimes big money can entice."

"That's a really vague answer, Shawn."

"Maybe, but you're a reporter, and I happen to like my job—well, part of it."

He was scared she would make him lose his job? She would've thought he'd known her better. Though, admittedly, she'd argued that he didn't have the right to say he knew her. Sometimes finding the truth proved exhausting. "Fine. Officially, until we find safety, everything you say is off the record."

He exhaled. "When sabotage happens you can't help but wonder why. So I started to wonder if there really was a plan to address the needs of the Greater Sage-Grouse, like the geothermal plant impact report indicated. Otherwise, why would environmental groups get involved?"

"Are sage-grouse like little birds?"

"Well, they can get about two feet tall, but yeah." He shrugged. "Part of my job is understanding the wildlife habitat of the land. Sage-grouse are a big deal in this area."

"Why are you so sure an environmental group is responsible?"

"This type of sabotage... It's mild and aimed at the construction."

"I wouldn't call murder *mild*."

He was silent for a second. "A valid point, but we don't know if the sabotage and murder are connected, do we? The saboteurs didn't touch a thing while the control building and the air-cooler structure assembly was being built. The only thing left is pad preparation for the drilling rigs to be assembled. The sabotage started when they got closer to the grouse habitat. It just makes sense to suspect it's all about the grouse."

"Did it make sense to your supervisors?"

He shrugged but kept his face forward, watching the trail carefully as they climbed. "When I told my boss, he didn't think the sabotage warranted extra resources."

"So you suspect he plays a part in this?"

His spine straightened for a second. "To be fair, he doesn't have much to work with. We are notoriously short-staffed."

"Then what's the big deal about this kind of grouse?"

"People travel from all around the world to witness the famous male courtship call. The male bird changes shape and the call is kind of comical, but their numbers have decreased at an unprecedented rate. Since they're an umbrella species—"

"What does that mean?"

"Saving their habitat would mean we're also saving a bunch of other species that rely on the same habitat."

A howl broke the stillness and sent a chill up her spine. Other howls and yips followed, some long and soulful, others more like a pack of teenage girls screaming. They carried on for a few minutes, and she didn't bother trying to speak over their party of sorts.

"They're just dogs," Shawn said.

"Yeah, dogs that can eat you."

Maybe she found coyote packs a little scary, but logically, she knew there was minimal risk. She didn't want to think on the subject much longer, though. Darkness was closing in fast. "So you called in the sabotage tip because you wanted to keep the government accountable," she said instead. "I can get behind that. We *all* need accountability. It's why I believe in my job."

"Without enough manpower to protect the land and find out for myself, I had to know. If the mitigation plan for the grouse was working, then why would environmentalists see the need to sabotage?"

She mulled over his words. "I can't let myself make assumptions when writing a story, but your answer is better than I got from anyone at the plant. You seem to know this area well."

He took an unusually long stride on a steep decline and turned to help her, with both hands again, to make the same climb. He held both of her gloved hands for an extra second before he smiled and turned back to the trail. "I've always liked the wilderness, you know that. I enjoy my job—well, except for the law enforcement part."

"I have to say that, given a murderer is after me, I don't find your honesty to be very encouraging at the moment." She tried to use a teasing lilt, but the incline made her breathing a little strained.

He shook his head. "Just because I don't enjoy it doesn't mean I'm not good at my job." He turned and smiled. "And you're clearly good at yours, asking all the right questions."

"I'm glad you think so because I have one more question."

He turned and pointed. "Go ahead. I think we're almost to the top."

She hesitated, but the past kept flooding her brain with questions she might be able to finally put to rest. In high school, she'd dated Shawn in secret to avoid her twin brother, Eddie, making things all weird. The night of Shawn and Eddie's graduation, they'd gone to a party they should never have attended. Eddie had left intoxicated, driving Shawn's car.

The last time she'd seen Shawn was in a hospital hallway where she waited while her parents stayed with Eddie, who was unconscious with a broken back and a poor prognosis. Eddie had managed to prove the doctors wrong, though. Two years later he had fully healed and worked his way back to full functionality. Not that Shawn had ever bothered to find out.

He hadn't so much as said goodbye.

She should leave the issue alone, but her heart and mind refused to quiet. Now was her chance to find out the whole truth. "Why'd you leave?"

Shawn's heart beat harder as the trail turned into a steeper, thinner incline. Jackie's question made his head hurt. Part of him had wanted her to ask, to get everything out in the open, but the other wanted the past to stay buried deep.

"I would've forgiven you." Jackie's voice was soft. "I mean, I did anyway—it just took a little longer since I had to forgive you for leaving like that, too."

His jaw tensed. He shouldn't have needed to ask forgiveness in the first place. What he had really needed was someone to be on his side. It wasn't his fault Eddie had sneaked off and played a drinking game. Everyone assumed Shawn had known Eddic had been drinking when he'd taken his keys.

Even with the fabric of the gloves separating their touch, he wanted to let go of Jackie's hand. He took another step up the path. Duty kept his grip firm and secure. He would get her to safety. "If I had to do it all over again..." He had hoped saying something like that would put a quick and easy end to the subject, but he wasn't sure how to finish the sentence.

"What? What would you do different?"

Honestly, he didn't know. Each time he replayed the sequences of that night, he still wouldn't have had the knowledge that Eddie had been drinking, so he didn't see how any of it was in his control. If the night happened all over again, Eddie *still* would have taken his keys and ended up in the hospital, and Wolfe would still say he never wanted to see Shawn's face again. Jackie probably didn't know that tidbit, but he wasn't sure what good it would do if she did.

"I... I'd say goodbye," he finally answered. For that, he truly did regret. But he'd never forget the disgust and accusation in her eyes that night. Between her, Wolfe and the entire town, Shawn had endured shame that he didn't deserve yet could never fully erase.

He took his eyes off the trail for a second to gauge their progress. Three more steps and they'd reach higher ground. The cold had begun to seep past his defenses. He wouldn't ask for his coat back, though. He just needed to get his bearings and get them to that trailer. Walking through the snow that already had several inches built up would take a good half hour at minimum to go a single mile, though.

He reached the top and pulled her the rest of the way up to him with a final heave. Directly above them, the stars and the moon had brightened the darkness. He glanced down and could still see the hurt in Jackie's face. She knew he wasn't telling her the full story, but he wasn't ready.

He turned and trudged toward the edge of the forest. He glanced at his phone with the light on dim and pulled up the compass. "If we go due southeast, I think we'll run into the trailer."

"How many miles?"

He dreaded that question. "I'm… I'm not sure. Five?" It could be as many as ten, though. He wasn't sure now that he couldn't see where they were exactly. He'd never traveled there on foot.

Headlights swung to the east, one from a truck and another from what looked like a snowmobile. He pulled Jackie behind the closest evergreen tree to stay hidden from sight.

"Are those ATVs with the truck?"

"Looks like only a snowmobile. I didn't see an ATV."

"So maybe it's good guys," she whispered.

"Maybe." He reached for his holster out of instinct. The snowmobile took off again, revving off into the distance, but the truck headlights stayed on, as if stuck within the grove of trees. "Still, they look at least a mile or so away."

She peeked around the tree.

His muscles tightened as he tried his best to not shiver. The temperature dipped faster than expected and his back was still damp from the exertion. The wind howled past them. Thankfully, it hadn't started snowing yet. Fresh snow on top of the packed snow would make the journey even slower. Hiking in the dark, without so much as the use of a flashlight, was foolish. He didn't know this terrain well enough by foot to know all the dangers. What if there was another snow bridge?

"I think we might have to consider finding shelter for the night. This is the point where your dad would stop and make a snow cave, right?"

"Yeah, well, Dad had two other people helping him shovel so it wouldn't take eight hours. Plus, what if we don't give the snow enough time to harden and those trees get an extra boost of wind and dump enough snow on it to collapse, trapping us?" She spoke extra fast, probably to keep her teeth from chattering.

"At this rate, I'm a little concerned that we won't make it to that trailer tonight."

She gave him a side look. "Your turn." She took off the coat and shoved it in his arms. "Hurry before I change my mind. You can't rescue me if I have to drag you somewhere, and I'm pretty sure starting a fire right now would send a signal to those men that we're still alive."

He begrudgingly took the coat, determined only to wear it for a few minutes at most. "Let's keep moving, then, and see if it's friend or foe inside that truck."

He tripped over one of the many rocks and roots hiding underneath the snow. The progress proved slower than he feared. Jackie didn't complain, though. He counted silently to 120 and returned the coat to her. She raised an eyebrow but accepted. On and on they went sharing the coat back and forth until they got within a hundred yards of the red pickup truck.

"I know that truck." He could never forget, really. He *knew* that guy was the one who had dug up the wheel ruts left by the Oregon Trail pioneers, but he had no proof. "Darrell Carrillo. He's a metal detectorist, but the worst kind. He's also the hiker that's been missing. He wasn't supposed to be here." But that figured.

"So if he has a truck, maybe he just got lost?" She huffed. "But then why would the snowmobile lead him into the trees? Shawn, we have to assume he's in league with the man who tried to kill me."

He wanted to think of an innocent reason to explain the truck being in the forest, but his interactions with the man led him to believe otherwise. "Maybe." When they reached the small clearing within the trees, the lights took on an ominous glow. The truck appeared to have slammed into a tree.

Nothing about the day had made sense except for the constant current of danger. So while his normal course of action would be to rush to see if there was anyone injured inside, apprehension filled his core. He held a hand out to Jackie. “Do me a favor and stay back while I find out what’s going on.”

He placed one hand on his weapon and the other hand on the back of the truck, working his way forward. In the driver’s seat sat the missing hiker, his forehead leaning on top of the steering wheel.

Shawn surveyed the surroundings, his hand on his gun. No one else seemed anywhere close. The snowmobile tracks headed southeast, in the same direction of the path the construction workers would’ve used.

“Is everything okay?” Jackie asked, peeking out from her hiding place behind another tree.

He opened the driver’s door and the stench of alcohol wafted past him. “Definitely not okay,” he said. He placed two fingers on the man’s neck. No pulse. He moved to check the wrist, just in case there was any hope. “I don’t think he’s going to hurt you.”

Jackie stepped out into the open. “Oh? So it’s a friendly hiker?”

“Not exactly friendly, but we did find him.” He exhaled. “Unfortunately, he’s dead.”

FOUR

Jackie looked away from the man hunched over the wheel.

Cold. That foremost thought played on repeat and numbed her mind, even when presented with such shocking news.

The trees surrounding them gave them a little protection but not enough to hold the wind back. Although she was wearing Shawn's coat, her jaw quivered and every muscle vibrated.

Shawn took out his phone and grimaced. "If my fingers would cooperate, that would be nice."

"What are you doing?" She came closer—the last thing she wanted to do, as she could no longer avoid the sight of the hiker. At least there was no blood.

Shawn grunted and seemed to take a lot of effort to get his hand to stop trembling enough to touch a small symbol on his phone screen. "I just want to turn the flash off. The headlights may still be on, but if there are sudden flashes of light from my phone, we might get our unwelcome visitors back to investigate."

The light from the inside of the cab seemed dim but illuminated Shawn enough that she could see his lips had taken on a decidedly bluish tint. "We need to get warm, Shawn." They were running out of time before hypothermia became a risk. The wet spot on the back of his shirt was a surefire recipe for it. She moved to take the coat off. It was long past time to give it back to him.

"No. Keep it on." He pressed his lips together in a firm line, determination lining his features. "I have to move him."

"The body?" She couldn't keep the horror out of her voice but realized why he'd decided on the course of action. Trucks had heaters. The accident didn't look too bad, structurally, for the truck. The headlights were on, so the truck still had a working battery. They could probably drive back to the road and make it to civilization within a couple of hours. She'd find a hotel with a fireplace and hot cocoa and one of those thick terry cloth robes. Her shoulders rose to her ears, bracing against the wind. They just needed to get inside that truck.

"Yes. I have to move him. That's why I need to take photos." He moved his phone in several different angles around the body. "I hope the lighting is decent enough."

Crime scene photos, she finally realized. "You don't think his death was an accident."

His eyes darted to her and back to the phone. "That's not my call to make. It *appears* to be an accident. If I were an optimistic man, I would hope that the people on the snowmobile witnessed the accident and are heading back to civilization to call it in. If that's the case, our best chance for survival is to stay put and be found along with…" He bent at an odd angle to take more photos of the man's shoes near the pedals. "Along with him," he finally said. "But we investigate every death, accidental or not."

Shawn used to be an optimist. At least, that was how she'd always thought of him. The thought jarred her. They'd been apart for over a decade, but she'd still known him longer than she hadn't. People changed faster once they were adults, though.

"But where will we put him?" she asked. "I suppose the cold will help preserve the body." The branches of the trees surrounding them rustled with the breeze. She knew better than most what lurked in the shadows. "Won't animals…?" She didn't want to speak the question aloud, either. Law enforcement wouldn't be able to properly investigate the man's death if wild scavengers found him first. The haunting howl of the coyotes sounded again, confirming her thoughts.

"Thankfully, we have his keys." Shawn leaned over the man. He removed the key from the ignition but left the headlights on. He stomped over to the trunk of the covered cab. His entire hand shook as he tried to insert the key into the lock. "Getting them to work is another matter."

"If you're not going to take the coat back, at least let me help you." She took the key from his hand and unlocked it. The back opened to reveal a metal detector, a duffel bag, a jug of partly frozen water, a wool blanket, an emergency car repair kit and a backpack. A backpack usually contained snacks if someone was out hiking in the wilderness. "Shawn…"

"Go ahead and take stock of supplies, but please tell me the contents before you use anything."

He disappeared back to the front of the truck. She emptied the emergency car kit for its first-aid kit, emergency blanket and the day/night flare in case they needed it for a fire starter, but she left behind the jumper cables. The main zippered compartment of the backpack revealed beef jerky, a tuna packet, trail mix, four disposable water bottles that were on their way to being frozen but were still liquid, and a box of chocolate-covered almonds. "Oh, you were a good man." Her voice wavered as she realized that their best chance of survival was now because a man had died.

"I'm not so sure about that." Shawn stomped in the snow with—she gasped—the man in question over his shoulder. He grunted and maneuvered the man off his shoulder, into his arms and inside the bed of the truck.

The man wore a short, padded coat, jeans, a cap and tennis shoes. Shawn turned the man's face away from her view so she could only see the back of his head. A kind gesture, but try as she might, she couldn't fool her mind into thinking that he was just sleeping.

The wind gusted enough to shift the truck ever so slightly to the right. Desperation for warmth kept her from crying out over the dead man. The thought jarred her. Two men had died in one day and she'd almost been added to their number. Her eyelids felt like they might freeze closed as she blinked away the hot moisture.

"I'll check this one." Shawn reached across her and unzipped the duffel bag. On top of a pile of fabrics of some sort sat metal trinkets, some covered in mud, a pair of binoculars and what looked like an arrowhead. "He definitely wasn't up to any good if this is any indication."

Underneath, the items proved more interesting. "Shawn. Are those clothes?"

He pulled out gloves, a parka, extra socks and snow pants. Shawn gave a solemn nod. "Ill-intentioned or not, he was prepared for the elements." He gestured to the backpack. "Let's take this and the duffel and see if we can get the heat on."

They closed the covered bed of the truck. The back of her neck tightened with guilt over using the dead man's truck, but they couldn't start a fire without a couple of hours of gathering supplies and fighting the wind. Even if they managed to create a spark, the smoke and flames would act as a beacon to those who'd likely killed him. They really had no other choice but to utilize the supplies.

She stuck the duffel in the back seat for easy access and slipped into the passenger side of the truck. Shawn's open door made it feel like she'd entered a wind tunnel. She bit her lip to keep from telling him to hurry up as he took more photos of the empty driver's seat and the floor. She tucked her chin deeper into the coat until he finally slipped into the driver's side. The moment he shut the door, her skin burned with a strong intensity, as if her brain finally thought it was safe to give her body permission to acknowledge the full extent of what she'd been through. No more denial to survive, to keep moving. Everything hurt.

Shawn shoved the key into the ignition. "Let's hope this works." He clicked the key over and the engine revved to life. He flipped the thermostat to the reddest portion but kept the fan on low. She pulled off the gloves and held her hands up to the air vent. Cold air blasted, but it was warmer than outside.

Shawn twisted and contorted in his seat. "That parka looked warm."

"You should take your coat back."

"No, this will be fine." He struggled in the small space until he succeeded in putting on the thinner coat. But at least it had a hood. He cleared his throat. "He may not have been a law-abiding citizen, but I'd like to think he would've helped us." He shrugged. "I'd like to think that anyone would have compassion in such conditions."

There was the Shawn she remembered, the one who found the silver lining. Even though she knew from covering the news for years that the sentiment wasn't true, she remained silent. She bristled against his mention of compassion.

Now that she finally had reprieve from the wind and cold, her mind wanted to give full attention to the unsatisfactory answer he'd given her back on the trail. The only thing he'd do differently all those years ago was to say goodbye? Her throat tightened at the thought.

What had she expected him to say? *Oh, dearest Jackie, that night was the biggest mistake of my life. I should've begged for your forgiveness right then because I loved you, and I've never stopped thinking about you.*

She knew the pretend speech too well because she'd imagined Shawn proclaiming such things on a loop in the days after he'd left. She hadn't recalled the imaginary teenage interchange in years, though. If Shawn had actually said something similar on the trail moments ago, she might've felt more satisfied with his answer. But then what?

The question perplexed her, which probably indicated there would've been an awkward silence.

Shawn handed her a pair of wool socks. "Here."

Thoughtful gestures didn't help to put her mind to rest. Simply having dry fabric against her toes was enough to cause her eyes to well up with gratitude, but she refused to shed tears.

The air shifted. Heat!

Shawn turned the fan on full blast before she had a chance. In a few short hours, she'd be able to put all the internal drama in the back of her mind, where it belonged. Because even if Shawn had given an awesome explanation about the past, they couldn't pick up a relationship where they'd left off.

Her job was in Boise and his was hours away, in the middle of nowhere. He obviously still adored spending his time in the wild, while she refused to even camp. And how could she ever trust a man who left like that, without so much as a word? She leaned forward, anxious to focus on other things. "So can we head for the road now?"

Shawn turned to face her, his eyes widening. He stared at her for an uncomfortable few seconds, as if he expected her to remember something and speak first.

"What?"

He frowned and shook his head. "Jackie, we won't be able to drive this anywhere. I thought you'd realized."

"Thought I realized what?" She leaned forward, peering out of the windshield. "I know the truck hit the tree, but neither looks the worse for wear. I don't think the tree will fall on us if we back away. Is it a flat tire? I'm not happy about it, but I'm capable and willing to wrestle out the spare if it means we can leave tonight."

He shook his head sadly, so she pressed on. "I'm even willing to stand outside and guide you through these trees. It shouldn't take long to get to some solid snowpack. You know the area well enough that you won't drive us off a cliff, right?"

He didn't blink. "That's not the issue."

"We can beat the worst of the storm. It hasn't even started snowing yet." Like a cruel trick, thick snowflakes floated down to the windshield. Her shoulders sagged. "I still say we can make it to civilization tonight if we try."

"The back axle, Jackie. It's broken clean in two."

Please let him be wrong. She straightened. "Are you sure? I have a bit of experience with fix—"

"I know." He gestured to her door. "Whoever drove the truck here rode right over a massive log. The truck bed is being held in place by it. My guess is they planned to park this thing elsewhere, but after the break, they made do."

She peeked at the side mirror. The right tire tilted inward at a forty-five-degree angle. She should be thankful the truck sat fully upright. There went her dreams of nice warm accommodations for the beginning of her Christmas vacation.

She opened the backpack and pulled out two granola bars. Shawn accepted one and ripped off the wrapper. He finished it in three bites. She wasn't much slower. "Why do you think they meant to park the truck elsewhere? I'm guessing you don't think he died from a heart attack. Seems to me you're implying that it's murder."

He eyed her. "This is off the record, too, but surely you noticed his smell."

"Like he'd been dunked in whiskey? Yes." If she noticed things on her own, she didn't need him to be on the record. In fact, maybe if she got the scoop on the murders, she could finally get the promotion she wanted and never have to accept stories out in the wilderness again, despite her dad being the one and only Wolfe Dutton.

"Or some sort of alcohol," Shawn said. "The front of Darrell's coat had the strongest smell, but there was no liquor bottle in the car."

"He could've finished off his drink first. Elsewhere."

"True. But then I got into the truck without having to adjust the seat." He threw a thumb over his shoulder. "Darrell was a good five inches shorter than me." He glanced down at the coat. "At least he had a long torso."

So if someone else had been driving the truck, that person most likely moved the body to the driver's-side seat and staged the death to look like a drunk-driving accident. "You're saying that we're stuck in a truck that won't drive, with a dead man in the back who may or may not have been murdered by the same man that tried to kill me—or another dangerous murderer—and all with a blizzard on the way."

He rubbed both hands together and exhaled. Despite the truck's heater, his breath still made a foggy cloud. "I'm saying it's time to accept that we're operating in survival mode."

Shawn didn't regret his words, but he wasn't sure Jackie understood the severity of their situation yet. With the park closed so close to Christmas and the impending winter storm, murderers after them or not, every decision they made from this moment on would contribute to whether they lived or died.

He opened his photo album on the phone. He'd taken over a hundred shots because he never knew what would prove to be an important detail in the light of day. He flicked to the image that still perplexed him.

"So we're here all night?" Jackie asked.

"Yes."

"Are we hoping to be rescued?"

"I think the best we can hope for is that we aren't discovered by whoever planted Darrell's body here. I assume they were trying to make it look like an accident, so it seems unlikely they'd return, but I'm ready for them if they do." He patted the holster that sat on top of the console in between their seats.

She glanced at his phone and rummaged in her pockets until she pulled out hers. "I don't suppose we have a signal."

"Sorry, no." He tilted his screen in Jackie's direction. The photo that was bothering him only included the man's black ski jacket. He pointed at the white streak on the bottom hem in the photo. "That stain looked fresh."

She had her arms wrapped around herself but leaned forward, squinting. "You think it's an important detail?"

"Probably not, but you had a very similar spot on your jacket. Of course, you'd also slid off a cliff."

"That mark wasn't from the cliff. I accidentally brushed up against something during the tour of the construction site. They use some special latex paint for extreme temperatures. Each coat takes a couple days to dry, apparently. The foreman apologized and said it only needed another hour or so to cure." She shrugged. "I chalked it up to my good timing."

"So it's possible Darrell was at the construction site, as well."

She looked upward, as if in deep thought. "I noticed he wore tennis shoes. Seemed like an odd choice of footwear to be out in this thick of snow. Especially when he'd packed boots and had a metal detector."

"There's cement paths that I assume were cleared when you took the tour today?"

"Yes. I guess if he was going to stick to the paths, that makes sense, but still seems odd." She handed him back his phone. "Why'd you imply he wasn't a good man?"

He grabbed the wool blanket they'd retrieved from the duffel and folded it into a rectangle so they could both use half if he stretched it lengthwise. "It's a felony to even keep a metal detector in your vehicle on federal lands, let alone use it. We suspected him of ruining some historic sites."

"Why was he a suspect?"

"I don't have proof, but I've seen this truck on the land before. I spotted him a couple months ago through my binoculars on my rounds, from one of the higher vantage points. He had that metal detector with him, but he got away before I was close enough to get his license plate number. When the missing person photo came through with the vehicle description, as well, I knew it was him."

"Are hikers with metal detectors common?"

"Most detectorists follow the law and only search in legal areas with permission, but there's always a few that treat it more like a moneymaking scheme than a hobby. They don't care about preserving history. They think they're entitled to do or take anything they want on federal land." He shook his head. "I'm still angry about the gouges I found on a section of the Oregon Trail. Those wagon ruts survived all this time until someone took a shovel to them. Probably all for a rusty nail."

Her forehead creased. "What did you call him?"

"Darrell?"

"No, the other thing."

"A detectorist. Someone who uses a metal detector."

"Oh. I might've filled in the blanks incorrectly." Her wide eyes turned his way. "The murder I witnessed... The man didn't actually say he was upset about a detective."

He caught on instantly. "You think you misheard?"

"He said *detect*, but he was interrupted. My brain just finished the word for him. I didn't think there could be another option, but he might've been upset about a detectorist."

Shawn knew witnesses could be unreliable for that very reason. The brain had an uncanny way of trying to help along anything that didn't make sense. "So it's possible the two men were fighting about Darrell. Especially if it turns out he'd been on the property."

"Yes. But why would they be upset? What could he have seen or found? Or maybe he was behind the sabotage, but why?" Her face was animated and a good reminder that she was a journalist.

"If we knew that, maybe we'd know why two men are dead. It's probably best to let the matter rest." His phone screen taunted him with the words *No Service* still at the top of the screen.

Even with the new information, there was nothing he could do without calling for backup. His first priority was to get Jackie to safety. The archaeologist's trailer still seemed to be the best course of action. There would be supplies, a generator and, most important, a satellite phone. "At first light, we get to that trailer."

"I'm assuming you've never hiked this route to the trailer?"

"You'd be right."

She opened the glove compartment. "Maybe the guy had a terrain map of some sort?" She searched and found nothing except the truck's manual and registration.

At least she didn't argue that they should attempt to get to the trailer after nightfall. She knew as well as he did that hiking in such conditions was a recipe for death, but it'd been over a decade since she'd practiced wilderness skills, despite her memory of rappelling knots. It took training and practice to keep the skills up to par to face whatever the wilderness threw at him. But Jackie wasn't the type of person to keep her opinions quiet. At least, she didn't used to be.

In fact, he was a little surprised she'd let the topic of his leaving town abruptly go so easily. She hadn't said another word about it since he'd answered her on the trail.

She pulled out a container of chocolate-covered almonds. "I know we should probably ration our food, but that granola bar wasn't enough for dinner. And these are my favorite." She popped one in her mouth and offered him the container.

"Since when are these your favorite?" The moment the question left his mouth, he regretted it. A moment ago he was thankful she'd let the past go, and yet he'd just invited discussion. "I only meant I thought nuts were banned at your house."

She nodded and popped another in her mouth. "My mom is allergic to peanuts and tree nuts, but as soon as I went to college, I discovered that chocolate tastes better when paired with nuts. Even the chocolate itself tastes better. I'm serious," she said. "Just let it melt in your mouth and then spit out the nut, and you'll see I'm right. Better than normal chocolate. You know what I mean? Try it."

He couldn't help but laugh. He'd forgotten how enthusiastic she could get over the small joys in life, like food. "No, thanks. That's wasting a perfectly good source of protein and fat." He took a few from the box. "How is your mom, anyway?"

Her enjoyment of the chocolate dimmed. "Do you really care enough to know?"

He'd opened the door wide for discussion and perhaps even deserved that gibe. "Of course I do."

"Sorry. That was uncalled for. She's fine. Same as always." She set the box of almonds down. "I just don't understand how you could just walk away from us if you really cared. My mom always treated you like you were part of the family. We all did. Weren't you at all curious if Eddie ever recovered? I mean, he had a broken back. For all you knew, he could've died from complications."

He straightened, suddenly warmer than he should be despite the heater's setting. Had Eddie not told her anything? "I know that it took him two years, and he drove the physical therapists crazy, but he never gave up. He worked until he was fully recovered."

Her eyes clouded. "Why— How do you know that?"

"Eddie told me. The nurse told him I kept calling to find out his status. They wouldn't talk to me, though. I finally agreed to leave my number. Eddie called back. He apologized for wrecking my car. He kept me up to date for a while. It's been several years, but I heard he's running one of the branches for your father."

"So..." She stared out the window. "You spoke to him but not me?"

Her soft voice twisted his gut in knots. He'd hurt her. How could he explain that it was for the best, without sounding like a coward? The wind railed against the trees with such intensity that a giant chunk of snow slammed on the truck's hood and shook the vehicle. "Like I said, I probably should have said goodbye before I left that night. I don't expect you to believe me, but I didn't know that Eddie had been drinking when he took my keys. And even if I had, since when has anyone been able to control Eddie?"

She raised an eyebrow and faced forward but still didn't turn his way. "That doesn't explain why you left the *way* you did. A person who is innocent doesn't just run away."

"Because your dad said he never wanted to see my face again. The whole town was against me." The words rushed out with such intensity it was as if a storm had been brewing inside of him without any forecasted warnings. The memory still stung, and the day's events just emphasized his worst fear.

The truck underscored his proclamation with an ominous ding. He searched for the source of the sound. A bright orange gas tank lit up on the dashboard. Low fuel. Great. He felt like he was disappointing, all over again, the man he'd looked up to his entire childhood. He couldn't keep Eddie safe, and now he wouldn't be able to keep Jackie safe, either.

FIVE

Jackie tapped the digital clock. It was only eight o'clock at night even though her body felt like it'd already endured a twelve-hour marathon. Everything ached. She'd only spent three horrible hours in the elements, but a very long, cold night still awaited them without fuel to keep the truck running. "It's been twenty minutes with the heater on," she said. "We need to turn the truck off."

He frowned. "I know it's a bad situation, but I think when the warning light goes on we still have a couple gallons to go on. We also want to insulate ourselves. What else is in this duffel?" He handed her the man's boots. "Think you can make these work? Your flimsy fabric ones aren't going to do you much good tomorrow."

He was right; plus, they were wet. At least the man wasn't very tall, as Shawn had pointed out. His boot size was a men's size nine. She wore a size seven in women's, so they were still a little big, but not too bad with the thick wool socks. Shawn split up the rest of the items in the duffel to carry in between the two backpacks, in preparation for their early-morning hike. Then he stretched out the duffel bag and placed it on top of their wool blanket. "Every bit of fabric helps to keep us warm."

What she really wanted was to return to the subject of the past. Even if her father had flown off the handle at the time of Eddie's accident, couldn't Shawn understand? Her dad had been devastated when they'd been told of Eddie's injuries, and it was easier to blame someone else than his son, bloodied and bruised and waiting for surgery. All she remembered was her dad's disappointment when Shawn had left. But now she wondered if it was guilt.

She rolled her head clockwise in an attempt to stop her neck from complaining. Her muscles increasingly ached, and there was still a very long and cold night ahead.

Shawn shoved his hand deep into his backpack. "I think I have some pain reliever in here and a pair of tweezers in the first-aid kit."

He found the sample-size bottle and shook out a few pills into the palm of his hand. She took off her gloves to accept and his fingers brushed against hers. Her eyes refused to lift, refused to meet his. She wrapped her fingers around the pills and realized she'd been holding her breath. She swallowed the pills and Shawn beckoned her to show him her hands again.

She hesitantly offered her palms up. He set his phone in the cup holder so it shone enough to see and worked quickly. He cupped one hand at a time and went to work with the tweezers. She looked away. It hurt more if she thought about just how many splinters were embedded.

"If you could contact Eddie, why not me?" Her voice cracked with emotion she wasn't ready to feel.

His fingers stilled. "I guess I was scared I wouldn't be able to stay away." He set her left hand down gingerly and picked up her right. "I definitely couldn't bear seeing the way everyone would look at me in town. When people get that angry—even if they find out later they're wrong—it's hard to ever regain the same kind of relationship."

She tried her best to understand his reasoning but came up empty. "What exactly happened, Shawn?"

"There, I think I got them all."

"Thank you." She put on her gloves and took another swallow of very icy water that stung her throat.

"We were at the senior class party," he began.

"I remember. I was there." The worst part of secretly dating was that they could never attend or hang out at events together. So even though they'd dated for two years, it was easy to never get too serious.

"Yes. Eddie complained that the party was boring, so he walked off with his girlfriend. I found out later that they'd gone somewhere to do shots with some other couples." Shawn's voice took on a very monotone quality. "It was starting to get dark, but there was going to be a movie on the greens."

"We were going to sit together. By accident, of course."

His eyes shifted slightly in her direction. "Except Eddie didn't want to stay. I was in the middle of an intense discussion with some other guys about whether the Packers had deserved to win the Super Bowl and handed him the keys without a second glance."

That sounded like Eddie. "So why didn't you explain that to Dad?"

"He wouldn't hear it. He said I'd betrayed his trust and failed him." His frown intensified.

"But surely now..."

Shawn shook his head. "Eddie said your dad came around, but I never heard it straight from him. Like I said, it's been years since Eddie and I've talked."

Years. Seemed like such a waste. "But leaving was so drastic—"

"It wasn't as if anyone had my back. No one was on my side. Not even you."

"That's not fair. I didn't even know your side."

He shrugged. "You probably would've reacted the same way the town—"

"You're right it wasn't fair to blame you." Her forehead creased with a deep frown. "But I would hope you could forgive me for being in the wrong in the same way I had to forgive you for leaving without saying goodbye."

"Of course," Shawn answered, a little too quickly. "The bottom line is we never would've worked together anyway. Best to leave the past in the past." He leaned over and pointed at the pack in her lap. "Did I see beef jerky in there?"

She nodded, stunned, and tried to ignore the sudden smell of soy sauce and meat. If ever there was a clear indication of an ended conversation, asking for beef jerky had to be it. She knew all the reasons they wouldn't work *now*, but she didn't know of any reasons back then. So much of what he'd said confused her as if it held more than one meaning. Her temples issued a sharp warning pain behind her eyes of an impending headache.

"Sleep if you can," Shawn said, his brow furrowed low. "You experienced a lot of physical trauma hanging from that branch."

The pounding in her head and the soreness in her arms prevented her from asking more questions, but Jackie never let a mystery go unsolved without further investigation. She closed her eyes, just for a moment. The mysteries from the day were piling up too fast to mention. She would get to the bottom of what happened all those years ago, even if the truth meant she'd have to experience heartache all over again.

The snow had made a layer against the windshield and piled against the side windows. The seats weren't comfortable, but despite their attempts at blocking out the cold, the howling wind still slipped in and swept past his cheek. Shawn turned on the engine slightly earlier than planned. He'd been running it for roughly twenty minutes every hour to conserve their fuel. Jackie seemed to be in a fitful sleep. Blissful heat filled the cab again. The lines in her face smoothed and, thankfully, she didn't wake up.

At least the warmth had been strong enough to melt snow off the windshield and the side windows. He kept the headlights on, even now, to avoid raising suspicion should someone be watching. Under the cover of trees, there wasn't much to see except the flakes getting caught in the beam's gaze as they fell down.

Something flickered through the evergreen branches. He hunched over and squinted. Still nothing. He tried to move quietly as he grabbed the pair of binoculars he'd found in Darrell's bag.

The magnification took a few adjustments before he spotted the source of bobbing light. Men on ATVs and a snowmobile. He counted three. But what could be so important to risk riding on treacherous terrain in the middle of the snowstorm? Maybe the reason motivated the murders of two men and the attempted murder of Jackie.

They came to a stop. If he had to guess, the men had paused somewhere near the end of the crevice. A giant, high-powered beam turned on, flashing across the expanse of snow. The backlight illuminated the men as one walked forward and pointed it downward. Shawn's gut twisted. They'd said they would come back to make sure he and Jackie had died among the truck wreckage.

"Jackie, wake up." He hated to do it, but he couldn't take any chances. The men would know they weren't down there any minute and might start looking for them. "I don't think we can stay here."

She blinked and rubbed her face. "What?"

The beam bounced out of the deep pit and hit the tree line, heading straight for the truck. "Duck!"

He twisted sideways, getting his head close to the heater console while Jackie folded over, her head close to her knees. Sure enough, a second later, the light lit up the entire cab.

"But, Shawn, if they killed Darrell—"

He realized his mistake before she fully voiced it. If those men had been responsible for Darrell's death, they would've been expecting to see at least one person, albeit dead, behind the wheel of the truck.

A branch fell from the sky and hit the hood at the same time the sound of a gunshot reached his ears. Jackie flinched, a small scream filling the cab as she flung her arms over her head.

"They know we're here. They're coming for us, aren't they?"

"I'm afraid they are."

A loud crack and the windshield radiated with fractures around a circle. Shawn's head throbbed with the sound of impact. The beam still lit up the truck. He tried to contort to look upward and see if the bullet had actually made a hole, but he didn't find one. "Are you okay?"

She shivered. "No, I'm not okay! That was so close. They know, Shawn. They know."

A ping sounded again. This time a bullet went through the windshield and snapped the rear mirror in two. He narrowly missed the plastic hitting him in the forehead.

"We need to run, Shawn."

Since rescuers hadn't stumbled upon them with the headlights on, their chances of being saved now, so close to Christmas, reduced drastically. "You know the dangers of hiking in the night, and once we leave the vehicle there's no going back."

"I also know the dangers of being a sitting duck." She sat up and grabbed the backpack. The beam of light hit her straight on, and she bolted out of the truck.

Shouting could be heard, echoing through the open air. If the men hadn't known their location for sure, they knew now. The light disappeared. Engines revved.

He grabbed his pack, stepped outside and sank a good half a foot into fresh snow. The wind had stilled, and the sky, still thick with full clouds, momentarily stopped dropping flakcs. He rounded the truck with loud footsteps, his knees lifting to waist level with each step. The only good news about the vehicles heading straight for them was the bullets stopping for a moment while they drove around the crevice and up the hill. But that would only last mere moments. If they were the murderers who had planted the truck here, they knew the path. They had minutes at the most to get away.

Jackie ran deeper into the trees. She halted after about ten feet and spun around. The moonlight hit her wide eyes. "Where do we hide? They'll see our footprints."

"We can't outrun them. I'm guessing the field trailer is at a forty-five-degree angle, southeast of here. Let's at least start in that direction."

"But we stay in the woods and go deeper if we can. Remember how we tripped over all those rocks and trunks on the way here?"

He picked up her train of thought almost instantly. "Dangerous for a snowmobile."

"And not a picnic for an ATV. Especially if we get near trees grouped together."

He glanced up at the moon and lifted a hand in the direction he thought they needed to go. "They'll have to track us on foot, which gives us an advantage. Stay close."

"They're getting closer."

He didn't need her reminder. Their engines increased in volume, and by the sound of things, they'd reached the truck.

"What'd they do with the body?" a man shouted. The engines cut off. "Go in after them. They can't have gotten far."

Shawn couldn't hear the muffled reply. The trees were so thick that the men couldn't follow them on the snowmobiles, but it sounded like they were following on foot. If only they had more light. One wrong step and one of them could break a leg, fall into a hole or meet up with wild animals. The clouds shifted ever so slightly. The trees weren't as thick up ahead. The crunching of snow and branches followed them, pushing him to run faster, but he wasn't sure if Jackie could keep up. Without the promise of getting to heat, working up a sweat could mean hypothermia. Hope plummeted with each step. Their attackers had found their path. He heard it.

Jackie patted his back. He turned and found her holding up a flare. "I can distract them, while you try to take them down." She gestured to his gun.

In the night, outnumbered in manpower and ammunition, he didn't think it wise to start a shooting match, but the flare gave him an idea. "Distraction is a great idea. Not yet, though. Is it a simple road flare?"

"Day and night, handheld."

"Use the day side," he said in a quiet pant. He couldn't afford for the men to hear their plan. "At my signal, use wide circles so it fills the space, and then stick it in the snow, and stay low."

It didn't take long to find what he'd been searching for. As the tree grouping grew tighter on the south side, a large bank, covered with snow, rose up. A mix of evergreens and maples towered against the ridge, but they could still climb it. He wasn't sure what would be on the other side, though. Drop-offs were as common as trees in this section of land.

The moonlit shadows indicated the bottom of the bank was deep, somewhere between a ditch and a burrow. Running out into the open wasn't an option, so hiding in that space seemed like the smartest course of action.

The men were gaining on them by the sound of their footsteps. He pointed. "Right after you light the flare, go there." He stepped to the opposite side of the trees from where he wanted to eventually go. "Now or never."

Jackie twisted off the cap and orange smoke filled the sky. The day side of the handheld flare would produce a dense cloud of orange for at least a minute rather than the night side that burned short and bright. She didn't need to be told twice. She swirled the stick in a wide circle and the thick foliage trapped the smoke in the space.

"Drop it," he whispered. She stuck the bottom end in the snow and ran for the bank, just like he'd hoped.

The smoke continued to gather and form an orange wall within the trees. He pulled his gun and shouted, "Drop your weapons! BLM ranger!" He fired his weapon into the ground, ducked and sprinted to join Jackie on the other side of the orange cloud. A barrage of bullets sounded, all aiming for the spot he'd just been standing in.

Jackie stood waiting for him just past the smoke. He'd hoped she'd be in the hiding spot by now, but she'd picked up a fallen evergreen branch and swiped at his tracks until they reached the space together. The spot between the tree and the snowy bank proved tight. They could both fit, but would it be enough to hide?

He threw his pack into the space. Jackie took off her backpack and tossed it in, as well. He gestured for her to slide in first. They had roughly two feet of space in between the ridge and the tree branches, but they sat a good foot and a half below the trunk, with just their heads poking up. He managed to sit up, but at an angle, much like a recliner. Thankfully, the thick spread of pine needles, while not the most comfortable, protected them from moisture seeping into their clothes.

Jackie unzipped both backpacks and tilted the bags so the openings were facing them.

"What are you doing?"

"Zippers can be reflective, and we might need something," she whispered back. She grabbed a pair of pants and slid them underneath her like a seat cushion. Another reminder her attire wasn't as equipped for the elements as his.

The wool blanket on top caught his eye. He made

quick work with his pocketknife and cut two wide strips. "Wrap around your face and hair. Hurry."

The men were yelling. He kept the makeshift scarf off his ears and strained to hear.

"He's armed."

"We might've hit him."

"I'm not walking in there and making it easy for him to shoot me if we didn't. Is the girl armed, too?"

Jackie reached for his hand as if silently asking if he'd heard the danger nearby. He squeezed in response. Right now they needed to stay utterly still. The high beam swept across the trees. Jackie closed her eyes and tilted her head ever so slightly so all that faced forward was the gray wool blanket. Besides the added warmth, it hopefully made for good camouflage. A good idea, but Shawn needed to remain upright to see what was coming. He squinted through the thick pine needles. He could see movement, but not clear pictures.

Coyotes sounded in the distance, closer than before. An unbidden shiver ran up his spine, shifting the needles ever so slightly. The animal noises kept him from hearing the rest of what the men said. A flashlight beam shifted their way, reflecting off all the snow and shiny needles surrounding them. He held his breath and squinted but forced his eyes to stay open. The beam moved away.

The crunching of snow retreated and Shawn exhaled. Using slow movements, he carefully unholstered his gun and laid it on his lap for quick access. They may have narrowly avoided being shot, but they'd lost their only shelter. A wind gust shook the trees and dumped snow on top of his wool-covered head as if in response.

"Think they'll be back?"

"I'm sure they will. If they're smart, they'll return in the morning. They might even post men to watch the tree line closest to the road."

"That's not encouraging. Does that mean we should keep moving?"

"No, the risk outweighs the potential benefit. But we need to beat them by getting out of here at first light."

Morning couldn't come fast enough.

SIX

The minutes passed at an excruciating pace until the motors had revved far enough away that she felt it was safe to move. Shawn twisted to look into her eyes. "We should stay here until the sky lightens, and then get moving before they come back for a second look."

Logically, the verdict made sense, but she itched everywhere. The wool kept her face from feeling like an icicle, but she'd never been a fan of scarves over the nose and mouth. "It's your turn to sleep," she said. A quick glance at her phone showed the time as just past two in the morning. "I got several hours and I'm wide-awake."

He frowned and she geared up for an argument, but instead he handed her the Taser. "Wake me up if you see anybody." He leaned against the mound of dirt and closed his eyes. He probably wouldn't be able to sleep, as the rocky headrest had to be the most uncomfortable surface that—

His deep breathing fell into a pattern, instantly proving her wrong. Shawn had stayed awake for almost five hours with the silence and cold as his only companion. She didn't know how he'd done it without falling asleep himself.

She gingerly stuck her hand into the open backpack, taking care to be quiet but hoping to find something that would help them reach civilization fast or at least keep her awake. She trusted Shawn would be able to lead them to the archaeologist's trailer. Eventually. But she also knew the painstaking work of mountaineering. It wasn't an exact science.

She slid her hands underneath the backpack's contents and then into each pocket of the pack. Her fingernails brushed against something that crinkled. She cupped her hand around the flashlight on her phone so the beam wouldn't be strong enough to wake Shawn or be spotted outside of the trees. The paper seemed to be a brochure of some sort.

Carefully she unfolded the crude map onto her lap. Even with map-reading skills, she had a hard time making sense of what looked like a homemade document. Most of the map had been colored yellow, with a few black lines curving back and forth and across the paper. Those, she assumed, were roads. No elevations, peaks or legends could be found, not even on the backside. There was a rectangle in the middle with the word *Avoid* written inside it.

Above the warning was a hand-drawn pond—or maybe a lake, since she had no reference for scale. Trees surrounded it. Above the stick-figured trees, a green section filled the rest of the map. A crooked drawing of a square and triangle, vaguely resembling a house, had the penned words *New hut*, between yellow and green sections.

The quality of the map led her to believe the detectorist had created it. Perhaps the document was evidence and could help investigators retrace his steps. When her eyes couldn't handle the strain of studying the details in the dim light, she returned the map to the bag.

She rechecked the backpack before zipping it. A sliver of shiny aluminum caught her eye, sticking out of a pocket she hadn't noticed in the dark. Inside, she found a brand of hand warmers she'd never heard of before. Regretfully, she left them where they were. There was no guarantee when they would have warmth again, and they might need them later if the temperatures dipped even more. She shivered at the thought.

Once her phone was put back away, she forced herself not to keep checking the time. The sky gradually lightened. A hoot of an owl nearby caused Shawn to stir.

He pulled his scarf down and groaned. "We survived the night. I guess that's something."

"Two hikers were rescued today." She used her best newscaster voice. "When found, one remarked, 'We survived. I *guess* that's something.'" He didn't return her teasing smile, though. "Sorry, I've been told I'm a morning person."

"You speak in news bites now, huh?" He stretched his arms upward. "That's new. The 'morning person' part I remember. Should serve you well today. The faster we get moving, the faster you get rescued."

Every muscle ached as she turned to climb out of their tight quarters. She pulled down the edge of the scarf ever so slightly. To the east, the night sky had lightened enough that they could see the snow-covered trees with the stars still twinkling from up above.

"First light," she murmured. The half hour before sunrise had always been her favorite when she'd gone camping with her dad. They'd been the two early risers of the group while Eddie and Shawn inevitably slept until roused.

Those had been the best moments in the wild. Experiencing utter stillness and calm—before the birds sang a single note—heightened the beauty and majesty of nature. In turn, she'd always felt closer to God when surrounded by nothing but His creation. Although for the past few years she'd preferred a civilized version of it…like at a zoo or a resort.

Each step in the snow sharpened the fear that the gunmen might appear at any moment. Shawn took the same care in his steps for a minute before attacking the ground with a little more gusto. "If last night was any indication, we should hear them coming."

They struggled to find a pace that wasn't too fast—if they started sweating, their clothes would get damp, a sure recipe for hypothermia—or too slow so they'd never make it to the trailer by nightfall, or worse, before the storm hit.

"I really should've let someone know I was going to the wedding so they'd know to be looking for me."

She imagined her family getting all dressed up in a

few short hours, probably taking family photos without her. Twin Falls, as most would assume, was an unlikely place for a reality star to choose as his home base. But her dad had wanted his children to grow up as close to the wilderness as he had, while her mom wanted to live in a city. The compromise resulted in Twin Falls, a growing town surrounded by unique outdoor terrain with beauty on every side.

Her dad may have grown up camping and hiking, but his real love for survival skills had come during his time as an air force helicopter pilot. Wolfe Dutton never recounted stories from those days, not on his television show nor in real life, but her mom had once confided that he'd rescued many people, some who'd got into danger because they didn't know how to rescue themselves.

Jackie supposed that was what drove him to teach others his survival skills. When his show became a sneak hit, he started his own production company, whose first big purchase was a multimillion-dollar used helicopter that sat fifteen people. He could take his entire production crew out to the most remote areas. Too bad he wasn't in the area filming now.

She stayed in Shawn's footprints, directly behind him. They were both out of breath, which would make them sweaty, and their clothes would get damp. "And then you die," her dad would say. Her dad could take the mildest of decisions to prompt a story that ended with "and then you die."

"The trek would go a lot faster if we had snowshoes of some sort." The clouds gathering far in the west, low and thick, seemed ominous. She didn't know how long the weather front would take to reach them, but it seemed in their best interest to hurry.

Shawn kept trudging until he stopped in front of a tree. He pulled down his scarf and a slow smile spread across his mouth. "Doesn't hurt for Bigtooth Maple to be pruned in the winter."

She didn't need an explanation to know his intent. She picked out branches that were roughly three feet long and flopped them on the snow with the edges pointed upward. Shawn glanced at her choices and picked ones similar. "You're good at this," he said.

"Not really. Certainly not as good as my dad."

They worked in silence until they both had groupings of branches tied to the bottom of their boots. This time they were able to continue walking without sinking so much. The strain on her muscles, though, was no small thing.

Shawn opened his mouth and closed it, shaking his head.

"What? What were you going to say?"

"Is that the real reason you stopped wilderness trekking? Because you weren't as good as your dad? No one can expect to be at his level unless they've lived his life. And even he couldn't anticipate every fall or danger around the corner, even with a map."

"Kind of like how you can't control people or their mistakes, even with love on your side?" She didn't wait for a response. The words just tumbled out and her cheeks heated. She didn't want to start a debate. "Forget I said that. Besides, that's not why I stopped."

Her stomach twisted with the discomfort that came from getting too close to a subject that still brought her shame. “I should’ve seen the signs a cougar was tracking me, though. I should’ve been prepared.” The memories of the pain flared to life, easily encouraged by the strain her muscles had suffered last night. “A broken bone didn’t help matters.”

“That must have been terrifying, but I’m surprised you never went back to it. Eddie was, too.”

“You guys discussed me?” She put her hands on her hips, trying to be playful, but really she wanted to know what they thought of her. Her parents certainly hadn’t said much after the incident. Ironically, the biggest decision of her life at the time had warranted the least amount of discussion, like a taboo subject.

“Well, you weren’t my girlfriend yet.”

She huffed. “So I was fair game to discuss until then?”

“At least until Eddie could tell I was interested in you and made me promise not to date you.” He shook his head. “I always felt guilty for going behind his back. I never specifically agreed to his terms, but I never told him I didn’t, either.”

“*That’s* the reason we dated in secret? I thought we agreed Eddie and my parents would just make things weird.” She handed him a water bottle from the pack. Even though drinking cold water in the frigid temps was the last thing she wanted to do, they needed to keep from dehydrating.

“Well, there was that, too. But mostly because he didn’t want me to date you.”

For some reason, the brotherly protection warmed her heart, though it seemed completely out of character for her twin. Sibling rivalry was more their speed.

"I think we're almost there," Shawn said. "The trees thin out and then stop up ahead. The trailer will be in sight, but so will a lot of the rest of the land."

Jackie dared not hope. The hike had seemed to last for hours, but she had no sense of time without a watch or her phone on. They were close, but would they be able to step out of hiding in the trees without becoming targets? Shawn's forehead mirrored her concern, and they both stilled.

Shawn reached for his gun holster, almost out of habit. He bent over and untied the branches from his boots. Jackie followed suit without a word. While the bare-bones snowshoes helped with long walks, they prevented a stealthy approach.

"Do you have the Taser still?" he whispered.

Her eyes widened, and she pulled the weapon out from the pocket of his coat.

He'd forgotten she was wearing his stuff. "Okay, you can put that back. I'm sure you won't need it," he added hastily. "Just keep it handy. Stay behind me."

As they neared the edge of the clearing, a visual confirmed his worst fear. Two ATVs and a couple of snowmobiles were parked right in front of the archaeologist's field trailer. Two sizable men in full winter gear sat with their hands loosely resting on the handlebars, laughing at each other as if they were having the best day. He'd never wanted to write a ticket for motorized vehicles in unauthorized areas so badly in his life. If these men were responsible for the murders, they'd likely done much worse, but he didn't want to make assumptions.

His bones ached from spending the night in the frigid conditions. A generator, a mini-refrigerator, a hot plate and different kinds of tea and cocoa were all inside that trailer. He knew because on days he was too far from the field office to heat up his lunch when he'd brought leftovers, he'd stopped by the trailer and shot the breeze with Pete, who was often logging archaeological finds, usually minor.

Pete didn't have the best reputation for "street smarts," being considered more of an intellectual than a fieldman. Apparently the job market as an archaeologist proved competitive, and Pete, while disappointed with some of the duties of his position—such as checking to see if an outhouse would contaminate an undiscovered site of historic interest—seemed good at his job. He just hoped Pete had made it back home before the men loitering around his trailer caused trouble.

He placed his hand on the grip of his gun. They were so close to warmth and safety. As long as the men weren't armed, he could tell Jackie to stay back, and handle them.

"What's the status of the storm?" A third man stepped out of the trailer, speaking to the other two still seated on the ATVs. He placed the goggles on top of his head. Shawn hesitated. Were these the same men who had shot at them last night?

The smaller man held up his satellite phone. "Stalled longer than expected in the mountains to the west but expected to hit here in the next twenty-four hours. Supposed to dump an estimated two feet of snow with up to thirty-five-mile-an-hour gusts."

The standing man, seemingly in charge, grunted. "Okay, I think we can get done and out of here as long as the archaeologist cooperates."

"I think he can be made to—"

A gust of wind carried away the second man's words. Shawn's gut grew hot. Whoever these men were, they had taken Pete. He squinted, trying to make out the leader's face. Before he could take mental notes, his gaze caught on the man's belt. A holster.

The other man who'd been speaking also wore a holster. The third guy had a rifle strapped to his back. He couldn't count on the trailer as his means to get Jackie to safety. He stepped back farther into the grouping of trees to reevaluate. If he could just get his hands on a satellite phone…

A twig snapping behind him caught his attention. He spun around to find Jackie, who stood with her gloved hand over her mouth, her eyes as wide as saucers. A stick sat underneath her boot. She pulled her hand down, mouthing *sorry.*

"What was that?" a man's voice said.

Time to move. Except Jackie bent over with the broken fir branch and rapidly wiped his footprint away. That might have worked last night, but it wouldn't help a bit if the men discovered them standing there.

He went to grab her hand, but she brushed it away

and gestured for him to move. He hustled around the largest pine tree closest to them, one that had to be over a hundred years old, judging by its width. Jackie brushed their footprints away until she stood next to him.

He pressed his mouth against her hair. "They'll find us here in a second," he whispered. She pointed underneath the tree.

He almost groaned aloud but didn't have any better ideas. If they ran, the footprints would be a dead giveaway. They both dropped to the ground facing each other, as if about to start doing push-ups, with only an inch or so between their foreheads. He saw the question in her eyes and nodded. They rolled at the same time, until they were underneath the tree branches. Jackie reached out from the prickly cover to brush away their footprints with the same branch she'd used earlier, but her backpack caught on the branch they were hiding under. And judging by the crunch of footsteps, someone fast approached.

Shawn grabbed the branch from her hand. His backpack also caught, but he strained, his arms longer than hers, and jiggled the snow until it covered up the footprints. Before, the fresh, powdery snow had worked against them, but now he was thankful for how loose and fluid the flakes moved.

"I thought I heard something," a voice announced.

Jackie laid her head on her forearms. As the pine needles were sticking directly into his scalp like an acupuncture treatment deserving of a malpractice charge, he tried to do the same. The snow below him worked through the layers of insulation in the coat and caused his muscles to tense against the cold.

"I don't see any footprints."

"So animals rustling inside, then. We probably woke up some squirrel from nap time."

"Squirrels don't hibernate."

Shawn's ear was so close to the ground he could hear their boots making a swoosh sound with each step.

"They sleep a lot in winter," the other man responded.

"That's exactly the same thing as hibernating. Nobody there," the voice that'd given the weather report announced.

"It's absolutely not the same thing," the third man groused.

A gunshot rang out and hit the tree next to them.

They both flinched, but somehow kept quiet.

"A little warning next time," one of the men shouted.

"Just making sure you didn't miss something."

"Now they know where we are."

"Good. We've put them on the defensive and they'll get on the move." The older man who seemed to be calling the shots had no shortage of confidence. "They can't hide within those trees forever. If they want to escape the blizzard, they've got to come out into the open. I'll take a spin around the perimeter and make sure you didn't miss tracks. Carl, you take the other side. Spencer, you stay here with Mr. Wooledge. Make sure he stays on task. The clock is ticking."

Shawn felt fingers touch his hand. He fought to look up and found Jackie's hand wrapped around his. She could only lift her head a few inches, as well, but it was enough to read the concern in her eyes. The trailer was no longer an option and the men were hunting them. They were fast losing their chance at survival.

SEVEN

The man was right. They couldn't hide in the trees forever. Evergreens of all sorts made good Christmas trees, but they were not in any way, shape or form good for a deadly game of hide-and-seek.

"Let me make sure that Spencer guy went inside the trailer," Shawn whispered.

His movements made the branches above her wiggle and dump copious amounts of snow on the back of her head. She deserved it, though. She'd been the one who stepped on and snapped the branch. It was just like the incident with the cougars all over again. She should've checked her surroundings—

"Jackie," Shawn whispered. "Come on. I know where we have to go."

He reached a hand out, and as soon as she gripped his palm, he tugged, dragging her out, past whatever had snagged her pack.

Shawn touched his finger to his chest, indicating she should follow him. They moved slower than before. They hiked up a steep incline, only partially obscured from view. The trees thinned in number. Each step was a test of will, as her legs had already been pushed past normal endurance levels.

Jackie found a foothold on a snow-covered boulder. She put her weight on her right foot and the rock shifted. She cried out as she slipped. Strong hands grabbed her waist, lifted and pulled her backward.

"I've got you," Shawn said.

"I'm sorry I yelled. Do you think they heard me?"

A quick look over his shoulder didn't reveal the men, but their motors could be heard in the distance. "Let's hope not." The sporadic wind gusts played with her hearing, and she was no longer sure in which direction the ATVs and snowmobiles were headed.

He tapped the broken rock. "Looks like sandstone to me. Breaks off easily. This hillside is full of it."

"Great. It's going to be slow going, isn't it?"

"Time is not on our side." Shawn reached for her hand. "Let's work together."

Holding his hand felt more natural, though they were both wearing gloves. Trying to escape people who wanted to end their lives left no room for awkward moments.

Almost in tandem, one of them climbed up a few paces, testing the footholds, and then the other caught up using the proven footsteps. They repeated the routine until it felt like they would be taking turns for the rest of their lives.

Shawn hesitated for a second. The small break in momentum gave her a chance to catch her breath. At least he'd chosen a route a snowmobile couldn't mimic.

She chanced a glance over her shoulder and spotted the top of the trailer. "We've gone quite a distance," she said. "Too bad we can't keep an eye on those ATVs."

"They're probably checking the roads closest to Darrell's truck. They're assuming we would head for the most common route to civilization."

"Aren't we?" Her voice shook with exhaustion. Without the tough physical task of climbing that took all her mental and emotional energy, she felt at risk of falling apart.

He glanced down at her with one eyebrow raised. "Eventually. Our route is just a little riskier to avoid their perimeter searches. Do you have the Taser?"

She nodded. "I don't have a holster, though."

"It's safe enough to carry in your pocket. The pockets in that coat can zip if you're worried about it falling out. You know how to use it, right?"

"I think so. I took some self-defense classes a few years back." As a single woman living on her own, she'd made it a priority when she was in broadcast news. For some reason, it didn't seem as important now when only her byline showed up in print. "It works the same as the ones available to private citizens, right?"

"The ones on the market incapacitate for a full thirty seconds so you can drop the Taser and run away—better still, drive away. The range is about fifteen feet for personal use, while police-issued ones travel twice that."

"So how long do the ones rangers carry incapacitate? Double the amount, like a minute?" The thought of accidentally setting it off terrified her even more.

"Uh, no. Ones designed for law enforcement only last five seconds."

"What? Why so little?"

"To avoid using force unless absolutely necessary. If we're close enough for the Taser to reach its mark, that should be all we need to disarm and apprehend the suspect."

"Wow." She laughed. "I guess you're not supposed to run away."

He smirked. "Generally not. Unless you're outnumbered with no backup and want to keep a friend safe." He exhaled. "My favorite part of my job is teaching people about the land and the animals. There is so much to appreciate here that isn't noticed by the average park goer."

An unusual swoosh sound followed by drums of some sort reached her ears. "Shawn?"

He took a few steps to the northwest. Through a sliver of bushes and evergreens, a valley could be seen below. "It's the sage-grouse—those funny little birds I told you about."

The birds gathered next to a grouping of what looked like tumbleweed. One of the birds flashed pointy feathers and strutted. It puffed up its chest and made the most ridiculous sound. Whenever the bird walked, its ring of fur rose to its neck like a puffy white collar. "I can't believe that was a *bird*."

"Quite a courting call," he said with a laugh, waving her forward. Every muscle wanted to stop for a while, but his smile encouraged her to keep going. Shawn pumped his arms to get over a particularly thick portion of snow. "I've often wondered if he knows how silly he looks and sounds, and if the female agrees."

"It takes vulnerability to show how much you care about a person. At least she knows she's wanted."

The grouse stopped their song and the air stilled with uncomfortable silence. She'd said too much. Despite her resolve to let the past go, her tongue had a will of its own, determined to sneak in little jabs of reminders. What they needed was a change of subject. "Am I off base or should we be worried about your archaeologist friend?"

He turned to her, his face pale. "You picked up on that? Pete Wooledge is his name—off the record."

"I could find out his name for myself if I wanted. He's in a public position. We are running for our lives, and frankly, at this point, I think everything that's happening is as much part of my personal story as the Bureau's."

"And that's my fault."

She hesitated, choosing her words carefully. "If you hadn't called in that news tip, someone else probably would have. Maybe someone from the construction crew—the foreman was beyond frustrated—and I still would've ended up here."

"Thanks, but I know better."

"How about this—if we get out of this alive, you can proclaim 'off the record' all you like. For now, can you tell me why we're going this way? Where is this risky route taking us?"

"The only hope of the archaeologist surviving is if we get to a phone and get backup." His hand drifted to his gun. "I think we're dealing with looters."

She felt her eyebrows jump. “What kind of looters?”

“If I had to guess, I would say tribal antiquities. The Bureau finds new tribal sites every year. It’s estimated that there are likely thousands more undiscovered sites on Idaho public lands. It’s why we have to be so thorough and involve the archaeologists before we so much as put an outhouse on the land.”

“So you think these looters are holding Mr. Wooledge hostage and making him find these tribal sites for them?”

“More likely they’ve already found one and they’re making him catalog or unearth it or something. Looters are the most likely group of people to hold an archaeologist hostage. We have a most-wanted list back at the field office. I didn’t recognize those men, but I wouldn’t be surprised if they’ve changed their hair or aged since their pictures were taken. Sometimes they sell what they find for personal gain, but others sell to fund terrorist groups.”

“Doesn’t it seem unlikely that there are so many sites you haven’t found?”

“I’m responsible for millions of acres. Millions, Jackie, with all sorts of topography. On top of it all, the Oregon Trail crossed over here and split off into the California Trail, as well. We don’t even know all the places the gold-happy settlers tried their hand at mining, even if technically it wasn’t their land. So yes, I think given the history and statistics I’ve been given, it’s very likely.”

She surveyed the land with new eyes. Nothing seemed flat, but everything seemed beautiful. What other mysteries did the land hold? “So you’re saying you have a plan.”

"We can't go back the direction we came if those men are looking for us, so we're going to take a bit of a roundabout and sneak behind the back of the plant." He pointed southeast. "If I remember right, somewhere past this grouping of foothills, there's a rise that builds up to a plateau. If we can get to that, it curves all the way around to the eastern edge of the construction site. I know that the control building of the plant already had a generator and emergency landline installed."

"But that's where the murder—"

He held up a hand. "I know. But that's why we walk on top of the plateau until we get closer to the cement pads. We'll rappel down and sneak behind the construction site until we get to the control building. It's the best option for us to get help, to keep you safe."

"You're not going to try to get the archaeologist first?"

He stopped and stared right into her eyes. "You're my first priority."

The timbre of his voice and the meaning of his words made her heart race. She averted her gaze and turned to the west. From this vantage point she should be able to see mountains instead of a wall of fog. Or was it the storm front?

The thick clouds above made her think of inversions in the Boise area, where air would get stuck in the mountains and become stagnant. Residents were asked to stop using their wood fireplaces during times like that. Here, it meant she couldn't tell where the sun hovered in the sky. "What's the prevailing wind here?"

"West." He pointed to her right. "Come on. Just a little longer and we'll reach the top."

A bullet rang out through the sky and hit the snow ten feet in front of her. "Shawn!"

"It's a man with a rifle. Keep going!"

She hunched over and kept her gaze on the finish line. Almost there. Then they'd be on the other side, hidden. Until the shooter caught up on his snowmobile, at least. She couldn't focus on the despair growing in her chest. Another bullet kicked snow up to her left. The ground gave way and her foot dropped through the snow.

"Jackie!"

Her entire body plummeted through the snow and greeted nothing but air. A scream tore from her throat as she dropped toward a sharp descent. She flung her arms wide and stuck out her feet, crying out as her backside made contact with the thick snow.

She lifted her left knee and twisted it inward, trying to use her boot as a rudder or a brake. Her right leg remained as straight as she could keep it as she sped down the steep snowbank, topping any speed she'd ever achieved on a pair of skis.

"Hold on," Shawn called out.

To what? She kept her arms wide, tucked her chin to her chest and fought to keep her shoulders off the ground. She'd never wanted to be a human toboggan. If she kept the same trajectory she'd slide right over a flat surface with an upward slant. It was likely a rock covered in snow but might as well have been a skateboard ramp.

She dug her left heel and left shoulder into the snow and veered. But not enough. Once again she hit air, except this time she landed on a hard, flat surface and rolled until she came face-to-face with a wolf.

She dared not break eye contact, but she didn't want to appear like she was challenging the animal, either. He opened his mouth and bared his teeth. She pushed herself up to her hands and knees. The wolf growled, a sound that sent shivers down her spine.

She felt the impact of Shawn landing somewhere behind her. His grunt confirmed he'd survived. "You and cornices really don't get along," he muttered.

"Not the time," she said through gritted teeth.

She straightened, holding her hands out toward the wolf. If it made any sudden moves, though, she wasn't sure what she'd do. And she really didn't need to be reminded that she was not cut out for this. Once again, she'd made a mistake with no hope of rescue, because right behind the wolf stood an entire pack, glancing up from some sort of animal carcass.

Shawn gasped. She could hardly swallow or take a breath. "I think we've interrupted their dinner." She forced herself to lift her arms, slowly, making herself look as tall as possible. Trying to force her face into a fierce expression wasn't working, though. She'd written an article once on fear having a particular scent that animals could smell. This was the only time she wished that her reporting proved to be garbage.

"I really hope we don't look better than the planned menu."

Shawn's breath came out in heaving puffs that floated away, like clouds, in the breeze. They were on borrowed time before the gunmen caught up. At least they were on flat land for once, and Jackie didn't appear to have any broken bones. He didn't, either, though his lower back was likely to file an official complaint later.

The growl from the wolf six feet in front of Jackie didn't help his heart rate recover. He took a step closer and the growl intensified and caught the interest of another wolf that had been content feasting nearby. He squinted for a closer look. The average wolf pack was made up of six to eight wolves.

He spotted twelve. *Please tell me I accidentally counted twice.*

"We don't have time for this. That gunman might have to go a longer route to get here, but he'll tell the others. They'll catch up." Jackie held her arms up in a threatening manner, but the wolf didn't seem the least bit deterred.

Shawn noticed the tip of a three-foot branch caught up in the laces of Jackie's boots. While not very thick, the stick might help their cause. He bent over slowly, not wanting to give the wolf any reason to pounce. "Don't stare into his eyes," he said firmly. "You'll feel a tugging on your boot. Hold your stance."

"It's hard to look at him without looking into his eyes!" Her voice grew in volume and she shook her arms at the wolf. The wolf took the slightest step backward.

"Good." Shawn wrapped his hand around the branch and took a step beside her while swinging the branch upward. The wolf took another step backward. Unfortunately, two more of his buddies developed an interest.

"Shawn—"

"I know. They're probably just guarding their food."

"Okay. Okay. So we back up slowly, right?" She rose on her tiptoes and waved her arms. "Back off!"

He hollered and waved the stick in front of him in an arc. "That's it. Yeah, let's back away until they aren't interested, but we can't run or—"

"We die. I know. Let's just hope this time I don't fall off a cliff."

He knew she was recalling her incident with a cougar all those years ago. "I admit you don't have the best record with falling."

"You finally understand why my family used to call me Grace."

At any other time he might've chuckled at the memory. They *had* teased her, but that'd all stopped after she'd gone missing. He'd never told her what it was like for him, waiting until the search team had found her. He'd experienced the same feeling when she'd disappeared in that mound of snow at the top of the hill a moment ago.

Shawn waved the stick in front of him again because he wasn't about to go through the feeling of terror again. "Don't show fear, either, and step behind me." He felt Jackie's fingers grab the back of his coat. She tugged, leading him backward. "That's right," he said. "Good. Let's stay together."

"You keep them back. I'll watch our step," she said.

He let his feet slide backward across the snow some more, still wielding the stick that would easily be treated as a toothpick in the jaws of a wolf. Two of the wolves turned and trotted back to the dinner party.

The final wolf, the one that had started the standoff, took the slightest step back but kept his teeth bared.

Their boots crunched over the snow. The topography changed. The snow didn't seem as soft underneath their feet. It also seemed icier.

"I think it's working," Jackie said. "He's losing interest." The wolf took four more steps back, huffed and turned away to follow the other wolves.

Shawn couldn't celebrate, though. He'd made a fatal flaw in situation awareness. Even the flat areas of the Idaho wilderness should've had giant lumps from snow-covered tumbleweed or bumpy areas of terrain. There was only one logical reason to find such smooth topography. He should've noticed by now, but the gunman and the wolves had made the blood pound in his head and had turned off all other senses.

She continued to pull on his pack, shuffling backward. "You're going to think I'm crazy, but I thought I felt something move under my feet. It—"

"Jackie, stop!" Even as he said it, he felt the shift. The cracking reached his ears, but he was too late. Gravity tugged on him, breaking through the ice below. His legs hit the icy water before his brain could react. His arms shot upward, losing his grasp on the stick.

"No!" He felt Jackie tug on his backpack, the pressure pulling his arms backward for a minuscule portion of a second before she lost the fight against gravity. She'd pulled the pack off his back, without him in it. His fingers spread apart, desperate to grasp anything but only able to touch the icy water. He sucked in a giant breath before the water closed over the top of his head.

He kicked his legs, frantic to keep from plummeting deeper, but the lake didn't care. He continued to free-fall before bobbing upward. He reached his hands above his head. *Please let me come right back up to the hole.* His palms slammed against a thick slab that might as well have been rock. His throat tightened with a held-back scream, almost releasing what little oxygen he had left. He thrust his legs in a scissor motion, shoving his fists against the ice.

Unyielding.

I don't want to die yet. Don't leave Jackie alone up there with the wolves and murderers. I'm not ready. Please!

His thoughts and prayers ping-ponged in his brain so fast he couldn't comprehend much.

So cold.

The water was almost light enough to see through. Something brushed against his leg. He flinched, spinning around to see—a fish. And there, more light. And a hand? A hand holding the stick he'd lost. It thrashed frantically in the water, stirring up the current.

His arms wouldn't move as fast as he wanted. He reached out for it. The burning in his lungs intensified. The ache in his ribs, desperate to expand, almost consumed him. His legs wouldn't kick the way he wanted anymore. Still, he reached.

His right hand touched the slippery wood and his fingers wrapped around it, as if on their own volition. He stretched his left hand and tried to do the same as he closed his eyes. Just for a minute. To make the pain go away. He vaguely sensed he was moving until his face hit frigid air. He sucked in a breath.

"Shawn!" Jackie yelled in his face. "Don't give up!"

He blinked, as if coming out of a nightmare, except pain like he'd never experienced—like lightning—rushed through all his muscles. He fought to focus. Jackie lay flat on her stomach, on the ground—no, the ice. She could fall through at any second, as well. Adrenaline surged through his veins.

She grabbed his right hand and pried it off the stick to move it to her back. "Grab on to my pack."

He did as she asked. She pulled the stick from his left hand. "Both hands on my pack, and don't let go," she ordered. In a smooth motion, she twisted slightly away from him. The momentum pulled him up enough to get his elbows on top of the ice, but the resulting cracks couldn't be ignored. Her back arched and she stabbed the ice with the end of the stick. "Don't let go of the pack! Try to climb!"

He reached six inches past his first grasp. The pack had twisted to her side from his tugging. She pulled on the stick and slid farther away. Her grunt and the strain it had to be causing her gave him newfound strength. He would not let her die for him. Coming out of a frozen lake that was threatening to pull him back in proved to be the hardest pull-up he'd ever endured. His chest hit the ice.

Crack.

"Hold on." She clawed at the ice, slithering away, pushing his pack in front of her as she went. The movement proved enough to help him get his knee out. He vaulted off that pivot point and slid fully on top of the ice. Water poured off the top of his head.

The threatening cracks paralyzed all movements. Jackie twisted around. "I'm going ahead of you, army crawl all the way. Spread your legs. Spread your weight."

He did as she said, though he wanted off the ice as fast as possible. His muscles threatened to stop working.

"Come on, come on. Only a little farther. Keep moving. A little farther." Jackie continued talking until she came to a halt. Shawn followed her gaze. The wolves had stopped eating and all stared, as if enjoying the show. The sound of motors grew louder, though.

"We can't think about them yet." She slithered on, making sure he followed.

The moment she reached the snowy bank, she scampered up, reached for the back of his parka and pulled him the rest of the way to solid ground. He collapsed into the snow, panting.

"Listen very closely," Jackie said. "You must do exactly what I say without question." Her voice shook and her eyes were the widest he'd ever seen. "Do you understand? We've only got four minutes left to save your life."

EIGHT

Five minutes until hypothermia set in, and they'd already used up at least a minute if not two or three just getting him out of the water and off the lake. If she didn't get him past the immediate danger point quickly, she'd have no means to stop his death. The thought seemed to shut down all other emotion. A type of autopilot she didn't know existed overtook her.

She dropped the sopping wet backpack she'd pulled off his back into the snow. "Keep moving. Keep the blood flowing. The adrenaline is what's going to save you. Embrace it." She spoke rapidly as she unzipped his pack and pulled out all the contents as fast as she could. The water had yet to seep fully into the heavy canvas of his bag. The wool blanket was still dry, as well as the food and a host of other items. The water had managed to soak through the bottom of the pack, but that was where he'd stored the rappelling rope.

She grabbed the snow pants, a flannel shirt and the ripped wool blanket, balled them all up and shoved them into his hands. "Head for behind those trees.

Now! You know what to do." He rushed forward in a stumbling type of run to the grouping of bushes twenty feet away.

She turned to the wolves, only a hundred feet or so away from them. She raised both arms, this time unafraid. "You do not want to mess with me right now." She almost didn't recognize the firm, deep voice as her own. For a split second, the wolves turned their heads left and right, almost appearing like domestic dogs trying to decipher a command. But then they went back to their food like the dangerous hunters they were, and her bravado faltered.

A sob had been stuck at the back of her throat for too long. Almost losing Shawn was too much, but they weren't out of danger yet. She couldn't focus on the hard work ahead. She needed to focus on the strength she had. Her father had taught her that. Focus on the positive.

"Except I'm on empty," she whispered. The confession came out more as a prayer. She pulled her shoulders back and lifted a request for His strength before pushing forward. She forced herself not to run, so as not to tempt the prey drive in the wolves. She did walk fast and purposefully, though, as the sound of engines still echoed in the air.

She stopped short and called past the foliage that Shawn had disappeared beyond. As cruel as it seemed, with no fire available, survival training recommended removing wet clothes and rolling around in fresh snow, in hopes the snowflakes would absorb as much moisture as possible.

"Have you taken off the wet items and rolled in the snow? Have you put on the snow pants and blanket?"

"Y-yes." His teeth chattered so loud she could hear it through the brush. "S-s-so cold."

Her eyes flickered to the hills, as the engine sound grew louder. A snowmobile crested one. The gunman had found a way to the top. She didn't need to see what he was reaching for. She turned to run and a bullet tugged on her backpack. She fell down and pushed with her toe into the closest bush.

She crawled forward. A bullet hit the tree above her and bark sprinkled over her like sharp confetti. She forced herself to keep crawling, to keep moving deeper into the foliage. Where had Shawn gone?

"Are you moving?" The amount of restraint needed to keep from yelling in a life-and-death situation tensed her neck muscles to a painful degree.

Silence was the only response.

The bullets stopped. At least the gunman couldn't see her anymore, but it was only a matter of time before he called for the other men to join him. She hadn't seen an easy route for a snowmobile to safely maneuver to the lake area without a steep drop, like they'd endured, but it wasn't as if she had a map of the area to confirm her suspicions.

"Shawn, I need you to talk to me."

She dived through another set of bushes to find him curled up in a ball, shivering with the wool blanket wrapped around his torso and the snow pants on. Definitely meant for a shorter person, the hem of the pants stopped six inches above his ankle.

She ripped off her own backpack, ignoring the bullet hole at the back corner, and pulled her gloves off. While water-resistant, they certainly didn't qualify as waterproof. She searched inside the pack until she found her very chilled, but dry, socks and the fashion boots she'd been in last night.

She sat on the backside of her pack so she could avoid sitting in the snow and took off the detectorist's boots and wool socks. The wool socks were men's size anyway and should fit Shawn, while her thin black ankle socks from last night probably wouldn't have made it over his heel. She made the switch into her old socks and boots as quickly as she could.

"Good thing these socks are long. Put these on." His movements were too slow in responding, so she shoved the wool socks on for him. "These boots are likely to be tight, but at least they're dry."

He looked up and blinked rapidly, his arms still wrapped around himself, covered in the wool blanket. The blue-and-yellow pattern on the flannel he wore would normally have done good things for his complexion, but gray-tinted skin didn't look good on any one. He needed to get his blood flowing properly again.

"We have to get you moving." She held out a hand. He grabbed it and she almost flinched at his cold touch. "Please start talking to me. I need to know that you're lucid." She reached back in her pack to see if there was anything else she had that could help. "The hand warmers!" She'd forgotten her discovery early that morning.

She found the pouches and quickly scanned the directions. Air-activated, they had double-sided adhesive to strategically place the warmers in boots, on the backs of shirts and in gloves. The glove option was no longer possible since both of their pairs had suffered from the dunk in the lake. Still, she helped him stick two on his socks and two on the back of his shirt. He wrapped the blanket tighter and stuffed the ends underneath the overall-like straps of the snow pants to hold it in place.

She moved to take her coat off.

"No."

She hesitated at his fierce objection. "We need to get you warmer."

He shook his head. "I have the blanket and now these warming pads. You've already given up decent boots."

"That's not enough to actually increase your core temperature, Shawn. Here, let me take the wool blanket."

"No, I got it damp now. I'll be fine."

She knew well enough not to mess with his steely-eyed gaze. His mind was made up. "But what are we going to do? If we make a fire—"

"It'll be like a beacon."

"At this point, I'm willing to take the risk."

He frowned. "I… I don't know. We should at least get farther away from the wolves and gunmen before we decide. The last thing I want is to narrowly avoid death, fall asleep by the fire and wake up surrounded by fangs and guns."

"Agreed." She peeked out of the brush. The snowmobile was no longer visible, but maybe he'd found a path down to the lake. Once again, something triggered her mind. East of the lake, a tall giant rocky plateau rose up in the distance. That had to be the plateau Shawn said would help them sneak back to the geothermal plant site.

The gray clouds hovered so low she couldn't see how far north the tabletop rock extended, though. Some foothills bumped right up against the plateau while another set wrapped around the south end of the lake. They loomed above them like guardians, but south of the hills was a majestic pine forest.

The pieces of their location clicked in place. She was staring at the same locations highlighted on the homemade map. The rectangle must have been the archaeologist's trailer, which meant…

She pointed southeast. Her hand still stung from sinking her fingers into the icy waters. "Shawn, is there a warming hut on top of that foothill?" The hope in her voice almost physically hurt. The desperation to be right was so strong she was terrified of disappointment.

His brow furrowed. "That's USFS land. I think so?"

USFS had to be the Unites States Forest Service. That also confirmed her suspicion. The yellow section of the homemade map was likely Bureau of Land Management property, probably to match the color of their shirts and logo, and the green section would match the Forest Service.

"That's a tough hike," he said, his teeth chattering. "But getting indoors sounds amazing."

She handed him a beef jerky. His fingers were like ice cubes. He may have dry clothes on now, but he wasn't out of the danger zone of hypothermia. They needed to get his body temperature up within the next fifteen minutes, which meant she'd drag him up that hill if necessary. "Eat. Let's keep moving."

He blinked, appearing slightly disoriented. Oh, that was a bad sign. *Please help us make it in time.*

Shawn had never lost control of his body before. Maybe that wasn't what was happening, but his arms and legs vibrated at such an intense rate, far beyond any type of shivering he'd ever endured, that he fought to stay calm. Jackie's deepening frown every time she looked back at him didn't help matters. Maybe he looked even worse than he felt.

She dropped his hand. "That's it." A second later she'd tied one end of his rappelling rope around his waist and one around her own. "As much as I'd like to, I can't throw you over my shoulder and hike up this hill. I need to pump my arms to scale this incline and so do you." She grabbed a handful of chocolate almonds and shoved them in his palms. "Stuff these into your mouth and chew. Your metabolism is through the roof right now in order to keep you warm. Keep eating nonstop."

He did as she asked because it seemed simpler, though he wasn't entirely sure why. Every ranger knew the symptoms of hypothermia. He'd spent many winters educating cross-country skiers about the dangers but never thought he'd fall into the trap. He'd lose street cred if anyone else found out.

"Street cred?" Jackie's voice rose.

He hadn't realized he'd spoken aloud.

"Mental confusion is stage two…or three," she said. "I can't remember, but it's not good." She ripped off her coat. "Don't refuse me now." She forced his arms into the sleeves. She took a wool scarf and wrapped it around his head. That wasn't comfortable at all, as the icicles in his hair pressed against his forehead. She put a hand on each side of his face. "Stay with me."

The rope around his waist tugged him forward. She was ahead of him. He grabbed it with both hands and found he really wanted to follow but kept forgetting why.

Wind whipped her hair, clouding her vision. The intensity didn't seem to show any signs of stopping, either. Her heart pounded so hard she thought it would jump out of her chest. The clouds opened and snowflakes as big as quarters drifted onto her head. Any thicker, and she'd lose her way. The prevailing wind came from the west, Shawn had said, which meant she was still heading in a southeastern direction, unless the wind shifted and she got them lost.

The incline eased and she almost shouted for joy. Her heart raced from the exertion and the heavy breathing hurt. She almost walked into a posted sign against a wire fence that read Don't Walk. Baby Forest Growing Here. USFS.

A hundred feet in front of her was a crescent-shaped snow-covered space with the smallest tips of evergreen trees poking up out of its white blanket. Surrounding the space were magnificent trees that could easily compete for the honor of being lit at Rockefeller Plaza. And to the east, nestled into the front line of trees, was the shape of a wooden cabin.

She cried out. A burst of adrenaline pushed her to grab Shawn's hand. Her gentle prodding to jog for the building didn't work. He shuffled in the snow, his eyes half-closed, whether from confusion or from his muscles refusing to loosen up enough to run, she didn't know.

So close. They couldn't come so close only to die.

NINE

Shawn woke up in a sweat. He ached everywhere and felt a giant weight on his chest. He blinked slowly. The dim lighting made it hard to identify his surroundings, but he was dry and warm, and staring at a wooden ceiling. Something shifted next to his legs.

"You're awake." Jackie sat propped upright, her back up against a wall, underneath a massive set of windows. From his vantage point, prostrate on the floor, he spotted blankets of vertical fog—likely snow—coming down on the mountain peaks in the distance. The sky looked precariously close to darkness.

"This place faces west, so we can keep an eye on what's going on," she said. "Unfortunately, you can't see as far as the geothermal plant. I think we need to get to that plateau you were talking about to get a good look." She put down what looked like a pamphlet, shifted and moved to her knees. She placed a warm palm on his forehead. "Your fever broke."

She stood and moved to the smallest stove he'd ever seen, where she picked up a cast-iron kettle and poured liquid from it into a metal cup. "The Bureau really needs to reach out to the college students that built this warming hut so they can build more of them in the area. I've been reading about it while you slept. They built this as an experiment to see if a solar heating pump would work for a warming hut for snowmobilers. Then the trail society put in a propane stove as an added bonus." She crossed the room and set down the cup. "Do you think you can sit up?"

He yawned. The smells of pine and cedar and faint remnants of the fire ashes filled the room. He replayed everything she'd just said when he was barely awake. "Yeah." His voice sounded more like a frog croaking.

She tried to reach for his arm to pull him up, but he didn't need the help. He had a headache, his muscles felt a little sore and his skin a little tingly, but other than that, he seemed back to normal. "I can't believe it's actually toasty in here."

She cringed. "I'm afraid we might be running out of heat soon. I cranked the radiator to the max setting. The brochure says six hours of use with the solar pump." She pushed the warm mug into his hand. "Drink. Warm liquids will make me feel better about your core temperature."

The water was, in a word, disgusting. The metallic taste didn't help his mood, but the rest of his body seemed to appreciate it. The next few minutes he endured her orders to eat and drink more until his mind finally cleared enough to engage.

"I'm fine, Jackie." He reached for her hand, then

looked out the window and groaned. “Any sign of the gunmen? What time is it?”

She shook her head and powered up her phone. “Still no signal, by the way. It’s just after four o’clock.”

He groaned again. “That means we only have an hour before sunset. We’ve been here for *hours*.”

“I know, but your safety was more important to me, and I wasn’t sure what to do. Leaving the heater behind is going to be hard to do.” She gestured to the side door. “Do you know they also have a bathroom? Compost toilets.” Her eyes twinkled. “You really have got to get the Bureau to upgrade—”

“The Bureau manages more land than the Forest Service, but *they* get a bigger budget and three times as many employees.” He held up a hand. “Not that it’s a competition.”

She grinned. “Ah, so I’ve touched on a sore subject.”

“The sore subject is what we do next.” He picked up the pamphlet she’d left on the floor. “We need to get to that control room that has a phone, and call for help.”

Jackie lifted her chin to look out the window. “The wind isn’t messing around, Shawn, and I don’t like how that storm front looks.”

He followed her gaze. The blizzard was fast approaching. “Exactly my point.”

“But there’s a woodstove here. If the blizzard hits before we make it to the building, we’re talking white-out conditions for those looters out there, as well as us. If we stay here, we might be able to risk a fire. They wouldn’t be able to see it.” She crossed the room and pointed to a door. “There’s a changing room that would be big enough for me to sleep in so we could each have privacy."

He wasn't sure how to tell her…

Her expression clouded as he finally met her gaze. "We can't stay here, though, can we?" she asked. "The archaeologist."

He nodded, relieved she understood. "Besides, if those men know the land like they seem to, they'll eventually find their way here. I know I haven't been much help today, and my first priority is to get you safe. But I also can't ignore the fact that those men have Pete and might leave him to die in the blizzard."

Even more likely, the men might murder Pete when they no longer needed him, but Shawn couldn't bear to voice that possibility.

"I understand." She placed a hand on top of his and her cheeks flushed. "You feel warm again. That's good." She stared hard for a few seconds before her shoulders sagged. "I was so scared you were getting close to the dangerous zone. I couldn't remember all the stages of hypothermia."

"Your quick thinking and—" he reached down to pull off the itchy warming pads still in the boots "—ingenuity in what I could do to get warm made all the difference." He frowned as he noticed an extra coat on top of him with the USFS logo.

"I figured out how to open the ranger's closet. There wasn't much except that mug, some cleaning supplies and an extra USFS uniform, including the coat. I figured rangers are—at least philosophically—coworkers in a sense and wouldn't mind. I just piled it all on top of you in lieu of blankets."

He took the pile of clothes she handed him and stepped into the restroom for a moment to change. While it seemed like a small act of betrayal to wear the green forestry uniform instead of his normal tan, he'd never been so thankful for dry, warm clothes. He opened the door to find her at the propane stove.

"You saved me," he said. "Thank you." He noticed the two folding chairs pulled up close to the radiator with his clothes hanging on them, drying. She'd stayed busy while he'd slept.

"Well, it's my fault you needed saving."

He folded his arms across his chest. "Maybe my mind is a little fuzzy, but I don't follow. How do you figure?"

"Like you said, I really don't get along with cliffs."

He felt his eyebrows jump. "You don't really think you could've avoided that fall through the snow today, do you? Even the great Wolfe Dutton—no pun intended—wouldn't have been able to avoid the wolves, especially with someone shooting at him. Is that his real first name? Because I don't think I questioned it growing up." He had to stop for a second. What other thoughts did he need to revisit from his childhood? "And, even then, Wolfe experienced his share of falls—"

"Only dramatized falls. The time he fell through a cornice, he'd already canvassed the area with his crew and knew it'd be a safe drop. And no, his real name is Walter, but that doesn't sound nearly as adventurous as Wolfe, does it?" She shivered. "Although I'm not as fond of the name after coming face-to-face with wolves."

How could she really think today was her fault? He studied her face and the lines around her eyes. "Are you really still affected by that night all those years ago? When you were stuck on that ledge," he added. "That night was more traumatic than we all imagined, wasn't it?" His last question came out in a gentle whisper.

He averted his gaze the moment he asked. He hadn't meant to get so personal or sound so caring. Maybe he could blame his sudden emotional weakness on the lasting effects of hypothermia, but he'd be fooling himself. The more time he spent with her, the more he wanted to be with her. The tenderness in her eyes had been knocking down all the guarded areas of his heart and leaving him vulnerable yet again.

The atmosphere in the room seemed to shift at his unexpected question. "It doesn't occupy my mind all the time," she finally said. "But I also can't seem to get away from my dad's reputation, so I constantly feel pulled back. My first real job was as a reporter for the local news station. It was the same station you called."

He shook his head. "I didn't know that."

She shrugged. "The job was a short-lived stop in my career. I told everyone that the sensationalist nature of television didn't appeal, but that was only half the story." The tension in her ribs started to dissipate as she spoke. "The news director wanted to have a weekly feature where I would attempt survival stunts."

His eyes widened. "Wow. I take it you refused?"

"Until it became an ultimatum. They felt certain, given my relationship to the great Wolfe Dutton, that it would boost ratings—even if I failed horribly, which I knew I would."

"Probably even more viewers if you failed."

She laughed at the thought. "You might be right, but I moved to reporting for the paper instead. I figured if they couldn't see my face, then they wouldn't be tempted to make it an issue."

"But you still get assigned the stories in the wild."

"With a lot of encouragement to reminisce about my childhood and experiences with Wolfe Dutton. I *did* have a lot of wonderful adventures as a child, but they're my stories, and I don't know if I want to share, especially not for my job." She sighed. "I look forward to writing a feature big enough that I can call the shots on the stories I'd like to write without having to go as far as changing my name."

"So the hardest part of trying to say goodbye to the wilderness has been your job?" His question had a joking lilt to it, but something raw stirred within her, maybe because of lack of sleep.

She moved to help him finish packing up the gear. If she kept busy, she wouldn't seem as vulnerable. Shawn handed her one of the makeshift scarves she'd placed near the heater to dry. She wrapped it around her neck. "When I was little, it was all about proving I was just as good as Eddie. But I never loved the adrenaline of conquering the wilderness like my dad did."

"I suppose that's natural when you have a twin brother."

"Maybe, but when I gave it up, I felt a little like I gave up the one thing my dad and I had in common."

Shawn chuckled, shaking his head.

She crossed her arms across her chest. "Why is *that* funny?"

"Because you and your dad are two peas in a pod." He held out his hand and tapped his index finger. "I've never met two people so determined to achieve their goals." He tapped his second finger. "You're both the most passionate people on the planet." He tapped his third finger. "Fierce and full of grit with the most out-of-the-box ideas to make things happen—"

"Even if you're right, I'd still like to reach my dreams on my own merit."

"No one really is self-made, Jackie. Maybe if you embraced who you are and stopped worrying about trying not to be like your dad, then you'd have already written the features you wanted."

She bristled at the notion that he understood her job better than she did. The topic had turned the focus too much on her, but the moment of vulnerability poked at her heart, tempting her to say the thing that had been flittering in the recesses of her mind all day.

He sighed at her silence. "I probably spoke out of turn. We need to hurry," he said. "The sun and our reprieve from the weather are disappearing."

The temptation grew to bursting. "Before we walk out that door together, can we set the record straight so I can move on?"

Apprehension lined his face. "Okay?"

"That's more of a question than an answer, but I'll take it. You said that we would've never worked out. I understand why we wouldn't *now*, but why back then? We had a plan to go to school together. No more secret dating after Eddie left for the army..." She held her hands out, unsure whether she really wanted the answer or not.

He dropped his head and shoulders. She almost didn't recognize the suddenly defeated man in front of her. "You probably won't understand, but I knew I'd never be good enough for you or your family. Probably not for anyone. It's that simple."

That was the last thing she'd ever expected. "My family isn't perfect. I'm not perfect. I think you already know that, though. This is about the night of Eddie's accident."

He crossed the room to put away the mug. "The whole unconditional love thing is either a myth that some people are too stubborn to admit, or it's real but only for people who grow up with it."

She crossed her arms over her chest. "What if it's neither? I'm pretty sure God's the only one truly capable of perfect love. We can decide to love like that, but we're sure to royally mess up along the way."

He pointed at her. "See? That's just what I'm getting at. The messing up is what hurts people. This way, whatever I do only affects me."

"You can't believe that. Even if you live in the middle of nowhere, give me a week to investigate and I guarantee I can prove your choices still impact others."

He studied her for a full ten seconds before the intensity of emotion seemed to magnify in his face, as if he'd just solved a problem. "Is that why you became a journalist? To investigate how choices impact others?"

Every time she started to think that he didn't know her very well anymore, he pulled some profound observation out of his hat. It infuriated her that he was right. "Somewhat." A reflection out of the window caught her eye. "Shawn. Get down!"

She crouched, her fingertips holding the windowsill. She lifted her chin until she could peek over the edge. "I saw light reflecting off the snow below." She pointed. "There's the beam again. Some ATVs are on a corridor of some sort between the foothills."

He groaned. "They doubled back, then. I knew they'd check this route. That's the way the construction workers take to get back to town. The path avoids the lake."

"Why didn't we take that?" The thought that they needlessly suffered through an interchange with wolves and a frozen lake was almost too much to bear.

"Because to get on that path, you have to be to the east of that field trailer, out in the open. We would've been seen. I kept us on the most covered route to avoid being discovered."

She grabbed the binoculars out of the pack and focused on the ATVs. After three tries with the dials she finally got the focus right. "I can't see their faces, but they sure look like a couple of the same men." She let out a long breath of pent-up frustration. "Where does the route go?"

He paled. "It will lead them straight here."

TEN

The lights bounced up and down like a roller-coaster ride. Shawn accepted the pair of binoculars from Jackie. "I'd guess they're half a mile away." A snowplow appeared to be attached to the nose of the first ATV. The second vehicle stayed close, dragging a small trailer, like the type that would usually transport such a vehicle.

"Do you think they've got the stuff they've been looting in that trailer?" Her fingers gripped the window ledge. "You don't see the archaeologist on either of the vehicles, do you?"

He took another look. "I only see two men on the ATVs, but it's possible they're carrying antiquities. If so, they might not need Pete anymore." He pressed his lips tight together. If they hurt him...

"You think they are coming straight for us?"

Shawn lowered the binoculars and frowned. "Since they're carrying a trailer, we can hope they aren't hunting for us."

Jackie shivered. "Unless they plan to kill us, put

us in the trailer and stage an accident like that Darrell guy."

He raised an eyebrow. He hadn't considered a person being in there. What if Pete was trapped in there? "Most likely they're headed for the closest town. Due east. They'll take a sharp turn and head away from us on the snowmobile paths." If only voicing his hopes aloud made them come true.

"If we're that close to a town now, can we follow them at a distance?" She wrapped her arms around herself. "I've never missed central heating so much. Oh, and a real meal, not trail mix or jerky." Her stomach gurgled loudly.

He blew out a long breath and tried to ignore the way his own stomach churned. "If only. On a snowmobile or ATV it'll take them half an hour—maybe longer at their current speed—to get there. It would take us twenty times as long on foot with constant steep inclines and declines to hike."

She exhaled. "Judging by the clouds to the west, the blizzard is almost here."

"We definitely wouldn't make it to town before we were trapped. In whiteout conditions, I don't know that area well enough to lead us." He gestured with his head to the north. "I think we have a better chance of getting on that ridge and sticking to plan A."

He handed her the binoculars so she could see for herself. "Notice how it's at a diagonal? We would travel more as the crow flies, and it's all downhill. I'd guess we'd only have a mile on it until we'd reach the lowest point where we could rappel down. From there, we'd just need to sneak to the back edge of the plant. That might take us another hour, but then we'd be to the control building with a phone and a generator to run the heat."

"So we have a plan, but that doesn't account for the fact that those men are heading straight here, right now." Her voice rose and wobbled as she returned the binoculars to him.

He accepted and reached for her hand. "Don't worry. There's no need to stop here. They'll make a slight left and be on their way without so much as—"

The ATV with the plow rounded the top edge, now level with their location. The headlights bounced over a bump and swung to the right, directly into the warming hut window. Right at them.

"Duck!" they both said at the same time.

She grabbed his backpack and slid it in his direction, across the slick floor. She zipped up her coat and threw on her pack in a heartbeat. The design of the warming hut didn't leave much in the way of hiding spots. The ranger closet might be a possibility, or the bathroom with compostable toilet, but if the men checked either one, they would be trapped without an exit. The hut had been built with fire escape in mind, though, so there was a back door. Unfortunately, the back wall was practically made up of windows, as well. There was nowhere decent to hide.

The other ATV motor approached and quieted. One of the men shouted in the distance, his words muffled by a gust of wind that howled against the door. Footsteps crunched against the snow.

"Back door," Shawn whispered. They ran across the floor together and burst into the cold. He cringed at the sudden change in temperature, remembering all too well the level of cold he'd experienced hours ago. He never wanted to go swimming again.

Jackie raced ahead to a spot without windows and pressed her back against the thick wooden siding. Shawn mimicked her actions a half second later. The shadows worked to their advantage, covering the side of the building in darkness. A man shouted something about the heat and the oven still being hot. He looked upward. Couldn't one thing go right today?

"It's time to give it up," another man yelled. "I saw you fall into the lake. It's time to show yourself if you want to live."

"They know we're here," Jackie whispered. "One look out the back window, and they'll see our footprints."

Shawn searched the area for a solution. They couldn't outrun the men, especially if they returned to their vehicles. His muscles felt like they'd just endured a marathon after the ice incident. He had replaced his holster, so he had his gun, but there were at least two armed men out there. He slipped the gun from his belt.

Jackie stared at his hand with questions in her eyes.

He couldn't shoot to kill without risking Pete's location dying with them. He needed to arrest them, get to a phone and call for backup and a search party. "If we can separate them, I can disarm them, one at a time."

The moon highlighted the closest tree, a giant oak that didn't so much as budge with the wind, towering above them. Without leaves, the branches wouldn't offer them any camouflage, but the close proximity to the roof would allow him to gain a good vantage point and be able to use the element of surprise. Rarely did people look up.

He pointed to the tree. "Climb." If ever there were a degree for climbing trees, Jackie would've earned it by the time she was in third grade. So he had no reservations that she could still do it.

She nodded. "Lead the way."

He almost argued, but he was slower than her. Strategically, he grabbed at the lowest hanging branch and vaulted up the tree. Years of practice meant he didn't need to study physics to know how to scale the oak using the least amount of energy and strength possible. His feet took much of the weight, but his body had taken a beating over the last couple of days, so every movement hurt. He glanced down to see if Jackie was right behind him.

She wasn't there. His stomach flipped. He searched frantically, poking his head on either side of the trunk, looking for her. Footprints reflected off what little light still shone from the sky. He spotted her at the edge of the grouping of evergreens. His heart raced. It took all his self-control not to yell, "What are you doing?"

Two bullets rang out into the night sky. "I'm losing my patience," a man hollered. "We're going to catch you sooner or later. The faster you show yourself, the faster we can all get warm. Unless you'd prefer to die in the blizzard..."

As if they'd forget about the two murders the men were responsible for and surrender? He'd take their chances with a blizzard any day. He couldn't see the men, not even the one who was doing all the yelling, and he still had no idea where they were. They had to be out front searching for them. Jackie spun around at the tree line and her gaze found him. She held up one finger as if to say "one second," and then she made a second path, heading right back to his tree, but this time walked backward.

Instantly, he understood. She wanted to make a fake set of tracks to make it appear as if they'd run deeper into the forest. A diversion would give them time to escape, maybe even commandeer their vehicles and go straight for town. A smart idea, if only they had more time. Any second—

One of the men rounded the east side of the building. Shawn froze, paralyzed at the thought of what was about to happen. The man pulled out a handgun and aimed it at Jackie. She didn't see him, though. She was too busy keeping a lookout on the opposite side of the building.

Shawn kept one hand on the tree trunk, aimed and yelled, "Drop your weapon!" The man spun in his direction, gun still in hand. Shawn fired and the man dived to the ground.

A bullet whizzed past Shawn's ear from the opposite direction. He twisted to see the second man below, aiming a gun directly at him. A rustling of tree limbs in the distance caught their attention.

"Go after her," the second man yelled to the first. "She's getting away!"

Shawn used the distraction to make his move. He lunged for the roof, except his backpack caught on something. He struggled against the branch's pull on the pack, as the first man took off after Jackie. Shawn slid out of the handles.

The second man moved his aim back to Shawn. "What goes up must come down," he said with a sneer.

Shawn grabbed the dislodged pack and threw it. The pack met its mark, hitting the gunman's nose. Shawn leaped from the thick branch to the roof, no longer worried about stealth. He needed to get to Jackie before the other gunman did.

He landed and dropped into a crouch, doing his best to sink his feet and fingers through the snow to find a grip on the roof. Not much stuck to the metal shingles, but it proved slicker than he would've liked. He scampered up one side and slid down the opposite side of the roof. Without a gutter to stop his descent, he slammed into the ground, dangerously close to the ATV plow, in the giant mound of snow the blade had pushed aside. He rolled off and climbed up the side of the ATV. The keys weren't left in the ignition.

His hamstrings stung from the effort of jumping to standing, but he pushed through the pain and launched into a sprint, banging on the trailer as he passed. Jackie's imagination got the best of him and he feared she might be right about the trailer being used as hostage storage. Not a single noise, though. Unless Pete was already dead. Shawn shook off the thought and darted into the first grouping of evergreen trees. Jackie was somewhere within them, along with the other gunman.

He lifted up a silent prayer that he'd be the one to find her first.

Jackie's heavy breathing would give her away, she was sure of it. She couldn't run in the deep snow, her feet crunching with every step, without being found instantly. The grouping of evergreens, taller than the likes she'd normally seen, discouraged passage. The sunset gave way to darkness in the forest. The branches, heavy with snow, hung down like giant fingers eager to grab her.

The snow had come down harder here—or, more likely, the sun's rays didn't quite make it through the thick vegetation to melt the snow as easily. The heavy buildup underneath the trees meant there'd be no hiding places.

The crunching of footsteps behind her grew closer, faster. An unleashed scream continued to build, tightening her chest and neck, until she wasn't sure how much longer she could hold it inside. She pushed past two tree branches.

The land opened. No more trees. In front of her an expanse covered in dark shadows stretched for at least a mile, lit up only by the moon rising. The sun had completely disappeared behind the mountains to the west.

With every step she took, four crunching footsteps could be heard rushing her way. There was no time to hide her tracks. *Please cover me, Lord.*

Her toe caught a rock and she tripped. Pine needles

slapped her face as she fell to her hands and knees, right through the branches. The clouds shifted and the moon shone over the beautiful expanse of rolling hills. Tall grasses poked out of the blanket of snow, and a few monoliths stood guard in the distance. Giant boulders peppered the field and wore stacked snowflakes like Santa hats.

Not a single tree to be found on the lot in front of her, though. Nowhere to hide. She would have to run in the deep snow, flat out, for five minutes before she reached one of the towering monoliths. Even then, there was likely nothing behind it besides more open space. She'd be an easy target. And what about Shawn? Had he escaped or was he—

Judging by the footsteps, there was definitely more than one man following her, which could only mean one thing. They weren't after Shawn because they'd already got him. Her eyes burned hot with sudden tears, the moisture leaking slightly and stinging her skin. But she needed to see clearly. Now wasn't the time to lose it.

She blinked rapidly. This was her fault. She kept listening to her gut on instinct, the way she'd been trained, but when was she going to get it through her thick head that she wasn't her father? She had no business trying to help. She should've just gone up the tree instead of trying to fool the men into following her fake tracks.

The sound of other footsteps stopped. Her ears strained. Whispers filtered through the branches. "You go that way. I'll take this side."

They were going to ambush her, then. They had guns. She had nothing but a Taser she'd foolishly stuffed in the backpack with everything else, in too big of a hurry to be more strategic.

If Shawn had managed to stay alive despite the gunshots she'd heard, she needed to keep her wits about her. If they caught her or tried to shoot her, he would come for her. The certainty surprised her. This was different from the night of the accident, the night he'd left.

She'd seen the determination to get her to safety in his eyes ever since he'd rescued her. Whatever messed-up notion he carried about not being good enough, she knew he wouldn't let her die without a fight, which meant he would die trying to save her.

She couldn't allow that. With a new rush of determination, she picked up the rock that had tripped her, bolted upright and sprinted for the boulder fifteen feet away. She kicked her foot out and dropped to the ground, sliding behind the boulder like going for home plate. The moment she squeezed between the tall grass and the boulder, she popped up on one knee and threw the rock at the closest evergreen tree. She hit her mark and snow cascaded down from that tree and another whose branches intertwined it. The snow would cover her tracks.

She dropped down into a seated position and leaned over, her head between her knees. *Please cover me and protect Shawn.* The prayer ran on a loop in her head as the seconds felt like minutes.

She couldn't afford to move in the snow without the men hearing her. She wrapped her arms around her legs and covered her mouth to muffle her heavy breathing and the cloudlike vapor it produced. Her heart pounded hard against her ribs. Her throat stung with the shallow inhalations of freezing air.

Branches rustled. “You see her?”

“No. You?” the deeper voice of the two asked. A light beam traveled over her head to the ground not more than three feet in front of her. She held her breath.

The bushes moved, but not from wind. Something had erupted from its slumber. A squeak escaped her lips as the flock of dozens of birds that took flight covered her mistake.

The beam of light moved upward, illuminating the animals. The funny-looking birds, the sage-grouse, flew low to the ground, their wings fluttering so hard they sounded like a fleet of miniature helicopters taking off.

A bullet shot into the night. The sound of wings continued flapping, drifting off into the distance. Her heart beat against her chest so hard she was sure the men would be able to hear.

“You missed,” the deep voice said.

“Warning shot. What were those freaky, bearded chicken things, anyway?”

“I don’t know, but you’ve just given away our location to the ranger.”

“He missed me. He’s not a good shot.”

“What if he didn’t mean to hit you? He told you to put your gun down.”

“Either way, then, we don’t need to worry about him making trouble when we leave.”

Hope soared. The ranger they'd mentioned had to be Shawn. So he was alive. But if they weren't worried about him making trouble, what did that mean? The beam of light bounced around the ground again.

Jackie forced herself to raise her head just enough to see over her knees and get a better view of her surroundings. As soon as the men were gone, she'd need to leave her hiding place. No cliffs or drop-offs were apparent from this vantage point, but there were a lot of things to trip over. The areas in front of the monoliths seemed to have less snow, as if they'd been groomed before, almost like snowmobile paths. Odd.

"I'm not going any farther," the scratchy voice concluded. The light clicked off. "You know why. Maybe she doubled back and went into the trees, headed the opposite direction."

"Or you could think of it as your motivation not to get on the boss's bad side and check it out just in case," the deeper voice responded.

"That job wasn't supposed to be part of the deal. I'm not going back there, so drop it. You got the ranger's gear?"

Their conversation didn't make any sense. Where didn't he want to go? What job wasn't part of the deal? She really hoped he meant killing them wasn't part of the deal.

"Yeah, I got it." A zipper being opened sounded closer than Jackie liked. "Water bottles, food, a blanket… He's not going to make it to town before the blizzard. No way they're going to survive without this stuff."

"What about the warming hut?" The crunching of snow followed his question.

"We'll disable it on our way back. Things will be worse for us if we don't stay on schedule."

She relaxed ever so slightly, pulling her coat tighter. If the men took what she'd deduced was the snowmobile path, they would round the bend and see her. She needed to find Shawn and hide. It would take those men a few minutes to weave their way back through the forest to the warming hut. Still, she waited until there was utter silence.

She moved to get up. An owl broke the quiet with his song. She froze. The owl called out again. Wait. Though it sounded remarkably similar to a real one, if she listened closely, this "owl" was increasingly enunciating his sounds. That was no owl. The call almost sounded like *Who cooks for you?*

Her dad had once taught them that the word choice allowed them to mimic the cadence of an owl call better than a simple repetition of "hoo." They used to play epic games of hide-and-seek in the mountains, teasing each other with the calls. She hesitated. Was her voice strong enough to sound authentic?

She took a breath and tried. Footsteps answered her own high-pitched call, though she slurred her words together more to sound realistic. The trees moved slightly and Shawn stepped out into the moonlight. Her heart almost stopped at the sight of him standing there. She rushed for him. He followed her lead and ran toward her. Without thinking, she opened her arms, and they embraced.

She pressed her cheek on his chest, his coat open enough that she could hear the rapid beating of his heart underneath the forestry uniform. He wrapped his arms around her tightly, pulling her closer. His chin rested on the top of her head. “I was so worried about you,” he whispered. “I didn’t want to risk shouting your name. I’m thankful you remembered.”

She laughed but didn’t move away. “Your call was a little too enunciated.”

“I was afraid you would think I was a real owl.”

“You’re not *that* good,” she teased.

“It’s been a long time, though.” His voice softened, as if his words held more meaning.

“Yes.” It had been a long time since they’d adventured together, but the embrace brought back sweet memories, as well. A motor revved, giving her confidence they could talk louder. She lifted her head to look in his face. “Did you hear them talking? They’re on some sort of schedule, but they’ll be back to disable the warming hut.”

He dropped his arms. “Let’s step into the line of trees.” They huddled side by side among the trees as the ATV motor grew louder. Huh. She really thought they would’ve passed through by now and she could only distinctly hear one. It almost sounded as if they were trying to warm up the engine, maybe because of the frigid temperatures.

“They didn’t want to go after me in the open field,” she said. “Seemed odd to me.”

“They probably didn’t know if you were armed or not.”

"It almost sounded like they'd been here once, though." She supposed it didn't matter now. "How'd you get away? I heard shots."

He exhaled. "By the skin of my teeth. How'd you?"

"I think God answered my prayer. Maybe that sounds ridiculous, but I was able to hide and the sage-grouse offered a diversion. I think I see why you like those birds."

"Doesn't sound ridiculous to me." He smiled. "I like them even more now. Your dad was the one that helped me appreciate the way the ecosystem was created. I'm not against progress or hunting. I just want to protect the land." Howls filled the night sky and a gust of wind drowned out the noise. "At the moment, I'd be fine if the land had less animals that could eat us."

A shiver ran up her spine.

Shawn put an arm around her shoulders. "Are you okay?"

"I should be asking you that. You barely recovered from the lake. And were they right? Did they get your pack with the supplies?"

"I'm afraid so." He sighed. "All the more reason to start moving. I feel like a hypocrite hiking in the dark when I spend my days preaching against it." He picked up a stick and handed it to her. "You know the dangers, too, but I don't see any way around it."

"Do you know this area?" Jackie asked. They were saying goodbye to their last chance at shelter, so she fought against his impatience to leave if those ATVs would just move on to wherever they were going.

"Enough," he said. "I've groomed a portion of the snowmobile trails nearby. The USFS land juts into our

Bureau territory for only this bit. The rest of their land is all south of here. We need to cross north over the trail the ATVs used and we'll be on the plateau. If we stick to the backside of it, closest to the trees there, we will be covered. Then when we get to the narrowest point we can rappel down."

Jackie rifled in her pack. "I have one bottle of water left, a couple snacks and one of your ropes. But that's it." She gasped. "Shawn, my purse is still in my pack! Don't you see? That means I still have my car keys. Even if we can't find a phone, if we get to the control building, my car is there. We should be able to drive away."

For the first time since the nightmare had started, she finally felt like they could do it. They could get to safety.

He grinned. "That'd be great, but let's not get our hopes up. Driving in a blizzard—"

"I have chains in my trunk and a shovel." She shook her head, beaming. "Nothing will be able to stop me."

He raised his eyebrows. "Which tells me you're still a survivalist. You just prefer the urban jungle."

"And you prefer forestry over enforcer?"

He laughed. "Wrong agency, but yeah."

She moved the key to the front zippered pocket of the pack, for quick access, and returned her pack to her back. She was ready to face the storm now that they had a plan *and* a backup plan.

The click of metal sounded and in an instant she knew their plans had been destroyed. "Hands up," the gruff voice said. "No turning around."

She dared to glance at Shawn, only to find his face

pale. The man behind him pressed a gun into the back of his coat.

"Face forward," he barked. The sound of static filled the air. "I've got 'em. Right at the tree line. Over."

"Got it. Be right there. Over," the younger voice answered.

The motor instantly died and only the sound of wind whistling through the tops of the trees took its place.

"Seems I owe my partner some money. He had the idea of running the ATV motor nearby so you two would think you were safe enough to find each other. Didn't think the motor would cover up all my footsteps but guess he was right."

The man in question joined them almost instantly, his rifle pointed right at Jackie. He'd been the one to shoot her pack earlier, then.

"They were just talking about the danger of hiking," the gruff voice said. "I think that sounds like a fine idea. Get moving."

She wrapped her fingers around the makeshift walking stick still in her hand and stared into the ever-darkening sky. Did she dare try to use it as a weapon? One little stick couldn't overpower a rifle and a handgun before someone pulled a trigger, though. She dropped her head against the wind and took a step forward, having no idea where they were being led.

Shawn wasn't the only one who warned against the dangers of hiking at night. Her father had drilled the sentiment in her own mind, as well. No matter what happened tonight, she knew without a doubt they were about to face death.

ELEVEN

Shawn zipped up the coat he was wearing as the man shoved him forward with the end of his gun. They seemed to want them to go straight ahead, away from the ATVs and the warming hut.

"I wasn't kidding," the man with the rifle said. "I don't want to go out there again."

"You don't have to do anything but make sure they follow my directions."

They trudged forward. Jackie took a step closer to him and their shoulders bumped. "Sorry," she said. "The gusts are getting stronger."

"Keep moving," the man said.

They quickly discovered the bumpy portion of the terrain, tumbleweed, rocks and bushes hidden underneath the thick layer of snow. Jackie tripped and fell forward, crying out.

Like a punch to the gut, he couldn't stand to see her in pain. Even for a second. He dived for her, but the man grabbed the back of his coat. "Oh, no, you don't. Keep the hands up."

"He still has a weapon," the younger man yelled. He gestured wildly with the rifle. "Take it out of the holster and kick it."

He pressed the release in his holster. There went the last bit of protection he could offer Jackie. He tossed the weapon to the side then leaned over to help Jackie. His eyelashes filled with flakes a second after he'd blinked them away.

"Are you okay?"

She nodded but didn't attempt to speak. That wasn't good. Jackie only stayed quiet when she was really upset or hurting. He wanted to pull her into a hug again. The way she'd reached out to him earlier…

The surge of feelings took him by surprise and left his throat and gut feeling hot and tense. She reached for his hand and he pulled her up to standing as the men started yelling for them to hurry up.

He adjusted his stride to match hers so she wouldn't fall again without his arms there to catch her. Very few thoughts crossed his mind, since the work of hiking in the storm took great concentration, but their recent conversations replayed in his head. Even if he did get a do-over from that night he'd left, if he had a chance to properly say goodbye before they parted ways, he had a sinking feeling this time it would be much harder to let her go.

Still, she remained utterly quiet. Maybe she'd been injured and didn't want to tell him. Like the splinters from earlier, she'd rather keep her mouth tight than complain of pain. Her competitive streak could be exasperating at times, but it served her well when grit and endurance were required. She'd never leave him without a fight. The thought took him by surprise, and with a jolt he also realized the gun wasn't pressing into his jacket anymore. He glanced over his shoulder. The two men stood a good six feet behind them.

"Keep going," the man yelled.

Shawn hesitated. Why would they make them walk all this way just to shoot them in the back? How would that ever be construed as an accident? This wasn't hunting land. The snow grew thinner, smoother.

Tripping over tumbleweed, he let go of Jackie's hand on instinct to catch himself. His hands sank into the packed-down snow.

"Shawn, are you okay?" She crouched next to him.

The winds eased but still blew her hair across her face. Her vibrant blue eyes made his heart pound harder.

He'd been the one to leave her without a fight all those years ago. He knew he'd grown up a lot since his teenage years, but the thought smacked him upside the head. Why had he never realized the irony before? The very hurt he'd been running from, the very hurt he'd been trying to prevent, he'd inflicted on someone else. On Jackie. Why couldn't he have seen that before now?

Yes, she still hadn't defended him that horrible night, but he hadn't really given her a chance, had he? What if he'd stayed? It was a stupid question because he couldn't change the past. Being submerged in ice water must have frozen some of his brain cells.

His hands sank deeper in the snow. He shifted to try to get up before the men yelled another threat. Jackie offered her hand and he accepted it. As he stood, he lifted his knee and stepped into a lunge to fully stand. The earth shifted underneath his front foot. His heel slipped forward. Jackie clung tighter to his hand. "What—"

The snow shifted and started to move, like quicksand. Jackie pulled on his arm then slipped past him. She screamed. The snow disappeared beneath them and they plunged into darkness.

Stale, cold, black air engulfed them. He tightened his fingers around her hand, determined not to let go, and reached out with his other hand to grab on to anything. *Anything, please!*

His grip found a hard ledge of some sort and his fingers dug in deep, pain radiating down his forearm from the strain. His torso slammed against rock from the sudden jolt. He groaned at the impact and squinted into the dark. His feet dangled. Musty air swirled up and around him, escaping into a hole above, into the night sky.

"Jackie?"

"You can let go of me." Her voice was quiet and weak.

"What? Never." He tried to tilt his head to see her. He blinked rapidly, his eyes beginning to adjust. A mine. They had to be in a mine. A mine was always an unknown. The chute could be fifty to hundreds of feet straight down into the earth, depending on when it was built.

"It's fine," she whispered, gasping. "I think I've got something, but I need both hands."

His left arm stretched as far as it could go without his socket threatening to jump ship, but if he let go and she didn't have a good grip…

He couldn't bear the thought. "Are you sure you have footing?"

"I think so. You have to let go, Shawn. My arm can't—"

"Okay. One, two, three." Their fingers slipped apart from each other. He moved his hand to join the other on what seemed like an old piece of wood. His feet tapped the tunnel or enclosure they were in. The walls had to be made out of rock. He found a foothold that helped ease the strain on his arms and tried to catch his breath. "You still with me?"

"I think I'm fine." She broke into a coughing fit. "I'm standing on something. Where are we?"

"Shhh," he whispered. He strained his ears to listen. The men knew about this mine. That was why they'd stopped when they did. They knew they'd fall right in it. That *would* make their deaths look like an accident, and he'd walked right into the trap. They'd never have justice. But on the bright side, they were alive. They just couldn't let the men know it lest they tried harder.

Every second he clung to the side without being able to truly see his surroundings was like a python tightening around his ribs. It hurt to breathe. Finally, mercifully, he heard the slightest rev of an engine. The ground above them vibrated, dust and snow slipping past him. Were the men really gone or pulling a fast one again?

An ominous creak of metal echoed around them.

"Shawn?" Her voice wavered.

He pulled out the phone from his pocket and clicked the side button so the screen would light up their surroundings. His hand looked more like a claw gripping on to a rung of an old wooden ladder, but he was hanging straight down while the ladder was attached diagonally, as was the mine chute. He shifted to balance his foot on a ladder rung. He twisted carefully, and the wood creaked with every movement.

He tilted the light in her direction, this time flicking on the flashlight app for a more concentrated beam. Jackie clung to another partial slat of wood that served as a framework for the chute, but her feet rested on the trunk of a blue car, pointed vertically down into the earth. The car groaned and shifted, testing whatever rock formations temporarily suspended it.

She glanced down at her feet and cried out. "It's my car!"

A couple of creaks echoed through the air. She screamed as the car plunged a few inches, and she barely was able to keep her fingers on the wood frame. Shawn dropped the phone as he reached for her. The light bounced all around the rock tunnel as he spun on the ladder and tried again, reaching for her with his other arm. He grabbed her wrist. "Let go of the wood!"

She looked up, her eyes wide. The car creaked against the rock again.

His phone had landed on the rearview window of the car. The light illuminated the inside of the vehicle and reflected off a construction vest on a dead man who was pressed in between the windshield and the dashboard. Shawn fought against a wave of nausea. He didn't know the man well, but he'd been the associate field manager for the geothermal site. He had to be whose murder she'd witnessed in the first place.

Metal groaned again.

The walls of the tunnel shifted enough that rocks and debris sprinkled on them from every direction. "Jackie!"

She let go of the wood and her other hand grabbed his arm. She dangled from his grip, but he couldn't let go of the ladder, despite the snow falling onto the back of his neck from above. He strained the muscles in his back, pulling her toward him. One of her feet found a foothold on the wall, and her other leg stretched to find a rung on the ladder.

A squeal of metal breaking apart pierced the air, and the car plunged. All the air rushed out of him in shock. The car must've dropped fifty, a hundred feet down. If not for his lost phone, they'd only see darkness. Jackie climbed up his arm. He had to stay bent over until she managed to get both feet on the ladder. She wrapped one arm around his right ankle. "You can let go of my hand now."

"The ladder could go at any minute. Keep hanging on to my ankle." He let go of her and moved to climb up the ancient wood.

"Okay. Let's climb together. Move your right foot first."

He did and her fingers stayed wrapped around his ankle. He could feel her movement on the ladder. They moved in slow motion during the precarious climb, until the tunnel curved enough that he could see how they'd slid down.

"It's like the world's worst underground slide," she said.

"Something like that. An abandoned mine." He reached the top rung. "Okay. This is the hard part."

"You've got to be kidding me. Please don't tell me we haven't done the hard part yet."

"I know." He hesitated, panting, trying in vain to catch his breath. "I'm sorry. I'm going to lean over you, take the rope out of your backpack and give you one end. Then I'm going to need you to let go of my foot so I can rock climb my way out and pull you up."

"Just another day at the gym, right?" Her voice shook, but her bravado kept him going. He embraced the attitude. Just one more pull-up. He could do it.

He had to or they would both die.

She couldn't watch. The right thing to do was to encourage him, she knew that, but internally she was screaming. More rocks bounced past her and she bit her lip. Shawn groaned and she finally lifted her chin.

His feet dangled above her before he maneuvered over the final ledge and climbed out of the hole that had sucked them inside. The quiet and darkness of the mine seemed to amplify the moment she was left alone.

The packed-down snow area she'd thought was from snowmobiles had to be the earlier work of those men on ATVs, especially the one with the plow. They'd tried to cover up the death of the man she'd seen murdered by putting him in her car.

Her breathing turned shallow. If they succeeded at killing her, how likely would it be that her family would ever find her?

"I think I've got the rope secure," Shawn called out. "Test it without letting go."

Not exactly the best pep talk she'd heard. She closed her eyes and lifted up what seemed like the hundredth prayer for help. She twisted a section of the rope around and around her forearm and gripped it as she shifted.

"So far so good. Keep going. I'm holding it, too."

She took another tentative step and the wood cracked but held. Each step challenged her trust in God, the rope and Shawn. She reached the ladder's top rung and dared to look up. The space between the ladder and the ground above might as well have been hundreds of feet because she didn't see how she could climb it.

Shawn took a deep breath, sprawled on his stomach in the mouth of the mine, his arms hanging down and holding the rope with both hands. The sight was enough to make her want to scream in frustration. "What's to keep *you* from sliding down again?"

"I've got the middle part of the rope around my leg, and the last bit wrapped around a boulder. Ready when you are, Jackie."

She held on to the rope tightly and stared right into his eyes as she stepped off the ladder, launching off the same foothold Shawn had found earlier. He let go of the rope with one hand and grabbed the back of her backpack. The brief halt to gravity pulling her back down was enough to find another foothold and press up. A moment later she collapsed onto the firm ground and cried out. Every fiber of her muscles felt like it had been stretched and pulled.

"Are you hurt?" Shawn checked her over, helping her stand. As soon as they were far enough away from the mine, he untied the middle of the rope that had been looped around his foot and freed the end tied around a boulder.

She groaned at the effort her abs required for her to get back to her knees. "I told you I never wanted to be out here again. I never wanted to be a survivalist." She wasn't sure if she was talking more to Shawn or the Lord.

"I know, but we can't focus on that right now." He reached for her hand, still gasping for breath, as well. "Come on, Jackie. I can't do this without you."

"Since when?" she asked. "You said you like to rely only on yourself. You don't want to be needed, and here I am, utterly dependent."

"I never said I didn't want to help people, and we need each other."

She shook her head, unwilling to process what he was saying. She couldn't hold on to the pain in silence any longer. It all hurt. Physically, emotionally, mentally, she felt desperate to give up. To stop feeling pain.

She sucked in a breath and hated the cold air she had to breathe. "I can't do this. I can't. Did you see him? The man? Dead Geothermal Plant Employee Found in Journalist's Vehicle in a—" Her voice trembled. "What'd you say it was? A mine? I can't even finish the headline. And even if I could, it would be too long. Just like this entire weekend. It's too much."

Her heart rate and mouth wouldn't slow down. They'd almost died. Never again. She'd promised herself she'd never again be in a situation like this. And yet here she was.

"Yes," he said solemnly.

"Is that all you can say?"

"His name was Bob, and he was the associate field manager." Shawn walked farther away from the hole and beckoned her to follow him. "Some mines go straight down like a chute or are hidden in rocks like that. Just breathe, Jackie. You've been amazing. I need you to hang on a little longer."

She wasn't in the right mindset to listen to encouragement. When she'd seen the dead body in her car, she'd reached her breaking point. "I thought you knew this area. Didn't you know about the mine?"

"If I had, there would've been wire sealing off the entrance and a giant orange sign that said Stay Out, Stay Alive." He threw his arms up in the air and exhaled. "There are hundreds—thousands, maybe—of abandoned mines we haven't found yet. Ancient. You know that." He dropped his hands and his shoulders rounded. She saw then. He was shaken, too.

The wind gusted and seemed to suck out the air from her lungs. "You're right. I'm sorry I'm letting all this get to me." The snow pelted her face without any sign of stopping.

"What worries me most is whoever we're dealing

with knows the land better than I do." He dropped to his knees.

"What are you doing?" She realized they'd been following their footsteps back to the tree line. "We have to keep moving. It's too late to stop. Let's get to the other side. Sturdy rock over there, remember? Are you okay?"

He froze and looked up. He lifted his gun. "Much better now." He stood and holstered his weapon.

A light flashed in the distance. "Was that light going or coming?"

"I can't be sure. Let's assume they turned a corner. Please, follow me."

She held up a hand. "We should use the rope now, right? We don't know when one of us could fall through another snow bridge."

He hesitated to answer.

"Is it a bad idea?"

He shook his head. "No." He tied the rope around her waist. "I'm scared, though. If I fall, you go down with me. I can't stomach seeing you hurt," he said softly.

She stared at him in confusion. What had happened to the man who wanted to go everything alone? He turned away from her and they pressed on. Once they reached the trail the ATVs had taken, she forced herself into a jog to get across.

Shawn kept glancing back, his face turned into the wind, to check on her, and she waved him ahead. There was no use talking. The weather wouldn't let him hear her even if she shouted. The cloud shifted and the moon got its chance to light up the sky. The snowflakes dissipated.

They reached the rocky plateau. It had a downhill slant just as he'd told her to expect. She took another step and her leg gave out, sending her tumbling into the snow.

Shawn jogged back, his hands outstretched. "Are you okay?"

Her cheeks burned from the wind and the heat of embarrassment. She trained to stay physically fit, but never before had she asked her body to endure so much. "Aside from needing a massage and a hot shower, I'm peachy." She glanced down at her pants. They were almost soaked through. His were, as well. If they didn't get to some warmth soon, they would both be facing the real threat of frostbite. "My boots don't have the best traction."

The light bounced again and she studied the trajectory of the beams. "They're definitely coming back this way already."

"We spent a lot of time getting out of that mine."

Although they'd made it across and above the trail to the plateau, they would still be in perfect line of sight as soon as the vehicles curved around the final bend. The moon and stars to the east provided enough light to make out a shadowed line of shapes farther down the hill, though it was hard to see in between the gusts of blowing snow. "Shawn, there's nowhere to hide."

"I know." He turned to her. "What would Wolfe Dutton do?"

She barked a laugh. "Oh, the cold *really* must be getting to you to ask that."

"I'm trained in survival skills but not running for my life. You and your dad had the imagination to come up with all sorts of scenarios for his show and how to get out of it."

"I don't know what my dad would do. He never did an episode like this."

"So forget that. What would Jackie Dutton do?"

She reared back in surprise. "What?"

"The only idea I have is burying ourselves in the snow before they round those next two bends and see us."

"You're so determined to make a snow cave! But we're soaked in wet clothes with no hope of drying off, and digging enough room would take too long."

"The worst thing hikers can do is press on in the darkness, especially in a storm," he fired back.

"Most hikers don't have other men hunting them down."

"So we run and hope they don't notice us."

"We can't travel that much distance that fast by foot." She knew what he was doing with the rapid-fire exchange. Forcing a debate, challenging her, encouraging the best in her to rise up. She pushed away all other emotions and focused on the danger at hand, and she knew what they had to do. "Glissade."

The term was really a fancy way to say they needed to go sledding without a sled. His eyes widened and he looked behind him at the thick rock plateau that took them straight downhill for a good mile. "We don't have an ice ax to slow us down. We could go too fast and not be able to stop and—"

"And die," she finished for him. But if they stayed put, they would surely die, as well. She moved her backpack to the front, putting it on backward so the padding covered her chest. If they slid down, she didn't want her pack being ripped off of her from the speed. "I don't see any other way. Do you? We're exhausted, our clothes are wet..."

"The angle could be deceptive. We still have ropes around our—"

"If one of us goes off course, then the other has a chance to stop them."

"Agreed. It's the best idea we've got." He sat down in the snow, his legs slightly bent. "It's now or never. As soon as we get to that line of trees, we do everything in our power to brake."

She sat beside him and made sure her pants, even though damp, were still tucked into her boots. "Let's pray there's not another abandoned mine."

"I've already prayed that prayer." He nodded gravely. "Say when. Any second and they're going to see us."

She leaned back ever so slightly. The snow proved packable, and if not for the horrible conditions and utter exhaustion, the break in the weather would be ideal for a snowman. "Now."

A slight shove-off with her hands proved all that was necessary with a sloped terrain. She picked up speed at a surprising rate. She tucked her chin in as snow pelted her from every angle. Faster and faster. They had to be pushing over thirty miles an hour at this rate. The shapes in the distance came into focus. The trees approached rapidly.

She pressed her heels down deeper, hoping to slow down, but instead, her pace increased. She threw her legs and arms out wide, clawing the snow with her heels and fingers. She dared a look to her left.

Shawn lifted his right arm, clearly struggling with the sheer speed, as well, but he pointed. He shouted a word she couldn't hear, but there was no questioning that he was trying to tell her to go to the trees. He twisted, falling over onto his side, which forced his legs to point in her direction. He slid diagonally, right for her.

If she didn't make adjustments, he'd barrel right into her. Or the rope that connected them would make her go that way whether she wanted to or not. She mimicked his movements, but a wrong calculation would mean slamming into a tree, which at this speed would break bones or worse.

TWELVE

Shawn aimed his trajectory for one lone tree that stood a good twenty feet away from the other thicker grouping. Satisfied with the angle, he flopped back onto his back. The snow pelted him from every direction. At this speed, the flakes felt like sand pelting his face.

He squinted through the blowing snow. If he aimed left of the tree and Jackie aimed right, it would catch the rope in the middle and force them to stop. But not necessarily before they hit the rest of the trees.

Either way, this was going to hurt.

Shawn flipped over onto his stomach and dug his arms and feet deeper into the snow. Mercifully, his speed slowed. Hopefully Jackie was doing whatever she could to slow down, too. He dug his feet in deeper. His speed decreased. The low branches of the tree slapped his back. They'd passed the tree. *Please...*

The snow thickened, hardened, underneath the north side of the tree. His knees objected, as if sliding along a hardwood floor. He gritted his teeth against the discomfort. Slower, slower. Pressure tugged at his waist from the rope hanging up on the tree trunk, but he stopped, panting, shivering, before the rope dug deep. He flipped over onto his back. The evergreen trees wore thick white scarves made of snow on each row of branches. The clouds above them parted enough to show the most dazzling spectacle of glittering stars.

The snow insulated him from the wind for a brief moment. He heard Jackie's movements nearby.

"What if this is the last Christmas we ever have?" she asked.

That was the last thing he'd expected to hear from her. "What? Don't talk like that." He jumped up to a crouch and ran toward her.

"We might not survive, so it could be. My favorite Christmas memories are walking into the dark living room with nothing shining but the lights on the Christmas tree and dawn's first light barely seeping through the windows."

He reached her and took a knee, worried she'd hit her head, as she hadn't moved from her sprawled position in the snow. "Are you okay? We've descended far enough they shouldn't be able to see us."

"What was your favorite Christmas memory?" She shivered and held her stomach tightly. The rope tied around her waist had likely bruised her, and he realized she was buying time to recover before she needed to move. He would do anything to have her home right this minute, but he knew he had more to ask of her if they were going to make it to safety.

"Your parents gave good gifts. I still have the multitool your dad gave me. Made to last," he said.

She raised an eyebrow. "Really? That's your favorite memory?"

He exhaled. "Fine. Christmas dinner. I liked the way everyone teased each other but in a good-natured way." Those dinners were the only time he'd witnessed how a real family interacted.

She gave a self-satisfied smile. "Knew it." Her smile dropped.

"Jackie, be honest. Are you okay?"

She waved him away, her hand still on her stomach. "I will be. I have to be. Just give me another second. Pretend we're in a snow cave." Her smile wobbled and she pointed at the trees above, from her position in the snow. "Someone once told me that Martin Luther walked home one Christmas Eve and became stunned by the beauty of the shimmering tree in the moonlight. He went home that night and decorated a fir tree with small candles. I don't know if it's historically accurate, but it's easy to believe. The snow does glisten like little lights from this angle. It's beautiful."

Shawn held out his hands and helped her to a seated position, though he wasn't ready to let go of her. "I thought we have Christmas trees because the branches are pointing upward and the evergreen tree reminds us of eternal life."

"Whatever the reason, I'd just like to imagine this one is *my* Christmas tree."

He pointed to the tallest one in the middle. "This one? Good choice. You can see it from the valley below. I hope every year that no one gets a permit to cut it down." The adrenaline faded ever so slightly, even though his heart continued to pump as if running a marathon.

A star rocketed through the midnight sky to the east. “Do you think the wise men were glad they didn’t have to follow *that* star?”

He laughed. “Okay, now I’m worried about what the cold is doing to *your* brain.” He tugged gently on her hands. “Time to get up, out of the snow. Not much farther now.”

“The cold is winning, that’s what it’s doing to me.” She groaned as she stood and moved the backpack from her chest to her back. The wind whistled around them, but the tree provided just enough shelter to catch their breath.

He stared into her eyes, also glistening from the reflection of the stars. It was like his heart had been dormant in a winter slumber for ages, and despite the freezing storm about to attack them, his heart seemed determined to thaw in her presence. “I’ve always known you were amazing, Jackie, but I’m reminded over and over just how much.”

Her eyes softened. Even with her wet hair and red cheeks, she radiated beauty from the inside out. She stepped closer and opened her mouth to reply when their Christmas tree exploded in bullets.

“No!”

Shawn covered his arms over her head as they both cowered. They’d been too late, then. The men on the ATVs had spotted them from above. An intense wind gust swayed another tree in their direction. Snow flew up in their faces. He grabbed Jackie’s hand and tugged her deeper into the trees. "Stay down." They brushed in between two trees, and a second later, another gunshot cracked the branches.

"I'm trying not to touch the branches," Jackie yelled.

"More concerned about the bullets touching us at the moment."

He spotted a drop-off point. It might not have been the one he was initially thinking of, but he didn't have the time or lighting to find the best vantage point. He turned to the closest tree and searched for the thickest branch.

He pressed his boot into the needles and hopped on the branch until it bent down. Jackie offered an arm to help him balance, and he kicked at the weakest point of the branch, until it snapped off.

Her eyes widened. "Are you serious? We're trying a snow anchor?"

She understood his intention. Good. "The drop-off point is too far away from the trees, but we are angled away from the path the ATVs must be on. I think if we time it right, we can get off the cliff without being shot," he said.

"But the snow? Do you think it will hold us?"

"You saw how it packed."

She closed her eyes. "Okay."

"No other ideas?" If she didn't debate him, that actually gave him peace. It meant it really was the best idea they had.

"None. I can't believe I'm *choosing* to go over a cliff this time. Has to be better than doing so by accident, right?"

Man, he loved this woman. The unbidden thought stole his breath before the wind could. He couldn't process it right now. "They appear to have stopped shooting for the moment, but that might be because they're headed this way. Keep your head down in case I'm wrong and they shoot." He'd been wrong more times than he'd like to admit, but he prayed that this time he'd guessed right.

He rushed forward into the open snow and stopped two feet short of the edge, in case he fell victim to a snow bridge or another cornice. He dug frantically in the snow, until about a foot down.

Jackie reached his side, anxiously scanning the tops of the trees in front of them. She dropped to her knees. "We're doing the T-Trench snow anchor?"

"Yeah." He grabbed the rope between them and slipped it on the middle of the stick before he shoved the stick underneath the lip of snow he'd packed down. Jackie rapidly refilled the trench from the back edge while Shawn made a much thinner trench on the top of the snow for the rope to follow.

Engine noises carried through the wind. "I'm really beginning to dislike that sound," he muttered. He looked up. "You ready?"

She hopped over the trench area and they checked their ropes, together. She dropped to her knees, eyes closed. "Lord, be with us."

"Amen." He threw the extra rope over the side, even though the ends were still tied to their waists. They would need to work their way down to the end. They dropped to their stomachs, stuck their legs out behind them, both holding on to their sides of the rope, and began inching backward.

Jackie stopped for a second and removed a six-inch branch from within her hair. "I never thought I'd have a love-hate relationship with pine."

"Those are spruce. Both trees have vitamin C but pine tea tastes more like turpentine. Spruce isn't too bad. Motivation to tell the difference."

She laughed but kept inching backward. "Keep talking. I prefer to think we're doing a crazy stunt than running away from men who want to kill us and throw us into a mine."

His feet met air and he stilled for a moment. She gasped as hers did, as well. "Stay there a second."

He tugged on the rope. So far the trench anchor had worked. "Here goes." He slid down farther, always keeping a hand on the rope. He dropped, his body fully away from the edge, and swung with the wind until his feet pushed against the rock wall, taking some of the sting off his shoulders and arms. He stuck his legs out so he was sitting on air and glanced down. The moon weaved in and out of visibility but he spotted the cement pads and drilling equipment below them. They just needed to get to that control room and call for help.

Now, if only he could guarantee they didn't run out of rope before they reached the bottom.

The moment her feet reached air she wanted to cry out. She enjoyed rock climbing. Indoors with fake rock and a padded floor below, though, and only after she'd been sedentary for the rest of the day at work. Hanging by a rope, being tossed about by gusts of wind after her body had already been tested to its limits, was not the same thing.

She fought between wanting to use her feet as a clamp around the rope, which would take the brunt of most of her body weight, and needing her feet to keep her far away from slamming into rock. Each time the wind stilled, she'd lean back as far as possible, both hands gripped around the rope. She relaxed her palms and feet just enough to slide down as rapidly as possible. She felt Shawn's hands as he grabbed her ankles and pulled her closer to the rock face, wordlessly.

She slid down at a slower pace, not understanding why he wanted her so close to the rock face until his hands grabbed her waist. She let go and he set her down on the ground. If he hadn't pulled her, she would've landed in a thicket of some sort.

His fingers worked rapidly on the knots around her waist. "Quietly," he whispered, his lips against her hair. That was when she spotted the flickering light just past the cement pads. Freed of the rope, Shawn's arms moved lightning fast, pulling the rope until it fell completely from above and dropped at their feet. She turned around so he could stuff it back in her pack rapidly. The wind whistled so hard now she could hardly hear herself think, but she thought an engine roared nearby.

His fingers reached for her hand. "Work our way around to the control building. Stay close to the rock."

They made it about ten feet, single file, behind prickly bushes poking into their arms and legs, when a giant beam of light bounced on the rock above them, narrowly missing them. "Shawn, they have those radios, remember? Someone down here is helping the gunmen on the plateau look for us."

He grumbled. "Great."

Two steps forward, the rock wall had a five-foot-tall vertical crevice, maybe two feet wide. "Can you fit in there?"

Without discussing it, he ducked, twisted sideways and stepped inside. She followed him wordlessly. The air seemed warmer and drier than she'd expect. Whether from the break in wind or the geothermal heat, she didn't know. She didn't care. She wanted more warmth and for her nose to stop feeling like an ice cube, despite her efforts at keeping the lower half of her face tucked in the coat. Another larger, wider crevice opened up to the left.

Shawn stepped into the space. "This way the light won't catch us. Seems this cave winds deeper, but how about we stop here for a minute while they look?"

He guided her steps in the darkness until they fitted snugly, facing each other, in a narrow space. "I hope there aren't any hungry animals hiding in there."

"Do you have your Taser handy?"

She twisted to unzip the backpack and slipped the Taser into her coat pocket, but her forehead bumped against his chest in the process. She readjusted the backpack and faced him. "Sorry."

He leaned over and kissed her forehead as if to say it was okay. She didn't mind, though. They'd just been through a lot together and were so close to the nightmare ending. It was perfectly normal to show some sort of affection. Especially in the form of a friendly kiss to the forehead that didn't mean anything.

The warmth of his breath moved to her cheek. Her heart jolted and her breath caught. She was scared to believe the kiss to the forehead meant more. He kissed her cheek. She closed her eyes. Just as she was about to ask him what he was doing, his lips brushed gently over her mouth.

Heat rushed through her of an entirely different kind. Her hands reached for the front of his coat and she pulled him closer. His arms wrapped around her shoulders and his kiss deepened. Light flickered through her closed eyes.

They broke apart. Where could it be coming from? Deeper within the rock wall, the light reflected a second time, except it wasn't originating from the initial crevice they'd entered. There went their chance at talking about that kiss.

"Shawn?" she whispered. The flicker illuminated an orange cord wrapped tightly around the curve of rock. She looked down at her feet and spotted it behind her heel, weaving all the way outside. The light intensified into more of a glow around the corner. A shadow crossed it, interrupting the beam. Shawn looked at both the entrance to the cave and the corner. She imagined he was debating their options. She didn't have anything constructive to offer.

Her mind, body and heart were reeling from the last few days, especially the past few minutes. Her skin felt raw from the wind, in a way similar to the blistering sensation from a sunburn. Ironic. She desperately wanted to change clothes or get a warm blanket. The temperature had dipped enough that the snow had stuck to her trousers in clumps, frozen, not melting but still there, ensuring she would stay chilled even with shelter over her head.

Maybe the glow around the corner meant warmth. The crevice also had flickering lights. They were trapped. The light outside definitely came from the gunmen, but the light from within was still a mystery. Shawn turned and tiptoed toward the glow. At the corner he waved her back. He removed the gun from his holster and held it up to his chin.

Jackie stayed behind him but followed his example by holding the trigger of the Taser, though she kept her hand within the coat pocket, as the dry warmth of the pocket was too tempting to give up. She kept her eyes on the opening to the outdoors, lest someone sneak up on them.

Shawn peeked his head around the corner. “Pete?” Shawn’s voice came out in a whisper. Without giving Jackie enough time to react, Shawn strode around the corner. “Pete!” He didn’t quite shout, but his loud whisper bounced around the cave.

Jackie hustled around the corner after him. A man wearing the Bureau’s winter uniform crouched in front of a light the size of a basketball, with a small chisel and a brush in his hand. Presumably, this was Pete the archaeologist. The dirt around him had been excavated into a perfectly square recessed floor, with various pots and artifacts covered in dust on their side. A squat statue roughly a foot high sat right in front of him.

The man stiffened. "Shawn?" His eyes widened, and he frowned, then straightened out of his crouch to standing.

"Are you okay?" Shawn asked. He put his gun back in the holster, but kept his hand on it as he approached. "Have they hurt you?"

"Uh…no. But you shouldn't be here. It's not safe."

"Yeah, neither should you. How long have they had you?" Shawn shook his head, staring at the artifacts. "I knew they were looters. Come on. You can tell us on our way out."

A space heater across the room practically put her feet on autopilot. The orange power cord had split into other extension cords. The engine sound she'd heard earlier had to be from a generator. She stood in front of the heater, as close as she could without setting her clothes on fire, as Pete set down the tools in the dirt and licked his lips. "I've lost track of time. Listen, they're always watching the entrance. I don't know how you got in, but you should leave while you have a chance."

Shawn reached his hand out for Pete to grab. "You're right, but you're coming with us. We have a plan."

Pete hesitated for half a second, and Jackie might've imagined it but she thought Pete glanced at Shawn's gun before he nodded. Maybe he wanted to make sure Shawn could deliver on his promises before taking a chance at escape. She'd seen firsthand evidence that the gunmen out there—especially the bald man—had no problem killing to suit their needs. If Pete thought the safest answer was to do what the looters wanted, though, he was sorely mistaken. "I saw one of those men murder someone," she said. "And they've been trying to kill me ever since, likely because I'm a witness. You've probably seen too much, as well, Mr. Wooledge. Give those men what you want, and they still might kill you."

The click of a gun sent chills up her spine.

"Finally, a smart girl. I get so tired of people underestimating me. Too bad for you that you came back to test me." The bald man, the one who'd killed the employee, aimed his weapon right at her chest.

THIRTEEN

Shawn stepped in front of Jackie in one move, his gun pointing at the man. “Bureau ranger. Drop your weapon.”

“No!” Pete waved his hands in front of Shawn.

The gunman frowned at Pete. “What are you—”

“Don’t shoot them,” Pete interrupted. “I promised I’d finish the job. If you shoot them, I’ll stop helping you. You’d have to kill me.”

The man squinted hard at Pete, his weapon still trained on Shawn, as if weighing his options. “Fine. If he puts down his weapon.”

Pete caught Shawn’s eyes and nodded, as if he had his own plan that Shawn should follow. He felt Jackie’s fingers grasping the back of his coat. She stayed close to him, closer than usual. “Don’t do it,” she whispered.

He didn’t trust the gunman any more than Jackie did, but he also didn’t see another solution. If he tried to shoot, the gunman might still get off a shot and hit Pete or Jackie. The man stepped closer. “I agree not to kill you and the girl if you drop your weapon. What will it be?”

Shawn set down his weapon and kicked it over, hoping the man would stay away from Jackie. The man picked up the gun. "You two sit down. Against the wall." He waved the gun at Pete. "Come here. A word."

Jackie slipped behind Shawn and angled herself on his left side, closest to the gunman. She pressed herself so closely into his side that he had no choice but to put his right arm around her shoulder as they sank to the ground, all eyes on Pete approaching the gunman. "I don't trust him," she muttered, barely loud enough for Shawn to hear.

No surprise. He didn't trust the gunman, either. If he'd killed Bob, the associate field manager, and Darrell, the detectorist, there'd be nothing to prevent him from killing all of them once they were out of an area that could ricochet bullets. Jackie moved her right arm diagonally to her left shoulder and grabbed his hand that was resting there, as if she wanted to hold hands.

The motion surprised him but he eagerly held her hand. He hoped with one squeeze she understood how sorry he was that he'd failed. His declaration that he'd only rely on himself, that unconditional love wasn't for him, seemed so foolish now. He'd wasted his time shielding himself, under the delusion that as long as he took care of the land, he'd be satisfied enough. Two days of time with Jackie, the woman who despite the years gone by still knew him best, and his heart felt renewed and desperate to have a chance to live life to its fullest. But there was nothing in his own wisdom that he could do. They'd lost and would have to rely only on God and the hope that the gunman would make a mistake.

Jackie didn't seem to get any of that sentiment from their brief moment of handholding. In fact, she seemed annoyed. She tugged at his fingers, sliding his hand down the side of her arm. He finally understood what she was trying to communicate when she placed his hand at the side of her waist. His fingers brushed against the hard plastic outline of something in her pocket.

The Taser! She was trying to get his hand close to her pocket where she'd placed the Taser. She tilted her head and looked up at him with questions in her eyes. He couldn't explain the problem without the gunman hearing, though. If the man still had a gun pointed at one of them, using the Taser inside the cave would be too dangerous. The man might be able to get a bullet or two off, especially if he was facing them, before hitting the ground.

"Get back to work," the man barked at Pete. Pete turned around, his eyes flashing with anger, but he didn't reply as he walked back toward them. The man stepped forward. "Just so you know, Carl and Spencer are on their way back here with the trailer. The blizzard has arrived and is intensifying by the minute, so this will be the final trip. No exceptions. If you know what's good for you—" his eyes darted to Shawn and Jackie before returning to Pete "—have them help."

Pete set his jaw and turned to stare at the gunman an unusually long time. The gunman raised an eyebrow, as if unsure how to make Pete do what he wanted for a moment. "I'm going to check on Carl's progress," the man said. "But I'll be right at the entrance." He waved the second gun at Shawn. "Anything suspicious and I get trigger-happy."

The moment the man had turned his back on them, Pete knelt down, as if to start working on the antiquities again, but he whispered to Shawn. "His satellite phone doesn't work in the cave—the rock walls are too thick unless he gets close to the entrance. While he's busy you can tell me—what's your plan to escape? Is it ruined now since he got your gun? Is backup on the way?"

Shawn blinked, unsure of what to say that wouldn't dash all hope. He needed Pete to stay positive and focused and not try anything stupid. Being held at gunpoint pretty much changed everything, though.

"Before we tell you," Jackie hastily said, "what surprises might we be dealing with? How did you end up here, anyway?"

"Jackie?" That same look of distrust she'd flashed at him all those years ago appeared in her eyes now, except it was aimed at Pete. And why did she insinuate they still had a plan to escape? With a gunman blocking their only route, there was little chance they could get to the control room anymore and call for help. Even if they were able to stealthily take away the man's satellite phone, they would need to get outside for it to work.

"He can tell us while he works." Jackie leaned forward, away from the rock wall, and offered a small, encouraging smile to Pete. Shawn was baffled at her response but stayed silent.

Pete looked over his shoulder, making sure the gunman was still far enough away. “You know Bob Hutchison, the associate field manager?”

Shawn felt a little sick. “Not well,” he said. Though it was enough to recognize the man’s profile, dead, in Jackie’s car.

“During the feasibility and impact study required before approving the geothermal permit, he found this place. He apparently realized what he’d stumbled on—”

“And what’s that?” Jackie asked.

Pete flashed Shawn a questioning look as if asking why he should talk to Jackie. He was tempted to apologize for her natural journalistic tendencies, but he’d give her a few more minutes because her instinct seemed right. The more they knew about what they were dealing with, the better they could plan an escape. Though they were running out of time. If those ATVs turned around off the plateau and came back on the corridor path, they had minutes to spare before more gunmen arrived.

“An Oregon Trail campsite,” Pete answered. “For whatever reason, maybe illness, lightening their load or an ambush outside of the cave, they left a vast number of items behind. Once the looters Bob had hired started digging, though, we found an entirely new layer underneath.” He gestured behind him. “Tribal antiquities. Untouched stonework—I’d have to guess from the 1300s.”

Pete’s eyes lit up. “If this weren’t for looters, I’d be thrilled at the discovery. I’m not ready to say which tribe, but I know enough to recognize this statue is the crowning jewel. At least half a million dollars for her alone. I've almost got her free." Pete blinked rapidly. "Anyway, Bob realized the dig was bigger than anticipated, so he started sabotaging the construction to give him more time without being discovered. I got curious, found out what he was doing, and before I knew it, I was a hostage."

"How many other looters? Gunmen, specifically," Shawn asked.

Pete shrugged. "Can't say for sure. They kept me working."

"We know there's three for sure." The radio squawked, and Shawn held a finger over his mouth for a moment to listen, but he couldn't hear the conversation at the edge of the cave. Frustration built. "Have you counted more?"

"Did you know the assistant field manager was murdered?" Jackie interjected.

Pete raised an eyebrow, but it seemed more out of irritation than surprise. "Like I said, the site was more lucrative than Bob realized. The looters disagreed with how he was managing things and killed him." He turned to Shawn. "It was a sad day."

Jackie leaned forward, away from Shawn's arm. "So the storm approaching worked in their favor, right? They knew the park and all the roads would be closed. They could make multiple trips with the trailer and ATVs and never be spotted or tracked. Up until the storm, during the construction, they'd been stashing everything at your field trailer, right? Which is perfect, because no one would suspect artifacts in a Bureau trailer would be stolen property."

Pete shifted uncomfortably. "They took me hostage. I don't know what they were doing or planning."

Shawn nodded. "So the three gunmen we've spotted is all you know about?"

"Yes, yes, that sounds right."

"You didn't know what they were doing in your own field trailer?" Jackie placed her left hand down on the ground and moved to a crouched position. "The sabotage has been going on quite some time, so the looting had to have started before that. Right? That's what you said."

"They weren't at my field trailer before this storm." He shrugged. "When are you going to answer my question? Is help on the way?"

"What about the boss?" she fired back.

Shawn's pulse raced at the way she was questioning him, almost as if it was more an interrogation than an interview. A crunch of shoes on rocks pulled his attention. The gunman rounded the corner and walked toward them, carrying a radio in one hand and a gun in the other.

"Or maybe I'm looking at the boss." Jackie lowered her voice to a whisper. "Let's speak plainly. There's no way you think we're getting out of here alive, is there, Pete?"

Shawn reared back. "Jackie, the man's a hostage and my friend—" But the moment he said the words, pieces that hadn't made sense started clicking into place. Was she really insinuating that Pete was the one in charge of the looting? Could it be true?

He had a sinking feeling that it was too late to matter. A bullet cracked through the air. A sharp searing pain threw him backward and he slammed against the dirt floor, gasping for air.

Jackie sprinted forward. The Taser had met the mark. She hadn't realized the gunman would be able to get off a shot when the darts made contact, but at least he'd been way off on his aim. Five seconds. She had only five seconds to disarm him.

She shoved the Taser in her pocket and stomped on the man's wrist until he released the gun. Then she kicked it away. She leaned forward and grabbed the gun he'd taken from Shawn, which he'd stuck in his front waistband. She then leaped five feet away to pick up the kicked gun before the man could move to attack her.

Both guns now in her hands, she spun, arms wide to point one weapon at Pete and the other at the bald man on the ground. Pete glared at her from the floor, his hand covering his jaw, as if considering whether to take her down himself or not. She needed to know if he was hiding a weapon. He wasn't wearing bulky winter clothing like Shawn and her, but she needed to be sure. She pointed the gun at him. "Hands up, Pete."

"I'm an innocent victim here," he said. "Just ask Shawn. Hand me the other gun. I'll help." She swiveled her attention to Shawn, but he seemed to be having a cramp of some sort. He was sitting up, bent over, groaning—

He lifted his head, and in a gap between his open coat, she saw blood seeping through his shirt from a circle on the left side of his chest. She gasped and ran for him. "No!" She lifted the back of his coat. Nothing. The bullet was still inside him and could have ricocheted to other organs.

She dropped the hem, her heart rate racing. She still had to keep an eye on the gunman, who was sitting up, and Pete, whom she didn't trust despite his claims of innocence. After all her years of interviews, she could tell when a story was being fabricated. His details and timeline didn't add up.

And there *was* a boss. The bald man had mentioned one on the radio when they were stuck on that ledge. Besides, Pete had slipped in his story and had said "we found" before he'd got to the hostage bit. More than that, her gut told her he wasn't to be trusted.

She took a knee in front of Shawn. "I'm so sorry. So sorry. It's my fault."

He didn't answer. He moved his left hand up to cover the wound. Of course, he had first-aid training. He'd know what to do, but he might not be thinking straight. She pressed her two fingers against his neck. He flinched. "Cold," he muttered.

Yes, and they'd lost a lot of the sensitivity to touch. She wasn't ready to think about frostbite yet, but mercifully, she felt the warm pumping under his chin. Too rapid. That was to be expected, but the bullet had entered his chest. Even if it didn't hit the heart directly, the pathway would open up a large destructive tunnel in the cavity and could have injured tissue dangerously close to the organ.

"Jackie," he croaked. "Handcuffs."

She stared at him a second before understanding what he was talking about. She handed him the second gun. He propped his right arm up with his knee so it was pointed at the man thirty feet away. She found the pouch on Shawn's holster that held his cuffs. "Good idea. Keep pressure on your wound. We're going to get out of here, Shawn. You just have to hold on a little longer."

She turned and pointed at Pete. "Hands up."

He balked. "You have to be kidding. You're tying me up? Shawn, tell her."

"He doesn't need to tell me. I've got his back," she said. "And right now that means if you're innocent, then we'll figure it out soon enough."

"You basically shot him."

She tried not to cringe. "Yeah, well, Shawn already knows I make mistakes."

Shawn coughed. Or maybe it was a laugh. She couldn't afford to look yet.

"And you still want to handcuff me? How about taking care of the actual criminals first?"

"Stop talking, Pete," she said.

Once he had his hands on the back of his head, she twisted each wrist until she'd placed them in handcuffs, careful to watch for any signs he would put up a fight. She wasn't as smooth as she'd like, but at least she knew the basics after taking a citizen's police academy class a few years ago.

The gunman, roughly twenty feet away, pushed himself from sitting to standing, pulling out the Taser darts still attached to his chest. She pointed her weapon at him. "If I were you, I'd sit back down on your knees. I'm an even better aim with a real gun."

He sneered but did as she asked. Jackie removed the rappelling rope and used it to tie Pete's wrists together, just above the handcuffs.

"Isn't that a bit over the top?" Shawn asked. His question came out as a groan. "You don't know for sure he isn't a hostage."

"You don't have to talk if it hurts," she said. "Do you have more than one pair of handcuffs?"

"No, but knots..."

"Are my specialty." She attempted to smile. "That's what you were going to say, right? Because I may not be my dad, but if I'm going to embrace what I'm good at, then one of those skills would be knots." She pulled the rope tight to check her work and used the small key to take off the handcuffs.

She moved to approach the bald man and fought to project a brave face. The way he'd murdered that man so callously with the injection wasn't something she could forget. She glanced at Shawn before she got very close. He gave her an encouraging nod as he aimed his gun at the man, although his knee was the only reason the gun was propped up at all. She did the same routine, first with the handcuffs, but with him she kept one foot resting on the back of his knee, ready to step there forcefully if he tried anything. As soon as he was handcuffed, she pressed the gun in his back and grabbed the satellite phone from his pocket. She was surprised to find a pair of keys there, maybe belonging to his ATV? She stuffed both in her own back pocket.

Then, using the end of the singular rope she'd tied Pete with, she tied the men to each other, with a ten-foot gap between them. That way it wouldn't be as easy for one to run away. Now, if she could just get to the entrance of the cave and call for help.

Shawn moaned slightly, closing his eyes briefly. She took his gun from him so he could use both hands to put pressure on his wound. The stomping of feet ahead meant visitors would be joining them. A gun in each hand, she shook with adrenaline and pushed back the intense nausea that came with extreme levels of exhaustion. She pointed one gun at Pete and the bald man and the other toward the entrance of the cave. The men called Carl and Spencer rounded the corner. Spencer pulled a gun in less than a second, aimed directly at her. Carl moved to grab his weapon.

"Don't you dare," she said, and Carl froze, his hand hovering six inches from his weapon.

"Please don't shoot," Pete said again. "I'll do what you want. It's this crazy lady."

Spencer's eyes flickered in between Pete and the other man, indecision in his gaze. And for the briefest of moments, Jackie questioned if maybe she'd interpreted Pete's testimony poorly and been wrong. "Drop your weapon," she said.

Spencer shrugged. "Maybe I'm done with the whole lot of them."

"Drop it or the statue gets it," Shawn said behind her.

Jackie took a step closer to the wall so her peripheral vision could spot Shawn while still keeping an eye on the gunmen. Shawn held the top of the statue's head. Dirt clumps were still stuck to the bottom half, and the stonework dangled precariously over a very pointy boulder.

Pete's eyes widened. "Are you crazy? You could've damaged it, pulling it out of the dirt like that. Put it down, carefully!"

"You said it's worth at least half a million dollars, right?" Jackie asked Pete.

The man tied to Pete rolled his eyes. "Give it up. You're not fooling anyone. They know you're with us. Carl and Spencer, how about untying me, shooting the whole lot of these folks and cutting our losses? We have more than enough to get a couple million for the archive of the loot."

Pete's face blanched. "The seller will only work with me."

"Guess it's time to find a new seller," the gunman said dryly.

"If I don't check in with my contact every night, your names and photos are going straight to the FBI. I'm not stupid. This was a foolproof plan." Pete twisted to Shawn. "You know me, Shawn. I'm meticulous, a visionary. I've got profit margin to cut you in on the deal."

If Carl's and Spencer's expressions provided any indicator, these men weren't on board with splitting their profits with anyone else.

"That's a problem," Jackie interjected before the men fought any more. "Because to answer your earlier question, Pete, there is a *lot* of backup on the way.

That's the reason you wanted us to believe you were a hostage, right? To find out if there was any real threat on the way? Loads. Plus, I'm still holding two guns and I'm a great shot." She looked at Spencer. "You two drop your weapons and I'll let you go. You still have ATVs outside, right?"

As if in answer, the lights flickered. Once, twice, then darkness draped them all.

FOURTEEN

Shawn fought to keep his balance, but without his vision to help, he wobbled. He struggled to stop his right hand from letting go of the statue.

"She's behind me now. Don't shoot," Pete yelled.

Shawn stumbled forward, tripping over stoneware of some sort—hopefully a sturdy pot.

"No!" Pete growled. "If you dropped that statue, I'll kill you myself."

Shawn had no choice but to let go of his wound and grab the statue with both hands, gently dropping it to the dirt. He didn't care what Pete said. He cared about preserving a people's history, one that didn't belong to the archaeologist to sell to the highest bidder. Saving Jackie's life was a higher priority, though, so he didn't stop to feel around and see if he'd succeeded in keeping it in one piece.

"I still have a gun," Jackie said. "Be quiet." A second later a light illuminated her face.

The bald gunman, however, had already made his move, his leg up, his foot kicking out toward her. Shawn's fist moved on instinct, plummeting into the man's stomach. The action broke his trajectory and the man folded up, stumbling backward, the rope taking Pete with him. They fell into a mass heap. Jackie took a shaky breath. "Thank you."

"My pleasure."

She thrust the weak light from her phone to the entrance of the cave. "The other two are gone."

"Looks like they took your idea and decided to cut their losses."

She reached up and pressed on his coat. He flinched from the pain of the pressure. "Your wound."

"Jackie, we have to get somewhere safe before I can focus too much on that. Preferably the sooner the better." He almost told her about his fight against falling and passing out, but he didn't want the men to know he lacked strength.

"Well, we also need to give you the best shot." She cringed. "I didn't mean that pun. I meant the best chance at healing properly, which means you have to keep pressure on that." Shawn grabbed her hand. The pain was making him see stars in his peripheral vision.

The bald man struggled back to his feet, a challenge with his hands tied behind his back. Shawn dropped her hand and took his gun back. "The generator probably went out. If he was right and the blizzard has set in, the air intake can suck in snow and malfunction."

"Back to the original plan?"

He nodded. "The control room generator will be designed for the elements, and will have running water, central heat and insulated walls if we have to wait out the blizzard. Except, what about them?"

"We take them with us?" Jackie pulled her hair back, twisting it and tying it into a knotted bun.

Shawn hated the idea of escorting the men, but they also couldn't leave them behind. There was shelter, sure, but nothing sturdy enough to tie them to while they waited for help. For all he knew, they had other weapons hidden on the property. "I don't have any better ideas. We'll need to watch for those ATVs, though, in case they're just regrouping."

Jackie cautiously stepped on one end of the rope and slid it with her foot until she was far enough away to stoop and pick it up. "Ever heard of Wolfe Dutton?"

Pete's and the man's eyes flickered in recognition.

"Well, I don't like to brag, but he's my father, and he taught me *everything* he knows. A blizzard isn't going to stop me from shooting straight. So tread carefully. Walk in front of me. Now."

She held the phone with one hand, flashlight on. Shawn could see from the screen pointed his direction that the battery had only 7 percent left. He could also tell from the men's expressions that they didn't consider Jackie a threat no matter what she said.

"You heard her. Move," Shawn barked. He took the opportunity to stay one step in front of her, though. If they did try to pull anything, he wanted to be the one to take the brunt of it.

They stepped outside and the wind took his breath away. His muscles tightened involuntarily and the pain surrounding his wound almost made him cry out. Instead, he grunted. "Move faster. Get past the bushes."

The wind had created drifts three feet high in portions surrounding them. The majority of light from the moon and stars was dimmed by the thick clouds dumping flakes the size of quarters. Getting across a couple of acres with these men in tow would be next to impossible, especially if they decided to fight.

Jackie held up the satellite phone. “I’m not getting any signal yet.” She hollered over the wind.

“Works better when you can see the sky. With a cloud cover this thick, it might take a few tries, but we’ll get through eventually.” He was certain of it.

She handed him the phone. “Okay, you keep trying. You know how to work these better.”

They trudged on; the men in front of them seemed to be stalling. Granted, stomping through snow with their hands behind their backs probably wasn’t easy. Paths left behind by the ATVs could be seen in the snow. But only ten feet away, the trailer the ATVs had been hauling earlier that day had been left behind. They likely didn’t want to fight the drag a trailer created in the winds if their goal was to get away.

A sharp pain hit his stomach and his feet flew out from under him. The half a second of looking at the trailer had proved detrimental. The men had used the ropes in between them to take him down. A bullet split the howling wind once, then twice, and the world spun.

Jackie spread her feet wide and watched the men turn to her in shock. She’d fired close enough to the side of each man’s face to cause them serious, but hopefully temporary, ringing in their ears. She may not enjoy practicing survival skills in the wilderness, but she still enjoyed frequent visits to an indoor shooting range.

She'd definitely succeeded with Pete, as he howled and pressed his ear against his raised shoulder.

"Get in the trailer." She had to yell to be heard over the wind. She needed them out of the way to make sure Shawn was okay. Despite her blood burning hot that they'd hurt him, the freezing temps seemed to suck all oxygen out of her lungs each time she opened her mouth, and it was a fight to refill them. And her nose stung so bad from the cold she felt certain full recovery wasn't going to be possible. She'd permanently be able to play the part of Rudolph the Red-Nosed Reindeer every Christmas without makeup.

"I'm not getting in a trailer." The bald man curled his lips in a level of disgust and contempt that almost made her shiver. She could practically hear his mind thinking of ways to kill her.

"That was your warning shot. Next time I won't waste bullets." She dragged open the trailer door and gestured inside. Shawn still wasn't moving from the ground, and it was killing her not to run to him.

Pete staggered forward, and though it took them minutes longer than it should've, the two men begrudgingly stepped into the roughly six-foot-by-nine-foot space.

"Step all the way to the back," she yelled through the wind. The moment they did, she threw the rope inside with them and moved to close the swinging door, except she needed both hands. She tried slamming it against the wind, but it was a slow process. A second before it was fully closed, she felt movement, and the trailer shifted. The men were running at the door. Her fingers shook, fighting to get the long pin into the lock. If she didn't succeed and the impact of their bodies against the door threw her to the ground, they might overtake her.

The tip of the pin got into the hole just before initial impact, enough to keep the door from opening, but the hit moved the lock mechanism and the pin slid right back out. She pushed her entire shoulder against the door as two hands joined her efforts.

"Hurry." Shawn's face looked ashen, but he pressed with all his might as she fully slid the long pin into the lock. The door vibrated again. They'd taken another pass, but now they could bruise their shoulders all they wanted, ramming into the door, without going anywhere.

"Are you okay?" She reached for him and he draped his right arm around her shoulders and leaned slightly onto her.

"I think I fainted. Can't say it won't happen again."

"Keep pressure on the wound." She swung around, frantic to find any signs of the ATV the gunman would've been driving. The gust carried the loose snow into a whiteout in front of her. The clouds shifted ever so slightly and the moon reflected off metal in the bushes, twenty or thirty feet ahead. "Stay there."

"We might lose each other," he called. He grabbed her hand. "I'm okay with losing the men who tried to kill us. I'm not okay with losing you."

The way he looked in her eyes brought her more warmth than physically possible in the conditions. "Okay." She didn't want to argue. But she also feared he wasn't going to last much longer on his feet before he fainted again or worse. "Only if you lean on me. And try calling with the phone again."

He agreed with a nod. He held up the phone to his ear. "Ranger Shawn Burkett requesting emergency assistance," he shouted over the wind. He groaned and dropped the phone. "Only lasted a few seconds before it cut off." He looked up and the thick cloud cover had returned. "Our best chance is the landline in the control building."

"Then let's get there." She took his right hand and matched his stride. Her left foot had to move with his right foot to enable them to step in sync. They needed the momentum to step through some of the deeper snow. Finally they reached the ATV.

Shawn moved to sit in front. She held up a hand. "No offense, but if you faint while driving, things might get even worse."

He offered a weak smile but didn't argue. "You know we have to take them with us. If a rescue team reaches us, they can't go searching a couple more acres in a whiteout for them."

"And we can't leave them to freeze." She sighed because she could easily justify leaving them, but Shawn was right. It took a few tries, but she managed to get the vehicle started and drove back to the trailer. Using the hitch, she attached it to the back. After what seemed like hours but was likely only minutes, she sat back in the driver's seat.

She revved the engine, but realistically she couldn't see farther than a few feet ahead.

Shawn wrapped his right arm around her waist for stability. He leaned forward until his scratchy face brushed against her cheek. "Into the prevailing wind. Take it slow. There might be a drilling well that's uncovered, for all we know."

She almost cried at the thought. With the steering wheel pointed directly into the painful wind, she put on the goggles she'd found tied to the console and drove straight into the blizzard. With each bump and hill, she strained to see farther into the blowing snow. They passed a drilling rig and then minutes later another. Her heart rate sped up. Were they just driving in circles until they froze to death?

She sent up a silent cry to the Lord. And then she caught the smallest glimpse of red, which gave her pause. She pressed forward. Yes, definitely red pipe. With lines of snow draped on top of the red, seeping through the grates above, it was the most beautiful fake candy cane she'd ever seen. When she'd made the decision to leave her car, she'd felt safe exploring because she knew the red pipe would lead her back to it. The car, even though it now resided in a mine with a dead man inside, had been parked very close to the control building. She pushed the throttle harder.

Every minute she strained her vision, her arms and her back against the blizzard, she felt the temptation to rest, even just for a second. The moment the building came into sight she almost cried. "We're here, Shawn."

Pressure increased on her back. "Shawn? Are you okay?"

He didn't answer.

FIFTEEN

She would not make it to a safe haven, only to lose him. Jackie maneuvered to get off the ATV, doing her best to keep him from falling into the snow. Instead he fell over on his stomach onto the seat. It took her ten minutes, but she found the industrial-sized generator and cranked it. Lights flickered on within the windows.

Emitting something between a growl and a cry, Shawn lifted his head.

She ran to him and tugged on his right arm until he was able to stand. "I wasn't going to leave you there in the snow," she said. "But if we don't get that bleeding to stop, I fear the next time you pass out, you won't wake back up again. Let's get inside."

"The snow is warmer than the air," he said with a groan. "That's messed up."

"So messed up." She laughed and this time he actually leaned on her for support as they shuffled for the door. The snow, mercifully, wasn't as thick on the paths that had once been shoveled a couple of days ago. "You have keys, right?"

He shook his head. "No." He gestured with his head to a rock peeking out of the snow. "They can take a door out of my pay. I might be asking for hazard pay after this week."

A sense of humor was a good sign. She propped him up beside a window, grabbed the rock and, with a heave, threw it at the window closest to the latch.

It bounced off.

If she weren't at the end of her rope, it might've been funny. Shawn leaned over and picked it up with his right hand. He stepped in front of the door, and with seemingly the effort of a tap, the rock snapped through the glass and fell through the other side.

Jackie rushed forward, reached her hand in the hole and opened the door from the inside. She looked over her shoulder at Shawn with a smile. "Even when injured, you can't leave me to save the day alone."

"The biggest mistake I ever made was leaving you, Jackie. I'd like to think I've learned from it."

Did he know his words rocked her to the core? He'd basically paraphrased the words she'd longed to hear a decade ago. The objections that'd once come so quickly to mind faded in the background after the kiss they'd shared in the cave. Dizziness washed over her. She hadn't realized she'd held her breath. She blinked rapidly, smiling. They could discuss everything later, after he was healed. Then it would be easier to think logically, to do the wise thing, and say goodbye. "That's... that's nice to hear."

She helped him inside and closed the door. "Let me find the thermostat, and I'll get the place warm."

He pointed to the far corner. "Phone first."

His breathing pattern started to resemble a shallow pant. Her concern grew. They reached the spot next to the enclosed fire extinguisher, where the phone, with a sign above it reading Emergency Use, had been installed on the wall. He grabbed the phone, leaned against the wall and slid down until he was seated on the ground.

Confident he'd be able to make the call without her, she rushed to find the thermostat and turned on the heat. At least the commercial generator had been installed with the weather in mind, underneath the awning on the northeastern corner of the building, the most protected from the blowing snow.

Shawn argued with the man over the phone. "There has to be some way. A four-wheel drive—" He blew out his breath. "Helicopter? You have my coordinates." He closed his eyes. Pale, and progressively more ashen, his skin color started to frighten her.

She gently took the phone from him. "Your ranger has been shot," she said into the phone. "He needs medical attention immediately. There are also two looters in the trailer outside and another two that got away. If I have to go outside to check on the men in the trailer, that's going to put my life back in danger."

"I understand, ma'am, but it's simply not safe for any of our law enforcement in these conditions. All the roads are closed. There's not enough visibility for our snowmobiles. Even the medevac can't fly. If ice develops on the blades, everyone's at risk. Where was Ranger Burkett shot?"

"Near the heart." Her voice shook, despite her attempts to steady it.

The man on the other end of the line hesitated. "Have you stopped the bleeding?"

"I'm not sure." She bent over and unzipped his coat. His eyes were still closed, his breathing uneven. Blood had soaked through the entire front of his shirt. She recoiled. "No," she whispered. Anything but, and every time he stepped up to help get them to safety in the last two hours, he'd put himself at risk.

"Do whatever you can to stop the bleeding, ma'am. Step on the wound if you have to."

"You have to be kidding me." She looked around the room, desperate for something to trigger an idea, an out-of-the-box solution. "What's the radar say? How long do we have to hold on until you can make it here?"

"I'm afraid I can't say."

She heard the negativity in the man's voice. Shawn didn't have much of a chance. The blizzard could hang on for days. Besides Shawn's safety, she couldn't leave those men out in below-freezing temperatures for much longer without endangering them. "Please hurry," she said and hung up the phone.

"It's okay," Shawn said.

"No, it's not." She took off the makeshift scarf from around her neck and folded it in squares. "Like you said, you're not going to leave me now."

She pulled down the hem of his collar and cringed. Congealed blood was everywhere, but still it ran from a gaping wound. She placed the folded square over it and kept her hand on it, trying to ignore the way the blood from his shirt stuck to the top of her hand. "I'm sorry, but this is going to hurt."

She pressed down and he hollered. "I'm sorry. I'm so sorry. I have to stop the bleeding. I have to at least slow it down. You've already lost so much."

He gritted his teeth. "It's okay. Man, that hurts." He exhaled and inhaled slowly.

How long could they hold on without medical attention? "Should we talk about something else to get your mind off…?" She didn't want to finish the question.

He nodded and cleared his throat. "Back there, bragging about your dad to criminals. Does that mean you're coming around to the ways of the wild?"

She laughed. "I see. Turn the attention to all my issues. Short answer is no. Long answer is I think you were sort of right."

"Wow. I like the sound of that."

"Not all the way right," she teased. "The ways I'm like my father I question the most, worried that I'm not good enough to be allowed those traits instead of just embracing that I have them in common."

He smiled. "I'm glad to hear it."

"So the next step," she said, "will be accepting the strengths while also being humble enough to learn my limits and being okay with that. Like…" She bit her lip. "Not assuming I know everything about Tasers or breaking down doors. Shawn, I'm so sorry. Pete was right about one thing. I basically shot you." Her eyes filled with hot tears that blurred her vision. "I could've killed you," she whispered.

"But you didn't."

"I know," she said. Though her mind answered *not yet, at least*. She pushed away the horrible thought.

"I can't believe I trusted Pete." His eyelids drooped.

"I'm sure it's going to take a long time to forgive him." His shoulders sank lower. She needed him to stay awake, to stay with her. She searched for more to say. "I mean, you can choose to forgive him in a flash, but the hurt and the temptation to hold on to the anger—both those things take a long time to get over. Well, you already know. You've had plenty to forgive in life, and it's understandable that—"

"Knowing and doing are two different things," he said, his eyes still closed. "But you were right."

"I was?"

He opened his eyes and sighed. "I didn't realize I was living—well, barely living—the same way I grew up. I've been in self-protection mode so long that once I had the freedom to live differently, I guess I didn't realize I was choosing the same solitary life as an adult that I hated as a kid." He licked his dry lips, his skin paler than before. "Like you said, if I'm a believer, then I should start acting like His love is more than enough for me, right?"

His blood started to seep through the folded scarf despite the pressure on the wound. Her own heart raced and her eyes burned. Did he know he was about to pass away and was trying to prepare her? She pressed harder on his wound and he flinched. *Please stop the bleeding, Lord!*

"Shawn Burkett, if you're telling me this so I can have peace after you die, then…well…you better save your breath until you're better because I'm not ready to give up. And you better not give up, either. Help will come sooner or later. We just need to stick it out."

He smiled. "I'm trying to tell you I finally agree that love is worth the risk."

Their eyes connected. What was he trying to say? Loving in general was worth the risk? Risk…

She felt her eyes widen. "Shawn, I have to make another call." She placed his hand on top of the wound. "I know it's uncomfortable, but you have to press hard while I let go. There's only one man I know who would think it's worth the risk to fly into a storm of this magnitude."

His mouth dropped open and his eyes twinkled with sudden awareness. "What would Wolfe Dutton do?"

She grabbed the phone and dialed. "That's what I hope to find out. Pick up, pick up. Please…"

Even though the pain radiated mostly from his chest and shoulder, every expansion of his ribs seemed to aggravate the tendons attached to that arm. The minutes had ticked by slowly. *Please help us. Hurry.*

Jackie hadn't been willing to move from putting pressure on his wound, especially after talking to her dad. But much longer, and they would have to let the criminals out of the trailer and bring them inside for more adequate shelter, though he hated the risk to Jackie that might bring.

The sound of a rapid-fire jackhammer accompanied by a loud, growing hum vibrated the walls. Two men ran inside, carrying a stretcher. Jackie frowned. "Felix? Cameron?"

They nodded and set down their first-aid kits. Shawn barely registered their movements as they packed his wound with gauze. Wolfe stepped in the door. Jackie ran to him. “Dad! Thank you so much for coming. I’ve never been so happy to be rescued.”

“I have to admit I was surprised to get your call.” He pulled her into a hug. “But I’d do anything to rescue you, honey. You never have to question that.”

Dressed in gear that looked like black canvas, and in his early fifties, Wolfe still looked like every bit of the hero that Shawn longed to be.

A cameraman came into view behind him.

“Oh, Dad, you didn’t…”

Wolfe shrugged. “That’s the only way the chopper’s liability insurance is covered in a scenario like this. The production company technically owns it.” Wolfe turned and looked at the camera. “Let’s edit that bit out in post.” He grinned. “We’ve measured the winds at forty miles an hour and the temperature at negative ten. This storm shows no sign of stopping. This winter rescue proves to be our toughest yet.”

The cameraman nodded his approval at Wolfe’s sound bite and ran back outside. Wolfe glanced at Shawn, and maybe Shawn imagined it, but there still seemed to be a coolness there despite Eddie’s assurances that Wolfe knew Shawn wasn’t responsible for his son’s accident. The men moved Shawn to the stretcher. “Let’s get you out of here.”

“We can’t go yet,” Jackie said. “Two men are in the trailer. The looters.”

Wolfe nodded. “We brought two rangers with us.

They're gathering and arresting them now. We've got to go. The longer we're here, the greater the risk of ice on the rotors."

Wolfe escorted Jackie outside. The medics picked up Shawn on the stretcher and jogged out the door. The intro for the camera wasn't an exaggeration. Shawn stiffened as the wind rushed past him. The medics stayed low, running to the helicopter, the blades still moving, albeit slower. Jackie and Wolfe were opening the back door to the helicopter, where a space without seats was ready to load the stretcher.

Movement past Jackie and Wolfe caught his eye. The two rangers Wolfe mentioned were walking with the gunman and Pete. Not surprisingly, both men had apparently helped each other out of their rope bindings. Except, Pete seemed to be talking a mile a minute, his arms flailing too much to be in handcuffs like the other man. Had he convinced them he was an innocent hostage, the way he'd fooled Shawn? Dread heated his bones. "Jackie," he yelled. "Do they know about Pete?"

Her eyes widened as she and Wolfe spun around to see the rangers. Pete reached for the ranger's holster and, knowing how it worked, set free the man's gun. Pete lifted the gun and pointed it straight at Jackie.

Shawn grabbed his gun, still in his holster, twisted on his side on the stretcher as it was being lifted high to fit in the helicopter, then pressed the trigger. The bullet soared in between Wolfe and Jackie and reached its mark. Pete's shoulder wrenched backward, and he dropped to the ground beside the ranger.

The medics pulled back and set Shawn on the

ground rather abruptly, as startled as he was. Jackie held a hand over her heart and dropped to the ground in front of him. "Are you okay?"

Wolfe looked back and forth between Jackie and Pete. "That…that man. He would've killed you if Shawn hadn't—" He turned to Shawn. "Thank you."

Before he could reply, the ranger on the left—one Shawn barely recognized from an introduction when he was first hired—approached.

"The archaeologist, Pete Wooledge, is the one that hired the looters," Jackie said before the ranger could ask questions. "He wanted us dead."

The ranger straightened. "I'll need statements at the hospital."

"Of course," Shawn muttered. "Can't wait for the paperwork, too." And with that, he finally allowed the darkness that'd threatened to overtake him for hours to sweep him away.

Jackie choked down her tears as her dad wrapped his arm around her shoulders. "Let's get in the chopper, honey. He's in good hands. I only hire the best medics for my crew, you know that."

"It's touch and go, sir," Felix said.

She choked a sob until she realized the camera was pointed at Felix's face. She looked to her dad. "Stunt or not?" she hollered over the ramping-up winds.

He helped her into the chopper. "In his state, I don't think so. Let's go."

She sat up front with her dad and put her headset on to be able to communicate with him, though she had full knowledge that both headsets were linked wirelessly as microphones to the camera, as well. "I can't fly above the storm now that we've gone this low," he said. "The air gets progressively colder as we ascend and, combined with the humidity, that means ice will develop on the rotors, guaranteeing we crash."

"So what's the plan?" She hated how high-pitched her voice had got. Had she convinced her dad to come to their rescue only to die in a fiery crash?

"The roads are closed, so we use that to our advantage and stay low until we're through the worst." The wind howled again, carrying a sheet of snow that blew against the windshield. "Let's pray my tech works. We'll be flying blind for a little bit with this whiteout."

He moved the cyclic stick in one hand and the collective rotor in the other, and the helicopter lifted. Jackie remained quiet for a moment, knowing her father needed to concentrate. She couldn't see his feet but knew the pedals were also controlling the tail rotor. She never had figured out what all the dials on the control panel meant, even though he'd explained many times. He rolled them slightly to the left, and the taxi lights, meant only for ground use to land, showed him the way to the highway.

She looked over her shoulder to see even the rangers, flanking the looters who were now both handcuffed, looked as shaken as she felt.

"I'm surprised you got them to agree to come."

"Turns out I served with Shawn's boss's brother," her dad said.

"By *served* do you mean rescued?"

Her dad, while boastful in all matters pertaining to his show, never bragged about his time in the service. "Does it matter? They were happy to help."

As he deftly flew the helicopter between pillars of rock and over cliffs, all the while avoiding power lines, her mind raced. The snow began to ease up enough that the lights at the nose of the helicopter began to be of use again. They were going to get past the storm.

She looked over her shoulder to the cameraman, noting he also wore a headset. "Could we stop recording vocals for a bit?"

He gave her a thumbs-up and clicked a button. Her dad glanced at her. "Should I have insisted a medic check you before we left?"

The beating her body had taken over the past few days begged for a pain reliever to stop the aching, but she had survived. She would survive. "I'm sure I'll be fine. Dad, did you know that he wasn't responsible for Eddie's accident? He said Eddie told you what happened."

Wolfe's grin dropped, and he kept his gaze on the path ahead of him. "I know I owe him an apology. But at the same time, I was a little mad that he left. I kept telling myself that if he came back, I would do it in a heartbeat."

"I get that, but, Dad, you told him to leave."

A frown deepened in his forehead. "I know I constantly told you to keep moving, to keep pushing, but when it comes to relationships, I can fool myself into doing nothing, saying nothing." He sighed. "Like with Shawn. Like with you." He nodded resolutely. "I should've made it right a long time ago. And now..." His voice broke a little before he cleared his throat and squinted to see through the glass. "Well, I owe him your life."

"Shawn said you and I were two peas in a pod." She enjoyed seeing her dad smile at that and was a little surprised that he didn't argue. A noise in the back of the helicopter caught her attention—a feat, given the overwhelming volume of the blades whooshing above them. She looked back to see the medics working feverishly over Shawn. What was happening? She turned back. "Did you know there is a bird that when it flies sounds a little like a helicopter?"

He nodded. "The sage-grouse."

"Of course you would know that." She smiled, even though her heart was breaking at the thought Shawn's life was hanging in the balance. "I love you, Dad," she whispered into the headset. A tear escaped as she realized she hoped Shawn heard her, as well. She should've told him earlier and now she might not ever have the chance. As the heat blasted on her legs and feet, the aches and pains came to the forefront and weighed her eyelids down until she couldn't hold them up anymore.

SIXTEEN

Jackie was startled awake by a beeping noise. Were they about to crash? Her eyes flew open to find a doctor over her, pressing buttons on the machine attached to her.

"Good morning," the doctor said.

"Morning?" She gasped. She glanced down to find thick hospital blankets on her. And every finger and toe was warm. Her mother sat at her side, holding her left hand and doing a crossword puzzle draped on her lap with her right hand. "Shawn! Is he—"

"About to go into surgery," her mom said. "They wanted him on fluids to rehydrate him first. He lost a lot of blood but thankfully not enough to warrant a transfusion. You both were severely dehydrated."

"I'm not his doctor, but in general, dehydration increases the chance of all sorts of surgical complications and can stop the anesthesia from working." The doctor took a thin white cylinder and clicked it. "Hopefully, like with you, the IV did the trick."

His bright beam of light studied each of her eyes and examined her face a little too closely. "I'm going with my initial diagnosis. Stage two frostbite, which means with proper care, you should fully recover. If any blisters arise in the next three days, we need you to come in immediately." He straightened. "You've got quite a few bruises, but other than that, I think you can be discharged and have a merry Christmas." He smiled, clicked off his light and left the room.

"Having you here, safe and sound, is the best Christmas present I can ask for, and it's only Christmas Eve." Her mom leaned over and kissed Jackie's head. "But I also have an early present for you." She beamed and handed Jackie a plush royal blue robe with white trim. "I think you have time to see him before they wheel him into surgery."

"You have a visitor," Wolfe said.

Shawn looked up to find Jackie glancing between him and her dad with questions in her eyes.

Wolfe stood. "The bullet must have hit the ground, then ricocheted upward. They think it's closer to his clavicle than his heart." He picked up his jacket. "I think I'm going to check on the other lady we rescued last night."

Jackie's eyes widened. "What other lady?"

"We found a car stuck in the snow on the highway right after you fell asleep. Pulled her out and brought her here with us." Wolfe beamed. "A winter rescue special was a great idea. I think we might make it an annual thing." He held up a finger. "All dramatized, though. Don't get any ideas."

"Never again, if we can help it, Dad."

"Okay, I'm going," Wolfe announced with a chuckle as he left them alone.

Shawn searched for the right thing to say, the right way to say it. "You must have gotten an upgrade on your hospital robe."

"Mom brought me one," she said. "They think I'm getting discharged later today. I'm properly hydrated again." Her smile faltered. "I wanted to make sure I saw you before— I mean, I wanted to tell you…" Her voice shook. "Are you okay?"

"Well, they gave me some localized pain medicine, but I'm sure I'll feel better after surgery."

An orderly with a gurney began to enter the room.

"I'm so sorry," Jackie told him. "Can I have another minute? We'll be quick."

The man hesitated but nodded and stepped back into the hallway to give them privacy.

The time crunch caused Shawn's heart to race, because though he thought he had a good prognosis, the surgeon had explained that gunshot victims always had a risk of complications. "I…uh…know I'm going to make mistakes and sometimes it's going to hurt, but as I've told you, it's worth it."

She tilted her head. "What?"

Her puzzled expression made him smile whether he felt like it or not. "I love you, Jackie. That's what I'm trying to say. I'd rather risk my heart breaking again than not tell you." He watched her closely for a reaction. Her forehead smoothed and her cheeks flushed a rosy pink. Down the hall, bells could be heard, and the soft singing of "Silent Night" started.

She stepped closer. "I heard carolers were allowed to visit today." She grinned. "I'm going to make mistakes, too, Shawn. A lot. But I love you, too."

He reached for her hand. Her warm fingers wrapped around his. "Since you can't get up, let me help you out." She bent over and brushed a soft kiss over his lips. She straightened. "Get some rest, Shawn. I want tomorrow to be the first of many Christmases with you."

"About that..." His heart pounded. "I know we have a lot to figure out, still, but if we're going to date again, I want to be honest with your brother. I need to ask him for his blessing."

She groaned. "A merry Christmas is in my reach and it all rests on my brother?" She winked. "I guess it's a good thing I have time to shop for his gift today."

He laughed and squeezed her hand as the orderly returned. "I have no intention of giving up, Jackie."

And with the promise of a future on her lips, she kissed him right before they wheeled him away.

Jackie rushed around her parents' house, gathering her purse and her coat. She wanted to visit Shawn at the hospital before enjoying the Christmas meal and presents time with her family.

Eddie and his wife, Sienna, who was now six months pregnant, entered the living room. Sienna placed a plate of gingerbread cookies on the coffee table and pushed Eddie's hand away. "It's not time to eat them yet."

"Will you tell Mom and Dad I'm making a run to the hospital before visiting hours are over?" Jackie asked.

The doorbell rang. Jackie looked at Eddie, who was smiling. "Go on and get it," he said.

She fought against rolling her eyes, stepped into the entryway and opened the door. Mom and Dad stood on either side of— "Shawn!"

She moved to hug his neck and stopped short, seeing the bandaging around his shoulder. He laughed and used his right arm to hug her. "I'm okay."

"Medical staff there are good friends," her dad said.

"Because you've brought them so much business," her mom said dryly. "They threatened to start you a punch card you're such a regular."

"And they let me sneak him out for a Christmas meal," he finished. "As far as anyone knows, he's just taking a walk in the halls for a couple hours. We just need him back by ten."

"Let's not keep them in the cold, honey," her mom said.

Shawn's mouth twitched from trying not to laugh.

"We have a quick errand," Dad said, "and we'll be right back to serve Christmas dinner."

"Everything is in the warmer," her mom added. They turned, arm in arm, and returned to the Range Rover.

Shawn stepped inside and Jackie closed the door behind him. He glanced at her purse and coat. "Going somewhere?"

She removed her coat. "I was on my way to see you. I have news."

"Oh?"

"The FBI caught the two men and recovered all of the antiquities."

His shoulders dropped and he beamed. "Good. That's a load off my mind."

"And my sources say Pete wants a deal, so he's giving them the information on the buyer. The FBI hopes to set up a sting and recover even more artifacts."

Shawn shook his head. "Pete always wanted to be responsible for a big archaeological find. Never imagined it would be from behind bars."

She looked to the floor, overcome by a sudden burst of shyness. "And I wanted to write everything down while it was fresh, so I've been working nonstop ever since I was discharged. I got word yesterday that two of my articles are scheduled to be printed. The article I was assigned about the sabotage will be front page tomorrow, and after your challenge, I decided to go ahead and write a piece on the importance of preserving history and heritage." She couldn't help but grin. "And that story will be in Tuesday's edition."

"Congratulations. I never doubted you."

"My boss wants us to talk about what other ideas I've been holding out on him. So thank you for the push to go for it."

"Hey, guys, the party is in here," Eddie called from the living room.

"Right." Shawn nodded as he inhaled, as if preparing for battle. He made a beeline straight for Eddie, and they did their special handshake that ended in a thumbs-up.

For a split second, it was almost like taking a time machine back to when they were kids, before Shawn really looked at her as anything more than Eddie's sister who tagged along for everything. "Hey, man. I don't have much time before your parents get back, so I need to get straight to the point. I'm here because I know you made me promise not to date Jackie because you were worried about—"

"Nope," her brother said, holding a hand out. "I wasn't worried about anything. That's not why I made you promise."

His wife reentered the living room with two cups brimming with coffee. She handed a mug to Eddie and perched on the armrest of his chair. "Made him promise what?" she asked.

"That he would never date my sister," Eddie said. Sienna exchanged a look with him that Jackie couldn't read.

Eddie reached for her hand as Sienna asked, "And why would you do that?"

Eddie nodded toward Shawn. "Because he dated Miranda even though I'd liked her first—when I knew good and well that he really liked my sister. When he finally got smart enough to break up with Miranda, she still wouldn't go out with me."

"But you're married now," Jackie interjected. Of all the immature reasons…

"Happily," Eddie said with a beaming smile and a nod. "I was young and foolish back then." His wife turned to him and they only had eyes for each other.

"I was young and foolish back then, too," Shawn said.

Eddie shook his head. "Nope," he said, in a teasing voice. "It's the principle of the thing. A promise is a promise." His wife laughed as if in on the joke.

"Even though you lied about the reason for the promise." Jackie rolled her eyes. "That's ridiculous."

Shawn turned to Jackie and reached for her hand. "See, the thing is, I love Jackie." He looked deeply into her eyes and her legs almost turned to jelly. "I only promised not to date you."

He took a step backward and dropped to one knee.

Eddie and Sienna gasped. "Are you serious?" Eddie asked.

Shawn didn't turn away from Jackie. "Would you—"

"Are you sure?" The question rushed out of her mouth before he could ask anything.

He grinned. "I've never been so sure. Will you do me the honor—"

"Okay, I changed my mind. You can date. Joke's over," Eddie shouted. "Great. Dad's going to kill me when he hears this is my fault."

His wife leaned over, grabbed the plate of gingerbread men and placed them in his lap. "Honey, let's just watch. It's a beautiful moment," Sienna whispered.

Jackie angled away so they weren't in her view.

Shawn took a deep breath and restarted. "Will you do me the honor of being my wife?"

"Yes." She helped him return to standing and kissed him heartily. "I love you, you know?"

"I love you, too."

"So much so that when we get back from our honeymoon, which will be in a proper hotel, I'll happily build a snow cave."

"You'd build a snow cave for me?"

"With you," she clarified with a laugh. "But I'd

like to be back to indoor plumbing and central heat by nighttime." The reality of their situation, however much she wanted to shove it back into the recesses of her mind, couldn't be ignored. "We have a lot to figure out, though. The long-distance..."

"I think I have a solution." He grinned. "Your dad offered me a job to start a Boise field office. I'd get to run all the survival courses I want and lay down my badge."

"That's not all," her dad said from the hallway. Jackie spun around, realizing her parents must have returned and pulled into the connecting garage this time around. "I sent my network the preliminary clips from the rescue and they want to have a chat with you about future possibilities."

Shawn's eyes lit up. Jackie realized they were so close together, having just got engaged, and she wondered how her dad would take it. She'd always imagined her future fiancé would've asked her father first. She looked into Shawn's eyes, wondering how he was feeling. Except, instead of any apprehension or embarrassment, he flashed her dad a thumbs-up before turning back to her. "Your dad actually told me that as far as he was concerned, I was part of the family."

Her mom and dad stepped farther into the room, holding wrapped packages with Shawn's name on them. Their little errand must have been to get him presents, then. "And Shawn told me," her dad added, "that with all due respect, he'd like to join the family in a different way, as an in-law. Can I assume this little conversation means we have some good news?"

Eddie held up a gingerbread man. "It was all my doing, Dad. Gave them the little push they needed. They're engaged!"

Shawn laughed and wrapped his free arm around her waist to pull her in closer. He understood their playful sibling rivalry almost better than she did. His lips gently touched hers. "Merry Christmas."

"Merry Christmas," she whispered as she returned his kiss. She was never so happy to be home for Christmas.

* * * * *

Tanya Stowe is a Christian fiction author with an unexpected edge. She is married to the love of her life, her high school sweetheart. They have four children and twenty-one grandchildren, a true adventure. She fills her books with the unusual—mysteries and exotic travel, even a murder or two. No matter where Tanya takes you—on a trip to foreign lands or a suspenseful journey packed with danger—be prepared for the extraordinary.

Books by Tanya Stowe

Love Inspired Suspense

Mojave Rescue
Fatal Memories
Killer Harvest
Vanished in the Mountains
Escape Route

Visit the Author Profile page
at LoveInspired.com for more titles.

VANISHED IN THE MOUNTAINS

Tanya Stowe

And that he might make known
the riches of his glory on the vessels of mercy,
which he had afore prepared unto glory.

—*Romans* 9:23

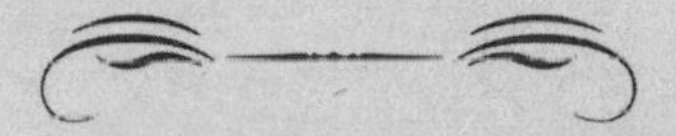

For my husband, Gary,
and one of the trips of our lifetime.

ONE

Dulcie Parker wound her long curls into a tight bun on top of her head and gave it one last pat. Messy, soft buns were the "in" look right now but for her, the tighter the better. First off, her super-curly hair was messy enough and second, she'd found that the sterner, harsher look worked best for her job. In fact, she considered it part of her work uniform: a tight bun, black pants, a crisp white button-front shirt and a black jacket. As a fairly young domestic violence counselor, she needed to be taken seriously, not only by the men she often met but also by her coworkers who considered her too young and inexperienced.

As if anyone is too young to know that words and fists hurt. Her cultured university-professor father taught her that lesson.

She closed her eyes and forced those thoughts from her mind. Going down that path was not the way to start out her workday...one that would end up with her being late to the shelter if she didn't get a move on.

With one last push to a misbehaving curl, she flipped off the bathroom light.

As she entered the small living room of her apartment, she frowned. An envelope lay on the floor by the door.

Puzzled, she picked up the plain white envelope, ripped open the seal and removed a single piece of paper folded neatly into thirds. A message was printed vertically down the middle of the sheet.

Mind your own business or you'll become a Missing One.

Dulcie's fingers trembled as she read the words.

A missing one…the exact words her client Doris Begay had used.

In Dulcie's line of work, threats came with the job. She'd been yelled at and threatened by angry husbands, boyfriends and family members of women seeking help, but this…this was different. This was specific and was not about her clients at the shelter. Or at least only a fine thread connected them.

One of her clients, a Navajo woman named Doris Begay, had been living with an Anglo man, Matt Kutchner. Recently they'd left the Navajo reservation in New Mexico and moved to Durango, Colorado. Once there, Kutchner's violence escalated and Doris's daughter, Judy, had talked her mother into attending group therapy sessions at the shelter where Dulcie worked.

Dulcie had almost convinced Doris to leave the man when sixteen-year-old Judy went missing. The police questioned Dulcie about the violence she had witnessed against Judy Begay. When the young woman's battered body was found at the bottom of a mountain canyon, Dulcie's statements led to Kutchner's arrest.

But the message in her hand wasn't about the Kutchner case. It was about the questions Dulcie started asking after his arrest.

Even before her daughter's body was found, Doris had referred to her as one of the Missing Ones…almost as if she knew her daughter was dead. Since moving to Durango a year ago, Dulcie had learned about the Navajo reluctance to refer to the dead by their names. Still, the mother's use of the phrase *Missing Ones* puzzled Dulcie. How many girls were missing? When she questioned Doris, the woman grew uncomfortable and mumbled something about many reservation girls disappearing.

Dulcie's business was domestic violence. She knew the national statistics. Native American women experienced violence and exploitation at a rate ten times higher than any other ethnic group. But Dulcie did a little digging. To her shock, she discovered the number of missing girls from their area was even greater. The city's close location to multiple Native American reservations, including the massive Navajo reservation, could account for the higher numbers. But to Dulcie, the frequency of the kidnappings indicated something more…something deadly, superefficient and, so far, undetected. Could a trafficking ring be operating in the Four Corners area?

Dulcie had barely started asking questions and

someone was already trying to silence her...someone who could still be outside her door.

The paper slipped through her fingers and floated to the floor. She dashed across the room and squinted through the peephole. As far as she could see, the hallway was empty, but someone could be beyond the narrow vision of the small sight.

Threats weren't much good without force. Was someone waiting for her to step out of her apartment?

Halfway to the kitchen counter for her cell phone she remembered something important. She'd only discussed her concerns with two people—her boss, Vonetta Lauder, and a municipal policeman. Officer Shaw had been the original investigator on the Begay/Kutchner case until they realized the victim lived outside the city limits. From that point on, jurisdiction lay with the county sheriff's office and their detective. Still, when Dulcie needed local statistics, she'd approached Shaw for help. He was the only one besides her boss who knew what she was investigating.

One of them had definitely shared the info. That proof lay on the floor at her feet.

Vonetta was the visible representative of the domestic violence center for women, the voice of those who couldn't speak for themselves. She sat on multiple boards, was always in the news and earned lots of recognition and donations for the privately funded women's center.

But Dulcie had a sense about people, a feel for their hidden motives and agendas. She could thank her dad for that deeply ingrained mistrust. She couldn't quite pin down the reason she'd never trusted Vonetta, but she'd had the same feeling about Officer Shaw. When the Kutchner case moved to the La Plata County Sheriff's Office and Deputy Austin Turner, she'd felt a sense of relief.

Deputy Turner! That's who she would call. She searched her list of phone contacts for his name. She'd liked the man from the minute they met. Not just because of his appealing, boy-next-door good looks. Something about him inspired positive feelings, maybe his deep, confident voice or the lingering pain she glimpsed behind his gaze. Whatever it was, the man understood…had the same sense about people that she possessed.

During the investigation he had given her his cell number. His phone rang and rang until his message clicked on.

Dulcie licked dry lips and tried to find the right words. "Umm, Deputy Turner, this is Dulcie Parker. Can you call me as soon as possible? Something… something has happened." Her voice broke and trembled as she recited her number.

Now she would have to wait. She stared at the paper on the floor, anxiety building with each passing minute.

Don't wait. Call the sheriff's office and hunt him down.

She dialed again. The receptionist sounded busy and a little more than irritated when Dulcie asked if Deputy Turner was in.

"I don't have the answer to that, ma'am, but I can connect you to his line so you can leave a message."

"Yes. Yes please." The fear must have come through in her voice because the receptionist paused.

"Hang on. Let me see if I can find him."

The line went silent and Dulcie took several deep breaths. Now was not the time to lose her hard-won control.

The receptionist clicked back on. "I'm sorry. He doesn't seem to be at his desk. Is there someone else I can connect you with?"

Dulcie paused. Someone else? No…she couldn't trust anyone else.

"No, thank you. I'll leave him a message."

"All right. I'll connect you."

After a short pause, Deputy Turner's deep, reassuring voice echoed in her ear again. Hearing it gave her a jolt of comfort that almost brought her to tears. "Deputy, this is Dulcie Parker. Please call me as soon as you can. It's important."

She ended the phone call, slid onto a bar stool at the counter and rested her forehead on the heels of her palms. How had she come to this again? Was she a magnet for trouble? Was her fear of being a victim creating conspiracies in her head? She looked at the paper resting on the floor.

No. This wasn't her imagination. She'd stumbled upon something deep and dark and someone was determined to keep her from exposing it.

She closed her eyes and whispered a prayer. "Please, Lord, help me."

Over and over again, she repeated the words, until

the darkness threatening to overwhelm her subsided. Then she took a deep breath.

Fear was the tactic all bullies used. The only way to combat fear was to face it head-on. These people—whoever they were—wanted her to stop asking questions. That's the one thing she couldn't do. She had to move forward, had to do something.

She slid off the bar stool and walked to the door. The hallway still appeared empty. She took a deep breath and placed her ear against the door. She heard nothing. Not even another apartment door opening or the deep hum of the elevator.

No door opening. The thought stuck in her mind.

What time is it?

She glanced at her watch. Twenty minutes before eight. Every day precisely at 7:45 a.m. her neighbor across the hall left for work. Joey Delacroix worked for the city and was precise in everything he did. In five minutes on the dot, he would leave. Dulcie could leave with him.

Taking a deep breath, she swooped the paper off the ground, folded it back into the envelope and shoved it and her phone into her purse. Grabbing her coat, she slipped it on and tugged the strap of her purse over her shoulder. Then she hurried back to the door. Easing the chain out of the lock, she released the dead bolt and pressed her ear to the wooden portal again, listening for any sound.

A minute passed and her heart pounded. What if whoever left this message was waiting near the elevator? What if there were more than one? What if they weren't afraid to attack her and Joey together?

Stop it. You're letting fear overwhelm you again.

Still she needed…wanted…some way to defend herself. She looked around the room. A small can of scented aerosol spray rested on the nearby end table. Sprayed directly in an assailant's eyes, it would make a great weapon. She popped the lid off, let it fall to the ground and gripped the can in her left hand. Then shc pulled her door key out of her purse and clasped it between her fingers, pointed edge facing out.

Now she was ready. She placed her ear against the door and waited. One minute passed. Another.

Where was Joey? Had she missed him? Did he call in sick? Her pulse pounded faster with each question.

And then, the door across the hall opened. It was so loud, she shook her head and stepped back. Of course, she didn't need to press her ear against the door. Every morning she heard Joey leave while standing eight feet away in her kitchen. Fear was stealing her common sense. She needed to get control.

Straightening her spine, she tucked the aerosol can just inside her large, open purse and twisted the doorknob with fingers still clutching the key. With the door wide, she paused and glanced both directions.

All clear. She looked her neighbor's way. Joey stood motionless, his key poised just above the knob and a frown on his face.

"Hey, Dulcie. Is something wrong?"

She swallowed and stepped outside her door to lock

it. "No, no. Nothing. I just… I thought I heard someone at my door earlier. Did you see anyone?"

"Nope. But I'm running a little late so I was rushing around. Might not have heard someone in the hall."

She nodded and swallowed. They locked their doors simultaneously, then walked down the hall side by side. Dulcie hesitated, waiting to see if Joey would take the elevator or the stairs. Since he was running late, maybe he'd depart from his usual choice and use the elevator. Either way, she was going the way he went.

He punched the buttons outside the elevator and turned to face her. "You sure you're okay?"

She tried to smile. "Just a lot on my mind. A busy day today."

The elevator dinged. Joey motioned for her to step in ahead of him. "Yeah, me too. We're getting close to month's end and I've got to finish a project before that."

End of October. Fall was sliding by. Cooler temperatures. Falling leaves. The golden aspens. All the russet shades and burnt oranges on the mountainsides. The colors she loved and had barely noticed this year. Life was slipping past her at the speed of light. She glanced at Joey, his pressed shirt, neat tie and overcoat. His daily "uniform." They were a lot alike. Caught up in their work, too focused to see the world around them. Maybe when all of this was over…

Dulcie looked away. Probably wouldn't happen. She had a hard time getting close to people, especially men. But one thing was certain—she was very thankful for his presence this morning. She started to tell him so when the elevator door slid open. Joey gestured for her to move ahead of him again and the moment was lost.

She paused at the front door of the apartment building, her gaze scouring the parking lot. It seemed empty, but still she hesitated. Joey reached in front of her to push the handlebar of the door.

Shaking her head, she said, “Sorry. I guess I’m not all here today.”

“No problem. It’s just that I’m in a bit of a hurry.”

That was her cue to get moving.

The cold, brisk air made her catch her breath.

Joey moved across the lot but stood outside his car door, watching her, waiting. She hurried to her own vehicle, released the can she’d been clenching into her purse and punched the fob to unlock her door. Dulcie slid in and locked it again. Joey already had his car backed out and she watched him pull away. Then she sat in her car in the near-empty parking lot and wondered what to do next.

She couldn’t go to work and face Vonetta or go to the municipal police station where Officer Shaw worked. Only one place remained where she could find help. She backed out and headed to the county sheriff’s office.

Austin Turner dropped his Stetson on his desk, ran a hand through his short hair and sighed. This was one of those days when he was especially glad that as a detective, he didn’t have to wear the typical county sheriff uniform. Not that he wasn’t proud of the uniform. He loved the job, the work he did and most of his fellow deputies with few exceptions.

No. The job wasn't the problem. He was. For a long time now, he hadn't been able to wear the uniform with pride. Ever since the death of his Navajo wife, Abey, and their unborn child in a car accident, he hadn't felt worthy of the badge or the uniform he'd so proudly donned twelve years ago.

Again, he ran his hand through hair too short to move out of place…a nervous gesture and a sure sign that the bad feeling he'd had since waking this morning was here to stay. He'd had lots of those days in the three years since he'd lost his family. No matter how hard he tried, he couldn't shake the feeling that he should have done more. Could have prevented their deaths.

He thought he was on the mend but the brutal beating and death of a young Navajo girl had fired up all his old resentments and everything else he'd tried so hard to suppress. Many a night he'd lain awake, seeing that poor girl's body at the bottom of a mountain ravine. Those long nights ended only after he arrested the girl's stepfather.

Truth be told, the social worker involved in the case, Dulcie Parker, had contributed to his unrest. Something about the woman stuck with him. It had to be because she was so worked up…not for any other reason. There was no room in his life for another woman. Abey and his baby still filled every corner.

No, Dulcie Parker bothered him because she pushed relentlessly for answers and action. He'd only interviewed her a few times, but he never lost the feeling that she'd be following the investigation from afar, watching, waiting for results.

He recognized the bright flame of restitution in her eyes. That flame was the only thing he had in common with the redhead and was probably the one thing he didn't need in his life. After he'd struggled for so long to suppress those feelings, Dulcie fed the embers into life again…not to mention the fact that she set his nerves on edge. She was touchy and flighty, jumping away every time he got close. He didn't doubt for a moment there was a story behind those actions. She had a history, a past he didn't know and didn't want to know. The last thing he needed was a woman as close to the edge as her.

And maybe his imagination was running a marathon. He shook his head. A prolonged vacation might be the only solution to his overactive mind. He was due for some time off and his lieutenant had been pressing him to take it. The case was over. The Kutchner trial didn't start for another month, a long time from now. Until then, he needed to put all those unwanted feelings and thoughts away. Maybe he should consider some time off.

Determined to discuss the idea with his boss, he hung his hat on the rack behind him and checked the work cell phone he kept on Silent. Sleep was hard enough to attain without reporters driving him crazy all hours of the night. Since he'd arrested Kutchner, they'd been harassing him relentlessly and he needed to talk to them even less than he needed to be around Dulcie Parker.

He had a message on his phone. He hit the play button, and Dulcie's voice, the very woman he was hoping to avoid, echoed over the line. She sounded…scared. That shouldn't have surprised him. She seemed pretty uptight and easily shaken. But still her voice sounded… more than just frightened. Terrified was the right word. He released a heavy sigh. This was the last thing he wanted today, especially since she asked him to call her as soon as he could.

Fearing she had a complicating issue with the Kutchner case, he reached for his desk phone and saw the message light flashing. Dulcie was on the office machine, as well. Something was seriously wrong. Before he could even dial her number, the front desk buzzed him.

"Hey, Turner, I've got a woman here who needs to see you. She's pretty upset."

"Don't tell me. It's Dulcie Parker." He shook his head. "I guess you better send her in." He knew she was trouble from the minute he met her. There was just something about her…

He rose from his desk. The officer led Dulcie into the large common room filled with deputies' cubicles. Even across the room Austin noted her pale features—so white the red freckles across her nose and cheeks jumped out.

Taken individually, her features didn't seem to fit together. Almost black eyebrows stood out against her pale skin. They were too dark for the rest of her face, even darker than her large brown eyes. Her lips had all but disappeared in paleness. Her curly copper-shaded hair might be pretty if she didn't pull it back so tight and flat against her head. But she plastered it against her scalp and frizzy little strands rejected those tight confines. They fuzzed around her face in fiery protest.

She looked more than upset…and that meant Austin's morning would probably go from bad to worse. He stopped a few feet away and nodded. "Ms. Parker, what can I do for you?"

Glancing around, she stepped closer—but not too close, he noticed. He'd seen that action the first time they met, that she didn't let him—let anyone—get too close. In a low voice she asked, "Can we talk…someplace more private?"

Austin hesitated. Whatever she wanted, he didn't need to provide. She was toxic to him…brought feelings to life inside that were better off dead. But her colorless features and large, frightened eyes got to him. He gritted his teeth and pointed to a small room off the main area.

As soon as he closed the door, she pulled an envelope out of her purse and handed it to him. He opened it and read the message inside.

Mind your own business or you'll become a Missing One.

Austin had heard the phrase only once, at a meeting Abey had helped organize. As a member of the Navajo Nation, she had been heavily involved in multiple social organizations. In fact, he'd first met her when he was doing overtime duty at a fundraiser for Native American teens. The slender, dark-haired beauty caught his eye the minute she walked in to give an impassioned speech to the young women of her nation. At that meeting, an older Navajo woman referred to the missing and exploited Native American women by using the term *the Missing Ones*.

Over the top of the paper, Austin studied Dulcie Parker. There was a serious issue with missing and exploited Native American women. It was true, and if he'd learned anything about the woman across from him, she was the kind who would meddle in someone else's business. She wouldn't be able *not* to meddle. If he knew anything about her, it was that. Just talking to her would mean trouble for him too, trouble he was pretty anxious to avoid.

He took a slow breath. "Whose business have you been minding?"

Obviously, she didn't catch the hint of accusation in his tone. "I have no idea. All I did was ask for some statistics on missing women in the local area."

Her voice trembled. At least she had sense enough to be frightened. Maybe she'd be smart enough to walk away.

"When Doris Begay said her daughter was one of the Missing Ones..."

Austin's senses perked up. "Is this about the Kutchner case?"

"No...yes." She closed her eyes and took a slow breath. "I don't know. All I know is almost from the moment Judy disappeared Doris Begay assumed her daughter was gone forever...or dead. I'm not sure which. When I asked her why, she mumbled something about all the missing reservation girls."

Austin's jaw tightened. "So, of course, you had to check it out?"

He couldn't keep the irritation out of his tone. This time she heard the cynicism peeking through. Dark eyes, that moments ago seemed frightened and unsure, focused on him with startling clarity.

"Yes, I did. I won't turn my back on a woman or child…ever."

There it was again. The blazing passion that backed him down…backed most people down. It was a little scary. What was even more frightening… He understood that ferocious passion. He had one just like it, locked inside, eating away at his soul.

That fact hit him in the face like a slap. Dulcie Parker put him on edge because she was exactly like him…just more honest and open about it. He'd run away from his problem, even tried to hide from it. But she spoke it, walked it and lived it. If he were honest, her courage made him uncomfortable.

Ms. Parker didn't appear to notice his startled reaction. It didn't even slow her down. Now that her passion had been ignited, she was on fire. "Do you realize how many local girls are missing?"

He tried to push the thoughts away, to douse the fire with a shift of his shoulders. "We're surrounded by Native American reservations. They have the highest statistics so of course our local numbers are going to be elevated."

"Thirty-eight, Deputy Turner. Thirty-eight local women and girls have gone missing in the last three years. That's almost double the amount in the previous ten years. Even accounting for the rise in sex trafficking that's an alarming increase. Are you trying to tell me that's to be expected?"

The number *was* alarming. Why hadn't he seen that figure on any reports passing through this office? Who generated that info? Definitely something he needed to find out.

Before he could say so, she went on. "Those numbers may be acceptable to you, but they certainly are not to me."

That rankled. Was she trying to get a response out of him? Trying to ignite the same kind of angry blaze inside him? He'd been fighting for three years to keep that emotion out of his work. And now, here she was, this barely-tied-down ball of rage, trying to make him react.

She wouldn't like it if he did.

He forced himself to keep tight control. "Of course those numbers matter. There's someone's wife behind each one of them." His emotions flashed with anger. Where did she get off sounding so high and mighty? "I've never seen those stats. Where did you get your information?"

"The Durango police department. Deputy Shaw."

Shaw. Austin knew him. Most folks in the local law enforcement did. The man made sure of it. He was ambitious. Austin had worked with Shaw and frankly, he wouldn't put it past the man to try to call attention to his work any way possible. But Ms. Parker didn't know that.

"I didn't tell anyone about my research except Officer Shaw and my boss. They are the only ones who could have passed that info on to someone else to create that note."

Austin didn't know Vonetta Lauder as well as he knew Shaw, but he'd met her, watched her on the local TV programs and read about her in every newspaper in the county. Like Shaw, she seemed to enjoy the limelight. Neither of them inspired confidence in Austin. That fact alone made him willing to hear Ms. Parker out.

"Let me get this straight. Shaw gave you some kind of report?"

Some of her anger seemed to fade. "No. In fact, he wasn't tremendously helpful. He gave me a couple of internet resources that didn't tell me anything. But I'm pretty good with research. Once I got started, I found the info I needed and put the numbers together myself."

He stiffened. "You put the numbers together?"

She tensed again. "I told you. I'm good with research. Actually, excellent."

"I'm not questioning your research capabilities, Ms. Parker. Just pointing out that there's the possibility of error in your info. We all make mistakes."

She stared at him, stunned, and he watched all the spark and fire fade out of her. "You don't believe me."

"I didn't say that. It's my job to find the facts, not make dangerous guesses. Here's something else to consider. You were just involved in a high-profile murder case. Those investigations bring out the crazies and your name was all over the news. Maybe some unbalanced person or a former client decided now was the time to get back at you with this scare tactic."

She looked away. When she spoke, her voice was very low and tremulous. "It worked. I'm scared."

Austin released a frustrated sigh. "I didn't say I would not look into this. I will. I'm just trying to point out how many explanations there could be. We can't just go around jumping to conclusions, pointing fingers and naming names before we have the answers."

She gave a slight, hesitant nod. "I guess that's true." She pushed the strap of her purse higher on her shoulder and studied him, her dark eyes fathomless with strong emotions behind her tightly controlled gaze. He didn't know what they were for sure…but they were there, held in check. The intensity put him off-step.

He lifted the letter. "Can I keep this?"

She caught her breath and hesitated. For the first time, she stumbled over her words. "It's…it's the only proof I have."

Mistrust. That was the intense emotion behind her gaze. Austin's jaw tightened and his resolve hardened. "I get it. You want my help but you can't find it in yourself to trust me."

Fed up, he shoved the envelope toward her. She gripped it with shaky fingers.

Austin spun and walked toward the door. "I'll look at all this and let you know if I find anything."

She fumbled with her purse, shoved the envelope inside as she moved toward him. She paused just short of the door. "Will you…can you call me even if you find nothing? I'd like to…know."

He nodded. “I’ll be in touch.” He opened the door. She ducked her head and passed him, but not before he caught the defeated look on her features.

Austin followed her into the large common room and watched as she walked away. His instincts were right. She was a woman looking for a crusade and she’d triggered feelings from his convoluted past. Good police work didn’t happen when the emotions were engaged. He knew that better than anyone. He needed to step back if he wanted to assess this properly…no matter how many defeated looks Ms. Parker sent his way.

He felt someone’s presence behind him and turned. Lieutenant Dale McGuire, his supervisor, nudged his chin in Ms. Parker’s direction. “What’s she doing here?”

Austin didn’t trust his own prickly attitude so he shook his head. “Nothing important.”

“Good. Can I see you in my office for a minute?”

Frowning, Austin followed his lieutenant. Dale had helped him get the job here at the station. He’d been a good supervisor and a great leader. Austin liked and respected him for all those qualities.

McGuire gestured to the door. “Close that.”

So…this was serious. Austin was instantly on guard. “What’s going on?”

McGuire stood behind his desk. “It’s pretty bizarre, that Parker woman showing up today. Not more than twenty minutes ago I got a call to watch out for her.”

“Watch out. What does that mean?”

One of McGuire’s eyebrows rose. Austin recognized it as his boss’s “I’m not happy” signal. But what was he unhappy about? The call or Austin’s questions?

He got his answer immediately. "I didn't ask questions. I just listened. You should follow my example." Dale's eyebrow still rode high on one side. "I was told that she's a troublemaker. She was fired from her last job after some scandal. Now she's looking to cash in on her claim to fame with the Kutchner case. That's the type of publicity we don't need. So back off."

Austin studied his superior. Even though he'd just had similar thoughts, it rankled to be ordered to stand down. "Since when do other people tell you how to run your staff?"

McGuire's eyebrow rose even higher. "I think what I said was to the point. I didn't ask questions and neither should you. She's trouble. Stay clear."

He picked up the file on his desk as if the conversation was over. When Austin didn't move, he looked up again.

Austin hesitated. He didn't like this. It smacked of collusion. He couldn't believe McGuire was okay with it. "Who gave you the call?"

His boss took a deep breath, obviously irritated. "Does it matter? We were advised. That's all you need to know." When Austin still didn't move, McGuire's frown deepened. "Is there something about this meeting you're not telling me?"

Dulcie said Officer Shaw was one of two people who knew about her research. Shaw belonged to the municipal police department and was a rising star. When he talked, people took notice. Did his popularity extend to the county sheriff's department too? How deep...or high did his influence go? And why was Mc-

Guire so resistant to giving Austin details about the phone call? For the first time, he questioned the motives of a man he respected and considered a friend.

"Is that an order, Lieutenant?"

His superior stiffened. "If that's how you want to take it."

"I think that's how I *have* to take it."

McGuire dropped the file to the desk. "That's fine, Turner. Take it any way you like. Just see that you do it."

Righteous senses bristling, Austin turned his back on his mentor and stalked out of the office to find Dulcie Parker's number. His boss's uncharacteristic actions just pushed him over the edge. Something was going on and Austin intended to find out what it was. Ms. Parker just became his number-one priority.

TWO

Dulcie slid behind the wheel of her car, locked the door and closed her eyes. When Judy Begay's murder investigation had been handed over to Deputy Turner, she was relieved. She'd liked the man and Dulcie couldn't say that about many people. Her background made it difficult for her to trust. But she'd had a good feeling about Deputy Turner. There had been something about him...the sense that he understood. That he was as serious about crimes against women as she was...and that he was kind. That was the most important thing. Kindness. Her early years had been dreadfully empty of that emotion. She craved it now like living water.

Her experience with Deputy Parker this morning had felt anything but that. She knew people, had strong instincts about them and was usually right. How could she have misjudged Deputy Turner so badly?

Did his boy-next-door looks turn her head, muddle her impressions? It was true he was handsome...and blond. Today was the first time she'd seen him without his cowboy hat, and she had to admit what was underneath that Stetson did not fail to appeal. He kept those golden locks short but they still had a stubborn wave in the front. His blue eyes were clear and so bright, they almost sparkled beneath the brim of his hat. He also had a cleft in his chin, a distinct little dent that set off his almost-too-pretty looks. Dulcie closed her eyes.

Okay. So… Deputy Turner's appearance had definitely made an impression and probably skewed her people instincts.

But he said he would look into it. She had to trust him and get on with her day. She reached for the key in the ignition but her fingers trembled so she couldn't grip it.

She gave her hand a shake and tried again. Still she couldn't take hold.

She was scared. Too scared to go to work and face Vonetta and too afraid to go home. She leaned back in her seat and closed her eyes. She felt like she was crossing the Grand Canyon on a tightwire with hundreds of feet of empty air beneath her. It had been a long time since she'd been this scared. Not since she and her sister hid in their closet with their arms around each other.

Her cell phone rang and she jumped a mile, bumping her knees on the wheel. Taking a deep breath, she stared at her purse. It was probably work wondering why she was late. Should she answer?

Of course she needed to answer. Otherwise they'd keep calling. On the third ring, she grabbed the purse and pulled her phone out. A sigh of relief slipped out as

Deputy Turner's name flashed across the screen. She couldn't slide the on button fast enough.

"Hello?"

"Dulcie, I'm glad I caught you." His voice was pitched so low she barely heard it. "I hope you're not already at work."

Should she tell him she hadn't even left the sheriff department's parking lot? It was embarrassing, but she needed to practice trust and honesty.

"No. No, I'm not. I haven't left yet."

"Good. There's been a…development. We need to talk. But not here. I'd like to take a look at your information. Can you meet me after work…say five thirty?"

She hesitated. Did she dare invite him to her apartment? All of her files were there and he could check out her place. But that meant letting a stranger into her sanctuary. All of her old fears rose to the surface, strapping her tongue down.

"Dulcie…are you there?"

That voice. So confident. So deep and sure. She could trust him. She had to.

"Yes, I'm here. All my files are in my apartment. We can meet there."

"Great. I'll see you at five thirty, and Dulcie… I'm going to need that letter."

"Yes, yes, of course. I'll have it."

"All right. I'll see you then."

"Umm… Deputy…what should I do? I mean…if there's been a development maybe I shouldn't go to work."

He was silent for a long moment. "Do exactly what

they said to do, Dulcie. Nothing. Mind your own business. Don't mention the letter, talk to anyone about it or do more research. I've got a couple of things to check on before we talk. Then I'll have a better idea of our next step."

Our next step. Dulcie sighed. That tightwire across the Grand Canyon suddenly felt like it had a safety net beneath it. She could do what she needed to do now.

"I'll see you at five thirty sharp." She gave him her address, hung up the phone and reached for the ignition key with only a slight tremor.

Austin parked on the side of the road, far down from Dulcie's apartment complex. He'd been there for almost twenty minutes watching the road. He wanted to be sure someone wasn't following Dulcie, so he waited, his fingers drumming on the wheel.

Dulcie's small white economy car came around the corner and pulled into the parking lot. Austin waited, his gaze roaming up and down the road, searching for any car that might have followed her. No vehicle stopped or even slowed. After a long while, he turned on the ignition and pulled into the driveway of the complex. Dulcie's car was parked in a spot marked with her apartment number. It looked like she was still sitting there. Was she waiting for him?

Probably. Maybe she was more sensible than he first suspected. He pulled into a visitor's space and climbed out. The night air was crisp. It would be even colder when he left. Autumn had swept into Colorado with an early storm and decided to stay. If winter followed the trend of the last few days, it would be long and cold.

He pulled out his sherpa-lined jean jacket and folded it over his arm. Dulcie didn't leave her car until he walked up. Then the door flew open and she slid out in one smooth movement.

"Did you think I wasn't coming?"

"No, I…just didn't want to go inside by myself." She looked down, almost as if she was embarrassed to admit she was afraid. She had every right to be frightened and he felt a little guilty about his disregard this morning for the danger she seemed to be facing. Dulcie's safety was just as important as the integrity of the department. She'd just come to the wrong person for protection. He didn't feel capable of giving her a fair shake.

But she *had* come to him, and he owed her his best effort…and the same kind of honesty she now seemed determined to give him. "I was here early. I parked outside on the street to see if you were followed."

She looked up, surprise in her gaze. "Was I?"

Austin tilted his head. "No. Not from what I could see."

She sighed. "I almost wish they had followed me. That would explain how they know so much about my movements." A small breeze riffled over them like a cold breath and she shivered. "I guess we should go inside."

He gestured her forward. She lifted her purse strap higher and paused. It took her a moment, then she straightened her spine and marched ahead. She was determined even though she was afraid. He didn't know if that was bravery or foolishness. But it made Austin like Dulcie Parker just a little more.

They took the small elevator up to her apartment. Dulcie scrambled through her large bag, looking for her keys. Just as she reached for the lock, the door across the hall opened and a man with brown hair, glasses and a full garbage bag in hand stepped out.

"Oh, hi, Dulcie." His gaze jumped from her to Austin then darted to his shoulder holster and the badge attached to his belt. Then he looked back to Dulcie. "Is everything all right?"

Her lips parted and to Austin's amazement, the woman who had no trouble expressing herself was at a loss for words.

Despite his surprise at her stalled actions, Austin stepped into the silent void for her. "No, no problem at all. Dulcie and I met a few weeks back and decided to grab a pizza some time. Tonight's the night." He smiled.

Dulcie's neighbor looked at her for confirmation. She nodded. "Joey Delacroix, this is Austin Turner. We met…a few weeks ago like he said."

A half smile, half grimace slipped over Delacroix's features. He looked so disappointed, Austin almost chuckled. Dulcie's neighbor looked back at him and Austin smiled, the biggest, most self-satisfied grin he could manage. "Nice to meet you."

Austin held out his hand. Joey grasped it, then the man looked away quickly. "Yeah…same here. See you later."

He gripped the bag and scooted down the hall like he was embarrassed. Puzzled by the encounter, Austin looked at Dulcie for an explanation. But she ducked her head and opened the door.

Was his arrival interfering with a budding romance? Did this mousey guy, who seemed afraid of his own shadow, know anything about his neighbor? His impression of Dulcie was of a driven woman who took no prisoners and left no one behind in her quest for justice for abused women. Mousey guy didn't have a chance. Austin didn't even try to stifle his pleasure at the thought.

He followed Dulcie inside, oddly pleased. Not that he had…or even wanted a claim on Ms. Parker. He just didn't think Delacroix should have one either.

Pushing aside his wayward thoughts, Austin surveyed the room. Dulcie crossed to the kitchen bar and set down her bag. The living room was meticulously clean. Furnished with a serviceable brown sofa and chair with a glass-topped table in between. It looked like standard apartment issue. But Dulcie had added her own splashes of color. Blue-and-green pillows and the same colors in a swath of material above the blinds. A soft, comfy-looking blue beanbag chair rested in one corner of the room beside a small, glass-topped desk. Paper files were stacked on top. Nothing was out of place. It almost felt too organized, too straight and neat…like the woman nervously looking around her home. But to his surprise, Austin found the room welcoming. He could sit on the couch and stay for a while. As much as he loved his own cabin on the mountain, it didn't have this "get comfortable" feeling.

He studied Dulcie as she slid out of her coat. "This is nice. You've made this small place feel…homey."

She sent him a shy, pleased smile. "Thank you. I'm not here much but when I am, I want it to be comfortable, you know? I'm glad somebody else likes it too."

She took his hat and coat from him, careful not to let their hands touch, and hung them both on a stand near the door. Austin couldn't resist teasing her just a little. "Did I just destroy a blossoming romance?"

"What? Of course not!" The pink tinge that came into her cheeks told him otherwise. Not to mention the fact that she refused to look him in the face. When she finally glanced up, he lifted his eyebrows in a question.

She sighed. "Really. I've barely spoken to the man. It's just…well, he walked me to the elevator this morning and I felt a little thankful. That's all."

Austin chuckled, almost to himself. "If you say so."

He lifted the blinds and checked the locks. No marks or spots where the window might have been jimmied. He peeked outside, saw that there was no balcony or a ledge wide enough to crawl along. Then he examined the door frame, searching for evidence of an attempt to pry the door open. At last, he tested the handle and found it sturdy and tight.

"Can I check the bedroom?"

"Sure." She sounded confident but scooted down the hall ahead of him. He didn't know what she was so nervous about. The bedroom was in the same meticulous order as the living room. Windows secure. Closet doors shut. But he checked inside anyway, just to reassure her.

"Everything is good, Dulcie. It doesn't look like anyone even attempted to get inside. Just keep the locks on and do your laundry in some public place. No dark basement rooms until we get this sorted out."

She nodded. "I will. Thank you."

He headed back down the hall. As he passed the bathroom, a soft scent drifted toward him. Flowery and green like grass or broken leaves. It reminded him of a soft spring evening. He liked it. Was it Dulcie's perfume or some sort of room deodorizer? If she let him get closer to her than three feet, he might know the answer. But every time they got anywhere near each other, she skittered away like a wild animal. He hesitated just a moment longer, taking in the pleasing aroma, but she halted, three feet behind him. What happened to the "no prisoners taken" woman? Was she only fearless when she was protecting other women and children? Shaking his head, he moved forward.

Back in the living room, he went straight to the desk. "Are these files your research?"

"Yes. Take a look while I order us a pizza. Can I get you something first…a soda or a bottle of water?"

"Yeah. I'd like a soda if you have it."

She picked up the cell phone and dialed. While she waited for an answer, she walked to the fridge and came back with a cola. "What kind of pizza?"

"Anything with meat."

He looked at the files on the desk. Each of them was at least an inch thick. She had four full folders. If she had done all of this on her own in such a short time, she *was* an excellent researcher. He carried the files to the sofa and plopped down. It was as comfortable as it looked. He'd had a long, tense day trying to avoid his lieutenant and keep busy. All he wanted right now was to lean back on Dulcie's front-room sofa, rest his head on the soft blue pillow and close his eyes. But the files lay heavy in his arms.

He opened the first and began to read. Name after name. Place after place. Most of the missing women had home addresses on the reservations. Not a good thing since all of those places were out of his jurisdiction. In order to start any kind of investigation, he'd have to ask permission and cross official lines. That by itself would be difficult.

The doorbell rang. Dulcie, who had taken the chair at the end of the sofa—as far from him as she could get—tensed. She was still frightened and since she was already uptight and determined not to get too close to him, this whole situation was looking bleak.

Austin shook his head and rose. She hurried after him and stood behind him. Austin took the pizza box from the delivery boy. Dulcie reached around him to hand the college kid a wad of money. Austin shut the door and reached for his wallet. "Here, let me..."

"Absolutely not. This is my treat. You don't know how much I appreciate this."

Austin studied her downcast features. There it was again. That little tremor of fear in her voice. She must have heard it too, as a wash of pink flushed over her cheeks. She seemed ashamed of her fear, embarrassed by it. She had every reason to be afraid and no reason to be ashamed.

He handed her the pizza and, with new resolve, went back to the files, searching for a common thread between the missing women. Dulcie brought him a piece of pizza on a paper plate. He reached up and cupped one hand under hers to support the plate. Her soft skin sent a jolt through his fingertips before she jerked away. Had she felt that little electric charge? He looked up into her startled gaze.

"Sorry. I'm still jumpy."

Right…and her nerves were contagious. He was beginning to feel as tense as she acted. How were they going to work together if they made each other feel like cats walking on hot tin roofs?

He turned away, tried to focus on the files beneath him. It worked. Soon, he was lost in the names, dates and places. Dulcie had already separated the cases by years, three to be exact. Roughly ten women each year, living in different locations, had disappeared. But the staggered dates and locations of the disappearances had perfect precision, as if they were planned out months in advance. These were not crimes of opportunity, but were systematic. Austin's insides tightened as that truth sank in. These people were smart, powerful and deadly…and he had no clue how to penetrate their web.

But he was only skimming the files. He had to go deeper.

"We need to tear these files apart. We need pencils and paper." After such a long silence, his words startled Dulcie and she dropped her pizza slice onto her lap. She peeled it off and flopped it on the paper plate, but a large spot of red sauce covered her black pant leg.

"Oh no." She wiped the stain with a napkin then rose quickly and hurried to the desk. She brought two yellow legal pads and a pile of pencils back to the coffee table. "I'll be right back. I have to change."

Austin nodded, grabbed one pad and jumped back into the first file. By the time she returned, he was deep into dates and barely glanced up when she entered the room. When he did, he almost dropped his pencil.

She'd changed into a long-sleeved top over stretchy workout pants. There was nothing particularly flattering about the outfit except the color. The purple toned down all the harsh carroty tinge of her freckles and turned her lips to the color of peaches. And her hair… Those orange wisps around her face had disappeared into curls the color of burnished copper that fell in glossy coils well below her shoulders. Brows that had seemed too large and too full now matched the deep brown of her eyes and the dark fire in her hair. She looked wild, barely contained and completely unfathomable.

He was staring. Knew he was staring but couldn't stop. Dulcie Parker was beautiful. She looked uncomfortable beneath his scrutiny. He tried to gather his thoughts and felt like he needed to apologize. For what, he didn't know.

"I'm sorry," he said at last. "It's just you look…so different."

"I know. My hair always seems to get lots of unwanted attention. That's why I usually pull it back."

Unwanted. Austin shook his head as understanding sank deep inside him. In one sentence, she'd hit upon the source of their tense relations. "It shouldn't be unwanted, Dulcie. A beautiful woman shouldn't be afraid to be beautiful."

He didn't dare look up to see what impact his probably "unwanted" observation might have on her. He was afraid if he looked up, he'd tell her how her hair was like a crown and made everything else fit into place. But he knew she wouldn't appreciate the compliment so he kept his gaze on the files in front of him.

"How did things go at work today?"

"Good." She cleared her throat. "It went better than I thought. Vonetta's attending a conference and won't be back for three days."

"No one else asked any questions? Nothing seemed suspicious or out of order?"

"Not at all. If I hadn't found that letter under my door, it would have been a perfectly normal day."

He nodded and finally dared to look up. "Well, my day was anything but normal. Someone sent an order to my lieutenant suggesting that I stay away from you."

Dulcie slumped to the chair at the end of the sofa. "Someone warned you to stay away from me?"

"Yeah, before you even arrived at the station."

She stared at him, stunned. "How did they know..." Words seemed to slip away from her and fright built on her features. "Is that why you called me? To let me down easily and tell me you can't be involved?"

His lips tilted upward. "Not likely. I don't take those kinds of orders."

Dulcie's lips parted in what seemed like relief and she swallowed. Her fire-wrapped hair framed her neck, made it appear long, white and incredibly soft. Once again, he felt himself staring.

She walked to the desk, pulled out another file and handed it to him.

"What's this?"

"It's important. I need you to read it."

He opened the file. It was an employment report from Dulcie's last job in California. A mother came to the shelter with a split lip and bruises, an obvious victim of domestic abuse. But it was her little girls who caught Dulcie's attention. She'd kept a tight record of their responses. The sisters showed no signs of violence and made no comments. In fact, they refused to speak, shied away from the touch of anyone…just like Dulcie. Obviously, their actions ignited her concerns. When the woman weakened and returned to her husband, Dulcie broke all her counseling boundaries and pushed the mother to the point of harassment. She resorted to waiting outside the woman's house and following her, begging her to return to the shelter. Eventually, the husband discovered Dulcie's presence and filed a complaint. Her supervisors had no choice but to let her go.

Austin looked up. Dulcie watched him with those dark, unfathomable eyes. What was behind that unreadable gaze? What did she want him to say?

It didn't really matter what *she* wanted. He had one very important question. "Did you convince the mother to return?"

She swallowed again. "No. I heard later that she

ended up in the hospital and the father disappeared… with the two little girls. They haven't been seen since."

Austin looked down. Anger rushed through him. Once again he felt that ruthless, vicious rage that he worked so hard to contain. He'd been right. Dulcie Parker wasn't good for him. Her past, her present—everything about her—ignited his banked rage.

He lifted the file. "You didn't have to show me this."

She nodded slowly. "Yes… I did. Because there's one more thing you should know." She licked dry lips. "I'm not so sure I won't do it again…cross the line, I mean. I couldn't live with myself if I lost more little girls."

All the passion inside Austin froze. She was talking about herself and didn't know she'd just put his own unspoken emotions into words. He couldn't live with himself if he lost something—someone—else, including a copper-headed woman with dark passion hiding behind her gaze.

The thought of Dulcie endangering herself, continuing to put her job and maybe even her life in danger for these women made his instincts flare like live wires. He dropped the file down on the table. "I hope you mean that because it looks like you've already put your life on the line."

Dulcie stiffened as Austin slammed the file shut. A frown creased the spot between his eyebrows and when he was angry, that little cleft in his chin twitched. She'd noticed it before, almost the first time they'd met when he was questioning her about Judy Begay and her relationship with her stepfather. That little twitch was a sign for Dulcie. Austin might try to act like he didn't care, but he did...deeply, and for that reason, his anger didn't frighten her.

He raised a tense gaze to hers and lifted the folder again. "It also says in here you handled twenty-five cases in the three years you worked with this shelter. They gave you this file and made a point of saying how well you had performed before this incident. That tells me they wanted to help you any way they could. What happened, Dulcie? Why did this case make you snap?"

She took a deep breath. "The two little girls reminded me of my sister and me."

It was hard to talk about it. But she had to tell him. She needed to make him understand. "My dad was a well-respected professor, a very popular teacher. But at home he was a monster. Anytime something fell short of perfection, he took it out on my mother. My sister and I would hide in our closet. Then one day my sister spoke up and he knocked her across the room."

Dulcie swallowed. "As soon as he left for work, my mother packed our bags. I remember her hands trembling the whole time. We took a taxi to a shelter. They helped my mother file a restraining order. Then they found her a job and gave us counseling. I wouldn't be here if not for that shelter. That's why I do what I do. I wouldn't have a life if not for someone who cared enough to be there."

His voice was low and maybe still angry. "So now you have to be that person. The one who cares."

She nodded. "I worked hard to have a normal life,

to overcome my fears and walk in the world with my head held high. I thought I was over my past. But that encounter with the little girls, and now this letter… They both sent me spiraling back again. They made me feel like a helpless child and I don't like that feeling."

Austin looked at the file, avoiding her gaze. But his jaw clenched and a muscle twitched. He didn't like what was happening any more than she did. That assuaged her fear.

"I know you care, Dulcie. You didn't have to show me this." He lifted the file.

She licked her lips and shook her head. "That's not why I gave it to you. I just wanted you to know it's not personal. I… I have a hard time trusting people, but I do trust you…as much as I'm able. Do you understand?"

He leaned back on the sofa and was silent for a long while. "Yes, I think I do."

He placed his elbows on his knees and linked his fingers. He had strong hands. They looked like they could handle anything. They made her feel safe. *He* made her feel safe. That was a new and startling feeling. She had a hard time growing close to anyone, and feeling secure with someone was way out of her experience. Austin Turner was sending her down new paths.

His amazing, strong jaw tightened even more, making the cleft twitch. "Look, I'm not going to lie to you. I didn't want to get involved. I still don't. My wife was a part of the Navajo Nation. I…"

His voice broke and he looked away. "I lost her and my unborn child to a drunk driver three years ago. I came here to get away. The last thing I want is to get involved in anything like this."

Shock waves swept over Dulcie. She didn't know he had suffered such a loss, and from the look on his face, he was still suffering. Three years and he was still in pain. She should have known, should have recognized that kind of pain, the kind of fear that held one back and kept a normal life in check. And yet, another very strong emotion had pushed him out from behind that wall. What was it?

"Why *did* you get involved? Why did you agree to help me?"

He looked up and his blue-eyed gaze was as cold as steel. "The fact that someone in the force is using their power to keep you quiet. I won't stand by and let corruption tear down the department. The men I've worked with… Most of them are good officers, good men. Whoever is behind this needs to be stopped. I won't let them destroy the only thing I still care about."

She took a deep breath. "I understand. I never thought I'd work in social services again. I was certain I'd end up a clerk in some government office. Vonetta knew my history, the whole story and hired me anyway. I was so thankful for the second chance, but now I'm right back in the same place. I've crossed a line I didn't even know was there."

Austin was silent for a moment. "Did you ever think there's a possibility Vonetta hired you because of your past?"

"What do you mean?"

"Anyone who has met you knows you're passionate

about the women you serve. She probably suspected you would cross lines again and that willingness would make you the perfect person to blame if things went wrong."

Cold trickled through Dulcie and she stared at him.

"Don't look so surprised. These people, whoever they are, are powerful. They got my boss to warn me off and he's one of the most upright men I know. Their plans are complicated, like a web. A group this organized probably has contingency plans for everything, especially the future."

Dulcie was stunned. "You don't really think she hired me because I'd be easy to blame, do you?"

He shrugged. "My gut says this group is powerful and smart. I want to move carefully. And I need that letter."

Dulcie didn't hesitate. She grabbed it from her purse and handed it to him.

Austin nodded his head in approval. "We've had our fingers all over it. I doubt the lab will find anything besides our prints, but it's the only solid clue we have. I'll get it to a friend and see if she can't put a rush on it."

That little cleft in his chin twitched as his jaw tightened. He gestured to the files on the table. "Most of these cases involve multiple justice departments, the municipal police, the county sheriffs and the Navajo police. Jurisdictions cross and recross. The tribal police have no authority off the reservation and the municipal police have none on tribal lands. Add the FBI and their particular duties to the mix and you have a fouled-up system. This group has taken advantage of that fact."

He shook his head. "I'm not sure how much help I can be. In the first year only two victims lived in my jurisdiction. No telling how many others are outside my boundaries. I can pull those two reports without drawing attention but asking for others might send up red flags—flags we don't need flying."

He picked up the first year's file. "And… I don't know how we can connect Officer Shaw. I haven't found a link to him, but someone in law enforcement is involved otherwise my boss wouldn't have tried to pull me off. Who knows how far up the chain of command it goes? Not to mention all the other questions we have to answer. How do they operate? Do they hold their victims in the local area or move them immediately? How do they transport them? But most of all, we need to find those first connections. How are these girls chosen? What place or people do they have in common and what sets them up to be targets?"

Dulcie shook her head. "That's the one thing I've been going over and over in my mind. Judy Begay had a best friend, Susan, from her days on the reservation. The two girls met every Friday at a bar. I always wondered how her stepfather found their meeting place. I could never get that info out of Judy."

Austin stared at her. "What are you talking about? There's nothing in the report about Judy meeting with another girl the night she disappeared."

"Judy rushed out of the center to meet Susan. I told Officer Shaw…"

They stared at each other—silent—until Austin shook his head. "Shaw left a very important detail out of his report so that puts him back at the top of the suspect list." His features darkened. "And that puts my whole case against Kutchner in jeopardy. We might have the wrong man in jail."

Dulcie shivered. Austin's features were frozen. He was coldly, silently furious. His job, the men he worked with, meant a lot to him and this betrayal went deep. Dulcie respected his feelings, even admired them. But somehow, she was a little disappointed. Had some deep, unspoken part of her wished Austin had agreed to help for her sake? Was her initial trust of Austin based on something else…those handsome all-American looks and a dimple that telegraphed his feelings? Was she attracted to him?

Of course not. Her instincts wouldn't betray her like that. She respected and admired his devotion. And of course, she felt compassion for his loss. He was a complicated man who intrigued her. That was all. Nothing more.

"Do you have any clues about the location of the bar?" His question drew her attention back to the issue at hand.

"No, I asked Judy multiple times, but she wouldn't tell me. The topic just slipped out one day when she was talking about Susan. They'd been friends since they were little."

"All the more reason why Susan should have been included in the investigation. Do you have a last name?"

"No, I'm sorry. If Judy said it, I don't remember."

"Well, we're going to have to find this girl. I have something I have to do tomorrow morning, but first chance I get, I'll question Doris Begay again."

Dulcie bit her lip. "She's not here. She moved back to the reservation when Matt Kutchner was arrested."

"It figures." Austin flopped back on the sofa and rubbed his face. "What's tomorrow?"

"Friday."

Apparently, his mind was starting to drag with fatigue. He shook his head. "Look, it's late and I'm tired. I need to tackle this fresh in the morning." He gathered the files into a pile.

He was leaving. Actually leaving. The thought of being alone in her apartment ignited her trepidations. "What…what shall I do tomorrow?"

He gave a quick shake of his head. "The same thing. Nothing. No questions. No research at work. Act like you are doing exactly what they want."

She gestured to the files and her hand trembled slightly. She dropped it quickly, hoping Austin didn't see the telltale shaking. "Why don't you leave those with me? I'll break them down for you."

"Are you sure? We need a lot of information culled out of them."

"I will not sleep anytime soon. I might as well make the time productive."

He studied her for a moment then nodded. "All right. Make separate lists for each year. Write down anything the cases have in common, names, places, friends, anything that doesn't seem right. We'll go over the lists tomorrow night when we meet again."

He started to stand then paused. "You'll be all right, won't you?"

Studying his weary features, she stomped on her jumping nerves and nodded. "I'll be fine."

"Okay." He stood, slid his Stetson into place, grabbed his coat and headed for the door. "Remember, keep a low profile tomorrow and call me if something comes up."

"I will. I promise."

He hesitated for one moment, then unlocked the dead bolt and opened the door. The minute he stepped out and closed it, Dulcie twisted the lock and slid the chain into place. Then she stood there, listening to his footsteps as he walked down the hall. After everything had gone silent, she finally stepped away from the door. Her knees were a little weak. She plopped down on the couch and closed her eyes.

Lord, I need to be strong. Need to help Austin. I need Your strength.

She spoke her favorite scripture out loud until her fear began to fade.

"And that he might make known the riches of his glory on the vessels of mercy, which he had afore prepared unto glory."

Riches of His glory He had prepared for her. She was unique and beloved of God. Her father had not valued and treasured her, but God did. He'd prepared riches for her even before she was born. One of them was her normal life. After the horror of her early childhood, her day-to-day living held a certain peace and was a blessing. The fact that she could be of service to other beaten and beleaguered women was another richness. They were His promises fulfilled, what He had prepared for her. She'd believed that for most of her life.

But for the first time, when she spoke the scripture, she felt uneasy…felt a question forming. First the woman and her daughters in California. Now this threat. Were these incidents God's way of telling her she was on the wrong path?

She shook her head. That couldn't be the source of her unrest. She was certain she was meant to fight for those who couldn't. That conviction filled her entire being. Something else was causing this unrest, but she couldn't put her finger on it.

Prayer would answer her question soon enough. In the meantime, she needed to get to work. She pulled her fluffy throw off the back of the couch, wrapped it around her and opened the first file.

She worked for hours. It wasn't until she'd gone through all three years of paperwork that she finally put the pencil down, leaned into the pillow and closed her weary eyes.

She didn't open them again until her alarm woke her the next morning. The buzzer was going nonstop in the bedroom. She glanced at her watch. The alarm had gone off at least a half an hour ago. She'd be late to work if she didn't get moving.

Throwing off the blanket, she dashed to the shower and dressed in record time. She didn't even try to do makeup. Pulling her wet hair back into a tight bun, she grabbed a protein bar from the kitchen and made it to the front room just as she heard Joey's door open across the hall.

Sliding the chain loose, she twisted the lock and opened the door. Joey paused. "Good morning. I guess we're on the same timetable again today."

She gave him a hesitant smile. "Barely. I didn't hear my alarm."

"Is everything okay? You look a little…frazzled."

"Oh, yeah. Everything's fine. I just hate being late."

She locked the door and headed to the elevator. Joey filed in right behind her. Downstairs, he opened the glass door for her, and she smiled again, this time trying to appear more confident. Her car was close by and she pulled her keys out as Joey strode across the lot to his. She waved, beeped her lock, then looked down at her handle.

The words *No Cops* were scratched into the paint just above it.

She froze for one long minute. Then her gaze shot around the parking lot.

"Are you sure you're okay?"

Joey stood outside his car, the door open. Dulcie swallowed hard and nodded. "Yes, everything's fine."

She slid in, jammed the key into the ignition and drove away. She waited until she was far down the road before she pulled over and dialed Austin's number.

He didn't answer. His voice message came on. Just hearing his voice gave her the encouragement she needed to keep from falling apart. "Austin, it's me, Dulcie. I know you said you didn't see anyone following me, but there has to be someone watching me. They know we met last night. The words *No Cops* were keyed into my car this morning." Her voice cracked and she was silent for a long time while the message kept running. At last, she found her voice. "All right. I'm going to work. Call me when you get this."

THREE

Lieutenant McGuire had sent Austin a text late last night asking him to come in early. Austin was right on time. Five in the morning was one of the few hours during the day when the station was quiet. The emptiness of the place, with no one loitering in the office area and no phones ringing, increased Austin's tension. Not to mention the fact that he hadn't slept well. With Dulcie's information and concern for how to deal with McGuire swimming around in his head, he'd tossed and turned most of the night. He marched straight to the break room for a mug of coffee. Sipping the hot liquid, he let it burn its way down his throat, hoping it might clear away the foggy fumes of frustration.

Dulcie's research had struck a nerve with someone…a person with a lot of pull in the force. That kind of power was bad for the department and bad for the men he worked with. He needed to find out who was pulling the strings and why. The only place he could start was here. McGuire's light was on in his office.

Picking up his coffee mug, Austin headed to meet

his supervisor. The last thing he wanted was to create a break between him and a man he considered a friend, but it had to be done. He knocked on the door frame. "You wanted to see me."

Seated at his desk, McGuire gestured Austin in. "Close the door behind you."

Austin obeyed and stood in front of the desk. Every muscle in his body tensed as his mind desperately searched for a way to wiggle the information he needed out of his boss.

McGuire handed him an envelope. "The search warrant for the Carson place came through late yesterday."

Mrs. Carson and her son lived in the San Juan Mountains just south of Silverton. Unfortunately, Mrs. Carson's property fell within the La Plata County boundaries, so Austin's team had inherited the case. Mrs. Carson and her thirty-year-old son were estranged because of his long history of crime. Unfortunately, during a good time in their relationship, Mrs. Carson had allowed him to move into a remote cabin on the edge of her acreage. However, their relationship soured again. She'd filed a report claiming he had threatened her and was using her cabin as a holding place for stolen property. Austin suspected Carson had already cleared out.

He took the envelope from McGuire. "You know this is probably a waste of time. Do you want me to handle it this morning?" He dreaded hearing the answer. The drive to the Carson property would take most of the day. He didn't want to go that far from Dulcie.

"Yes, and I've called Bolton and Cornell in early to go with you. It could get ugly."

Austin nodded and stalled, searching for a way to broach the subject creating such turmoil inside him.

McGuire beat him to it. "Listen, about our conversation yesterday."

Austin froze. "Sir?"

"I handled it badly. I was angry and I took it out on you. I don't enjoy conversations where a superior talks down to me, like I don't know how to handle my own men. And then, when I walked out and saw Ms. Parker here, it put me over the edge." He leveled his gaze on Austin. "I've never taken orders from anyone about my men…and I will not start now. You have my permission to ignore the instructions I gave you yesterday."

"You don't know how glad I am to hear that, sir."

The lieutenant had strong features, short brown hair streaked with white strands and a broad nose. One dark eyebrow rose in a tilted quirk. "I suspected there was more to that meeting than you mentioned. Anything you want to talk about?"

Austin hesitated. "Only if you want to tell me who issued the warning."

"Done. It came straight from the district attorney as a 'courtesy call.' One official to another from DA Havlicek. He did everything he could to convince me that Ms. Parker was trouble. Said she was fired from her last job and not to be trusted. I don't care about her employment record and his call was so far out of line I could barely control myself. Ordinarily I would have told him just what I thought of his 'courtesy call,' but

I held my tongue. Something's going on and I want to know what it is."

Austin was more than relieved McGuire felt the same way he did about the call. He only hoped his lieutenant would feel the same way about his other suspicions.

"You're right. Something is going on." He told his lieutenant everything Dulcie had relayed to him, right down to the statistics on the Native American women.

McGuire agreed with Austin's assessment. "I've seen some high numbers but, like you, assumed our location was the common factor. Those numbers might have gone unnoticed until Ms. Parker pushed and someone pushed back."

"My thoughts exactly."

"First thing you need to do is find out from Ms. Parker what the DA has on her. It could turn into something we don't want associated with this department."

Austin nodded. "I already did. They fired her from her last job for pressuring a client to come back to the safety of the shelter where she worked."

McGuire's eyebrow rose again. "That's tough."

"Yeah and now, barely a year into this new job, she stumbles across what looks like a sex-trafficking ring."

His supervisor's gaze jumped up. "You think it's that serious? Not just a couple of opportunistic grabs?"

"No way, sir. These guys are smart. They've got plans and—as you witnessed—pull. I didn't take Dulcie's story too seriously until you gave me that order. Then I knew powerful people are behind this. The

DA, Officer Shaw and Ms. Lauder, they carry weight in this town."

McGuire agreed. "I've known Vonetta Lauder a long time. She's an ambitious woman with an agenda. I've never figured out exactly what that agenda is, but I don't think her whole heart is in her work." He shook his head abruptly. "We need to keep a tight lid on this. If I take you away from your other duties, someone might ask questions we're not ready to answer. Until we know who we can trust, you need to look like you're working your other cases. I'll cover for you as much as I can, but I want this to be your top priority. We have to sort this out quickly and quietly."

Austin nodded. "So, I'm still heading up the mountain to the Carson place?"

"Yes, this has been your case. If I hand it off to someone else, it will look bad. Take care of that today, then we'll see what we can do about freeing you. I might even need to order you to take some time off." McGuire smiled a wry grin. "I've been trying to convince you to do that. Now it'll be an order even if this vacation wasn't the kind I had in mind."

Austin grinned. "Keeping busy. My kind of rest."

McGuire motioned him toward the door. "Get out of here and get back as quickly as you can. In the meantime, I'll see if I can check in to a connection between Lauder and the DA."

Austin gave him a mock salute and headed out, feeling better than he had since Dulcie walked into the department. He left a message for Bolton and Cornell to meet him at a coffee shop on the way out of town.

Then he grabbed his jacket and drove to the lab. His friend Cindy had done some expedited work for him before. He hoped he could convince her to make Dulcie's letter a priority. She agreed and Austin was back on the road in a heartbeat. By the time Bolton and Cornell arrived at the shop, he had coffee for them ready and waiting to go.

They headed up the mountain with the sun tipping over the high peaks and casting a warm, golden glow over the roads and trees. Austin had a hard time focusing on the work ahead of him. All he could think about was Dulcie's predicament. But he needed to get on track. This warrant for the Carson place might be a run-of-the-mill job, but McGuire was right. Bob Carson was dangerous, and Austin needed to be mentally prepared.

He tried to call Mrs. Carson and let her know they were on their way, but he'd waited too long. He'd lost cell service this high on the mountain.

The Carson house was even farther up, almost five miles off the main road, at the end of a bumpy, dusty trail. As soon as they pulled into the drive of the dilapidated house, Mrs. Carson came out to greet them. She told him the warrant had taken too long. Her son had been gone from the cabin for over a week and he was keeping company with Walter Benally. Austin knew the man well. He was a hard case. Five years in prison. Damaged vocal cords from a prison fight. Multiple assault charges after he was released. He worked for Johnny Whitehorse at his bar just outside the Navajo reservation…a dangerous gathering place for all the local criminal element. At one time, every thief, robber and drug dealer in the Four Corners area passed through Whitehorse's place called *The Round Up*. As far as Austin was concerned, Bob Carson had just taken a step up on the criminal food chain ladder.

Austin and his men traveled farther up the dirt road. The cabin was empty and vandalized. Carson had done serious damage to his mother's place before he left. It had broken windows with trash strewn about, but one thing struck Austin as unusual. A large U-shaped ring was screwed into the wall above one of the dirty mattresses on the floor. The heavy-duty ring didn't budge even when he slammed his foot against it. He couldn't figure out a reason or a purpose for the metal ring.

With nothing else to find, Austin and his men left the ramshackle cabin. Bolton and Cornell drove on down the mountain. Austin stopped to talk to Mrs. Carson and have her sign the paperwork. When she finished, he said, "If your son comes back, just let us know."

"I won't be here if he does. I'm moving to Florida with my sister. So he'll be your problem…or the new owners'."

"You're selling the place?"

"Already had an offer from Rocky Mountain Dreams, that big realty company in Silverton. They told me they had someone willing to buy it for more than I hoped for."

Austin's uncle Butch was a locomotive engineer who worked on the narrow-gauge railroad based in Silverton. They ran the old-time steam engines up and down the mountain from the mining-town-turned-tourist-center to Durango. His uncle had talked about the owner of Rocky Mountain Dreams, Kent Pierce, and his control of the town's chamber of commerce. Uncle Butch even suggested that Pierce had shady connections with the police department. Austin thought of the cabin, the mysterious ring and wondered if Pierce could have any connection with Benally and Carson. He didn't have enough info to put all the pieces together but his investigative instincts had flashed on to high alert.

But for now, he needed to get back to town and Dulcie. With one last glance at Mrs. Carson's retreating back, he hurried to his vehicle and headed down the mountain. The image of Dulcie's trembling fingers flitted through his mind. She had a way of tugging on one of her curls, winding it around her finger when she was upset. She'd done that almost the whole time they were together last night.

The image stuck in his mind because it was a measure of her fear…not for any other reason. Most definitely not because she had that wild woman/frightened child look about her. If—and that was a big if—he were to take interest in a woman, it wouldn't be one like Dulcie with her deep-seated fears. No. He wanted another warrior woman like Abey. But there wasn't anyone like his wife. She was one of a kind and any thoughts about Dulcie were based on concern. She needed help. That was all. Even if he wasn't the right person for the job, he couldn't resist helping someone in danger.

Shaking his head, he pushed the speedometer as he

hurried back to town. The minute he had reception, his cell phone buzzed with messages, three in a row. The first was from Dulcie. He was out of reception when she called, so he'd missed it. First chance, he pulled off to the side of the road and listened.

Austin, it's me, Dulcie. I know you said you didn't see anyone following me, but there has to be someone watching me. They know we met last night. The words No Cops *were keyed into my car this morning.*

He'd been so careful. He was certain no one was watching her. How had the gang found out they had met?

She'd sent him a second message around one that afternoon. *Hey, it's me again. I... I haven't heard from you so I'm a little worried. I'm at work, but I can't concentrate. I'm going home early and locking the door behind me. Call when you get this.*

Good. That was the safest place for her until he could get there. He had one last message and punched the button. It was Cindy from the lab.

Hey, you owe me a coffee. That letter was handled so much the prints were overlapping, but I found one on the inside of the envelope. It's a partial, but I'm confident I've got the right guy. His prints are on file because he works for the city. His name is Joey Delacroix.

Cindy kept talking, but Austin didn't hear a word she said.

Joey Delacroix. Dulcie's neighbor right across the way. The mousey guy she was so thankful had walked her to her car. He was the one sending her threatening messages and watching her every move right out her front door…and she was headed home again…straight into his arms. Austin had to warn her.

Dulcie pulled into her complex's parking lot and closed her eyes. Thankfully it was a Friday and she'd been able to get away early. Not as early as she'd hoped but still…she didn't think she could take another hour of trying to look normal when her insides were sloshing around like liquid.

She pulled out her phone. Still no call from Austin. She knew he was busy, but he'd said to call him. He promised to help but almost seven hours later…no response. Something was wrong.

But she couldn't just sit in her locked car and wait for him. She needed to get inside her apartment. Once there, she'd be safe, and she'd call the department and ask for him. There was only one problem… Getting to her apartment.

Carefully, she checked the cars in the parking lot. All were empty. She noticed that Joey's car was in its usual place. He was home early today too. That made her feel a little better.

One hand grasped her phone, the other twisted her keys in her usual "punch" grip, one key pointed out. Then she jerked open the door, hit the lock button and dashed for the apartment entrance. She ran through the empty entry to the elevator. The doors closed behind her. She sighed with relief. When they opened, the hall was empty too. She hurried toward her door, fumbling to get the right key out of the "punch" hold.

Just as she reached her place, Joey's door opened. She jumped but pressed a hand to her thumping heart at the sight of her friendly neighbor. "You startled me."

"Sorry. I've been hoping to catch you. I'm glad you came home early today."

She gave him a half-hearted smile. "Yes, I was feeling a little off and it was a slow day. How about you? Why are you off so early on this Friday?"

"I'm about to close the door on a very long project so I thought I'd celebrate."

"Really? That sounds like a fun evening."

He stepped closer. "Actually, I was hoping you'd join me. I mean...well, I wanted to give you time to get settled, but you've been here a year now and well... I just thought..." He hesitated. "The truth is your deputy friend was here last night and well... I'd like to put my hat in the ring if you're looking for...pizza-night friends."

Stunned, Dulcie stared at him. "I—I wasn't exactly looking for...friends."

"No, of course not. I put that badly. I just meant I'd like to spend more time with you. I thought we could start tonight. Something simple. Just a quick drink to celebrate my success."

Tonight. Three days ago, even two days ago, she'd have jumped at the chance but tonight... No way was she going out.

"I'm sorry, Joey. Not tonight. I'm a little under the weather. That's why I came home early."

He stepped even closer. "Please, Dulcie. It would

mean a lot to me. We can stay in. I'll bring over the drinks. I have everything. You name it—I've got it."

His plea sounded so heartfelt. If it meant that much to him…maybe she could make it work. After all, he'd helped her. She hesitated.

He seemed to sense her wavering thoughts and stepped even closer. Dulcie leaned away. He was invading her personal space. Old fears swept over her and her knees went weak.

What seemed like an earnest appeal seconds ago now seemed like a demand. Were her old fears taking over? Was she imagining the change?

"Come on, Dulcie. Just a few minutes of your time. I promise, I won't stay long. I'll tell you all about my project."

The undertones in his voice made her feel like she didn't want to know about his project. And still he crowded her. He was so close her back was up against her door with no room to move.

"Come on, Dulcie." His voice was low, insistent. "Let's go inside and talk." He reached for her keys. Dulcie stood frozen, her gaze focused on his hand, only inches from her keys.

Her phone buzzed.

Joey stared at it as if it were a writhing snake. His pleasant features turned to frowning anger.

Before he could speak, Dulcie tapped the phone symbol on the screen with her thumb. "Hello."

Austin's voice rang over the line. "I'm so glad I caught you. Where are you?"

Dulcie was so relieved to hear his voice, she sagged

against the door. "Outside my apartment, talking to Joey." She gave Joey a tremulous shrug. He smiled but it was more of a grimace, and he stepped back out of her space.

There was a conspicuous silence on the other end of the phone.

"Don't say my name, Dulcie." Austin's hastily spoken words froze her again.

"Okay. Why?" She looked at the man standing across from her.

"Listen carefully. Don't talk. Just listen. Joey won't do anything while you have someone on the phone. Tell him this is an important call. You have a family emergency. Tell him you have to go inside. You might even have to leave town. But whatever you do, don't hang up. Keep me on the line. Got it?"

Dulcie took a slow breath. "Yes, yes. I think so. Hang on."

She licked her lips. "I'm sorry, Joey. I have a family emergency. You must excuse me."

His features tightened. "I'm sorry to hear that." His sympathetic words didn't match the tight, cold frustration in his face. "Is there anything I can do? Let me help."

He stepped back into her personal space. Loomed over her. Images flashed through her mind, her father standing over her mother, his fists clenched, his face a mask of fury. Her mother's soft cries echoed in her ears. Time stood still. Her muscles froze.

The man in front of her seemed to sense her inability to move. A small smirk flashed over his lips and a look came into his eyes… A look she knew well. It telegraphed his sense of victory, his knowledge that he had power over her. He had won…and still she couldn't move.

Then Austin's words came over the phone. "Dulcie, are you there?"

His voice, strong, capable, certain. Warm blood coursed through veins. Fear-frozen muscles thawed. Numb fingers twitched. She clenched them around the keys in her hands.

"Dulcie, answer me!"

She took a deep, gasping breath. "Yes. Yes, I'm here. Thank you for your concern. I'm just…a little shocked."

That look she knew so well, that hateful, power-filled certainty, faded from Joey's features. She licked dry lips and addressed him. "There's nothing you can do, Joey. I have to go now."

"Good girl. Keep talking." Austin's voice…confident, protecting her over the phone. He gave her strength. Nodding goodbye, she turned her back on Joey.

Her spine tingled. She could almost feel his gaze shooting daggers into it. For one long, heart-pounding minute she was afraid he wouldn't let her leave, might grasp her shoulders and pull her back. Because of Austin on the phone, listening, guarding, Joey dared not touch her. She fumbled the keys and almost dropped them before fitting the right one into the lock and opening the door. She shut it quickly then slammed the dead bolt into place.

FOUR

Austin flipped on the lights atop his vehicle and sped down the road. Then he called McGuire and told him what had happened.

"Do you want me to send someone over to Dulcie's place?" McGuire asked.

"No. She's safe inside her apartment, but get a hold of Delacroix's license plate for me. We may want to bring someone in to follow him. I want to know who his contacts are."

"Agreed. I'll look into it and see who I can put on it."

Just as Austin pulled into Dulcie's apartment complex, McGuire got back to him with the license plate number and a description of Delacroix's car as well as the name of the deputy he was thinking of bringing into the investigation. Austin approved his choice.

"He's a good man. Hold on a second." He searched the parking lot but Delacroix's vehicle was gone. "He's not here. At least, his car isn't here. I'm going to get Dulcie out of here before he shows up again."

"Good idea. I'll have Bolton there tomorrow morning."

Austin signed off, parked and hurried up to Dulcie's apartment. He knocked very quietly on her door. A moment or two later, it swung open. Dulcie stayed hidden behind it. As soon as she closed and bolted the door behind him, she threw herself against him.

For one stunned moment, Austin stood with arms outspread. The woman who shied away from him every time he got near had her arms wrapped so securely around his waist he could hardly breathe. He held his arms wide…not sure if he should hug her back or not. Would she appreciate the gesture or feel trapped? He wasn't sure…but it felt good to have her close.

Wet tears soaked the top of his shirt above his bulletproof vest. The soft scent of spring drifted up to him and those wild, untamed curls tickled his cheek. He couldn't help himself. His arms wrapped around her.

"It's all right, Dulcie. I'm here now and he's gone."

She nodded, still clinging to him. "It was such a close call."

Stepping back, she wiped at her cheeks. When most women cried, their noses turned red and their lips and eyes puffed. Dulcie's did too, but on her, those changes softened her features, slightly blurred her bold eyebrows and full lips. Made her look soft and in need of another hug. He almost pulled her back into his arms before he caught himself.

"You're safe now." He sounded gruffer than he intended. But it worked. She straightened and met his gaze.

"You don't understand. He made me feel like I was ten years old again. I froze. Completely froze. I couldn't push him away, couldn't defend myself. I just stood there. If you hadn't spoken to me…he would have taken my keys right out of my hand…and I would have let him."

She shook her head and stepped away…taking that soft summer scent with her. Austin missed it the minute she moved.

He swallowed and tried to get his thoughts back on track. She was igniting his protective instincts…the ones that always got him in trouble. He needed to pack those responses in a case with steel bands around it.

"He caught you off guard. That's all. You thought he was a friend and he wasn't."

"You're being kind, but any other woman…any normal woman would have at least tried to keep the keys away from him. I just stood there."

Austin didn't know what to say to that. Abey probably would have delivered a flat-palmed punch to his nose…a self-defense move she'd learned in a class she'd brought to the reservation. But Abey wasn't like most women and nothing like Dulcie. He needed to remember that fact.

"All I know is his car is gone. We need to get you out of here before he comes back."

She gestured to a slightly larger than carry-on-sized suitcase. "I'm all packed."

"That's it? Everything is in there?"

She sent him a tremulous smile. "I'm not very high-maintenance, in case you didn't notice." Her tone indicated that was another fault, so unlike other "normal" women. But with Dulcie, the high-maintenance habits of other women were wasted. She had a unique beauty all her own…and it was a shame she didn't know it.

But moments ago, he'd vowed to lock thoughts like that away. Clenching his jaw, he gripped the handle of the suitcase. "Do you have all your files?"

"They're in my bag with my computer." She pulled her heavy winter coat off the sofa. Beneath it was a large satchel bulging with the files. Hitching it on her shoulders, she nodded. "I'm ready."

Austin opened the door a crack and looked up and down the empty hall before stepping out. Dulcie locked the door, and they hurried down the hall and out of the building. Austin checked the parking lot. Delacroix's vehicle was still nowhere to be seen. Nevertheless, once they were in Austin's vehicle, he drove around town for twenty minutes, making right and left turns every half mile to make sure they were not followed. When he was certain no one was behind them, he headed up the mountain to his cabin.

He texted McGuire to let him know he had Dulcie safely in his company and they were driving to his house. McGuire texted back to let him know to park his sheriff's SUV in the garage because he just put out the word that Austin was on vacation and Ms. Parker needed to do the same.

"You need to call in and tell work you had a family emergency and are on your way to California. Hopefully, they'll believe you and it will buy us some time to investigate."

Pulling her coat up tight around her neck, she nodded. "I think they'll believe me. Today one of my coworkers asked me what was wrong. I told her my sister was sick again."

"Again? Does your sister get sick often?"

Dulcie tugged on her coat again. Austin turned up the SUV's heater. "Thanks."

She gave him one of those small, shy smiles, like she was ashamed to ask for basic comforts. "My sister has a lot of health issues. She internalized so much of what we went through..."

Her words trailed off.

"Despite what you're feeling right now, it sounds like you've handled things better."

Her deep sigh filled the vehicle. "Only because my sister stood between me and my dad. She protected me. She took the brunt of his anger." Her voice cracked and she turned her gaze toward the window, away from him. Still, he heard the tears in her tone. "I always felt like the only way to thank her was to be the best I could be, to live a normal, happy life. I don't think I'm doing that very well."

Clouds covered the setting sun and now evening added to the growing gloom in the vehicle. It settled over Austin with a heaviness he recognized all too well.

"You say *normal* a lot. Like it means something. I don't even know what normal means."

That caught her attention. He could feel her gaze on him and this time, he refused to glance her way. He kept his focus on the road ahead.

"But you were married and had a baby on the way. That's normal, isn't it?"

He shook his head. "There was nothing normal

about my wife or the life I led with her. She was… amazing. Brave and full of goals and possibilities. It was all I could do to keep up with her." He glanced over. In the twilight of the car, her dark eyes stood out against pale features. "And I never expect to feel that way again."

She met his gaze. A slight frown creased the space between her brows. "I don't think I could live that way… Without hope of something better."

He shrugged. "It depends on what you mean. To me, better is not wishing or wanting something I will never have again. I spent three years of my life wanting her back…wishing things were different. That's a black hole I barely crawled out of. I never want to go back."

He couldn't just leave his thoughts there. He had to probe deeper. "Tell me truthfully. What does *happy* mean to you? What do you need that would give you that happy, normal life you think would be so perfect?"

"I… I don't know."

Shaking his head, he turned back to watch the road. "There you go. Wishing and wanting something you can't even define is a prescription for unhappiness."

He felt her gaze settle on him, as powerful as a touch. He could sense her probing gaze as if she was searching for understanding or answers…and he had neither.

At last she turned away. They were both silent as they sped along the highway, the headlights flashing against the black asphalt and the dense forest around them. He hadn't meant to darken her already complicated life with his own tragedy, but there was something about Dulcie that compelled him to be honest… to open up. Maybe that was her gift, the talent that led her to become a counselor. Whatever it was, he needed to keep his own depressing thoughts to himself.

Gentle snowflakes, the first of the season, began to fall. Soon a white blanket covered the road and the branches of the trees. It brightened the night. Made everything seem clean and white.

"It's coming down pretty hard."

Dulcie nodded. "Yes, and it's beautiful. It's light in the darkness and God's gift to us, to brighten our night."

He glanced at her quickly. She met his gaze defiantly. The little smile tilting her lips was confident, certain and beautiful. Looking at it warmed him, made him want to smile back. He wasn't sure the snow was a gift from God just for them, but he was glad she felt that way.

He turned back to the road. "We'll rest tonight. First thing in the morning, we'll head down to the reservation to see if we can find Doris Begay. I want to talk to her."

"Good. That means my day at work wasn't a complete waste. I looked up her previous address on our records."

"Let's hope she's there. The reservation is too big to try to cover it all."

"How big is it?"

"Over twenty-seven thousand square miles and it stretches across the Four Corners states."

"Wow. I knew it was big but… What if she's not there or we can't find her?"

"I still have a few contacts on the tribal police. We won't come away empty-handed."

He slowed and pulled off the main highway onto a dirt road. "Don't worry. I won't bounce you too much. I just live far enough from the road to silence the highway traffic noise."

Soon the dirt road opened into a clearing. An A-framed log cabin and a detached garage sat at the back of the clearing. Austin hit the button for the automatic door opener and pulled into the garage. A blue Jeep was parked inside. "I don't use it much, but we'll be driving that tomorrow. My sheriff's vehicle is a little too obvious."

He pulled her suitcase out of the back and led the way to the front porch. He flipped the switch, and light flooded his darkened home. He gestured to the left. "That's the kitchen. It's small but fits my purposes. I don't do much cooking."

"It's not any smaller than my apartment kitchen. Small kitchens work for people who don't spend much time in their places."

"Yeah, I guess that's true. There's a half bath tucked in the corner. The stairs across from us lead to the loft bedroom and the full bath. You'll be sleeping up there."

"Oh no, I can't take your room."

"Yes, you can, and you will. It's an open loft but it offers some privacy and besides, the desk is up there. You'll need it for your research."

She started to protest, but he held up a finger. "I sleep on that sofa more than I sleep on the bed. Trust me—I'll be fine."

She seemed surprised by that and didn't argue. Instead, she looked at the near-empty wall to the right. "Your windows are so high up."

"Yes, but I have quite a view from the loft and those windows catch a lot of light. They're perfectly placed for the sun's early-morning rays and they warm the house. The guy who built this cabin was environmentally conscious. Speaking of warmth though, I better get the fire going." He gestured to the sofa across from the rock fireplace. "Have a seat. I don't leave the heat on during the day, so first thing I have to do is light a fire."

Showing Dulcie his house made him realize what a utilitarian life he'd been living. There was nothing comfy or homey like Dulcie's place. That realization made him feel like he needed to apologize again. He seemed to have done that a lot since Dulcie stepped into his life. He didn't understand and what's more, he didn't like it.

He set her case down, stacked the kindling on the hearth and loaded the logs. In moments the fire was blazing. Dulcie sat on the edge of the sofa, shivering, looking like a lost child...who once again shied away every time he stepped near. They were back to that nonsense.

At her apartment she threw her arms around him and now she wouldn't let him step within a foot of her, like he was the threat. It was discomforting, made him unsure of how to respond. He settled for an apology he'd felt the need to give a moment ago.

"I'm sorry it's not as welcoming as your place."

She shook her head and a small, embarrassed smile

crossed her lips. "Your home is fine. It's me. I'm just tired. It's been a rough couple of weeks. Actually, a rough two months, ever since Judy disappeared."

Austin couldn't argue with that. Those terrible months were the reason he'd spent so many nights on the sofa. He'd come home exhausted, eat a frozen pizza and fall asleep in front of the fire only to wake up and do the same the next day.

Frozen pizza. It was the best he had to offer her. "How about some hot chocolate and something to eat? That might help."

She nodded, but her smile was conspicuously absent and…he missed it. Truth be told, he wouldn't mind her in his arms again either. He ached to comfort her in some way. But his arms would only frighten her more.

"Whatever you have is fine with me."

He turned on the oven and heated some water in the microwave for the hot chocolate. When it was done, he handed her the mug. She worked her fingers so they wouldn't touch his. Frustrated, he shook his head.

"I have to feed my chickens. I used to let them roam free but a mountain lion got a few of them so now I keep them in a coop. It won't take me long."

She nodded absently. Austin hurried out. The snow was still falling. His poor chickens were used to his erratic schedule and feedings. He tried to keep their feed bin full in case he didn't make it back in a timely manner. It was near empty so he filled it. When he returned to the now warm cabin, two paper plates and napkins rested on the small wooden table by the loft stairs.

Dulcie came from the kitchen holding the pizza pan

with two oven mitts…but she still hadn't removed her coat. "I hope you don't mind me rummaging through your cupboards. I wanted to help."

"No, of course not." He took off his Stetson, hung it on the rack near the door and washed his hands. Grabbing a knife from the drawer, he sliced the pizza and slid one piece onto her plate. She took two bites, then gripped the mug.

He still felt like apologizing. Was it for his meager accommodations or for her past? He wasn't sure. He just felt like he had to say something. "I'm sorry I don't have anything better."

She shook her head. "The pizza is fine. Really. It's my usual dinner. We have that in common too. I'm just overtired. If it's okay with you, I'm going to head up to bed."

"Sure. Let me show you where the blankets and towels are."

He carried her suitcase upstairs then went back downstairs and finished the pizza. As he cleaned up, he heard the shower running and before he sat down in front of the fire, the light by his bed stand went out. Austin eased back on his couch with a heavy sigh. Dulcie ignited too many contradictory emotions in him. One minute her jumpiness irritated him, the next he wanted to hold her in his arms and protect her from the world. Just the kind of crazy feelings he didn't need to have. She seemed to be as conflicted by him as he was by her. The best thing for both of them was to solve this case and get out of each other's way…and the sooner the better.

* * *

Dulcie opened her eyes. Gray light was peeking over the mountain through one of the loft windows. It was just bright enough to see the surrounding forest. She glanced at the clock. Barely six in the morning. Still, she'd slept almost ten hours. Closing her eyes, she stretched, feeling cozy, comfortable and relaxed. Just having Austin in the house had given her a sense of peace.

She would have stayed in bed longer, but she heard some stirring in the kitchen and soon, the smell of coffee drifted up to her. Her stomach growled. After throwing back the covers, she hopped out of bed and hurried into the bathroom to dress. She hadn't noticed last night but not one of the loft windows had blinds. Given the empty stretches of forest that swept out on each side, with no apparent neighbors, Austin obviously didn't feel the need for window coverings. And he was right not to block the spectacular views. As she made the bed, she marveled at the forest of trees sweeping down the mountain to the valley below. She wondered if on a clear day, you could see all the way to Durango.

Not knowing what they would be doing, she pulled jeans, a long-sleeved knit top and a comfy blue plaid shirt out of her suitcase. As soon as she was dressed, the smell of the coffee lured her to the kitchen where Austin handed her a mug. He looked rested but the dark shadow of a beard graced his cheeks and that wave on his forehead stood straight up. She'd never seen him any other way than clean-shaven and she was surprised by how attractive this slightly rumpled Austin looked.

"Good morning." He nodded but didn't smile. Apparently, an early-morning Austin was not only rumpled but grumpy. That made her smile. There was a boyish quality about him she found incredibly appealing. He looked like a younger, not quite so bitter Austin.

"There's milk in the fridge and sugar in the cabinet if you use it."

"I do. Thanks."

He took another sip. "Since I have nothing for a good breakfast, I thought we might head out early and stop at a place I know in Cortez. It's far enough out of Durango I don't think we'll be seen."

"That sounds good."

"Okay. If you don't mind, I'll grab a shower and we'll take off."

She nodded and he hurried up the stairs two at a time. Dulcie sipped her coffee. The cabin really was a nice place. It just needed a few finishing touches. The wooden ceiling beams were stained a golden color, like the sunshine. She walked into the living room area and ran a hand along the smooth river rock on the fireplace. Still warm from the blazing fire, it emanated a soft heat. She settled on the hearth and imagined what she might do to add some color to this fantastic open area.

Maybe a painting on the wall beneath the high windows…no…one of the beautiful natural handwoven Navajo blankets she'd seen in the stores downtown. A lovely two-handled Navajo horsehair vase, a ceramic in white with black cracks etched on the surface. Thick strands of real horsehair were fired in the pottery and burned away creating the black etchings. Dulcie had seen an example of the craft at the same Native American store where she saw the woven blankets and loved the unique black markings of the pottery immediately. A large piece would look perfect on the dark rock of the hearth.

She sat content, decorating Austin's empty house in her mind, until he came down the stairs, shaved and with his stubborn little cowlick combed into place.

She smiled. "Your home is amazing. You were right about these windows. They're spectacular."

"I didn't think you were so convinced last night."

"Forget about last night. I was sleep deprived." She really felt like a different person this morning, stronger, brighter, ready to solve the mystery ahead of them. She was sure she owed it to Austin and the confidence his presence gave her. "I had the best night of sleep I've had in months. Thank you."

Her heartfelt words seemed to move him. His crooked smile was genuine. "Well then, let me feed you before you start to feel food-deprived. It'll take me a few minutes to warm up the Jeep. I'll pick you up on the porch." He slid into his hat and coat. Tossing her the keys to the door, he stepped out. The brisk cold air swept into the room, making her thankful he'd volunteered to warm up his vehicle.

She ran upstairs and grabbed a knitted scarf from her suitcase. By that time, she could hear the idling engine just outside the door. After slipping on her jacket, she hitched her purse over her shoulder and locked the door behind her. Austin pulled his shiny blue Jeep close to the rock-lined walkway. The storm had brought two or three inches of snow that lay on the ground like a pristine blanket. It seemed as if her entire world had been washed clean. Austin's golden home full of sunshine. The sparkling snowy perfection around them and the handsome man smiling at her from the driver's seat brought her a joy she hadn't experienced in a long time… Maybe ever. It was hard for her to remember that men were chasing her, determined to do her harm. As if to preserve the perfect moments of the morning, she stayed in Austin's steps on the path, so she wouldn't disturb this soft winter wonderland tucked deep in the forest. Just before she climbed into the Jeep, she glimpsed a small wooden building with chicken wire surrounding it.

Austin took the keys and tucked them into the console. Then he headed down the snow-covered road. It seemed a shame to disrupt the beautiful white covering on the dirt road. Soon they came to the highway. Many cars had already passed over it. The snow had melted and the black asphalt slashed across the white scene with muddy slush on each side. Her winter wonderland was disappearing with every mile they traveled. But one question, one thought lingered.

She couldn't contain it and blurted it out. "Why chickens?"

He turned to her, with a half smile and a half frown. "What about chickens?"

"I mean, why did you choose chickens? Not a usual pet like a dog or a cat."

"Oh, my counselor advised me to find something to care for."

"You went to counseling?"

"I met with my pastor for over a year, trying to forgive myself."

His words gave Dulcie pause. "Why did you need forgiveness?"

He was silent for such a long time, Dulcie thought she'd gone too far, stepped over a boundary he wasn't willing to cross. She bit her lips, sorry that she'd pushed for answers he didn't want to discuss. She turned away.

Then he surprised her with words spoken in a low tone. "I was a sheriff's detective out of Gallup, New Mexico. I knew the dangerous, empty stretch of reservation road Abey traveled over that night, knew the statistics by heart. I should have stopped her from driving home. I…failed to protect… The one thing I took an oath to do when I signed on to become a sheriff. All I ever wanted was to protect people, to help…and yet I couldn't help the most important person in my life."

Dulcie wanted to protest, to tell him he wasn't responsible. She felt the need to reach out and reassure him even though all of her counseling training told her she needed to let him speak. It was all she could do to keep silent. What was it about this man that made her want to act against all she knew? Somehow, he reached deep inside her, passed all her trained barriers to her basic instincts. She didn't know if that was bad or good. She only knew she didn't want him to stop.

"The department counselors finally suggested a

transfer. So I applied for the La Plata County Sheriff's Department and made the move, relocated to Durango. I invested in my cabin in the mountains above town, bought a horse, two cows, and let chickens roam over my property. The pine trees and the green were so different from the flat dusty mesas of New Mexico, it changed things. Maybe changed me."

He glanced her way and then back to the road. "At any rate, it didn't seem fair to pick an animal that needed companionship when I'm gone so much of the time. It wouldn't be right to leave a dog home alone most of the day."

It made sense and was fair. But she had the feeling there was more to his thoughts. She wasn't surprised when he continued.

"And besides… I didn't want something I would become too attached to. I couldn't stand losing something else."

His words doused her lovely morning in cold. It was the saddest thing in the world to know that he had that beautiful place in the forest full of sunshine and peace and couldn't enjoy even a small part of it. It seemed so wrong for the caring man she sensed beneath his walled exterior.

She studied him. "Did it work? Did you stay unattached?"

He almost nodded, then a slow, wry smile slipped over his features and a small chuckle escaped. "Are you kidding? Did you see my chicken coop? As soon as I found out some of my chickens were missing and I saw the mountain lion tracks, I went straight to the lumberyard and bought enough wood to build the Taj Mahal of chicken coops. My birds live like kings."

He gave her another quick glance, filled with humor, and she smiled back. Some morning sunshine spilled into her heart. There was more she wanted to say but she left it at that. They both needed that morning sunshine right now.

They traveled down the mountain and through Durango, leaving the forests and the snow behind. They passed the entrance to Mesa Verde National Park, the park that preserved the largest collection of Ancestral Puebloan, formerly known as Anasazi, dwellings in the country. She'd heard all about the park and its cliff dwellings, but she'd never visited. She could easily have made a day trip but somehow, never found the time. That thought made her sad. She loved her work, loved helping the women. Why did she suddenly regret her choices?

Just a few more miles down the road, the snow disappeared. Only a few banks of mud and slush graced the sides of the streets in the small town of Cortez, just fifty minutes away from Durango.

They stopped at a small roadside café and ate a quick breakfast but were back on the road soon. They left the foothills behind and dipped into the open flatlands that led to northern New Mexico. The change of environment came so quickly, Dulcie was in awe. A panorama opened up for her. She could see for hundreds and hundreds of miles. Mountains dotted the vast open area, popping up out of seeming emptiness. To her right was a massive, flat-topped mesa. The sun had not come out in full force, so everything was tinged with soft purples that blended into the dark shadows.

"I've seen numerous paintings of the area, but I never understood why the painters used so many purple and lavender colors. Now I do. It's a true reflection of the land. It's beautiful," she murmured.

Austin nodded. "Yes, it is. We're heading into New Mexico. At sunset, those purple mountains will turn mauve then gray. It looks like a vast empty desert but hidden in all those purple shadows are canyons and wonders. There's a reason New Mexico is nicknamed the Land of Enchantment."

The tone of his voice gave her pause. "You love this land, don't you?"

He studied the view ahead of him. "It's my home, where I grew up. It's a part of me. But it can be a harsh place...unforgiving. I'm not sure I can say I love it anymore."

He pointed to a road up ahead. "That leads to the Four Corners marker where New Mexico, Utah, Colorado and Arizona meet in one spot. You can stand on the marker and be in all four states at one time. The spot is on tribal lands. There're some concessions and a few refreshment stands. Not much to see besides the marker. But you can take a picture with both feet in all four states."

He gave her a small smile that made her wish they could stop right now and take that picture. Not for the first time Dulcie wondered about the effect Austin Turner was having on her.

They traveled for over an hour with Austin pointing out interesting spots and different mesas. At long last they turned off the highway onto a dirt road. They drove for almost thirty minutes on the rough, bumpy, pothole-marked trail.

"I can't believe anyone lives out here. There's nothing. Just a few telephone poles and electric wires."

"Some places don't even have those. The traditional Navajo reject modern conveniences. They stick to the old ways. Plus, the government broke the land into allotments and gave each family a place. In those days they needed lots of land to graze their sheep, so they appreciated the distances between. Things are different now, but they still love their land and the open spaces."

Dulcie allowed her gaze to follow the power lines to where they crested over a hill and dipped down out of view. Sure enough, as the vehicle came to the top of the hill, they looked down on a trailer with several wooden outbuildings and a pen with a few goats. A woman stood in the pen with the animals, pulling apart a bale of hay. As they drove closer, Dulcie recognized Doris Begay. As soon as they were near enough for her to identify them, her body language changed. She shook her head and sent them a scowl meant to keep them at bay.

"Looks like we're not very welcome." Dulcie frowned.

"That's putting it mildly."

Taking a deep breath, Dulcie climbed out of the truck and walked with determination toward the woman. Doris was dressed in jeans and a faded plaid shirt. Her long hair was tied back in a ponytail with wisps of hay caught in it. She turned back to her work so that when Dulcie got close, she had to speak to get her attention. "Hello, Doris."

The woman turned sharply. "Why are you here? Judy's dead and Matt's in jail. What else do you want from me?"

Dulcie halted in her footsteps, shocked by her bitter hostility. She looked at Austin and he continued forward, not backing away from the woman's obvious anger.

"Yes, Matt is in jail. But we think we might have the wrong man."

She shook her head. "He killed my girl. I know it. You need to keep him locked up for the rest of his life."

Austin nodded. "You're so sure he did it, Doris?"

She nodded vigorously. "He did it."

Doris glared at Austin, daring him to deny it.

Austin ducked his head. "I think you're right. Matt killed your girl, but was he alone? Did someone help him?"

The rage fled and her features washed cold and white. The belligerence bled out and she shook her head. "I don't know nothin' about that. Nothin'."

She was lying—Dulcie knew it and so did Austin. He pressed her for more info. "Who was Matt hanging out with before Judy disappeared?"

The woman shook her head. "He didn't need no drinkin' buddies. He did that all by hisself."

"All right, where did he do his drinking?"

She shook her head. "I told you. I don't know

nothin'. Now go away and leave me alone." Spinning, she headed toward the house, too angry to say more.

Austin shook his head in frustration. Dulcie couldn't let her get away without more answers.

"What about Susan, Doris? Where can we find her?"

Doris halted in her footsteps. After a long pause, she looked back over her shoulder. "That one is her grandmother's problem. Ask Bea Yazzie."

"Where can we find her?"

She hesitated a moment longer. "At Tséyi. Her hogan is near the White House Trail." With that, Doris Begay marched to the front door of the trailer and slammed the door shut behind her. Austin nudged his head toward the truck. They both headed toward it.

As soon as they slid inside Dulcie said, "Is that it? You're a sheriff. Are you just going to let her shut you out like that?"

"I told you. I have no authority on the reservation."

Sagging, she leaned back on the seat. "I'd forgotten. So, what is Tséyi? Do you have any idea?"

He nodded. "It's Canyon de Chelly, one of the Navajos' sacred places. It's close." He started the engine. "Did you notice she didn't use Susan's name?"

Dulcie caught her breath. "She called her *that one*. Do you think she believes Susan is one of the Missing Ones?"

Austin nodded. "Maybe. One thing is certain—Doris Begay knows a lot more than she's willing to tell us. We're going to need more help."

"What kind of help?"

"I know someone on the tribal police force. I'll call him. But first we'll pay a visit to Susan's grandmother."

He jammed the Jeep into Reverse and backed up. As he turned the truck around, Dulcie's side of the vehicle swerved close to the front of the trailer. Just inside a small window beside the door, she glimpsed Doris peeking out from behind a white curtain and she had an old-fashioned phone held up to her ear. As soon as she saw Dulcie, she jerked her hand away and the curtain fell back into place.

"She's talking to someone on the phone, Austin. I thought you said living out here she wouldn't have any modern conveniences. Do you think she's calling Susan's grandmother to tell her we're coming?"

Austin's features tightened into a grim frown. "Not if Bea Yazzie lives in the canyon. There's no electricity there."

"Then who is she in such a hurry to talk to?"

"That's the million-dollar question, isn't it? Fortunately for us, anyone we need to worry about is in Durango, three hours away. We'll have time to talk to Susan's grandmother and get out of there before they can reach us." He slammed the gearshift into forward motion and kicked a dusty cloud up behind them.

FIVE

As he drove to the highway Austin's mind traced over the time it would take them to get to Canyon de Chelly and back again. They were less than an hour away. Half an hour to trek down the trail and a half hour back up. They might cut it close, but they could make it out of the canyon before the people Doris Begay had called could arrive. One thing about the reservation—it was spread out.

Doris's actions seemed clear to him. She was convinced that Matt Kutchner had killed her daughter and thought he should stay in jail. But she was afraid of the men he'd been hanging around. Too afraid to even name them. She'd come back to the reservation to hide, and now she was willing to buy her safety by reporting their visit to the men she feared. Austin was almost sure that's who she called. Now he and Dulcie had limited time to get in and out before anyone could respond to Doris's call.

But they had to locate Susan Yazzie. Right now, their whole investigation hinged on finding a clue to her whereabouts. If they didn't find that new direction, their trip today was a waste of time…time that was running out. Austin's internal clock was ticking away. Things were coming to a head. He could feel it.

"Tell me about Canyon de Chelly."

Dulcie's question pulled him out of his thoughts. It took him a minute to change gears. "Well, let's see. It's one of the longest continually inhabited places in America. The Navajo have been there since before the Spanish came and some ruins of the Ancestral Puebloans are preserved there too."

"So people have lived in Canyon de Chelly for over a thousand years?"

"Yes, the Ancestral Puebloans lived there for generations before the Navajo people. In fact, Anasazi, the name we used to use to label the Ancestral Puebloans, came from the Spanish. They used the Navajo word for ancient enemies. It doesn't properly describe the people who lived in those dwellings so we stopped using it."

"I thought the only cliff dwellings were at Mesa Verde."

"No, they're dotted all over the Four Corners area. In fact, we'll see some in the canyon. Severe drought and difficult times forced the people of the Chaco culture out of the flatlands into the mountains where there was more water. They built their homes in crevices and clefts for protection using wood and plaster. Some of them look like modern-day apartments with multiple stories. They accessed the top floors by going through rooftop doors and ladders on each level. In some places the only access to the dwellings was by hand-and footholds."

"Navajo still live in the canyon?"

"Some stay there year round. But most just live there in the summer when it's warm then leave during the winter. Some traditional folks have hogans, round houses made of logs with mud roofs and a door facing the east. A stream runs right down the middle of the canyon so there's water for their sheep and crops. Navajo sheep are still important to the people. They say their wool is the best for weaving. Many families make their living from weaving rugs and blankets. Abey's grandmother was a weaver."

His voice dropped off as thoughts of his wife flooded his mind. He'd talked about Abey more today than in the past year. Dulcie seemed to do that to him, ignite thoughts he'd tried to suppress. He wasn't sure he liked the feelings those thoughts uncovered.

"Abey…it's lovely. What does it mean?"

"Leaf. It means leaf. Her grandmother wove a blanket for us using wool from her own sheep and natural dyes from plants. The pattern she used is called a storm design, geometric shapes all in earth tones, but she put green leaves in places. It's a true piece of art."

"Where is it?"

"Packed away. I haven't brought it out since I moved."

Dulcie shook her head. "I'm sorry to hear that. It sounds like a beautiful tribute to Abey and her culture. You could hang it on that empty wall in your living room. It would probably look spectacular."

His jaw tightened. She did it again, challenged all the protective barriers he'd put in place, and now he was certain he didn't like it. "It would be a constant reminder."

She nodded. "Yes, but it would be the right kind, a reminder of the good things in her life, not the tragedy of her death."

Austin sent her a sharp glance. "That's strange advice coming from a woman who still suffers panic attacks and freezes every time she gets a reminder of her own past."

The words were out before he could stop them, and he instantly regretted them. Dulcie's features faded and she looked away. But her hurt response only lasted a moment. She turned back to him. The color was gone from her cheeks, but her lips were set in a firm line.

"Who better to give you that kind of advice than someone who constantly fights to keep the fear at bay?"

His shoulders sagged. "You're right. I'm sorry. I was out of line. I just… I don't talk about Abey."

Her expression was achingly honest. "I understand, Austin. I truly do. I couldn't talk about my childhood for years. It was too horrible. But finally, I started remembering some good times. And that's how I fought the bad. I try to remember the wonderful blessings the Lord sent to comfort me through the bad times. Sometimes I struggle to find the good things, but it's worked…until now."

He was certain she was referring to her recent bout of dangerously debilitating fear when faced by Delacroix. He wouldn't add more fuel to the fire of her disappointment. Right now, she needed encouragement more than truth...especially after his unkind comment a moment ago. "Give yourself a break. It's not every day a person's life is threatened. It's not surprising you've suffered a setback."

She sighed. "Maybe, and maybe the Lord has a new lesson for me."

Austin smiled in spite of his conflicted emotions. "You're finding the good in your bad situation, right?"

She laughed, a sweet little sound he hadn't heard come out of her. She had laughed little, if at all, since they'd met. "I guess. See? It's a good habit to form."

He tilted his head. "It's not a habit I need. Blessings don't come my way."

"Or...you've forgotten how to recognize them when they do."

He slowed the Jeep as they came into Chinle, the town leading to the canyon.

"I think we need to grab some lunch. There's a drive-through up ahead. Will that work for you?"

"Sure."

He pulled in and ordered some burgers and fries. Keeping busy gave him an excuse not to talk. He handed her the bag and pulled onto the road. Eating also gave him an excuse for not talking, but it didn't shut down his mind from churning.

Was she right? Had he forgotten how to recognize the Lord's hand moving in his life? He never gave up believing that God was out there...somewhere. He just felt that the Lord had stopped working in his life. He'd clung to his pastor's counsel, attended church most every Sunday and yet…his faith life had been empty. He felt like God had abandoned him the night Abey died.

Is that how he really felt…? Abandoned? Had he just been going through the motions of his faith?

He couldn't remember a single instance where he'd felt loved by God…even *felt* the Lord's presence. Dulcie was wrong. He hadn't forgotten how to see God. He had been abandoned. One dark night, on a lonely stretch of highway, God turned His back on Austin Turner.

"Doris alerted the ring about our visit, didn't she?" Dulcie's question broke into his thoughts. Her tone was so low, he almost couldn't hear her.

In spite of her determination, it seemed she couldn't keep her concerns completely under control. His mind searched for the right way to answer, one that wouldn't trigger her into a frozen state. "She didn't come home to find her 'roots.' We still don't know *who* she's hiding from, but she's definitely hiding."

"It doesn't make sense. Why would she call them? How could she help the men who murdered her daughter?"

"She blames her husband for her daughter's death, and since he's in jail for that crime, I don't think she sees it as helping them. Besides, she's afraid to end up like her daughter. She'll give those men what they want to protect herself, even if what they want is us."

Dulcie slowly nodded. "I understand that. My note said I'd become a Missing One too. It frightened me into unexpected actions."

Austin tried to reassure her. "Look, the reservation is a big place and the canyon has a lot of visitors. People will surround us and it's almost a three-hour drive from Durango. By the time any of our suspects can reach the canyon, we'll be long gone."

His phone rang. McGuire's name flashed on the screen. He punched the button on his console to answer.

"Hello."

McGuire's gruff voice rang over the air. "Glad I caught you. I've got some bad news. The municipal police got a call last night to investigate a break-in. Someone trashed Ms. Parker's apartment."

Cold washed over Austin. He looked at Dulcie. Concern was reflected in her gaze.

He gripped the steering wheel. "They were looking to snatch her and destroy her research."

"That was my thought."

"Who called in the report?"

"The couple in the apartment below Ms. Parker heard banging, things falling and reported it. By the time the officers got there, the intruders were gone. I've asked for a complete report from the munis."

"I'll be surprised if Officer Shaw doesn't try to suppress the info."

"Officer Shaw hasn't reported for duty in two days. According to one of his fellow officers he's missing."

"A missing police officer? That didn't trigger an all-out search?"

"It did. It was good to have the munis on board and…they found some suspicious activity on Shaw's computer."

"I'm surprised he didn't wipe it clean before he left."

"Maybe he didn't know he was leaving."

Austin's churning thoughts came to an abrupt halt. If Shaw was missing… "What about Delacroix? Did the officers question him?"

"They tried but there was no answer at his apartment. A resident said they saw him leaving the day before around three p.m. This morning his car was found at the bottom of a cliff on Wolf Creek Pass. There were skid marks and two sets of tire tracks."

Austin knew exactly what that meant. Delacroix was dead…probably at the hands of his partners in crime. He glanced at Dulcie and tried to frame his words in a way that wouldn't terrify her.

"Sounds like they're eliminating all their weak links."

"And all our leads."

Austin took a slow breath. All their leads except Dulcie. His efforts to reframe his words failed. She'd connected the dots and was afraid.

"Did they find anything in Dulcie's apartment that might lead us to the perpetrators?"

"No prints, nothing tremendously helpful except for one thing. It wasn't a break-in. Someone picked the lock, a professional job. I had Bolton create a list of all the local criminals with that skill."

McGuire read the names but Austin knew one that would be on there before his lieutenant even said it. Austin was very familiar with Walter Benally and his career of crime. The man's involvement sent another spike of worry through Austin.

He glanced at Dulcie, fearful that his concern might show. She'd clamped her lips tight with tension and turned her gaze away.

"Things are getting dangerous, Austin. I want you and Ms. Parker back as soon as possible."

Austin hesitated. "We're twenty minutes out from Bea Yazzie's place. So far Susan Yazzie is our only lead. We need to find her."

McGuire was silent for a lengthy pause. "All right, but you need to make Ms. Parker aware. It should be her choice. If she decides to go on, I want you to stay in touch."

"We won't have reception in the bottom of the canyon but I'll do my best."

Austin clicked off. The gang was sending their members into hiding or maybe even killing them off. They were risking exposure to cover their tracks and eliminate any evidence. Those actions increased Dulcie's danger incrementally…not to mention the fact that if Benally was involved, there was a good chance Johnny Whitehorse was involved too. Benally worked for Whitehorse, who owned The Round Up bar located just off the reservation. The men after Dulcie could be closer than he thought and he'd just talked McGuire into letting them go farther away from safety. Was he wrong? Was he taking too big a risk, expecting too much from Dulcie…and maybe even himself?

He glanced her way again…once…twice. She wouldn't meet the unspoken question in his gaze and her lips were pinched in a tight line.

"You heard about Delacroix?"

She nodded, a tight dip of her head. "But I'm not sure I understand the significance of two sets of tire tracks."

Austin inhaled. "The skid marks mean Delacroix tried to brake and stop his descent. The other set of tires means another vehicle was behind him, pushing him off."

She jerked. "You think his partners in the ring pushed him off the road?"

"That looks like a possibility, yes."

Shock washed over her features. "He was one of them…he tried to kidnap me…for them. If they'll do that to one of their own…" The obvious conclusion hung in the air between them.

"We don't know exactly what turned them against him, Dulcie. He might have done something wrong. Maybe he felt guilty about his treatment of you and wanted to speak out. McGuire has put in a request for a search warrant for Delacroix's apartment. Perhaps we'll find an answer there."

She looked ahead, her churning emotions clearly written on her face. Then her features froze. "I was his project," she murmured.

Austin turned to her. "What do you mean?"

"When we were standing outside my door, Joey said he was about to finish a long-term project. I was his project, Austin. He'd been spying on me, watching me the entire time I lived there. When I discovered the ring, he was about to turn me over, but I escaped. He failed and now he's dead."

Austin nodded slowly. "It makes sense. He tried to

run so they followed him." Reaching across the space, he grasped her hand. "Dulcie, they're eliminating all their loose ends and you are a loose end. They'll be even more focused on catching you now."

She closed her eyes and took deep breaths. Austin linked their fingers and squeezed.

"McGuire gave us permission to go on but like he said, the decision is up to you. We can go to Bea Yazzie's hogan or we can turn around and head back to safety right now."

He gripped her hand tightly. His touch seemed to give her strength.

"No," she murmured, struggling to find her voice. "We have to go on. Susan is a loose end too. She's somewhere out there, hiding or running or maybe in their grasp. We have to find her."

Relief swept through Austin. He released her and gave her a one-sided smile.

"That's my girl."

She rubbed her hands up and down her arms as if a sudden chill had entered the Jeep cab. He was happy she agreed to go on but concern assailed him. If her fears finally overcame her, he'd have to leave her in the vehicle while he hiked down the two-mile trail by himself.

Wait…could Dulcie even hike down the trail? Right now she looked about as fragile as a porcelain doll. Maybe she wasn't up to that kind of strenuous activity. How could he have been so stupid as to not consider that possibility? If she wasn't up to it, he'd have to reformulate his plans.

"Hey, I forgot one little detail. The trail is two miles down and back. Are you up to that kind of walk?"

Dulcie took a deep breath, looked at him beneath lowered brows and sent him a mysterious, sort of flirty smile that knocked his socks off. Where did that come from?

She pushed her long russet-colored locks over one shoulder and said, "I can probably beat you down and back up."

Austin chuckled. He couldn't help himself. What had suddenly made her so confident?

"Was that a challenge?" He couldn't keep the teasing out of his tone and he didn't try. He liked this slightly sassy, flirty Dulcie.

She flashed a brilliant, hundred-watt smile that literally took his breath away. This…this was the wild, untamed woman hiding beneath the waiflike little girl. Here was the real Dulcie, the woman she kept tamped down with tight hairstyles and ugly, baggy clothes. The real woman afraid to come out from behind the frightened child. Did she know how her sun-burnished curls and brilliant smile could light up a day…his day?

"I think it *was* a challenge. Are you up to it, Deputy Turner?"

His chuckle was out before he could stop it. How did she do this…keep him off-balance and pull emotions out of him…emotions he hadn't felt in a long time?

He wasn't sure. He only knew that for a change, he was enjoying himself. "Just so you know, in my division, I ran the fastest mile in our POST…peace officers standards test."

Her eyebrows perked up and she tilted her head back and forth in another sassy movement. "Was it faster than nine minutes? Because that's my best."

"Whoa, are you serious? That's pretty good for a woman of your stature."

A sad smile wavered over her lips. "What you really mean is a scaredy-cat like me."

Not giving him time to answer, she said, "You shouldn't be surprised. Heavy-duty exercise means good endorphins to fight depression. I've been a runner since my first therapist recommended it when I was fifteen. I admit most of my running these days is on the treadmill in my apartment complex's gym. But I do love hiking too. If I'd known about Canyon de Chelly's trail, I would have tried to make it here before now."

Austin eyed her askance. "Do you really think the trail could have lured you away from your needy women?"

She turned to him, her expression wide open and so vulnerable it was almost painful to see. "No," she said. "Probably not the trail by itself."

Austin's breath hitched. Was she hinting that he might coax her out for a hike? All his teasing fled and he focused his gaze on the road. What was he doing?

Encouraging a broken woman to open up to a man who had nothing to give was wrong, just wrong. He needed to stop this right now. He couldn't think of anything to say, a way to apologize or explain, so he just kept silent. Fortunately, they'd arrived at the parking lot of the trailhead.

He pulled into a parking space among the others.

Many visitors stood near the ledge overlooking the canyon. Dulcie walked toward the lookout as Austin pulled two bottles of water from the box he kept in the back of his Jeep and tucked them in his jacket pockets. Living and working in such isolated places, he'd learned to keep water and supplies on hand.

A cool breeze swept up from the bottom of the canyon and lifted the ends of Dulcie's burnished curls. A slight smile wavered over her coral lips as she stared at the sight on the sandstone cliff across from them. Dark pigment washed down from the canyon rim above and covered parts of the cliff, giving it the shiny gleam called desert varnish. Six hundred feet below the rim, tucked in a narrow, horizontal slice in the bluff were the ruins. Time-washed plaster turned white covered some towers and upper buildings and had earned the site its Navajo name, Kinii' ni gai… White House. Below the cliff rooms, on the canyon floor, were more abodes.

"Archaeologists say the towers were once tall enough to reach the top level. That's how the builders got to the upper rooms. That's unusual for pueblo ruins. Usually the inhabitants used ladders and hand- and footholds to climb up and down."

"It must have been a difficult way to live, and yet…"

Her gaze travelled up and down the canyon below. A wide sandy wash swept down the middle, dotted with water-loving cottonwoods. Both those trees and the willows along the bank of the *arroyo* had lost most of their leaves. But the empty branches had a regal look.

Even with winter nipping at its edges, the canyon still carried a beauty all its own.

"It's unique and amazing," Dulcie said.

Her words sent a spike of pleasure shooting through Austin. He was glad to know she valued the canyon in the same way he did. But it was also one more thing Austin needed to ignore. If he wasn't careful, Dulcie would break through his protective wall and that was not a good thing. She wouldn't understand that his wall was there for other people's protection. The man behind that wall was empty, drained, living a half life. Dulcie and her innocent ways needed to stay on the other side for her own emotional safety.

"We don't have time for sightseeing. We need to get going on that trail. Dark comes early to the canyon." His words sounded gruffer than he meant, but maybe it was best that way. Dulcie would be safer.

Austin started for the trail, leaving Dulcie standing alone on the edge. She trembled at the full realization of the threat facing her. Her senses, every nerve in her body weakened.

Joey had threatened her, pushed her against the wall intending to trap her so he could hand her over to the violent men of the ring. The feeling of powerlessness he'd ignited inside her washed through her again. She felt trapped, suffocated...powerless...and now...the man who had made her feel helpless was dead...probably murdered by the very men who were his partners.

Austin's words echoed in her mind. *The decision is up to you.*

Up to her. She had choices…options. She was not a trapped little girl, powerless to take action or even move. Her gaze darted to Austin as his tall form took the trail. He seemed full of strength and purpose. She could have kissed him for the courage he gave her. Instead, she took another long, deep breath and followed him.

Dulcie concentrated on moving one foot after the other. She felt awkward and weak at first, but soon, her body found a rhythm. The exercise felt good. Stress and fear poured out of her and into the ground with each pound of her foot on the dusty trail. Soon the path narrowed and they walked along bluffs of sandstone. Large red boulders dotted the sides of the trail and piñon trees and evergreens sent the smell of pine into the air.

Soon, she felt stronger and maybe even peaceful. Yes, men were chasing her. Yes, other women were in danger…and maybe lost forever. Those were realities. But she felt guided, purposeful and she owed it all to the man in the cowboy hat and dusty boots leading the way.

Matching him stride for stride, seeing an outcropping or a bird darting across the sky, she'd turn to see Austin noticing the same thing. They saw things, enjoyed the small delights of nature in the same way. This walk along the trail—being with him—gave her a sense of companionship she'd only known with her mother and sister. It was unique and thrilling. What would it be like to see the Grand Canyon with him, or the red rocks of Sedona? She could think of a myriad of trips she would enjoy sharing with him. He'd called her his girl. If only…

Dulcie almost stumbled over her own feet as surprise washed over. In her life, there'd never really been an "if only" moment with a man. Of course, she'd hoped for moments like this, but with most men, she'd always found herself tensing up, closing in on herself. The second they raised their voices, all her old fears flooded in and any burgeoning relationship would end. She'd had those moments with Austin too, especially in the beginning. But now that she knew him better, those moments came farther and farther apart. So many other things about him gave her peace… The concern he tried to hide for the missing girls. The respect he had for her gave her confidence and she felt herself unfolding like a flowering bloom. It was an unexpected blessing and she thanked the Lord as they hiked down the trail.

They passed through two tunnels carved into the rock and finally came to a flat area. Off the path, tucked around an outcropping of rock, Dulcie glimpsed the edge of a round, wooden structure. A sign along the dirt trail leading to the hogan commanded them to respect the privacy of the occupant.

"This is it." Austin stepped onto the path leading to the home.

Dulcie scooted to catch up with him. "Are you sure? The signs are very clear about not trespassing."

"This is the only hogan on the trail. It has to be the right one."

Around the corner, the outcropping of buff-colored

rocks concealed more flat land with small corrals and pens. A Navajo woman crossed from the hogan to a trough with a metal bucket in her hand. A black-and-brown dog trotted by her side. Sheep in the small pen headed for the trough when they saw her coming. Dulcie smiled. The woman's animals knew her and responded, an action Dulcie didn't expect to see from sheep.

The woman wore traditional clothing, a full-length skirt that looked like dark blue velvet. A long-sleeved blouse of the same material. And a silver concha belt was looped around her tiny waist. Her silver hair was tied in a traditional Navajo bun. As they drew closer, Dulcie realized the woman was much older than she'd first thought. Susan's grandmother didn't look strong enough to carry the heavy bucket of water. Her face was long and weathered from days in the sun, but her features wore a serene expression Dulcie would not forget for a long time. There was such peace in that expression. She longed for that kind of peace.

"Ya ta he." Austin called out the greeting.

The woman turned. She was neither startled nor frightened by their presence, but she tilted her head and squinted her eyes, trying to see them clearly.

"Ma'am, my name is Austin Turner and this is Dulcie Parker. I'm a deputy from the La Plata sheriff's department. We'd like to talk to you about your granddaughter."

"So, you have found her?" The woman's voice was low and raspy. It took both Austin and Dulcie a moment to understand her. When they did, they glanced at each other.

"No, ma'am. We weren't sure she was missing."

"She has been gone two months but my nephew was on a long trip. When he came back, I told him to go to the men at that place…that tribal police. They said they would make a report."

Dulcie and Austin shared another glance. If a report was generated, Officer Shaw obviously had done his work and suppressed it. Austin shrugged. "I'm sorry, ma'am. I didn't receive the report, but I'd like to help you find her."

She studied him, then looked past him to Dulcie. Finally, she nodded. "Come. We will have coffee."

Heading toward the hogan, she never looked back.

Dulcie grabbed Austin's arm. "We don't have time for coffee. You said we had to get in and out before someone has a chance to follow us."

"We don't have a choice. It would be disrespectful not to take the offer now that she's made it. If we want the information, then we will drink coffee."

Dulcie followed him but couldn't help but glance back at the trail and up the cliff's face. The path was empty, and that took some of the edginess off her nerves.

A small table with chairs stood just outside the hogan. The woman had already returned from inside with three mugs and an old-fashioned metal coffeepot. Steam poured out of the spout into the cool air. The smell drifted toward Dulcie, roasted and rich and more appealing than she would have imagined. They settled at the table and Bea Yazzie poured.

Austin engaged the older woman by asking if she

used the wool of her sheep for weaving. She answered yes, and they chatted for a while about her Navajo sheep and the natural dyes she used for their soft wool.

"I use my grandmother's loom. It's very old. Even older than me." Her dark eyes twinkled and Dulcie found herself warming to the woman. Austin deftly and gently brought the conversation back to her missing granddaughter. Dulcie noted that although she didn't refer to Susan by name, she didn't speak of her as if she was already gone.

But Doris Begay had referred to Susan as a *Missing One.* What did she know that the rest of them didn't?

According to Susan's grandmother she had been missing since the night of Judy's murder. Bea Yazzie had thought her granddaughter was living with a friend, but since she had no cell phone, she had to wait to call Susan until her nephew returned.

"I knew she was in trouble. My granddaughter, she always talks about Doris Begay's man. He is a bad father. I told my granddaughter...both girls, you come live with me in the canyon. Stay away from that bad man. But they wouldn't come. Now look what happened." She shook her head. "Young people today want all the wrong things. Those girls want to look like movie stars. They always worry about makeup and clothes and go to that drinking place to show off."

Across the table, Austin tensed. "What drinking place?"

"That one, just off the reservation. You know, John Whitehorse's place."

"You mean The Round Up?"

She nodded. "That place is no good…no good for no one. Not men, and for sure, not young girls."

Austin asked her a few more questions, about other friends of Susan's he could contact, other places she frequented. But the young woman lived in Durango and only visited occasionally. Her grandmother knew little about her life in the city. Austin seemed eager to leave now, more than anxious. He thanked the woman many times but rose firmly. "It's getting late. We must leave the canyon before dark."

The older woman nodded. She studied his face and looked deep into his eyes. "Yes, you are the one. You will find my granddaughter."

He gave a shake of his head. "I will do my best. But I can't make any promises."

The old woman nodded once more. "You will find her."

Austin rose and strode toward the trail. Dulcie said goodbye and followed him. He inspired good feelings in all women, not just herself. But that fact didn't seem to please him. He hurried up the trail and Dulcie was hard-pressed to keep up. Almost out of breath she said, "Are you taking my dare seriously? Are we racing up the trail?"

He paused and turned back to her, his features set and hard. "I made a mistake. I was so anxious to get to the truth, I was overconfident. I should have known better…thought it through."

"What do you mean?"

"I should have known Whitehorse is involved. He's

got a hand in every crime racket in the Four Corners states." He started up the trail again.

"So? That just gives us someone else to investigate."

"You heard Bea. Whitehorse's place is where vulnerable women go to get noticed. Only it's probably not the kind of notice they're looking for. Whitehorse also has the right men, the kind who can muscle a girl into a truck and transport her."

Dulcie halted. "You're saying you think Whitehorse is the leader of the gang."

Austin kept his gaze on the trail and hurried forward. Dusk was slipping into the canyon very rapidly and the trail was disappearing. Another few moments and the cliff walls would block all light. A chill came with it, settling over them with a gloom that went deeper than a simple setting of the sun.

"I don't know if he's the leader. He has the muscle, but I doubt he has the means to contact a buyer on an open market. That would take someone with a little more national or international exposure."

She hurried to catch up. "Someone like DA Havlicek or Kent Pierce."

"Yeah. Exactly like those two, but which one? And most important of all, how do we prove it? We haven't pulled up one single piece of evidence except Delacroix's fingerprint on your threatening letter and he's already been eliminated."

Out of breath, she halted. "It also doesn't explain why we're running up the canyon wall."

Austin paused long enough to grab her hand and pull her forward. "I told you—I took the wrong chance.

I assumed we could beat the people looking for you out of the canyon but I was wrong. Doris Begay is terrified of someone, and now, I'm pretty sure that someone is Johnny Whitehorse. When she made that call, it was probably to him and his place is only an hour away. His men might be on their way or already here."

Dulcie's heart skipped a beat and she stumbled behind him but Austin didn't let up his pace. He marched ahead, climbing so fast Dulcie's legs and lungs burned. They passed through the first near dark tunnel. Then climbed past the piñon pines to the second tunnel where Dulcie pulled her hand loose and stopped. Her lungs were on fire and she needed to stop for a moment to catch her breath.

Austin halted too. In that moment, they heard voices. Two men talking quietly, their footsteps scattering rocks as they made the descent on the other side of the tunnel.

Dulcie stared at Austin, wide-eyed, her heart pounding when they both heard one man say her name. It echoed through the tunnel, muted, but clear enough to understand. They were here for her. Without another word, Austin grabbed her hand again and bolted back down the trail.

SIX

Fool! Idiot! Stupid!

Austin called himself names as he pulled Dulcie down the narrow trail. How could he have been so foolish? He should have known Whitehorse would be involved in an operation this big. When Dulcie saw Doris Begay on the phone in her trailer, he should have escorted Dulcie back to a place of safety. Now she and Susan's grandmother were in danger. Not only did he have to get Dulcie away from the men behind them, but he had to make sure they didn't make a stop at the Yazzie hogan.

Darkness was looming. Shadows made the trail difficult to see. They came to the second tunnel and Austin had to use the light on the cell phone to get them through. It was a beacon for the men above them to follow, but it was better than tripping and falling.

How many voices had he heard? At least two distinct ones but there could be other silent men with them. Could he hold off two or more men on his own? He had his service revolver but no way could he afford bullets flying everywhere. Dulcie could be hurt. Better to get to the canyon floor where they could hide in the myriad of curves and pitch-black crevices of the cliffs. Then they could find another way out of the canyon trail. But first…they had to get past the Yazzie hogan. The last thing he wanted was for the men to harm Susan's grandmother.

They came out of the tunnel and he switched off the light. At this section of the trail, piñon trees covered each side, hiding them from view. Just ahead was the turnoff trail to the hogan. A rocky abutment hid the home but a wide-open space between the trail and rocks was clearly visible from the trail above. He wanted to make sure the men following them saw and knew that they didn't take the path leading to the Yazzie place. He would need to time it carefully so the men could see that he and Dulcie had run down to the canyon floor.

Just as they hit the open space, Austin pushed Dulcie ahead. "Keep going. Don't stop. I'll catch up."

"Why…"

"No questions, Dulcie, just get going!"

She spun and ran to the next turn in the trail, out of his view. Austin scanned the face of the cliff. Two dark figures emerged from the tunnel. Good. Only two men. And their exit out of the tunnel was perfect timing. He could see their excited hand gestures in the gloomy darkness.

They saw him. Suddenly…one man pointed. There was something in his hand. A shot reverberated through the canyon. A bullet pinged off the ground ten feet away from Austin, followed by angry words echoing in the canyon. One man wasn't pleased his partner had fired. Austin didn't wait to see which of the men had the gun. Spinning, he followed Dulcie down the trail.

So, the men were definitely armed. That confirmed his suspicions. He couldn't risk Dulcie getting caught in the crossfire. Nor could he risk getting trapped in a rocky culvert with no way out. He knew there were other trails out of the canyon, but he didn't know where they were and would probably miss them in the dark. Somewhere down the canyon someone might have an ATV or a means of transportation, but they could be miles away and asking for their help would put those people at risk. Chances were most canyon residents had already left for their winter homes. Very few of the families were like Bea Yazzie, who was set in her ways and lived in the canyon all year long. That left only one place they could hide where they would have an exit.

The ancient ruins. Austin hated the thought of possible damage to the ruins but if it meant saving Dulcie, he would do it.

For years, he'd assisted a friend with the yearly inspection of the ruins and had explored them up close. There were two levels, a ground floor and another level resting on a ledge high above the bottom. The ground floor had a tower with multiple levels. It was too damaged to climb, but there were many rooms on the floor level and even a niche deep at the back, beneath the massive bluff. If necessary, he could tuck Dulcie in that crevice and lead the men away. Besides, if the men had to search each small cubby room in the ruins, that would give Dulcie and Austin time to get out and head back up the trail. Hiding in the ruins was their best option.

He came around a corner and almost ran into Dulcie coming back up the path. "I told you not to stop."

"I heard the shot. I thought you might be hurt."

"Everyone for a mile in both directions heard the shot. Let's hope one of them has the means to get help." Grabbing her elbow, he hurried her back down the path.

"Do you think those men would hurt Susan's grandmother?"

"If one of those men is Walter Benally—he would hurt his own grandmother if there was money involved." His words came out in a low tone. They reached another bend in the trail below with a view of the front of the hogan. It was silent and dark, as if no one was there. Even the sheep had moved into the corral beneath the ramshackle covering against the rock wall. "I think Bea is used to taking care of herself. Besides, I made sure they saw me. My guess is they're more intent on getting their hands on you."

At least that's my hope. He glanced one more time at the hogan and sent up a prayer for the old woman's safety…and theirs.

The trail flattened out. Piñon pines gave way to tamarisk and olive trees—non-native, invasive trees taking over the park and most of the Southwest. Right now, Austin was thankful for their coverage. They came to the flat, sandy wash of the riverbed. The snowstorm had blanketed the mountains but had not yet reached the desert, so the wash was dry. Across the streambed, a wire fence surrounded the ruins, blocking them off from trespassers. With a glance at the cloud-filled, moonless sky and the cliff above, Austin led Dulcie from bush to bush, hiding and darting to avoid being seen. At last they made it to the other side. He followed the fence to the rock cliff where it ended with massive wooden posts. Gripping the fence, he climbed over.

Dulcie's harsh whisper echoed beneath the bluff. "We're stopping here?"

"It's our best chance. Come on."

Without another moment's thought, she climbed over, evidence of her trust in him. Too bad she trusted him so much. So far, he hadn't done a very good job of staying ahead of the gang's plans. But wasn't that the story of his life?

He shook off his negative thoughts and led the way to the ruins. "Be careful. Step where I step and don't lean on any walls or supports." He kept his voice low so it didn't echo in the empty chambers. Dulcie didn't speak and he didn't look back to see if she acknowledged his order. Finding his footing took all of his concentration.

There was no way to enter the ruins proper from the left side. They had to cross in front…in plain view from above. Austin could only hope the men following them were focused on the trail. Ducking, he pulled Dulcie across the open space and around the remains of a large kiva—a deep, circular pit. Austin headed between two walls and led her all the way to the back, where a narrow door with a T-shaped frame fed into the dark interior. On the opposite wall, another door led into a warren of rooms that once served the small but bustling community. Other doors led farther and farther back until the ruins dipped beneath the massive cliff wall. Austin didn't want to enter the deeper parts of the ruins if he didn't have to. But if he did, the small doors and rooms were hard to traverse and would slow their pursuers down. Hopefully that would give Dulcie and him time to escape from the other side. At least that was his plan.

Please, God, let this work. Let me do this part right.

At the back of the narrow passage, two wooden beams supported the wall to their right. It was a good place to hide since the shadows there were deep, but he could still see down the narrow opening and across the riverbed.

"Sit down and lean against the supports…but only the supports, not the walls. Rest while you can." Dulcie nodded in response to his whispered words and eased down on ground worn hard and smooth by years and use. Unfortunately, both their raspy breaths echoed in the empty passage.

Austin crouched down beside her. "Take some deep breaths. Let's slow it down."

She nodded. With silent gestures, he motioned for her to follow his deep breaths. She obeyed and several inhalations slowed and silenced their heavy breathing…and just in time.

They heard the low voices of the men standing outside the fence around the ruins.

"I'm telling you. That's the only place they could have gone."

"Nah. They could be hiding behind any of those trees down the wash. We need to keep going."

Austin's worst fear was realized when he recognized the raspy voice of Walter Benally. Bob Carson's mother told Austin her son was running with Benally. Was Carson the other man?

Whoever he was, he was insistent. "I'm telling you, man. They're hiding in those old rooms. Let's go look."

Austin tensed.

"I'm not gonna waste time searching all those rooms when they've probably gone down the trail," came the raspy reply. "Besides. I don't go near the houses of the ancient ones."

Ancient ones. The people of the Navajo Nation often referred to the Ancestral Puebloans as the ancient ones...and they had tremendous respect for their ruins. The man's use of the term confirmed his conviction that Benally was one of the men.

"How far is the next house on the wash?" the other man asked.

Benally sounded irritated. "I don't know. I don't spend no time here if I can help it. The place gives me the creeps. Besides, we don't want anyone to see us. You already caused enough noise with that shot, Carson."

Austin clenched his fist with conviction. He should have paid more attention to Carson's mother when she told him about the connection. He wished he'd followed through and done more. If he had, they wouldn't be here now.

"Sorry. I thought it might scare him into stopping. So what are we gonna do?"

"Let's go down the trail a ways. See if we can't get to a high spot where we can look down on the floor. We can see most everything from there."

They moved away from the fence and down the trail. Austin listened until he could no longer hear their movement. It was long enough for Dulcie to settle herself from their strenuous run down the trail. She had begun to shiver. Austin pulled the water bottle out of his pocket and cracked the lid. Even that small sound echoed in the cavernous passage. They both tensed. When nothing happened, he handed the bottle to her and she drank. Austin opened the other bottle and took his own sip before carefully and silently creeping toward the opening so he could look down the wash. The men walked along the white edges of the sandy riverbed. Suddenly, they paused and stood for a long while. It appeared they were arguing again. Then one of them spun and stalked back their way. Austin hurried to where Dulcie sat, knees drawn up, head resting on her folded arms. Her whole body shivered.

Lifting the snap on his firearm holster caused her to raise her gaze. Austin knelt low and whispered, "They're coming back our way. If one of them crosses the fence, I will shoot. If I fire, I want you to run to the back. There's a deep crevice in the rock wall. Go as far as you can and hide. I'll try to lead them away."

She started to shake her head, but he held his finger to his lips. The men's muffled voices reached them and Dulcie held whatever protests she'd been about to make.

The two men stopped at the same place along the trail and once again, their voices carried over the wash. Austin pressed back as close to the fragile wall as he dared.

He wished he could lean out far enough to get a glimpse of their faces. He wanted visual proof that they were who he thought. If he and Dulcie got out of this canyon safely, he'd be on the radio to McGuire to have them arrested. But if Carson convinced Benally to climb the fence and cross to the ruins, they wouldn't get out of here unscathed. Austin gripped his pistol.

"I still think they're hiding in those ruins." Carson's voice caused Austin to tense and hold his breath. He dared not even remove the safety on his gun in case it clicked loudly in the narrow passage.

"I told you. I'm not going in there!" Benally was adamant. Austin released his breath.

Benally continued, his tone marking his irritation with Carson. "For all we know, they could have hidden in the trees along the trail. We could have easily missed them in the dark."

"Too bad the moon's not out. You really think they got behind us and doubled back to the parking lot?"

After a long silence, Benally said, "I don't know. Let's go back. If his Jeep is still there, we'll wait for them. They have to come up sometime."

"What if they climb out someplace else?"

"We have a better view of the whole canyon from the lookout. We'll see them if they move up or down the wash. Besides, it's miles to the closest help."

Austin heaved a sigh of relief and closed his eyes as the men walked away. He couldn't believe how fortunate they'd been. Only Benally's deep respect for the ancient Puebloans had saved them. Relief swept through him making him sag. He waited a long while before he crept to the opening of the passageway and peeked out. He watched the trail leading up the side of the cliff. Two dark shadows moved across the opening below Bea Yazzie's hogan. The small house was dark and showed no signs of life. He hoped Benally and Carson believed it was empty, but Austin didn't move until he saw them crossing the next clearing above the path to her place. Releasing his breath in a long sigh, he holstered his gun and walked back to Dulcie.

She sat huddled on the ground, shaking from head to toe. She looked so cold and tired and miserable. All he wanted was to pull her in his arms and hold her. But he wasn't sure how that gesture would be received. One minute she appreciated his help. The next she shied away.

He eased down beside her, his back against the support. After a minute of watching her abject misery, he couldn't stand it. Opening the folds of his coat, he pulled her close and tucked the sides around her to warm her. To his amazement, she fell into his arms and nuzzled her face beneath the fold of his coat. Her wild curls tickled his chin. Her flowery scent drifted up to him, wrapping him in feelings of warm spring and new things and he couldn't resist. He dipped his head and buried his face in the soft caress of those wild curls.

Was that a kiss? Austin's breath warmed the top of Dulcie's head and she felt certain that his lips were buried in her hair. Wild pleasure surged through her and she sighed with relief as his warmth enveloped her. She wanted nothing more than to snuggle deeper into his arms. She'd cooled off too quickly and now she couldn't stop her body's natural reaction. She trembled and shook for a long while before she could finally take a deep breath. Austin smelled crisp and clean, like leather and soap. Burying her nose deeper beneath his jacket she held on tighter. His arms held her close. Secure.

She felt safer in Austin's arms than she'd ever felt in her life and it had nothing to do with the body heat they were sharing. It was all about his kindness, the way his jaw set in a determined line when he thought of the missing women. How he constantly underestimated his abilities. The clear blue honesty in his gaze when he told Bea Yazzie he'd do his best to find her granddaughter.

Austin was authentic. Real. Not full of boastful pride or overbearing assurance. He might not believe it, but he could right wrongs and make the world safe for women who never felt that way. She rested her cheek against his chest and listened to the steady, strong beat of his heart.

"I'm sorry." His words rumbled deep in his chest and startled her. "I should never have brought you here. I wish I'd put two and two together and taken you back to Durango after McGuire's call. Whitehorse has a finger in every crime in the area. If I was thinking right, I would have realized he'd send men right away."

She did not want to rise from the comfort of his

arms so she didn't. It felt too good. "It would have been a waste of time to take me back to Durango. Time we don't have. Now we know Whitehorse is involved."

"We know more than that. I'm pretty sure those two who followed us are Walter Benally and Bob Carson."

This time she raised slightly to look at him. "Are you sure?"

He nodded. "I recognized Benally's voice. It's distinctive. He's Whitehorse's muscle and does all the man's dirty work. I just tried to serve a search warrant on Bob Carson. His mother claimed he's running with Benally so I suspected he was Benally's partner. I was right."

She eased back down onto his chest and into the comfort of his arms. "Does that mean you can identify them and arrest them for shooting at you?"

"I'll try…if we get out of here in one piece. They're waiting for us up in the parking lot. I've been going over the trail in my mind, trying to think of a way I might climb up the rocks and get to my Jeep without a fight."

"Maybe they'll give up and go home."

He made a humorous sound that rumbled deep in his chest. Dulcie liked it.

"They will be sitting in their warm car all night. I think we'll give up before they do."

She shook her head. "You'll figure out something."

He stilled. "You sound complacent for someone about to spend a freezing fall night at the bottom of a canyon."

Complacent. No, not complacent. Content. She was

content in the arms of a man who made her feel safe, who instilled confidence in her, who made her feel like all the world could sometimes be good. A man whose heart belonged to someone else and maybe always would. That thought should have frightened her and sent her scurrying away to the security of her own corner. But it didn't. She had never felt like this before, never even thought she could feel this way about a man. For a little while…or maybe even just for as long as it lasted, she would enjoy this moment.

"Not complacent," she murmured, trying to express herself without giving away too much. "Confident. I'm confident you'll find a way."

His chest rose with a deep breath. "You shouldn't have confidence in me, Dulcie, especially not after what just happened. I slipped up, made…mistakes."

Something in his tone struck a nerve with her. It sounded like pain—a deep, ongoing pain. "*We* took a risk today, yes. But it wasn't a mistake and it was worth it."

He gave a sharp shake of his head. "Risks are never worth it."

This time, Dulcie rose to meet his gaze. His Stetson shadowed his face and she couldn't see his blue eyes, the ones that said so much more than his words expressed. She wished she could see them, see how deep the pain went. But she didn't need to. She knew exactly what troubled him.

"This isn't about me, is it? It's about Abey."

He didn't answer. Instead, he shifted and moved so he could climb to his feet. Dulcie scooted back, gave him room. She felt the cold emptiness the minute he stood. It wasn't fair. She'd told him her life story, confided things she'd told no one, not even her counselors. But he wouldn't talk to her about his wife. Her disappointment went bone deep. But this wasn't about her, about the attraction she felt for him and he obviously sensed. This was about something more.

"I'm not the only one who trusts you. You inspire confidence in other women. Susan's grandmother is certain you will find her granddaughter."

Refusing to look her way, he shook his head. "Determination doesn't always lead to success. I'm determined to find these men. Doesn't mean I'll succeed."

"But it makes it more likely. You won't give up easily, Austin, and people sense that in you. No matter how many times I had setbacks in my counseling, I pulled myself together and went back. I never let it stop me and look where I am now."

Spinning quickly, he fixed her with a hard look. "Yeah, look at you now. Frozen every time a man gets close."

She caught her breath. His words pierced again. Hurt washed over her so deep, she couldn't even speak. The ache must have shown on her face because Austin shook his head again, spun and walked away to stand at the edge of the passage. Once there, he shoved his hands in his pockets and his back was stiff and straight.

Dulcie felt the misery go through her like a wave of heat. She let it sweep through because she'd learned one thing in all her years of counseling… Once the pain washed away all the false hopes and crushed dreams, the truth would stand bright and brilliant. So she let the waves of pain clear away her ragged emotions until one thing rang true.

She shied away from men. She had trouble trusting them… All except for one.

"Not you," she whispered to his rigid back. "I trust you."

With that admission came another. Just because she trusted him, was willing to share her life stories with him, didn't mean he felt the same way. Just because he was special to her didn't mean she was to him. She wished she could be special to him, wished he felt he could trust her the way she trusted him. She wanted to be the one to crack the impenetrable wall around his heart. But it was a foolish wish. He'd just proven that. She could never be the kind of woman his wife was, a strong person, a leader among her people…and now a martyr to lost hope. Dulcie wasn't sure any woman could live up to Austin's memories of his dead wife. And that made her even sadder.

The cold bit into her body. She needed to get moving, get her blood circulating. Austin was right. Tonight would be miserable…especially now that she wouldn't be in his warm arms. She paced back and forth, stretching her stiff legs and swinging her arms. It didn't help much. The cold was piercing. It wasn't long before she was shivering again.

Austin came back. She barely glanced his way. She kept up her brisk pacing.

He slid his fingertips back in his pockets. "Dulcie, I didn't mean..."

"Yes, you did." She glanced up. Her words caught him off guard because he froze in surprise, fingertips still linked in his front pockets.

She shook her head. "You don't have to apologize for speaking the truth. Besides, I shouldn't have pushed you for info you don't want to share."

He released a heavy breath. "It's not that I don't want to share. After she died, I talked to counselors until I couldn't talk anymore. I know how to do that. That's not the problem. Being here on the reservation has been hard. I've tried to block the memories from my mind, to concentrate on our investigation, but I can't. Meeting Bea Yazzie was especially hard." He looked down and around. Any place but at her. "Abey's grandmother was a weaver too, but when Abey was a teenager, she wanted nothing to do with it. After she found out she was pregnant, she decided that she'd stop all her volunteer work, slow down and make the time to learn the craft. She was spending long hours at her grandmother's hogan. That night she stayed until after dark and that road..." He shook his head. "I should have made her stay at the hogan and not let her drive home on that lonely stretch."

This time Dulcie didn't stifle her thoughts. He'd been unkind twice, so this time she thought it only fair if she spoke the truth back to him. "From what little you've told me," she said in a low voice, "I don't know if you could tell Abey what to do. It sounds like she had a mind of her own."

She caught him off guard again. His jerked his fingers free from his pockets and his blue eyes flashed in the shadows. He obviously didn't like her pointing out the truth. His sharp reaction told her that. She was glad. She might not be the one to break down the barriers around his heart, but he didn't need to live with a guilty conscience. That's one gift she might be able to give him.

"I should have said more, done more."

She shook her head. "We have that in common too. I thought if I could just reach that mother in California, I could save those little girls. It didn't work."

"Why not? Why didn't God honor your commitment and your struggles? For that matter, why did He let a woman and an innocent babe die like that, in the middle of a dark road alone and afraid?"

She shook her head slowly. "I've asked myself a similar question over and over again. Why couldn't God make my dad love me? Why couldn't Daddy just let go of the anger and love us?"

He pinned that piercing blue gaze on her. "I hope you got answers because I didn't."

"Oh, I got an answer and I'm sure you did too. You probably just didn't like it."

He glared at her. She could barely see his features in the dark but the pale moon, partially covered by clouds, still reflected off the hard set of his jaw.

"Sin is here, Austin. From the moment the angels turned away from God, sin entered the world. Bad things happen to good and innocent people. God weeps but He allows it to happen so we'll understand that His mercy is our only hope. He's the source of all good and our best reason to go on. *Romans* 9:23 says it perfectly. 'And that he might make known the riches of his glory on the vessels of mercy, which he had afore prepared unto glory.'"

She met his doubting gaze. "We were prepared for glory, Austin. That means we're unique. Special and loved. I cling to that every time I feel defeated. It's hard to hear His still, quiet voice in the world we live in. But He's there, listening, whispering in our hearts." She paused and looked up at the sky, at the brilliant bright stars. "Maybe the Navajo have it right living way out here. It strips away all our mechanical tools and illusions of power. His glory surrounds us in the skies and stars, so close we can almost touch them. I think it's easier to hear His quiet voice here because there's nothing to block out the sound and nowhere to hide."

The moon finally came from behind the cloud. She glanced back at Austin. His jaw was set and his blue eyes were hard and angry beneath the brim of his hat. The smooth line of his jaw tightened even more and the cleft in his chin twitched. He turned and stalked to the front of the passage.

With a heavy heart, Dulcie began pacing again. She was so cold, her teeth chattered.

Austin ran back to her, his voice pitched low. "Someone is coming down the path with a light." He grabbed her arms and pushed her toward one of the T-shaped openings into another room. "With that light, they'll be able to see right down this passage. Go deeper. But be careful. One wrong move and the wall could come tumbling down on you."

Dulcie gingerly stepped over the lip of the doorway and crouched down in the corner. Austin followed. They turned back to look through the doorway just as light flashed down the passageway they'd just vacated. The light beam swayed from corner to corner.

"Hey, you two, come out of there before you freeze. Let's go get warm."

The light flicked away. Dulcie and Austin stared at each other as Bea Yazzie's low voice echoed through the ruins.

SEVEN

Austin motioned Dulcie to wait while he checked outside. Sure enough, the old woman stood on the other side of the fence, her dog seated beside her.

"Come on. It's safe."

Dulcie scrambled out of the cramped space and they moved down the passage into the opening. Austin had to help Dulcie over the fence, a sure sign of her cold, numb state. When they reached the older woman, she shook her head. "You should not go to the ancient ones' houses where you will freeze. Why did you not come back to me when those two left?"

"How did you know they were following us?" Dulcie's teeth chattered when she spoke.

Bea clicked her tongue. "Those two…they sounded like a team of horses galloping down the trail, arguing and carrying on. I waited a long time after they left to come find you."

"We didn't want them to bother you, ma'am. They may be noisy but they're dangerous."

"Yes, I heard the gunshot. Fools." The vigorous

shaking of her head showed even in the shadowy light of the moon. "Come on. I made you some Navajo tea. It will help."

They climbed the trail, the older woman moving ahead of both them. Their bodies and limbs were sluggish from the cold. When they entered the hogan, a battery-operated lamp sat on the table, casting a white glow over the single room. The cast-iron stove in the middle of the hogan radiated heat. Austin's face and fingers immediately tingled. He couldn't imagine how Dulcie was feeling. Bea handed her a heavy Navajo blanket and pushed a chair from the table closer to the stove.

"Sit. Both of you, sit."

Austin helped Dulcie tug the blanket around her as Bea poured a mug of tea. Dulcie wrapped cold fingers around the steaming cup and sniffed the liquid.

"What is it?"

Austin pulled another chair close to her and sat down. "An herbal tea made from a local plant. It's called greenthread. Go ahead and drink. It's full of antioxidants and good for you."

"I don't care how good it is for me. It's warm." She flashed him a little smile. Her dark eyebrows rose in an expressive gesture and her long curls bounced against her cheeks. Although she'd just spent four hours in the freezing winter temperatures, she looked wonderful. He couldn't turn away from her brown-eyed gaze or her peach-colored lips as she sipped the tea. Thankfully, Bea handed him a blanket and a mug.

He drank his tea and let the heat from the fire sink

in. His harsh words echoed through his mind. He felt bad about what he'd said to Dulcie, almost accused her of being weak and useless. She'd probed a painful wound and he'd lashed out…unthinking. It was cruel and he regretted it. But she seemed to handle it better than he did. She was over it by the time he'd returned and even spun it back on him with truths he couldn't deny.

Was she right? Did they have many things in common, like a need to save the world? It was why he joined the sheriff's department in the first place, to help make a difference. But when he'd lost Abey, he'd felt useless and thought he'd given up the notion of making a difference. But here he was again, trapped in a hogan at the bottom of a canyon with men waiting for him above…all because he thought he could help a frightened waiflike woman with the same need to help. He believed that need was dead…along with his faith in God. But he was wrong. Obviously, he hadn't given up all hope. He still had a sliver of faith that the Lord meant him to do some good and Dulcie had sensed it, had dragged it out of him. Otherwise they wouldn't be here now.

If she was right about that, maybe the rest of what she said was true too. Maybe they were prepared for glory. Maybe the Lord had plans for them…for him. He certainly hoped so. Or else all his efforts to help Dulcie would end tomorrow morning.

The old woman pulled more blankets off a shelf, and Dulcie helped her arrange them into pallets near the stove. When they finished, Dulcie grasped her hand.

"Thank you. I don't think I could have lasted out there through the night."

The old woman nodded her head. "Tonight, you sleep. Tomorrow will take care of itself."

Yes, tomorrow will take care of itself. As he settled in his pallet near the warm stove, one last thought drifted through his mind. *Please, Lord, don't let me fail her.*

Austin opened his eyes slowly. With his senses tuned to any sounds outside the hogan, he hadn't slept well, and he had a crick in his neck.

Bea was already up. Water boiled in the kettle on the stove for more Navajo tea as she mixed bread in a wooden bowl. She pulled large pieces of the dough loose and dropped them into a cast-iron skillet next to the kettle. The bread sizzled and the smell of pork stew drifted over the air. His stomach grumbled without warning.

"You need to eat," Susan's grandmother said with a chuckle. "When you see people on the trail, then you can go. Those fools won't touch you when others are around. They are cowards who don't want to get caught."

Austin smiled, amazed at the older lady's wisdom. She might have led a secluded life but she was one smart woman. Dulcie stirred and rose from her pallet. She asked how she could help. Bea told her to set the table and she found bowls and spoons on a shelf. When the fry bread was done, the elder lady spooned the stew into bowls and they ate on their pallets, close to the fire.

All the while, Dulcie's gaze wandered back to the loom. It wasn't long before Bea explained how it worked. She talked about her craft, how so much of a Navajo woman's heart and soul went into the making of a Navajo blanket. Austin listened and remembered Abey's grandmother saying the same things. But this time the words didn't hurt.

Maybe Dulcie was right. Talking about the good things eased the pain of the bad.

About nine o'clock, he heard voices and looked out to see two couples making their way down the trail to the ruins.

"It's time." He stood and Dulcie helped him fold and stack all the blankets.

Dulcie turned and grasped Bea's hands. "Thank you. We wouldn't have made it through the night. You saved our lives."

The old woman nodded. "Yes, it is because he is the one who will find my granddaughter and bring her home." She turned to Austin. "Do not forget. I am waiting."

Two days ago, her words would have filled Austin with guilt and trepidation. But today, thanks to Dulcie, he half believed the old woman.

And that he might make known the riches of his glory on the vessels of mercy, which he had afore prepared unto glory.

We're unique. Special and loved. Dulcie's favorite scripture and words echoed in his ears. Austin wanted to believe. He needed to. People were counting on him.

He nodded toward the old woman. "Thank you."

She nodded back at him with a half smile that made Austin think she understood everything he was thinking. He gave her another quick dip of his head and moved toward the door .

Dulcie gripped the older woman's hands and said, "May I come and visit you again?"

"Yes. Come. I'll teach you more about the weaving."

Dulcie's responding smile was beautiful. Austin could have stood by the door forever, watching her dote on the older woman. But they had a long trek ahead of them. He forced himself to turn and walk away.

Austin stepped outside to check the trail and the lookout above them before he allowed Dulcie outside. Bea stood in the door of her hogan and waved as they headed up the trail. Dulcie seemed particularly subdued. Just before they moved out of sight, Dulcie turned back and waved. When she saw Austin watching her, she gave him a shrug. "I never had a grandmother."

That thought occupied his mind for a long while during the trek up the trail. He couldn't imagine not having a grandmother. Even though his lived far away, he knew Abey's grandmother well. She used to laugh at his jokes so he saved all the corny ones to tell her. The memory pleased him.

Now that they were rested and fed, the trek up wasn't as difficult as he expected. No one met them coming down. He wished someone had. He would have liked to ask about the parking lot, how many cars and who was there. But they met no one descending, and sooner than he expected they drew near the top. As they reached a corner, he told Dulcie to pause.

"Wait here for me. I'm going to leave the trail and climb over those rocks so I can see the parking lot. If it's clear, I'll call you."

Dulcie's warm, soft hand grabbed his, made him want to linger, but she gave it a squeeze and let go. "Be careful."

He climbed the steep hillside and crept over the large boulders marking the parking lot. He lay flat and peeked over the edge. The lights of a tribal police car flashed. The vehicle was pulled up behind his Jeep and a tall, slender, familiar figure walked around it. Austin sighed with relief. Rising to his feet, he waved Dulcie up and climbed the rest of the way.

"*Ya ta he*, brother."

Cade Hatalhe paused and turned, "*Ya ta he.* It's good to see you walking around in one piece."

"You don't know how glad I am to see you too."

Cade shook his head. "We got a report of a gunshot. When I saw your Jeep, I was sure I was going to climb down there and find you with a hole in your head."

"You almost did."

"Your lieutenant has been burning up the airwaves looking for you. What kind of trouble are you in now, brother?"

Dulcie came running up. Both men turned. She'd spent the night on the dirt floor of a hogan and hid in dusty ruins and still, she looked amazing. Her russet curls shone in the early-morning sun, and her eyes were expressive and sincere as she examined Cade. Austin felt a sense of pride…that was quickly squelched when he caught Cade's speculative glance.

"Who is this?"

"Dulcie Parker, this is Deputy Cade Hatalhe from the tribal police. He's my…" Austin hesitated.

"Clan brother," Cade finished for him. "Even though my clan sister is gone, I still claim this one." He nudged his head in Austin's direction. A thankful flush of warmth washed through Austin. He didn't deserve Cade's faithfulness or affection. He'd walked away, turned his back on the people here, people who loved him, who were hurting too. He shouldn't have left. They could have shared the pain, walked the path of grief together. He felt humbled that they still wanted him back. And he owed that realization to the slim red-headed waif beside him.

"Our office got a report of two men on the trail and a gunshot early this morning. I was headed out here to talk to Bea Yazzie so I got the order to look around."

"Are you working the Yazzie girl's case?"

"Yeah, not that I'm getting very far, very fast. I've hit another dead end. Any idea who fired at you?"

"Walter Benally and Bob Carson."

Cade shook his head. "Benally. That one is trouble. I heard he was running with a man from Durango but I didn't know who. So why are they after you, brother?"

Austin trusted Cade implicitly, so he related the events that had led them to the canyon. Cade listened with an occasional shake of his head and a muted sound of frustration.

"You know if Benally is involved, Whitehorse is the one giving him direction."

Austin nodded. "I suspect Whitehorse's bar is one place the victims all have in common. They snatch the girls from different locations but I'm sure they spend time at The Round Up bar. The girls would probably recognize Carson and Benally from the bar and not be on their guard. It would make their kidnapping easier. I'm going to pay it a visit."

"So, you think Susan Yazzie didn't just run off. You think she's one of the ring's victims?"

"I think so, yes."

Cade looked away, frustration in his taut movement. "I thought she might have gotten tied up in that situation with Judy Begay and her stepfather, but once he was arrested, I believed it was over. I had no information about this ring."

"And I had no clue about Susan. The ring has been suppressing info. We've discovered that much for sure."

Cade shook his head. "This is bigger than all our departments. You need to report this to the FBI office in Farmington. We can use their resources."

"As soon as I get Dulcie someplace safe, I'm going to The Round Up."

"It's my case too. Let me help. I'll go to Whitehorse's place while you take care of Dulcie and go to the FBI. I'll put out an APB for Carson and Benally. Any idea what those men are driving?"

"No, we were already in the canyon when they arrived. But Carson's mother said he owned a white panel van. As soon as I have cell reception, I'll contact my lieutenant. See if he can't get Carson's registration. We'll get the ball rolling on our end too."

"Interdepartmental cooperation." The tall man grinned. "May be a first."

"Let's hope it's not the last. Be careful at The Round Up. You could be walking into trouble. Whitehorse and his cronies know they're suspects. There's no telling what they might do."

"I'll tread carefully" Cade patted Austin's shoulder. "In the meantime, get to Farmington. This case is crossing too many jurisdictions and we need help. Ask for Agent Bostwick. He's our contact."

"Will do."

"I'll follow you until the turnoff to Whitehorse's place. I want to make sure those two aren't waiting to ambush you on the road."

"Good idea."

Cade waved. "It was nice meeting you, Ms. Parker." He headed to his vehicle. Austin took his keys from his pocket and they loaded into his Jeep.

They pulled out of the parking lot onto the main road. When they drew closer to the highway and phone reception, Austin's phone buzzed with consistent messages. "I suspect my lieutenant has been trying to reach me." His wry tone made Dulcie smile.

He punched the connect button on his steering wheel and called McGuire. When his supervisor answered, his voice was taut. "You'd better have a good excuse for not checking in for the last twenty-four hours."

Austin shook his head. "How about getting shot at

and trapped at the bottom of a canyon? Is that a good excuse?"

McGuire made a frustrated sound. "I knew something was wrong. This shouldn't have happened. I need to know where you and Ms. Parker are at all times."

"Agreed. I won't make that mistake again."

"So what did you discover in the canyon?"

Austin filled him in on all that happened, right up to the meeting with Cade.

"Carson's mother was right. He's neck-deep in serious trouble. Listen, she also said he owned a panel van. Can you check his vehicle registration and get me a license plate ASAP? I want to get the info to Cade before he heads to Whitehorse's place."

"I'm on it now. I'll also contact the tribal police chief, and both the New Mexico and Colorado state police with the info. Your friend Cade is right. It's time to bring this case out into the open."

He clicked off and silence hung over the Jeep's cab. Austin glanced Dulcie's way and saw a small frown creasing the space between her expressive brows.

"What's wrong?"

"There are still so many unanswered questions. We don't know the leader of this group. Or where they take the girls. So many pieces of the operation are unsolved. I'd feel better if we could provide the FBI with answers…at least with the evidence I've already accumulated."

Austin shook his head. "Haven't you had enough? You've been threatened, almost kidnapped and now shot at. How much more do you want to experience before you say stop?"

"I keep thinking about those girls, about Susan Yazzie."

"It's been two months since they murdered Judy Begay. If they have Susan, she's probably been transported out of the area already."

"Maybe, but you said yourself there haven't been any more disappearances since Judy's death. Isn't it possible they stopped everything, waiting to see if Matt Kutchner would talk?"

"He hasn't. Never said a word about the ring. We didn't have a clue that there was a bigger operation going on."

"Exactly. They promised him something. I don't know what they could offer him. He'll spend the rest of his life in jail."

"That's exactly what they offered him. His life. A gang this powerful could easily arrange to have him killed in prison."

Dulcie released a heavy breath. "You're right…and they've frightened Doris Begay into silence too. We have to find the leader, Austin, and make sure we stop this gang."

"We will. Once the FBI gets involved, more resources will be at our fingertips. We'll find them."

"That's why we need to retrieve my information."

She studied him, a hopeful expression in her gaze. "You want me to take you back to my house."

"Do you think we can?"

Austin shook his head. "Aren't you afraid? We just spent the night in hiding."

A sweet smile floated over her lips, a tender, soft look that went straight to his heart. "I told you, you make everyone feel safe. You make *me* feel stronger."

He didn't like acknowledging that her words made him kind of happy, a little warm inside so he didn't answer. It wasn't long before his phone rang again. McGuire had Carson's license plate number.

"Everyone's on high alert. I made sure Deputy Hatahle's department was informed. He has the plate number too. We've got every law enforcement department in the Four Corners area looking for those two."

"Good. Since we're covered, we'd like to go back to my place and fetch all of Dulcie's info for the FBI."

"Probably not a bad idea. But with all of this gang's resources, they might have your address. I'll send Bolton up ahead of you to make sure the area is clear."

"Thanks. That makes me feel better."

"Just remember to stay in touch. The gang's game is out in the open and that will make them desperate. They'll want to escape and they won't care who they take down in the process. If I don't have constant contact from you, I'll be sending my men to find you." He clicked off.

Not long after Austin called his lieutenant, Cade flashed his lights.

"Cade is giving me the all-clear signal before he turns."

Dulcie watched as the deputy's cruiser pulled off

the main highway. "Do you think Benally and Carson were waiting for us somewhere on the road and Cade scared them away?"

"I don't know. I think it's more likely the tourists did a good job of that. Benally and Carson couldn't afford to have witnesses to our murders. Cade's backup made sure they left us alone."

Dulcie's heart hammered. "Do you really think that's what they're trying to do, murder us?"

"It might have been their intention just to frighten us away, much like Delacroix tried to do to you, but once Carson fired that shot, they had to find us. They knew if I escaped there'd be an APB on them. Firing on an officer of the law is a criminal offense I can testify about."

She eased back around in her seat. The road twisted and they left the vast plains and began to climb the hills. "I'm relieved it's out in the open now. We can go forward with the investigation. No more skulking around and hiding."

Austin lifted a one-shouldered shrug. "We still need to stay in the shadows. You heard McGuire. They're desperate now. Carson and Benally will be on the run. There's no telling what risks they might take and the rest of the gang will cover their tracks, making sure none of the evidence leads to them."

"Surely they can't expect to keep their activities a secret. We know what they're doing."

"Yes, but we only have suspicions. We don't have one shred of evidence that will stand up in court. We'll be able to identify Carson and Benally, but neither of us can say for sure who fired the shot or what connection they have to the missing girls. All we did was drive Carson and Benally to desperate measures."

Everything Austin said was true. Dulcie wanted to argue, but she couldn't. His words only confirmed her deep-seated need to get back to her research. "Maybe we pushed them out into the open, but we also have more pieces of the puzzle. I suspect that Vonetta uses her position to identify thc at-risk girls. Joey Delacroix proved himself a good soldier by keeping an eye on me. He probably also used his position with the city to suppress information about the crimes. Deputy Shaw loses reports and convolutes the already difficult communication between law enforcement agencies. Whitehorse's men do all the dirty work and kidnap the victims. But once they've been taken, Whitehorse wouldn't be foolish enough to hold them at his place of business, would he?"

Austin shook his head. "He's a snake, but he's not stupid."

"Do you think they transport them to their destination immediately?"

Austin was silent as he considered. "They take them from all over the Four Corners area, but the kidnappings happened at relatively frequent times. They wouldn't have time to transport them individually between snatches. I think there has to be a holding place of some sort."

"Or places. They'd have to move them around. That's the connection I have to find. I'm sure that will take us straight to their leader."

He gave her a quick sideways glance…then another.

She studied him. “What?”

“We’re hours away from pulling in all the FBI’s resources, but you still feel like you’re the one who has to do something.”

She didn’t know what to say to that.

A soft smile slipped over his lips.

“Never leave a woman or child behind, even when your own life is threatened, right?”

“Unless I get frightened and can’t move…like you said.”

“Dulcie, I’m sorry. I was angry. I don’t handle talking about Abey very well. Honestly, I admire your devotion.”

“But…”

“But nothing. Just believe what I say.”

Despite his words, she knew there was an add-on to that statement. She felt the need to help, to do something, to take action. But every time the chips were down she became a prisoner of her own body. She didn’t understand it. The Lord had led her out of her horrible situation, had helped her grow and find some peace. So why did He let this start again? Why did He allow the fear to control her? Was He trying to teach her something more? Was there something else she needed to understand?

Please, Lord, make me understand. Let me know what You want of me.

No answers came to her and so they drove silently into the mountains, straight into the dark clouds ahead of them. They climbed the foothills beside Mesa Verde and snowflakes started to fall. The streets of Durango were wet and slushy, piled high with the fallen snow from the day before. The drastic climate change between the desert floor and the mountain community surprised Dulcie. Once again, she marveled at this unique corner of God's creation. By the time they reached Austin's home, the snowfall was steadily increasing. She was glad when they finally pulled to a stop at the cabin. Officer Bolton was waiting for them. He came to Austin's window. "Everything's clear. No sign of anyone. Not even tracks in the snow when I first arrived."

"Thanks, Bolton."

The man waved and headed back to his car. Austin parked his Jeep near the walkway and they hurried inside. Austin rubbed his hands together and gave her that soft, rueful smile. "I still only have frozen pizza. I can microwave that and some coffee while you gather your files. We need to get back on the road as soon as possible."

That smile wrapped itself around her heart and tugged. She couldn't stop from responding to it. How could she? He was apologizing for his home and his lack of hospitality when all she wanted was to curl up on the couch and stay forever. His home made her comfortable…he made her comfortable.

How had she come to this place? She'd found a man who gave her hope, made her want to walk beside him, to sit with him in front of his fire and fight the bad guys. He made her feel like they could do anything, be partners for life, fight the good fight. They could be the dynamic duo crime fighters. The thought made her smile too. But this wonderful, handsome lawman deserved a true warrior, a strong woman like his wife, not the weak, frightened shell she turned into when faced with her fears. He wanted…was holding out for that kind of woman.

That thought made her turn away from his kind features and his soft smile. "Sure. That sounds good."

"Move as quickly as you can. We need to get back on the road."

She hurried up the stairs, not daring to look back, or to dwell on the image of the two of them on the couch in front of the fire eating pizza. It was too good of an image to hold on to. She couldn't afford to keep those kinds of images. They would make letting go of him even more difficult.

She slid her computer and her notes in her case and pulled the bag's strap over her shoulder. The smell of pizza drifted up to her. A glance in the mirror showed her that her night in the damp air had turned her hair into a frizzy, wild mane. But she didn't have time to mess with it. Pulling the strap higher, she headed downstairs.

Austin walked toward her, travel mugs in one hand and a foil-wrapped paper plate with pizzas in the other.

His thoughtfulness…everything he did pleased her, made her smile. "Pizza and hot coffee? Perfect."

He gestured to the door. "If you take this plate, I'll carry your satchel."

He stepped in closer to hand over the food. Reaching up, she tried to gather her untamed hair into a knot.

"Don't do that."

She halted. His blue-eyed gaze covered her hair with a look so possessive...so loving, her breath caught. She felt beautiful and worthy in all the right ways. He was close, so close his lips were inches away. He leaned closer. This...this was what it was like to be wanted by this man...to be treasured by him. She needed more of that feeling, craved his kiss, his lips on hers. Then the look faded. That was the moment he remembered the woman between them, the woman she could never match.

He stepped back, looked away and cleared his throat. "It doesn't suit you. You don't need some kind of 'uniform' to hide the real you."

Handing her the plate, he then spun and stalked to the door. Dulcie's knees gave out and she almost slumped to the couch.

His words still echoed inside her. He didn't really see her now, frizzy hair and all. He saw the woman she could be.

That thought pleased her. She could be that person. She might never have this man or be worthy of him, but she would become the woman he thought she could be. She would make it her goal. With new resolve, she followed him to the door.

Austin's cell phone rang. He punched the speaker button with his thumb as he opened the door. "I've got my hands full so you are on speaker but we're on our way."

McGuire's deep voice echoed across the room. "Sit down, Austin, I have more bad news."

He froze and turned to face her.

McGuire's loud voice pierced the air between them. "Cade's been shot. He was attacked shortly after he arrived at The Round Up. There was a gunfight and he was hit. He's being air vacced to the hospital as we speak."

Dulcie cried out. Austin closed his eyes in frustration. "I knew I shouldn't have let him go alone."

"Apparently he saw Carson's white van as soon as he arrived and called for backup. He didn't go in alone. But they attacked him before reinforcements arrived."

"How bad is it?"

"Pretty bad. I'm heading to the hospital now."

Emotions washed across Austin's face, fear, anger and then frustration. She knew exactly what he was feeling. He was stuck here with her when he wanted to be at Cade's side. "We can go. I'll go with you."

He gave his head an abrupt shake. "We can't risk exposing you to the gang."

McGuire heard their conversation because he said, "Actually, that's the only good news I have for you. Cade's backup arrived shortly after he was shot. They took three men into custody. Benally, Carson and Whitehorse are in handcuffs. Their rampage is over."

Relief washed through Dulcie. "You have to go, Austin. You need to be by Cade's side."

McGuire spoke again. "I've contacted the FBI. Their men are on the way from Farmington. But I'll send Bolton back up there to watch over Dulcie until they arrive."

Emotions battled on Austin's face, so Dulcie took the decision out of his hands. She gently pulled the phone from his hand. "Thank you, Lieutenant McGuire. I would appreciate Officer Bolton's presence."

"I'll send him back. He just arrived. He'll be there in thirty minutes. But Austin needs to get going."

The lieutenant clicked off. Austin stood there motionless, his body frozen stiff with indecision.

Dulcie gestured to the door. "Go. Your clan brother needs you. I'll stay here and find the link I've been looking for. I want to have all my information ready when the FBI men arrive. We'll get them, Austin. I promise."

He nodded. Maybe he saw conviction in her features because he believed her, the woman he secretly thought was soft and weak. He seemed to understand that she would give every breath in her body to find the link…and she would…for the sake of the captive women and for this man. His unspoken confidence in her made her feel special, strong…wonderful. For one breathless moment, he leaned toward her. Again, she thought he would kiss her. She wanted him to kiss her. But he straightened and walked to the door, leaving her feeling cold and alone.

"Don't open this for anyone except Bolton. He'll be here soon."

EIGHT

Snow was falling hard and wind whipped his vehicle sideways. Visibility was difficult on the icy roads. In all honesty, he should call McGuire and tell him to send Bolton home. This storm was getting too nasty to drive in. But the truth was he didn't want to stop. He wanted to get as far from Dulcie as possible because he was feeling things he didn't want to feel...like admiration and tenderness. He didn't want to remember how her dark eyes and sweet lips softened when he looked at her, how each time she opened up like a soft rose unfurling. A copper rose.

He shook his head. Those kinds of thoughts should be reserved for his wife. So, he ran from Dulcie and the things she made him feel. Yes, he wanted to be by Cade's side, but truthfully, he was running from his emotions.

He never thought he'd want another woman...a woman who was as different as night and day from Abey.

How could this have happened? How could he have

let it happen? He stared at the white sheet of snow in front of him. The storm was slowing him down, making his trip worse. The vehicles he encountered crawled along the road. Bolton would surely be delayed and Dulcie would be alone. That thought chased away all others.

He wouldn't…couldn't leave Dulcie abandoned no matter how he felt. He had to stop running.

Punching the phone connection on his console, he called McGuire. "Tell Bolton to stay put. This storm is getting worse. It's too dangerous to travel up the mountain, and I can't leave Dulcie stranded. Keep me informed about Cade."

"I was just about to call you. Those two men we arrested who identified themselves as Benally and Carson lied. They had no ID on them, so it took a while to confirm. They're not the two we're looking for. They're Whitehorse's flunkies who gave the deputies those names to fool them and give Carson and Benally time to get away. They escaped in one of Whitehorse's vehicles…a white single-cab truck. We got the call out to search and it was spotted almost immediately. They were passing through Durango but they lost the cruiser following them."

An icy certainty settled over Austin. "They're headed up here. I'm going back to Dulcie."

"Be careful." McGuire's voice was taut with concern. "We just got notification to shut down the roads. We've had hourly bulletins and the storm has turned from bad to worse. Hopefully, we'll stop Carson and Benally at the roadblock."

"Unless they got through already."

McGuire was silent for a long while. "I'll repeat myself. Be careful. They know we're onto them. They'll do whatever it takes to keep the evidence out of our hands."

"I'll stay in touch."

Austin waited for a truck to pass then turned around slowly. The road was slushy but starting to get slick. He'd made the right decision returning to Dulcie. It wouldn't be long before this road would be impassable.

He slowed as he hit a curve. Lights far behind him flashed as he turned the corner. He was a bit surprised someone was on the road. He would have thought the roadblocks McGuire and the deputies implemented would have stopped all traffic coming out of Durango. The vehicle made him nervous, but the snow increased and he needed to concentrate on the curves. Next time he looked up, the lights were closer. The vehicle was definitely white. He couldn't tell the make. The snow was blinding and it was still too far away. He took the next curve faster than he wanted but he needed distance between him and the white car.

Despite his best efforts, the car gained on him… which told him the driver was moving faster than he should on this slick road. Moments later, it caught up. It was a white single-cab truck. Because of his angle of view, he couldn't see the face of the driver but he didn't need to. Only desperate men would drive the way they were in this storm.

He hit a straightaway on the road and the truck sped up so fast, it pulled up beside him in the lane of the oncoming traffic. Now he could clearly see two figures inside. Benally and Carson. He jammed on the gas and his Jeep shot forward. But the bigger engine of the vehicle easily caught up to him.

If they kept this up, he'd never be able to get far enough ahead to secure the house. Maybe he should go past his home, try to draw them away.

No, they could double back and find the house on their own. His best option was to slow them down, somehow disable their vehicle.

It wouldn't be difficult. The snow was coming down so hard, visibility was almost zero. Whatever he was going to do had to happen soon. They were coming up on a stretch of road with twists and turns and a nonexistent shoulder between the road and the guardrail. But what could he do? How could he slow them without risking his own safety? Maybe he could block the road and hold them off until help could arrive. It was the only way to keep Dulcie safe.

He lifted his foot off the accelerator and slowed to a crawl. He just needed an open space to turn his Jeep around without spinning on the slick road.

The truck zoomed up so fast, Austin didn't have time to turn around. He pressed the accelerator again, determined to get out of the path of the oncoming vehicle. But the white truck kept coming, close enough to see Benally in the driver's seat and Carson on the passenger side. Benally crossed into the path of oncoming traffic and pulled up beside Austin's vehicle. Then the man jerked his wheel and bumped the side of Austin's

Jeep, pushing him toward the edge. He was trying to shove him off the road just like Delacroix!

Austin manhandled the swerving vehicle back onto the road and jammed on the accelerator. He sped forward through another curve, barely keeping his Jeep on the icy road. Another bump like that and he might spin out.

He had to keep his distance. He sped down the road but the truck followed. Only a few feet of space separated the two cars running down the slick road at fifty miles an hour. If either of them lost control, they'd crash. With his eyes on his rearview mirror, Austin watched the white vehicle gain on him once again. He pressed the accelerator all the way to the floor. The Jeep barreled ahead putting a few more feet between them but not much.

"Idiots! We're going to crash." He mumbled the words out loud and realized that's exactly what Benally intended. He and Carson had nothing to lose. This was their last gambit. Their operation was broken. Whitehorse was arrested. Cade might not survive to testify against them. Austin and Dulcie were their only other witnesses. The criminals were going to make sure the two of them didn't live. They intended to kill him first, right here on the road.

Any hope of escape or slowing them down flew out the window. Gripping the wheel, he focused on the black strip of highway rapidly disappearing beneath the onslaught of the snowstorm. Surviving the next few miles would take all his concentration. His cell phone rang. He couldn't answer it and didn't even have time to wonder about who was calling. The ringing cut off, as if he'd lost reception. Probably because of the storm. The icy road was ahead of him. A curve was coming.

Please, Lord.

He barely had time to send up the words before he was leaning into the turn and slipping…sliding to the edge of the drop-off. At the last minute, his wheels caught and pulled him up the hill. Straight into the next curve.

He took a quick breath and looked in his mirror. The truck made the turn too, sliding into the other lane of traffic. Veering into that lane again helped Benally close the distance Austin had gained. Benally's vehicle took the curve better than Austin's lighter Jeep and closed on him. Austin pulled into the other lane, praying officers had stopped the oncoming traffic. He sent up another prayer as he hit the next curve and slid once again. This time the side of his car skimmed the guardrail. Sparks flashed in the dark air as metal ground against metal.

He glanced back. The heavier white vehicle took the corner better again, not even coming close to the rail. It gained more mileage, driving up so quickly, Austin was sure it would hit his bumper. He took his eyes off the mirror. The next curve came upon him fast. He barely had time to turn into it. He released the gas pedal, hoping to slow. He felt his vehicle sliding and suddenly… the truck bumped him from the back.

It was all the impetus his slipping Jeep needed. He slid across the road, broke through the guardrail, flew off and hurtled down a short, flat incline to the side of the mountain and a hundred foot drop-off.

Long after Austin left, Dulcie's mind kept wandering back, remembering the look in his eyes, the one that made her feel beautiful. She could see the shape of his lips, still feel the yearning to touch them with her own. The way he leaned in…and then the shuttering of his feelings. The cold remembrance of a woman Dulcie could never match.

That's what had stopped him from kissing her. He remembered Abey, her strength, her compassion. Dulcie could never match that, could never be that woman. She didn't even want to try anymore. But it felt good to know his feelings for her were strong. That she almost made him forget. That gave her hope for another man and a future. It wouldn't be Austin. She knew that. She also knew she would always compare any man to Austin. But at least now she had the knowledge that she was capable of love, that a man could ignite those feelings and she could respond. There was a time when she thought that wasn't possible. She would always be grateful to Austin for protecting her and awakening her womanly emotions, for making it feel safe to love and be loved.

But there were other women who were not safe, who needed protection. That's what Dulcie should concentrate on now, finding the location of Susan and the other missing women. The gang had to have a holding place. But where?

Rocky Mountain Dreams… Pierce's real estate company. Austin told her that Carson's mother said Pierce had handled the sale of her home. She said he was representing property all over the mountain. Could that be the answer? Was Pierce finding different locations all over the mountain, multiple places to move the girls from one to another? It made sense.

She pulled up the real estate sales and searched through the listings. Rocky Mountain Dreams had facilitated ten sales in the last month. There were six residential homes, two retail businesses in town and two pieces of property without buildings. She looked up the first one and clicked on the satellite app to get a visual. It was hard to see through the pine trees, but there were no buildings on that property or the other.

Next she looked up the retail buildings. They were smack-dab in the middle of downtown Silverton. Even though they were large vacant buildings, neither place was a good location for holding women as prisoners. They were far too visible.

Frustrated, she made herself a mug of hot chocolate. The wind kicked up and howled. It sounded like the storm had turned into a blizzard. She thought of Austin traveling down the mountain and wanted to call but first, she wanted to have good information, something positive for him to hang on to as he watched Cade fight for his life.

Settling down on the sofa again, she pulled up the satellite photos of the remaining six homes Pierce's company had sold. Each of them had buildings, cabins or larger houses…making them viable locations to hide victims. But how could they know which one?

Would they just walk up, knock on the door and start asking questions?

She dug deeper, looking for the buyers of each property. A company called Equine Properties purchased two of them. Satellite images showed that both locations had smaller cabins with no outlying buildings, something like what Austin found on the Carson property. More suitable to hunting or weekend places rather than homes. Interesting.

Equine Properties' website listed itself as a small renovation company, ready to buy fixer-uppers. There was another blurb about turning renovations into dream vacation homes. But when she went to look up the owners, she found nothing.

"Who are you, Equine Properties?" Saying the name out loud made something click.

Wait…equine meant horses. Could Whitehorse be Equine Properties? She opened files in the county clerk's office and found nothing. She dug deeper and finally found the registration DBA for Equine Properties. Owner and sole proprietor… John Whitehorse.

Dulcie leaped to her feet and whooped. "I got you, you snake! I got you!"

This was the evidence they were searching for, enough proof to fill out a search warrant for the cabins. She wrote the addresses of the two locations on a sheet of notepaper. Snatching up her phone, she dialed Austin's number.

It rang and rang until his voice mail clicked on. "Austin, I have the link. Whitehorse has a shell company buying property around Silverton from Pierce.

They're working together! Two of the places look like the Carson cabin you described to me, and I've written down their addresses. I'm sure they're using those places to hide their victims. I hope that's enough probable cause for a search warrant... Okay. Call me when you get this."

She hung up. In the sudden silence, the storm howled. It was terrible and Austin was driving in it. For the first time a tingle of fear climbed up her spine. She hurried up the stairs to the loft to look out. All she could see through the window was a sheet of snow, falling so fast she could barely make out the trees around the property. Austin was outside...in this? Had he made it down the mountain?

Her heart stopped. *Will he make it back up to me? Am I stranded?*

The blood pounded in her temples as she ran downstairs to check the weather on the internet, but she couldn't connect. The storm had knocked out the internet. She tried her cell phone reception. Nothing. She was all alone in a blizzard. Panic started to sweep through her. Suddenly, the sound of a car engine made her pause. Had Deputy Bolton arrived?

She ran upstairs again to look down on the yard. A white truck she didn't recognize pulled to a stop in front of the house. Definitely not the deputy. Two men in dark clothing stepped out. She couldn't see their faces, but she saw enough to know they were strangers.

Panic surged through her and she ran back downstairs. There was no knock on the door or calling out. Instead, gunfire exploded and hit the door. The solid wood splintered, sending pieces across the room. Dulcie screamed and dove for the couch.

They had to be members of the gang and they were here to get her. They concentrated their shots around the dead bolt. They were shooting out the lock! Any minute they'd be inside. She looked around desperately searching for somewhere to hide. There was no place. No nook or cranny. Just Austin's wide-open home, the place she'd loved from the minute she saw it. Now it would be her trap.

Her notes! She needed to hide her notes. Most likely they'd take her to one of the locations she'd just discovered. Austin needed to know where to find her. Her mind stumbled at the thought. But what if they had no intention of kidnapping her? What if they meant to kill her? Her heart banged in her chest for one long moment before clarity came to her.

If they killed her, then Austin needed the evidence to stop them. She ripped the note off the pad and stuffed it under the sofa cushion just as the metal dead bolt flew out of the door and across the room.

A large hand reached in through the hole and turned the lock on the handle. The door slammed open. Two men stepped inside and marched toward her. Numbness crept over her. Everything slipped into slow motion. She wanted to scream. Wanted to turn and run…somewhere…anywhere. But she couldn't move. Couldn't make a sound as one of them grabbed her arm and shook her.

"Good thing you're making it easy for us," one of them ground out. "After all the trouble you've caused,

I wasn't of a mind to be nice." He had sandy hair and light-colored eyes.

The other man had darker coloring. "You just gonna stand there and let us take you?"

Dulcie didn't answer, couldn't. She was paralyzed but her mind still raced. She recognized the raspy voice they heard echoing in the ruins at Canyon de Chelly. This man was Benally.

He spun her around. Something tight and sharp pulled her hands together. She heard the distinctive zip of a plastic tie. "Maybe you don't fight 'cause you think Deputy Turner is coming to your rescue."

The sandy-haired man laughed. "Yeah, Benally. That's what she thinks. Why she's not even moving."

How did Carson and Benally escape the Navajo police custody? She wanted to ask, thought the words, even tried to shape them with her lips, but still, she was paralyzed.

Benally shoved her bound arms, turned her around to face him and pulled her close. His dark eyes glinted with something cold and cruel. "Let me take care of that right now. Turner isn't coming. Not now. Not ever. We pushed his car off a cliff into a canyon where if they ever find him, he'll be crammed so tight in that tin-can Jeep of his, they won't know where he ends and the metal begins."

For the first time since they'd entered, Dulcie was able to make a sound. She whimpered a mournful cry. Then her knees gave out. Benally caught her and threw her over his shoulder. Carson laughed all the way out the door.

NINE

Austin's Jeep landed with a bone-jarring thud. His airbag exploded in his face, momentarily stunning him. But the vehicle didn't stop. It was still rolling down the flat incline toward the drop-off. He couldn't see what was ahead, but he knew there was a hundred-foot cliff at the end of his slide. If he didn't get out, he'd be hurtling over it too. He gripped the steering wheel. Through the side window, snow flew by as his Jeep continued to plow through the deep drifts. They slowed his momentum but still, he needed to stop or get out before his Jeep reached the cliff.

Struggling against the airbag, he tried to touch his seat belt. Suddenly, the vehicle dipped into a ditch and lurched to a stop. Austin jerked forward but stayed cushioned by the seat belt and the airbag.

He sat motionless for a moment or two. His chest hurt from his slam into the seat belt. A corner of his neck burned where the belt had sliced him. But he had stopped and he was alive.

The nose of his Jeep was pointing downward. He

could hear the hissing of his hot engine melting the snow. At least he hoped that was the hissing sound.

Please God, don't let the engine be damaged. But the most important thing was that he was no longer headed toward the cliff. He leaned his head back against the seat and took a deep breath.

Thank You, Lord. Thank You.

Relief swept over him and a thousand unrelated thoughts jumbled his mind. He was glad to be alive. A few months ago, he didn't want to live. He'd wished for the numbness of death, but now…now he wanted to live. Dulcie's lovely, distinctive image with those dark eyes and wild hair flashed into his mind. How could he have ever thought she wasn't attractive?

She was unique. Tender but strong in her own way. She wasn't a warrior like Abey, but she was a capable fighter. She battled her way through her fears. Conquered her own desire to hide and pushed forward every time…even when *he* wanted to run away. She was special. He should have told her so and held her close when she trembled. He wished he'd kissed her when he left her at the cabin…and at the ruins. Instead, he'd criticized her. Said hurtful things and made her feel less than she was.

Please, Lord, give me the chance to tell her how I really feel. Let me show her how much she amazes me.

His thoughts came to a stuttering halt. Benally and Carson had just pushed him off the cliff. Now no one stood between Dulcie and those animals. He had to get on the road and back to her!

Galvanized into action, he released the seat belt. He

couldn't move with the airbag. He needed to cut it open, but he couldn't reach his pocket knife. The engine had stalled, but the key was still in the ignition. He shut it off and pulled out the key. Positioning it between his knuckles, he punched the key into the airbag holes at the bottom to enlarge them. It took three punches before the key finally pierced and deflated the bag. When he could move, he pushed on the door.

Cold, fresh air rushed in, but he couldn't open it more. The depth and weight of the snow he'd plowed through was piled against it and had it jammed. Finally, free of the airbag, he shoved the seat back. The extra room gave him the space to turn and push both feet against the door. It swung wide and he tumbled out, landing in the soft snow. He lay for a moment, letting the flakes fall on his face, once more thanking the Lord for his safety.

But he had to get going. He climbed to his feet and hurried to the front of his Jeep. The ditch he'd slid into wasn't deep. Apparently, the snow had slowed his descent enough so that the dip stopped his momentum. His bumper was crushed, but it looked as if his engine was intact.

Looking back up the slight incline, he could see that his Jeep had made a clear path for about twenty feet down. Snow was plowed away, down to black dirt in places, enough solid earth to give him traction. The guardrail where he came off the road lay broken and spread out over the boulders of the drop-off. It wasn't much of an incline, just about six feet, and a rough enough landing to trigger his airbag. But the four-wheel drive of his Jeep could make the climb up the incline to the road…if he could get it started and out of the ditch.

His legs wavered slightly as he realized how close he'd come to dropping to the bottom. But the Lord had been merciful. Now if he could just get his engine running again…

He ran to the back of the Jeep and pulled a hammer out of the toolbox. He pounded the plastic dash to break it open and release the airbag. After pulling it loose, he tossed the apparatus to the snow, climbed back in and put the key into the ignition.

Please, Lord.

The engine turned over. Laughing with relief, he shifted his four-wheel drive into Reverse and slowly gave it gas. The vehicle shifted but slid back into place. He sped up again. This time the car moved very little and mud flew back behind the Jeep.

The wheels were spinning, not catching in the slick mud and snow. The Jeep needed traction to pull out of the ditch. He looked around. About ten feet away, a snag, a dead tree trunk, stuck its ragged edges up to the sky. Maybe he could get enough wood or bark off the trunk to give his wheels the gripping power they needed.

Grabbing his shovel from the toolbox, he slogged his way through the snow and dug around the tree. The trunk was old and weathered enough that he could pull bark and strips of wood loose and carry them back to the Jeep. All the while, a ticking clock counted off the minutes in his head.

Fifteen minutes from this location to his house. Another ten to break in. Benally and Carson were already at his house. How long could Dulcie hold out against them?

He refused to let his mind answer the question. Instead, he stepped up his pace. At last he thought he had enough bark and wood beneath all four tires. He jumped behind the wheel and turned over the ignition. His Jeep lurched and climbed slowly out of the ditch. When its nose pulled out, he let out a shout of relief.

But he still had to climb back up the hillside and over the rocky embankment. It wasn't steep but the snow continued to fall as the temperature dropped. Even now the spots of solid ground he'd seen were covered with snow and probably icing over.

Slowly but surely, he drove over his path of descent. He was aware of every second passing and the knowledge that if his Jeep slipped again, the ditch might not stop him. He could still slide over the edge of the cliff. He refused to let that thought take hold. Reversing over his trajectory took all of his concentration.

He reached his last hurdle…the rocky edge of the road's embankment. Moving even slower, he inched up. His tires hit the rocks and spun and spun. He released the sway bar and tried again. Finally, one rear wheel caught and climbed. He gunned the engine and pushed the transmission.

"Come on, old girl. I know you can do it."

His murmured words seemed to work. One wheel climbed over the bottom rocks, giving him more traction. Slowly, rock by rock, he bumped upward. All four wheels eventually worked their way over the rugged incline until he struck gravel at the edge of the road.

His back wheels spun again, kicking up mud and gravel but this time, his front wheels were on hard rock and pushed him. He angled the Jeep, hoping one rear tire would catch the asphalt and pull him completely off the muddy gravel. Metal screeched as the edge of the broken guardrail scraped along the side of his Jeep, but he didn't change his angle. As the last wheel slid over the rocks and the vehicle banged downward, his back tire hit pavement.

This time Austin let out a whoop as he pulled onto the highway. He grabbed his Stetson from the backseat where the airbag had knocked it, settled it in place then slammed the shifter into Drive. "Hang on, Dulcie! I'm coming!"

The numbness paralyzing Dulcie left in one long shiver. Her senses returned with an awareness of cold. She lay on the floor of the truck. Her hands were bound behind her. She had no coat. Carson and Benally had not bothered to cover her after they dumped her on the floor. They had the heater turned up but very little reached her. It all seemed to be coming out of the upper air vents. Shock began to wear off and her whole body trembled and shook with cold and fear.

Closing her eyes, she took several deep breaths and silently prayed.

Help me, Lord. Strengthen me. I let these men take me without a word. I didn't even cry out. I have to do something. No one else will come. Austin is dead.

Pain washed through Dulcie. Kind, strong but sensitive Austin was gone. That thought made her want to cry out. Losing such a vital, wonderful man hurt her more than she could bear. She felt like screaming in protest. Maybe even yelling at God.

Why did You let this happen? Why didn't You take me instead? He is so worthy...so wonderful. The world needs men like him!

She stifled a sob and let the tears fall. After a long while, her favorite scripture came to her.

And that he might make known the riches of his glory on the vessels of mercy, which he had afore prepared unto glory.

She didn't feel prepared for glory. She felt lost. Forgotten.

Why did You bring this man into my life to open my heart and then allow him to be taken away? Austin was right. You don't care.

More tears streamed down her cheeks but her hands were tied. She couldn't wipe them away, so she buried her face in the corner of the floorboard and silently cried.

Drained and empty, she lay there, her face hidden, her hands tingling from the tight bonds and her heart broken. In the emptiness of her soul, Carson and Benally's conversation drifted toward her.

"We can't transport all of them in this truck. The cops are probably lookin' for it."

All of *them*? Did that mean they still had some of the kidnapped women under their control?

"As soon as we get to Silverton, I'll drop you off at the cabin and get us a new vehicle."

Were they taking her to one of the cabins belonging to Whitehorse? She'd left the locations of the cabins on that note hidden beneath the cushions of Austin's couch.

But Austin was dead. It would take days for anyone to find the note…if ever.

"That chick Susan… Her broken arm will slow us down."

Susan was alive!

Benally's gravelly voice rumbled across the cab. "She won't slow us down for long. We'll get rid of her first chance we get."

Dulcie's heart pounded. They were going to kill Susan.

"Pierce won't like it if we dump her here in his hometown. He likes the operation kept far away from him."

"He won't have a choice. The operation is blown. He'll have to find us a vehicle or he'll be just as exposed as we are. He won't want that, and I guarantee you, if I go down, he'll go down with me."

Dulcie's heart stopped. Pierce *was* the head of the organization. She'd just heard it with her own ears and it became the proof they needed. But what good was that? She was as dead as Austin. To be a witness, she had to live…had to escape. But how?

Despair swept over her again. She felt bereft, abandoned.

Lord, I could use some of the riches You speak of in

Your words. I claim Your promise! Show me a way to save these women... Please... Austin gave his life for them. Let me do this for him.

Fresh tears spilled out as Austin's smiling image flashed in her mind.

At that moment, the truck slid sideways. Carson cursed as Benally struggled with the wheel and they continued to slide. At last, the vehicle stopped and jerked back onto the asphalt.

Carson cursed again. "The sooner we get off this road, the better."

"Relax. The cabin's just a few miles ahead."

Carson's grunt of disapproval was his only response, and Benally didn't sound as confident as his words indicated. The storm had shaken both men…and maybe that was the answer.

Maybe this storm was the hand of God disrupting these men's plans. Perhaps their fear and struggles would give her an opportunity.

Faith means believing when all else has failed.

Senses that had been dulled by fear and hopelessness woke and tingled with awareness. *Please, Lord. Help my faith. Give me courage.*

The vehicle slid again and both men jerked. Benally cursed as he struggled with the wheel once more and Carson grasped the handhold above him while the other pressed against the dash. They tried to hide it, but both of these cruel, dangerous men were frightened. They had done horrible things—beaten people, kidnapped women, murdered one young girl and Austin—and yet, here they were, terrified by this storm.

They were just as susceptible to the hand of God as she was…maybe more so because they didn't know or have His promise to cling to. So why had she become paralyzed with fear when they walked in the door of Austin's home?

She didn't know. Couldn't remember. She only knew she believed the Lord's promise now and she would watch and wait. Her moment was coming.

Benally pulled off the highway onto a dirt road. Dulcie felt and heard the soft crunch of heavy snow as they drove over the thick snowdrifts on the side of the highway. They traveled into the depths of the silent white forest for what seemed like hours but was probably only minutes.

"At last," Carson murmured.

With her hands behind her back, Dulcie couldn't rise enough to look out the windshield at what lay ahead of them, but Benally pulled the truck to a stop. Both men opened their car doors and a blast of frigid air flew inside, causing Dulcie to shiver.

Benally disappeared. Carson opened the door, grabbed her feet and dragged her out. She stood on weak legs that wobbled and threatened to collapse. Carson didn't give her a moment to gain her balance before he pulled her around the door into the full force of the wind. Snow like sharp pellets hit her face and snatched her breath. She turned her head away. Carson shoved her toward the cabin's door. Light flared in the dark interior. She tripped on the porch steps. Carson caught her upright and pushed her forward. She stumbled into a cabin almost as cold as outside. Carson slammed the door behind him.

To her left, Benally shoved wood into a freestanding iron stove. In the opposite corner, five women huddled beneath a single blanket. Dulcie's breath caught. She couldn't see clearly in the shadows, but she was fairly certain the woman in the center, cradling her arm against her, was Susan Yazzie. She recognized her from the photos she'd seen.

Carson shoved her toward the women. A thin metal chain ran under the blanket and was attached to a hook in the wall. All the women skittered away as Carson came closer. Their blanket covering shifted. Dulcie realized that the chain ran through bands around each woman's ankle, looped back and through the hook on the wall. A lock secured the chain ends together.

Her captor shoved her toward the women. "Sit down."

The women made room for her, huddling closer together. All of them were thin, their hair matted with grease and dirt. A few had bruises on their faces. Susan's arm was bent at an awkward angle, definitely broken. A dirty white tank top braced the arm and was tied around her neck. She looked uncomfortable and her features seemed permanently settled into a frown of pain.

Susan had been missing for almost two months. Dulcie had no idea how long the other women had been captives. But they were all in bad shape. She started to speak but Susan shook her head in an almost imperceptible movement.

Benally slammed the iron door of the stove closed. Flames appeared through the cracks of the old-fashioned potbellied stove and soon, heat drifted toward them. One woman groaned with relief and leaned toward it. She quickly squelched the sound and sent a sharp glance in the men's direction, but neither one reacted. They seemed preoccupied.

"I need to get on the road." Benally's damaged voice grated across the room. "Come with me to the truck and get their food. After I'm gone, you can let them loose and feed them."

Carson nodded and followed him out. As soon as the door closed behind them Susan whispered, "Is it really you, Ms. Parker? I wasn't sure with your hair down like that. You look so different."

The thought of Austin and his words brought the hurt flooding to the surface again. She pinched her lips against the pain, then said, "I've been told that. But how do you know me? We've never met."

The young woman looked down, her features gripped in pain. "Judy talked about you all the time. Sometimes I waited in the car outside the clinic for her to finish her appointments. You always walked her and her mother to the door and stood there and waved. Like you were their friend. I always thought that was really nice. Judy deserved someone nice."

Dulcie gripped Susan's free hand. "You were with her when she died, weren't you?"

Her features flicked to angry life. "She didn't die. They murdered her. Her stepfather led us right to them. We never suspected he was a part of them. They paid him money. Cash for his own stepdaughter. She was so angry when she saw him take the wad of money, she ran at him. He said horrible things to her, called her names. She clawed his face and he pushed her off the cliff. Just pushed her off like she was a bag of trash or something. Benally and Carson were furious when Kutchner did that. Said he'd cost them money, so they wanted his payment back. Kutchner refused so they started fighting, throwing punches. I got shoved to the side and landed on a huge rock." She lifted her arm slightly. "That's how I got this. They beat Kutchner up and left him there, on the side of the mountain without a ride." She shook her head. "They should have pushed him off too."

"He's in jail, Susan. My friend Deputy Turner arrested him. His trial starts soon."

Susan sighed. "At least he's off the streets. We knew they were lying low and hiding." She nudged her chin to the door where Carson and Benally had exited. "Someone was going to take us away from here days ago but they refused to pick us up. They said it was too dangerous. After that, Benally and Carson moved us twice, from one cabin to another and now back here. We figured someone was looking for us. We hoped they would come..." Her words dropped off into empty silence.

Dulcie looked at the other women. She didn't recognize any of them. She would have thought at least one or two would have shown up in the police reports. Shaw had done a great job of keeping the reports stifled. Five women, from different places, with different looks: three brunettes, one blond and one redhead like Dulcie. All of them with varying ages. One looked as young as fifteen. Dulcie's rage increased. "They've kept all of you like this for two months?"

The women nodded. Susan spoke again. She seemed to be their spokeswoman. "We thought…hoped that all the moving meant the police were close. But now…" She stared at Dulcie. "Now that they've snatched you right off the streets, what hope do we have?"

She shook her head. "I wasn't just snatched, Susan. I was investigating the disappearances and got too close. They came after to me to shut me up, but the sheriff's department knows all about this ring. They…"

The door opened. Benally walked in. All the girls stiffened. Frustrated, Dulcie stopped talking and turned to face the man. He carried a large case of water bottles with boxes stacked on top. He set them on the table then pulled a handgun out of his jacket.

Dulcie shouldn't have been surprised but she was. She knew they had a gun because they'd shot the lock out of Austin's door. But when they'd taken her, they had not used a weapon. They didn't need one. She'd just stood frozen while they bound her and dragged her away. She looked at the frightened, haggard girls sitting around her and promised herself that would not happen again.

"Move back, girls." Carson gestured them away from the ring on the wall. They scooted as far back as the chain would allow. He opened the lock and they slipped free of the chain. They moved apart and tried to stretch their limbs.

Carson palmed his gun in one hand and with the other, lifted Dulcie to her feet and dragged her to the table where he placed the gun. Dulcie stared at it as he spun her around and slid a pocketknife between her hands. The zip tie slipped free. Blood rushed to her fingertips and immediately burned. Sharp pains shot through her shoulders and she shrugged them, forcing cramped muscles to move.

All the while, she kept her gaze on the gun. But she needn't have bothered. With her hands and arms numb, she couldn't grasp it even if Carson gave her the chance. But her moment would come. One way or another, she would set these girls free.

Her captor punched a hole in the plastic wrapping around the water bottles and pulled the tops off the boxes of granola bars. He shoved them at Dulcie. "Hand these out."

She obeyed even though her hands could barely grasp the bottles and bars. When she finished, she sat down with her own bottle of water and a granola bar. She could hardly force the food down but she didn't know when she might eat again and she needed her strength.

When she finished, she massaged her wrists. Cuts from the ties hurt like crazy, but she continued to work her wrists, trying to restore all movement. She was the healthiest and probably the strongest of the captives. If they were going to make a move, it had to come from her and she promised herself she would be ready.

Carson crossed to the cabinets, pulled a large old-fashioned transistor radio off the counter and returned to the table, where he placed the gun beside him once again. Then he began to fiddle with the radio's dials. Static filled the air. It was just the sound Dulcie needed to cover her movement as she sidled closer to the table.

The roads were so slick, Austin slowed to a crawl. He'd lost track of time during his efforts to get back on the road and the storm had knocked out all cell reception. All he knew for sure was that Benally and Carson were ahead of him. He prayed his sturdy home, with its high windows and strong doors would keep them out, keep Dulcie safe until he could get there. He even prayed that the storm would get worse, prevent them from reaching her. But as he arrived at the turnoff to his drive, the tire tracks leading up the dirt road told him the two men had traveled over it. He pulled into his yard, stopping where their tracks ended, and stared at his wooden door as it swung back and forth in the wind. Snow was piled on the tile of his entryway.

Demoralized, he climbed out of his cab and stomped through the almost knee-high snow. All of his efforts were for nothing. They'd blown away the lock of the door like it was paper. The lights were still on. The fire had burned to embers and Dulcie was gone. Her computer and files were missing too.

All of his fears settled over him like a frigid blanket. He had no idea where to go…where to look. She would disappear into the network they had been operating right under his nose. He'd failed…again.

He slumped to the stone hearth and hung his head. He should have known he would fail. All he'd ever wanted was to help people, to make a difference. And yet, he could not even save the most important women in his life. He was no hero. Never had been. The hope that had sprung to life inside him, the wish that maybe this time, he could make a difference, sputtered out and died. All of Dulcie's words about God's grace and the riches waiting for them were just words. If God existed, He was the same uncaring, unresponsive Creator Austin had come to know. He gripped his head as tears filled his eyes.

Dulcie didn't deserve this. She shouldn't have put her trust in him. But she had.

The words spilled out of him before he could stop them. "Lord, if You're out there. Help me help her. Don't let her be another victim."

No answering words came to him. No voice in the wilderness gave him courage. Shaking his head in disgust, he jerked off his hat and tossed it onto the sofa where it landed with a whoosh.

The edge of the cushion where his hat rested was tilted up, caught on its neighbor. He bent lower. Tucked beneath was a piece of paper, which he jerked free. It was a page from Dulcie's notepad with the words *Pierce's properties* at the top and two addresses below. Was this the connection Dulcie had been searching for, the places where the ring hid the kidnapped women? Inspiration struck and he pulled out his phone. He still had no reception but that last call he'd received had been from Dulcie. He was certain she'd called to tell him of her discovery but she was cut off. Still…she'd had enough presence of mind to hide this note from her captors. Hope and pride surged to life inside Austin.

If Pierce was the leader of the gang, then Benally and Carson were most certainly headed his way for help. If they all wanted to escape, their only option was to go through Silverton where they could wait out the storm and then go over the pass to Ouray. That had to be the direction they had taken…the place where he'd find Dulcie!

Austin strode to his broken door. After dragging a kitchen chair behind him, he secured the portal against the wind. Then ran through the stinging snow to his Jeep. The engine turned over. Austin said another silent *Thank You*. He wasn't sure if he was praying or if God would even answer. He only knew he was thankful. He spun the vehicle around and headed for the road.

Travel was slow going. Every mile was a struggle and with each one he gave thanks for getting another step closer to Dulcie. After what seemed like an hour, he saw the flashing lights of the police department's blockade on the other side of the road. They were stopping anyone from traveling down the mountain. But there was no blockade on his side. He was free to move forward. He hesitated for one moment, wondering if he should alert them. But his uncle's words about Pierce's connection to the local police department floated through his mind. Pierce had a strong influence in this small community. Austin didn't know how strong or how deep that influence went with the police. He couldn't trust them. He drove on, determined to reach the location of the closest cabin. If he didn't find her there, he'd go to the next and search until he did.

He drove through the almost empty streets of Silverton. Only a few cars were out and about. Just beyond the outskirts of the small mining town turned tourist-and-artist haven, Austin slowed. The road to the first cabin was close but it was difficult to find it when it was covered with at least three feet of snow. He had no cell phone reception to check his GPS but he had a map in his glove compartment. He could find it on the map, backtrack and estimate his mileage if necessary. He traveled a few more miles down the road until finally, afraid he'd missed the turnoff, he pulled to the side.

The storm had created a whiteout. Few people were driving but if he stopped, he could not be seen and might be hit. He needed to pull far off the road to check his map. He eased close to a pine, its branches laden with snow, and reached for the map.

Deep in the forest in front of him, headlights flashed. He paused and squinted through the trees. A white truck twisted and turned down a side road right before his eyes. He punched the switch on his lights off and watched in amazement as the vehicle crossed in front of him. He leaned forward, squinting through the blinding snow. Sure enough, the front fender of the truck was crushed on the right side…the side that had been used to push him off the road. He couldn't see the face of the driver but there was only one man in the cab.

Stunned, Austin leaned against the seat as amazement filtered through him. His descent down the hill… halting abruptly in a ditch before he went over the cliff, his Jeep's engine starting again, backing out and climbing onto the road. The paper beneath the cushion and now…one of Dulcie's kidnappers showing him the road to her location. Too many accidents. Too many perfectly shaped events to be coincidences. Was it possible God's hand had been with him all along?

The vehicle's driver paused at the road and turned onto the highway, driving right past Austin without even slowing. He never saw Austin parked to the side.

No way were these coincidences. God was guiding him…had been guiding him every step of the way. Emotions he couldn't describe swept through him. All he could do was raise his gaze to the heavens.

"I'm sorry. I was wrong. I don't deserve Your forgiving grace but thank You for leading me to her."

He jammed the gear into Reverse, backed out and turned down the road. Keeping to the tracks left by the SUV gave him traction on the winding path. Always conscious of the minutes ticking by, Austin leaned into the steering wheel as if he could push the vehicle to go faster.

At long last, he glimpsed light through the trees. Hopefully, the howling storm wind would mask the sound of his Jeep. Still, he stopped far away and killed the engine. He could barely make out the frame of a window in a decrepit old cabin. Smoke curled up from the chimney and swirled in the windy gusts. He popped the Jeep's door open and the smell of wood smoke drifted toward him. The wind caught the door and pulled it wide with such force, it slammed back against his shoulder. He turned away from the biting, icy pellets trying to shred his face. After easing the car door closed, he turned and trudged through the woods toward the cabin. He stopped behind a tree for a long moment, trying to decide what to do next.

The cabin appeared to have only one way in. He had no idea how many men might be inside. He prayed Carson and Benally hadn't been joined by others from Pierce's group. Thankfully, one man had driven away in the truck. A thought struck him. The missing man might be his way to get in. He pulled out his gun, checked his ammunition and moved forward.

He skirted the clearing in front so he could cross to the side of the building. Once there, he ducked around the corner and leaned into the cover of the building to escape the stinging snow.

Hopefully, the wind would be his friend. He took a deep breath and shouted into the gusts. "I need help out here."

His ploy worked. The wind picked up the sound of his voice and muffled it until it was barely audible. He held his breath and waited. Had they heard his cry for help inside? Did he need to say it again?

Just as he took another breath to shout again, the door swung open. A square of golden light spilled out onto the snow but no shadow covered it. Whoever opened the door was being cautious and stood to the side. Austin groaned loud enough to carry over the wind and waited. After a long while, the shadow of a man edged out from behind the wall…a dark gun was in his hand, clearly etched in the snow.

What should I do? Rush him? Or wait for him to

step out? Austin's whole body tensed and his pulse pounded in his temples. If he waited much longer, the man would grow suspicious and close the door again.

The shadow leaned farther out. Austin could tell by the movement of his dusky head that he was searching the line of trees in front of the cabin. Suddenly, a black object hit the man in the back of the head. He jerked and moaned then collapsed on the threshold. The object landed in the snow outside the door. It was an old-fashioned transistor radio.

Austin studied the lumpy shadow. No one ran to the man's aid so Austin cautiously stepped out from behind the corner of the building. Bob Carson lay unconscious on the ground, half in the door and half out. His gun had fallen free from his lifeless fingers. Austin ran to the door, kicked the small pistol into the snow behind him and lunged into the cabin, his revolver poised in front of him.

Five frightened women, clinging to each other, stared at him from across the room. Dulcie stood beside a table a few feet away from them, her face drained of color.

"Austin! You're alive!"

TEN

Austin stood before her. She couldn't move. Couldn't say another word. Then he shoved his gun back into his shoulder holster. In two steps he was in front of her, his arms around her, binding her close to him. He felt very much alive. She couldn't quite believe it.

Reaching up, she touched his cold cheeks. "They told me you were dead."

"Not yet. Thanks be to God." He pulled her head down and buried his face in her hair. "And thanks to you. I found your note under the cushion."

She smiled. "I should have known you were alive. God would not have given you to me only to snatch you away."

He stared at her. His blue eyes dragged over her features as if he were memorizing them. At long last his gaze met hers. "I don't understand the strength of your faith. But I want to. There's so much I want to understand, but there's no time. Benally could return any moment. We have to get these women…" He paused and studied the group still huddled on the floor. "All of these women into my Jeep and get out of here before he returns." He paused. "Is that Susan Yazzie?"

"Yes, they've been holding her since Judy was murdered, holding all of them, moving them between the cabins here in Silverton. They knew we were looking for them." She grasped his upper arms. "Pierce is their leader, Austin. I heard Benally and Carson talking. Benally is on his way to Pierce now to get a vehicle large enough to transport all of us once the storm clears. They know we exposed their operation and they're running!" She hugged him tight. "We did it, Austin! We broke the ring."

He didn't seem to share her enthusiasm. He gave a quick shake of his head. "All that means right now is that Pierce and his men are more desperate than ever. We have to get away from here...someplace where we will all be safe until McGuire can get up here with reinforcements."

"Can't we go to the local police?"

"Not yet. Not until I can get word to McGuire about Pierce's connection. I don't know who he might be controlling in the local force."

Fear that had spilled out of her at the sight of Austin crept back in. "Where can we hide until then? Susan is hurt and all of them are weak. They need food and water and most of all a warm place."

"I think I have an idea. We just have to reach my uncle's house. Come on. Help me move Carson inside."

They hurried to where the man lay and dragged him inside. "Let's lift him into the chair. I want to secure him so he can't interfere while we load into my Jeep."

Dulcie helped lift the man's dead weight into the wobbly chair. For a moment Dulcie thought it would collapse beneath him. Austin had to reach out and prop him up. He looked around for some way to tie him up.

One woman stepped forward, holding the chain and the padlock. "Here, use these. Chain him to the wall like he did to us."

Austin studied the chain then looked up into the face of the young woman.

Dulcie said, "Her name is Katharine. She lives in Cortez and she was taken two weeks before Kutchner killed Judy."

With a grim expression and a nod, he took the chain from Katharine's hands. "It's good to meet you, Katharine."

"Trust me, I'm thrilled to meet you, Deputy Turner."

He turned back to his task and dragged Carson toward the hook in the wall. "It sounds like you all did a lot of talking before I got here." He wound the chain around Carson, looped it through the hook and locked it in place. "That's a good thing because there's no time now for talk." Finished, he looked around. "All of you wait here while I get my Jeep. None of you are dressed warm enough to walk down there."

He started for the door and trepidation filled Dulcie. She grasped his arm. "Don't leave us unprotected."

Austin shook his head. "I kicked his gun in the snow. I don't know where it is."

He covered her hand with his own. "I'll be back in moments. I promise, Dulcie. I'll be right back."

A slight smile wavered over her lips. “There you go again, instilling confidence, being the hero.”

Shaking his head, he said, “We definitely have to have a talk. The only hero around here is you.” Then he spun and hurried out the door. Dulcie pushed it closed against the wind but left it open a crack. She couldn’t bear to let him out of her sight. She braved the icy cold and stood in the opening, watching as he disappeared into the woods. She thought she heard an engine start, but it was difficult to hear over the roaring wind. Then lights flashed in the trees. Her heart leaped and she turned to the women. “Come on. He’ll be here soon. Bring the blanket.”

They hurried to her side. One of them wrapped the thin blanket around Susan’s shoulders. Another supported her good arm. Their kindness in the face of such misery and torture warmed Dulcie’s heart. One way or another, they had to get these poor souls to safety.

Austin pulled his Jeep as close to the door as possible and jumped out. Dulcie pushed the portal wide and the women piled out. Austin held the Jeep’s door open and pulled the chair forward. They climbed into the narrow backseat. Two of the smallest girls had to sit on the lap of the others. Once they were situated, he helped Susan into the front seat and slammed the door. As soon as Austin was situated, he turned up the heat. Warm air flowed into the vehicle. “Hold on. It’s going to be a rough ride.”

The first curve they took pushed Susan to her side. She banged her injured arm against the door and a small groan escaped her.

"Here, let me help." Katharine loosened the blanket, folded it into a pad and placed it between Susan's shoulder and the door. When they took the next curve, she grimaced but the pain did not seem as bad.

The road was barely visible through the sleeting snow. Several times the Jeep slid over patches of ice. Austin shook his head. "The pavement won't be much better. Maybe we can follow the tracks Benally made on his way down. Let's just hope we don't see him coming back up."

They made it into town, slipping and sliding all the way. The streets of Silverton were empty. All sensible people were safely ensconced in their homes. Austin eased to a halt at a cross-street stop sign, mainly to check the depth of the snow on the street ahead of them. No tracks crossed the path and the snow was deep. "I don't want to risk getting caught in that. I'm going to back out and try another street."

He'd just reversed the car and turned in his seat when down the road, a large black SUV passed where they had been moments ago. "Austin, look. Someone else is out driving and it's a black SUV. Do you think it's Benally returning with Pierce?"

Austin eased the vehicle back out of view. "There's one way to find out."

Leaving the vehicle running, he opened the door and hurried to the sidewalk and around the corner of the building where he peeked out. Soon he came running back. "I can't be sure, but I think Benally is driving. I don't know who the other man is and…the SUV is definitely headed to the road we just came down."

Dulcie was silent for one long minute. "Do you think they saw us?"

"No. If they saw us, Benally would have recognized my Jeep and headed our way."

"How long before they find Carson and come back down?"

"I'm not sure. I just know we have to hurry." He turned the car around and took another route to his uncle's house.

Austin's mind raced as he negotiated the dangerous Silverton roads. Black ice was everywhere, and keeping the heavily loaded Jeep clear of the drifts and patches took all of his concentration. He searched his memories, trying to remember the day Benally was arrested. Everyone at the station knew his uncle worked on the railroad. Austin frequently talked about his uncle's adventures as an engineer on the steam locomotive line. Built in the 1800s, the narrow-gauge line ran from Silverton to Durango and was one of the biggest tourist attractions of the area. Austin tried to remember his conversations from that day. Had Austin talked about his uncle and his work? Would the criminal remember and draw the connection between them?

He didn't recall his conversations for sure, but he knew he couldn't risk hiding at his uncle's home. They had to find another place, one that was warm and would shelter the women. He knew a place and hoped his uncle would agree.

At long last, he turned onto his uncle's street. The small house sat on a slight incline above the road. Austin pulled to a stop and left the engine and the heater running. Then he dashed up the hill, slipping and sliding all the way, to pound on the door. Fortunately, lights were still blazing inside. His uncle was awake and he opened it very quickly.

"Austin…what are you doing here?" Uncle Butch stood in the doorway, his gray hair mussed, his flannel shirt untucked and fuzzy wool socks poking out from beneath his jeans.

"I don't have time to explain. I have six women in my Jeep. They're all victims of a trafficking ring operating here in our area. I've just rescued them from a cabin and I need a place to hide them and my vehicle."

"Hide? Don't be crazy. Let's call the police."

"Kent Pierce is the leader of the ring, Uncle Butch. After what you said about Pierce's influence over the local police, I don't know if I can trust them. I need to hide these women until men from my station can get up here. I thought about the railroad's roundhouse."

His uncle hesitated for a moment before he nodded decisively. "It's big enough for your vehicle and it has a couple of floor heaters. We can get the women secured there."

"We'll need your truck, too. I've got the women crammed into my Jeep and one of them is injured."

His uncle turned and pulled a key ring off a rack near the door. "Get it started. It'll be cold. I need to get my shoes."

"We also need blankets and food," Austin called out as his uncle moved down the hall.

"Grab what you need out of the kitchen and load it in the truck. I'll get the blankets."

Austin hurried to the garage and started his uncle's truck. Then he pulled microwave soup cups, boxes of cereal and packaged cookies into a bag he found near the door. He snatched a container of bottled water up with one hand and headed toward the garage.

His uncle met him in the hall, his arms full of blankets and heavy towels. Nodding toward the microwave cups peeking out of the top of the bag, he said, "It's a good thing I'm widowed and have tons of microwave food lying around."

Austin grunted. "It doesn't fill me with confidence to know this is how you eat all the time."

He pushed open the garage door and held it for his uncle, who paused. "You should talk. Frozen pizza is better?"

Shaking his head, Austin nudged his chin toward the car. "We don't have time for this discussion."

They'd had this talk many times, the one where his uncle told him it was time to stop mourning, to move on with life. Celebrate Abey and all she did by living life to the fullest. His uncle had said many times how disappointed she would be with the half life Austin had been living. Before, Austin had no purpose, no reason to change...until Dulcie. Now he had everything to look forward to...if they survived the night.

"We need to move someone into your truck so we can make Susan more comfortable."

His uncle nodded. "I'll see you down there." He punched a button. The garage door lifted. Austin ran down the incline to his Jeep and opened Susan's door. "Come on. Let's get you better situated."

The young woman was weak. She struggled to get out. Finally, Austin slid one arm behind her and another beneath her legs and lifted her out. His uncle parked beside him with his truck engine running. Butch opened the door and Austin slid Susan onto the front seat. Two other girls piled into the backseat and in seconds, both vehicles were headed down the road to the railroad's roundhouse.

He told Dulcie where they were going. "Okay," she said. "But what is a roundhouse?"

"It's a huge building where they do repairs and store the engines during the winter. Back in the day, the buildings were round so they could drive the engine in and around a circle and out. That's how they got their name."

"I see…a round house with round tracks."

"Exactly. The company doesn't run excursions down the narrow-gauge rails during the winter. It's far too icy and dangerous, so they store the engines and the railcars in the roundhouse."

Dulcie nodded and leaned forward as the large building loomed ahead of them. His uncle's truck stopped. He exited his vehicle, ran in front of the headlights, unlocked the tall metal doors blackened from the smoke of the coal-driven steam engines and then hurried back to his truck. He pulled inside and Austin followed, parking on the opposite side of one massive train.

Austin jumped out to help his uncle close the sliding door. "Go get the heat going for the women. I'll lock this."

His uncle nodded, then went back to where Dulcie and the others were helping Susan out of the truck. Austin didn't like the young woman's pale features and trembling posture. He was afraid she was going into shock. Apparently, Dulcie feared the same thing. He heard her tell the other women to make a pallet for her so they could get her warm.

A small area at the back served as the break room, complete with a microwave. Uncle Butch plugged in two large floor heaters. They had things under control, so Austin went to check out the building.

Steam engines filled the tall, long and somewhat narrow roundhouse. They'd barely had room to park their vehicles on the sides of the two huge train engines. He moved past the small break area to examine the rest of the building. The old roundhouse burned down in the 1980s and had been rebuilt. Only one original brick wall remained…and it was full of four-foot-high windows. Austin stared at the wall in dismay. No way could he secure those. If Pierce and gang figured out where they were hiding, it would be easy to break through those windows. He wouldn't be able to protect the women. One man and one gun against three men, probably heavily armed. There would be bloodshed.

Austin took a deep breath. But where else could they go? All they could do was keep the lights low and stay hidden. Hopefully, Pierce and his gang would not guess their location.

He moved back to the break area. The women sat on the floor, huddled around the heaters with blankets around their shoulders. Susan lay on a pallet. Dulcie pulled a foam cup of soup out of the microwave, blew on it and began to spoon-feed the young woman. A faint smile filtered over her lips.

The sight of Dulcie doing what she did best warmed Austin's heart. An hour ago, he'd thought she was lost. But here she was ministering to other women. God was good.

She was the only one without a blanket but his uncle had found her a bright yellow workman's jacket, two sizes too big for her. It hung over her hands but she'd rolled the cuffs up, out of her way. He shook his head. She wouldn't let anything like a little freezing cold impede her efforts to help these women.

How had he been so blind? He did not recognize that she was a warrior…different from Abey, but still a fighter. A champion of everyone except herself.

Austin decided then and there that if they survived tonight, he would spend the rest of his life showing her how wonderful, strong and beautiful she was.

Please, Lord. You came to me in my hour of need. Made me see how You've held me up. Pointed the way for me. Give me one last blessing. Let me spend the rest of my life showing Dulcie how valuable she is.

She looked up and caught him watching her. A sweet, soft smile filtered over her beautiful, coral lips… lips that were so expressive. They could go thin with displeasure and harden with determination. They were lips he wanted to kiss.

And please, Lord, if it is not Your plan for us to be together, let me kiss her just once.

His uncle walked toward him. Austin dragged his

gaze away from Dulcie and nudged his chin toward the back of the building. When they had stepped away, he shook his head and kept his voice low. "I forgot about that wall with windows. They make this place indefensible."

Butch nodded. "But it's warm and safe for now and they need to rest."

Austin agreed and looked up at the rafters. A giant mechanized lift that slid back and forth was attached to the roof. A ladder led up to the arm. It was the highest point and offered the best view out the high windows across the building. "I should be able to see pretty far out the windows from up there. Call me if you need me."

Butch nodded and moved back to the women. Austin climbed the ladder to the top. Wrapping his arm under the rung, he leaned back to look out the window. He could see for several blocks over the city. Snow covered the streets in a blanket of white. Two black strips of tire tracks marked their way to the roundhouse. An easy trail to follow if Pierce and his gang saw them. What would he do if they found them?

For the second time that night, Austin hit a blank wall. No ideas came to him. He didn't know what their next step would be.

He inhaled and clung to his rediscovered faith. The Lord had pointed the way once. He would do it again.

Time passed. Austin could hear the women quietly talking, his uncle's low voice and the soft laughter of the women. Leave it to his uncle to lighten their hearts. Uncle Butch told them how the road from Durango through Silverton to Ouray was called the Million Dollar Highway because it cost a million dollars to build at the turn of the century. Others said they called it that because of the million dollars' worth of discarded gold ore that went into the dirt used in the road's building. Butch told them how, at times, the highway paralleled the narrow-gauge tracks and in weather like this, the tracks were safer.

Austin smiled with the women. He'd never appreciated his uncle more than tonight, when he'd jumped into danger without a second thought and tried to make these desperate women comfortable.

Austin's arm, clinging to the rung, was getting tired. He needed to climb down and rest for a while. Conserve his strength. He was about to begin his descent when the flash of faraway headlights caught his gaze.

He froze and watched as the lights flashed again, pointing straight down the cross street of the roundhouse's location. Austin's pulse pounded in his temples. Adrenaline surged through him as a black SUV turned down their street.

Kicked into gear, he clamored down the ladder and ran to the women. His uncle and Dulcie looked up. The fear must have shown on his face because his uncle came to where he stood in the shadows outside the circle. Dulcie followed close behind him.

"They've found us." He couldn't keep the stress out of his tone. "Is there someplace in this building with no windows where we can secure the women?"

"I think I know a way to get us out." Uncle Butch gestured them to follow him to a small yellow engine about twelve feet long. "This is a speeder. They use it to get to the Tacoma power plant. It's in here for repair, but I got it running yesterday. It's in tip-top shape."

"How does that help us?" The speeder had sliding doors and a small enclosed area behind the driver's seat. Outside the speeder on the back was a wide bar with a narrow platform. A small basket-trailer for equipment was hitched behind it.

"I think we can get all the women inside and drive the speeder. There's no road to the plant. They can't get there by car. Just railway tracks over a bridge and five more miles up the snow-covered mountain. They'll never make it by foot in this wind and snow. The building is warm and secure so we can hold out there until the storm passes."

Austin eyed the speeder. "Do you really think we can get all the women inside?"

"It'll be a tight squeeze, but what other choice do we have?"

Austin didn't have an answer for that.

His uncle went on. "There's just two problems. There's a stretch of open, flat meadow before we hit the bridge that crosses the river. Those men could follow the road above and maybe catch us before we get there. The speeder doesn't travel very fast. But the second issue is the bigger problem." His uncle paused.

Austin eyed his silent relative. "What's that?"

"You've got to open the doors, let the speeder get through and hopefully jump on the back. I can build up steam and get us out the door quickly, but you might find it difficult to hop on…and someone else could get on with you."

Austin studied the giant doors of the building and the small bar at the back of the speeder. He wrapped his hand around it. The black metal was just the right size for his grip. The metal platform at the bottom wasn't even wide enough for his feet. But he could manage.

"Let's do it."

Dulcie gasped. "Austin, you can't! Even if you get on, you'll be an easy target for those men and their guns. They could shoot you!"

"I don't think they will risk a shot this close in town where citizens might hear. So far, they've tried to keep all of this under the radar."

"Then let's call the police. If they don't want their presence known, they must be trying to avoid the authorities. That means it's safe to call them."

Austin shook his head. "You saw how Deputy Shaw disrupted the proper order of operations. It only takes one bad egg to send files missing or to release prisoners. We can't risk something like that happening." She started to protest but he grasped her arms and said, "You are witnesses and our only real evidence. Do you want these men to go free to do this again?" He shook his head. "We've got to get you out of here now." He turned to Butch. "Let's get them loaded and take as much blankets and food as we can carry. We don't know how long this storm will last."

Dulcie stepped close and grabbed the lapels of his jacket. "Austin…please don't do this."

He gripped her hands. They were cold. Her eyes were wide and her amazing lips were so close…and they trembled. He wanted to bend down and kiss her.

A loud bang at the back of the building made them both jerk.

Austin pushed her toward the group of women. "They're trying the back doors. In minutes they'll find those windows. Get moving!"

The women were loaded into the speeder. Katharine held Susan's arm and led her while the others carried the bags of food, water and the blankets. Butch was right. It was a tight squeeze but they managed to fit everyone in with spots for Dulcie and Austin. But she waited outside for him.

Butch gathered enough steam and released the brake. The engine crawled along the tracks to the tall doors. Austin met Dulcie and they walked behind the slow-moving vehicle.

His uncle leaned out of the open window on the driver's side. "Give me a few minutes to build up speed. I'll punch it the minute the door is wide enough. You let go of that door and grab on. I don't plan to lose you, nephew. You hear me?"

Austin gave him the thumbs-up sign. Dulcie reached for him. He grasped her hand and pulled his gun out of his holster and placed it in her open palm. "I want you to take this."

She shook her head. "I can't. I don't know what to do with it."

He pointed to the lock. "Flip this open. It's the safety. Then point and pull the trigger. You probably won't hit anything, but you'll scare them."

"I can't, Austin. I'm afraid of guns. I'll freeze up again." She gave another shake of her head.

"Take it. If these men find a way to get to the power plant and I'm not there, Uncle Butch will need it."

Her lips parted. Now. Now was the time for the kiss he'd been wanting since that first night in her apartment when she walked in with her wild hair, distinctive brows and sensitive mouth. He ran his hand over her soft curls, gripped her head and pulled her close...

Glass shattered at the back of the building.

They were in!

He shoved Dulcie toward the speeder and ran past his uncle to the front of the building.

"They're here. Go!"

His uncle nodded. Austin reached the large metal sliding doors and looked back. Dulcie had climbed in. He unlocked the door and shoved it wide. His uncle nodded again and released the brake. The speeder shot forward. Austin stepped close as it moved past him. He grasped the black metal bar. It jerked him off his feet and dragged him as the speeder moved out of the building. It was still slow enough he was able to gain his footing. He hopped, trying to jump on the narrow platform. Just as the speeder took off, he gained footing on the back and pulled himself up.

Then he heard a shout. Carson ran toward them from the back of the building. Obviously Pierce and Benally found him at the cabin and set him free. Austin kicked him away, but he grabbed the basket at the back and tumbled into it.

Dulcie caught her breath as Carson tumbled into the flat basket attached to the speeder. Carson recovered quickly from his side tumble into the carrier and struggled to come to his knees. The basket wouldn't support the weight of the man so it dipped and swayed. He lost his balance several times. That gave Austin time to react. He bent behind the back of the speeder, out of Dulcie's vision.

All the women were turned, looking out the window. "He's pulling pins from the bar attached to the trailer." Waves of relief swept through Dulcie at Katharine's announcement.

Carson reacted too. Balancing on one knee, he lunged forward and snatched at Austin as he leaned over. Carson's growled shout echoed over the noise of the speeder engine and the women screamed.

Austin jerked back, pin in hand. Carson cried out in surprise as the basket carrier fell away. The connecting bar hit the tracks and tipped the carrier end over end, sending the man flying. He bounced, landed flat and didn't move as the speeder rushed down the tracks.

A collective sigh of relief flowed through the small cabin. Austin gave them a thumbs-up through the back window. But Dulcie wasn't satisfied. The storm still raged. Sleet bit into Austin's face and hands. He had to be freezing. She wanted…needed him inside with the rest of them. She faced the front as the speeder pulled away from the rail yard. They were still too close to the road but there had to be a wide, safe spot to stop so Austin could climb inside.

They all watched the railroad yard fall farther and farther behind. Dulcie thought they might make a safe getaway. Then she saw men run from the building and the black SUV pull onto the street, headlights flashing along the empty road.

She leaned toward Butch. "They just got into their car and drove away. Can they follow us?"

He nodded. "The highway runs on that flat space above us."

Dulcie glanced up the rocky cliff. A wide swath was cut out of the rock, wide enough for a two-lane highway. "But you said they couldn't reach us at the power plant. Where do the tracks pull away from the highway?"

He nudged his chin ahead. "Look up there, where that rocky hill crosses the tracks."

The tracks ran right through the middle of an outcropping with large boulders piled high on each side. "Just beyond that, a bridge crosses the Animas River. From there we're safely on the other side of the river away from the road."

She glanced back. Austin still gripped the bar, his features set as he ducked his head away from the flurry of icy snow striking his face. "Can't you go any faster? He's freezing."

"This is as fast as this little engine can take us. Austin's strong. He can hang on a little longer."

Yes, but could she? She relied on Austin. Counted on him. Needed him to lift her spirits, to give her courage and hope. She even had thoughts of staying in his house and filling the walls with beautiful treasures. She'd dared to dream of making it a home.

She loved Austin. Not just counted on him. Loved him. She had feelings for him from the moment she'd met him. For the first time in her life, she'd eased back on the throttle of energy and devotion that drove her to protect, to keep everyone and everything within her reach safe. She thought of the future, of what life could be like without the constant threat of loss or danger and she wanted it. Riding in the speeder with death so close behind them, Austin needed her help, and once again, she could do nothing.

The gun felt heavy in her hands. Abey would have known how to use it, wouldn't have hesitated to step forward to protect Austin. But it sat cold, heavy and deadly in Dulcie's hands.

She shook her head in frustration and looked ahead. The outcropping of rocks was only a few feet ahead. Butch said once they were past it, they would be free.

Please, Lord. Push us beyond those rocks.

They entered the narrow gap between the rocky boulders and were almost through it when a dark figure leaped from the side of the outcropping and lunged across the space. The women screamed but Dulcie lost her breath. The familiar paralysis of fear crept over her. She stood transfixed as the figure missed his footing on the speeder but latched on to Austin. The two of them struggled for a few moments. Austin punched and pushed to free himself, but the man hung on. Finally, unable to sustain his grip with the man dragging him down, Austin lost his hold and they both tumbled away, rolling through the snow.

The man was the first to gain his footing and marched toward Austin's prone figure. Dulcie recognized the determined features of Walter Benally. He grasped Austin by the coat, jerked him up and swung. His meaty fist connected with Austin's jaw. His head spun. Even in the dark, Dulcie saw blood spatter across the pristine snow.

Benally had the advantage of surprise and weight against Austin. Benally punched him again. Austin appeared almost senseless from the blows. Now he hung like a dead weight from Benally's grip on his coat. Austin needed help. But Dulcie stood in helpless, frozen fear, the gun in her hand.

The gun. She had the means to help Austin…if only she could move.

Benally struck another blow. Dulcie whimpered with pain. Austin needed her. She had to move…had to do something.

And that he might make known the riches of his glory on the vessels of mercy, which he had afore prepared unto glory.

Dulcie wanted the riches promised to her. She wanted the chance of a future with Austin. She wanted to claim the Lord's promise. A tingling started in her fingertips. Warmth built until a heated wave swept through her. Frozen lips parted and she screamed, "Stop!"

Her cry pierced the speeder. Butch jumped and turned to her.

"Stop and let me off."

He pulled the brake and the little speeder slammed to a halt. Dulcie pushed the sliding door open, hopped out into the knee-deep snow. "Get these women to safety!"

She slammed the door shut with a strength she didn't know she had. Slogging through the snow, she headed back to where Austin and Benally struggled.

Austin seemed to have regained his senses. Benally straddled over him but Austin swung his leg out with enough force to send Benally sprawling. Austin lay there for one long moment before climbing to his feet and striding toward Benally's prone figure. The older man fought his way out of a deep drift. Austin reached him and landed a punch to the man's exposed jaw. Benally fell facedown but lunged out of the drift and tackled Austin. Both men rolled across the tracks. Benally cried out as his shoulder caught one iron bar. But they continued to roll through the snow, close to the edge of the tracks and the narrow path they created along the mountain wall. For the first time, Dulcie heard the roar of rushing water and realized the icy Animas River was below the edge of the outcropping…the edge Austin and Benally were still rolling toward.

Austin finally broke free. Stumbling forward, he reached for Benally. The man, unsteady on his feet, took a wide swing. Austin blocked it with his arm and punched with his right hand. Benally stumbled backward toward the edge.

His arms swung wide as his foot hit empty air. Austin jumped and lunged, reaching, trying to capture Benally's arm. But he missed. Benally fell with a cry that echoed over the stormy wind.

Dulcie caught her breath and stopped. She stood on

the tracks, stunned, still far away from Austin as he leaned precariously over the edge.

A shot rang out, piercing the snow in a puffy flurry not five feet away from Austin. Dulcie looked up. A man with a long dress coat flapping around his legs stood above on the rocky outcropping of the highway. From her angle, Dulcie could see the black SUV, parked close to the edge. Smoke billowed out behind it. The engine was still running but the lights were off. They had raced along the road with no headlights so they could reach the outcropping undetected. That's how they'd beaten them to this point and how Benally had climbed down and lain in wait for Austin.

The man standing above them had to be Pierce. Even now he looked like the consummate businessman, not an assailant, taking aim again.

Austin was close to the edge of the cliff. Too close… and defenseless. She held his gun in her hand.

Austin ran for the protection of the boulders but he would never make it across the open space. Pierce fired another shot. This one hit the snow a few feet in front of Austin. The next shot would be closer.

Dulcie lifted the gun. Austin's words rang in her head. *Flip this open. It's the safety. Then point and pull the trigger. You probably won't hit anything, but you'll scare them.*

She braced her wrist, pointed and pulled. The shot echoed above the whine of the wind. The bullet went wide and hit the rocks below Pierce. The man jerked in surprise. Apparently, he had not seen Dulcie until that moment. She aimed and fired once more. The bullet pinged against the rocks. She fired again. Another ringing ricochet echoed over the icy wind. She fired one more time.

How many bullets did this gun hold? If she kept firing, would Austin make it to the safety of the rocks? What if she ran out of bullets and Pierce turned his aim on her? She stood out in the open with no protection.

It didn't matter if she was shot. Austin would be safe.

She pulled the trigger again and again. This time sparks flashed as the bullets hit the rocks closer and closer to Pierce, so close, the man dropped his gun, spun and ran for the car.

Now that Dulcie was firing, she couldn't stop. She pulled the trigger one more time. The bullet pinged on the rocks. The lights on the SUV switched on. Dulcie pulled the trigger and the gun clicked…out of bullets. The engine of the SUV revved and Pierce screeched away from the outcropping.

The man who had harmed and destroyed so many women couldn't face his own risks.

Dulcie continued to pull the trigger even though the gun was out of bullets, and the SUV's headlights flashed along the rocky cliff headed back to town.

At long last, her gut reaction to fight back eased. She took a deep breath, dropped the gun to the rocky dirt beside the tracks and wiped her hands on her pants.

Austin marched toward her, purpose and intent in every step. As he drew closer, she saw his chin and cheek were bright red, scraped and bleeding.

"Are you all…"

He grasped her head, wound his fingers through her hair and pulled her toward him. His cold lips covered hers. They were firm, demanding, needy. They took everything from her…even her breath. She felt lightheaded, weak. When she thought she couldn't give anymore, he broke the kiss.

Dulcie gasped for air and inhaled his soap-and-leather scent, the familiar scent that always sparked thoughts of warmth and comfort. She'd barely caught her breath when he tilted her head the other way and kissed her again. This time, his lips were soft, gentle, full of wonder as they shaped to hers, feeling their contours and depth. It was a loving kiss, one full of beauty and possession…a kiss of love.

When he finally released her, she stared into a gaze so full of tenderness, it took her breath away again.

Could it be? Was that love she saw in his eyes? Was it possible?

He gave a small shake of his head and his voice was low. "I promised myself if we lived through this, that would be the first thing I did."

She stared at him, his words barely penetrating the surprise filtering through her. "You…you wanted to kiss me like that?"

He nodded. "From the first minute you walked into your front room with your hair down."

"But you never…"

"I know. I fought every thought, every one of my natural needs. I even fought when the Lord told me to move forward. I was an idiot."

He lifted her head with a finger. "Almost as foolish as you, standing out here in the wide open, taking potshots at Pierce. Don't you know he could have killed you?"

She shook her head. "It didn't matter. You needed help."

He stopped the shake of her head with a firm but tender grasp. "And that, my foolish, brave girl, is why I love you. That's the most courageous thing I've ever seen."

His words jumbled in her head. Foolish. Brave. Courageous. Only one word clicked and had true meaning.

"You…you love me?"

"With all my heart, Dulcie Parker. Can you forgive me for being so blind, for not listening, for being prideful and angry and determined not to see and hear the signs the Lord sent to me?"

Once again, his words jumbled in her mind. "Signs? What signs?"

"You and your fierce, stubborn protection of the defenseless. Your determination to fight all your fears. You're a warrior woman in your own way."

"No…no, don't call me that. I'm nothing like Abey. Nothing. She was amazing."

He smoothed a hand over her wild, snow-dampened curls and shook his head. "Even in that you are wonderful. All the things I shared about Abey, all the ways I made her a star in my own mind…any other woman would have been jealous."

"I was." She ducked her head. "I am."

Tucking his thumbs beneath her chin, he lifted till her gaze met his once more. "Even in this you are incredible. You fight those feelings of envy with admiration. You could be angry or resentful but instead, you praise her and care about her memory. You value her strengths without ever recognizing that you have them too. You need to admire those traits in yourself, my lovely warrior."

She shivered as the truth of his words swept through her. This time she grasped his face and pulled his lips down to hers. This kiss was tentative, explorative… as if she didn't have the right to do it. But she grew bolder and kissed him as if he was hers. At last they broke off again.

Dulcie leaned her forehead against his. "Truth be told, I've wanted to kiss you from the first moment I saw that dimple in your chin. That's the only truth I know and I'm so glad you awakened those feelings in me."

Her words ended in a cold shiver.

"Trust me—I can't wait to explore those feelings. But first, we have to survive. We're three miles from town in the middle of a raging storm without transportation."

Dulcie shivered again and looked around at the empty path of the tracks that disappeared around a bend.

"What about Benally's body?"

"He won't bother us anymore. Come on. Let's go find our friends."

ELEVEN

Dulcie huddled close to Austin. They leaned into the wind and walked down the tracks in the direction the speeder had gone. Now that the danger was over, Dulcie felt the cold more than ever. They reached the outcropping and looked ahead. A narrow bridge crossed the river. On the other side sat the bright yellow speeder. Dulcie had never been happier to see anything… Well, maybe only a living Austin as he stood in the cabin door when she believed he was dead.

Grasping her hand, Austin tugged her forward and they ran across the bridge.

Butch threw the sliding door open. "I knew she'd save you."

As Austin helped Dulcie inside, the look he gave her warmed her body all the way through. "She saved me all right…in more ways than one."

As soon as Austin slid the door shut, Butch gunned the speeder and the pointed metal front plowed through the snow-covered tracks. They traveled more miles before a large brick building appeared in the distance.

Butch pointed to it. "They built the Tacoma power plant in 1905. I go there pretty regularly. I'm in charge of their speeder so I have my own keys to the facility. The main room hasn't many amenities but there's a control room that's nice and warm and I know for a fact, it has a microwave." Butch winked and the women laughed. Dulcie didn't know him very well but she was already beginning to love Austin's uncle Butch. She was certain they would be good friends.

He drove the speeder into a covered garage-type shed and they trudged through the knee-deep snow to the main building. Butch unlocked the doors and led the way upstairs to a narrow control room with complicated dials and monitors along one wall. On the opposite wall was a long desk below windows that looked across the river for a good view of the empty road.

They found the microwave and heated cups of soup for the women. Then they all settled on the floor next to each other and appreciated the warm room.

Austin ran a check of the building one more time before easing down to the ground next to Dulcie and leaning his back against the wall.

"I thought you'd be asleep by the time I got back."

She smiled at him and dropped her head on his shoulder. "I can't. My mind is spinning."

"What are you thinking about? I'm sure we're safe for now. Pierce and whoever is left in his gang are probably scrambling to find a way out of Silverton."

"I wasn't thinking about them. I was thinking… well…where do we go from here? What's next?"

He linked his fingers through hers and studied their

clasped hands. "There'll be a trial. Your agency will lose your leader."

She smiled. "I know all that. I'm not worried about the shelter or my work."

He leaned out slightly and gave her a look. "What's this? You're not worrying about someone else for a change?"

She squeezed his fingers. "No, I'm not. My work will not change, but I will. I don't want my life to go back to the way it was."

Lifting their clinched hands, he kissed the back of hers. "I think we both feel the same way."

She nodded. "I hoped so, but how do we change, Austin? Where do we begin?"

He let his head fall back against the wall and heaved a sigh. "I have no idea."

"Well, I know exactly what I want. I'm going back to visit Bea Yazzie at her hogan. I want to learn all about Navajo weavers."

She could feel his gaze on her but he didn't speak and she didn't dare meet his gaze. Would he agree or turn away from the path she could see so clearly ahead of her? Would their relationship be over before it even began?

At last she gained the courage to face him. "Will you go with me to visit her, Austin?"

A slow, sweet smile eased over his lips. "I would be honored." He kissed their clasped hands again.

She took a gradual, deep breath. "Would you do one more thing for me?"

A frown creased his brow. "If I can."

"Would you dig out the Navajo rug Abey's grandmother made and hang it on the wall below your front room windows?"

His smile faded. He was silent for a long, heart-stopping moment. Finally, he dipped his head. When he spoke, his voice was low. "It's time. I'll do it. But only if you'll help me. I'm not very good at hanging things."

Joy filled Dulcie's heart. She leaned in, kissed him again, then nestled her head in the crook of his neck. Safe in the shelter of his arms, she fell asleep.

When she woke, bright sunlight was flowing through the control-room windows. The storm had passed and the women were stirring. Butch was already up and had warmed soup in the microwave and passed out packages of fruit-and-nut bars.

Suddenly, Katharine rose to her feet and pointed across the river. "Look!"

A caravan of county patrol cars, blue lights flashing, followed a snowplow down the road to Silverton. All the women except Susan stood and cheered. Within minutes they were packed and loaded back into the speeder. It took time for the speeder's engine to heat up, but soon they were on the tracks headed to the engine roundhouse. When they were on the outskirts of town, cell phone reception returned to Austin's phone and he dialed McGuire.

"Am I glad to hear your voice." His supervisor's gruff tone echoed over the phone and throughout the speeder. "Where are you?"

Austin explained their situation and Pierce's involvement.

"Don't worry about him. I'll send men to his place and will keep the roadblocks in place. We'll get him. You just get yourself safely to the roundhouse."

Dulcie looked around at the women. Relief filled their features and brought tears to their eyes.

When Butch pulled the speeder into the open area of the railyard, flashing blue-and-red lights were everywhere. Ambulances, fire vehicles and police cars were all waiting to greet them. Dulcie even thought she recognized FBI agents in dark coats. The place was swarming.

Austin was the first one out of the speeder. McGuire rushed across the space and pulled him into a pounding embrace. "It's good to see you."

"It's good to be here. We almost didn't make it."

McGuire nodded. "It was a close call all the way around...for Cade, as well. But I'm happy to report he came out of surgery and doctors expect a full recovery. In addition, my men found Carson unconscious in the yard here. He's in one of those ambulances and... we already have Pierce in custody. They just stopped him at a roadblock."

"That's great news on both accounts." Austin nudged his chin behind them. "Walter Benally's back there at the bottom of a cliff. I'll give you directions."

"We'll take care of him." McGuire nodded to another officer and the man turned away to follow McGuire's unspoken order.

An ambulance driver tried to help Susan out of the speeder but she grasped Dulcie's hand as she passed. "I'm not going without you."

Dulcie sent a questioning glance at Austin.

He nodded. “It’s okay. Go with her. Those cuts on your wrist need attention.”

“I’m not going without you either.”

McGuire stepped forward. “That’s no problem. He’s going to the hospital too. He looks like he took a pretty solid beating.”

Austin grinned and grasped Dulcie’s hand. “That’s fine with me. I won’t be letting this woman out of my sight for a long time to come.” He paused and looked deep into her eyes. “Maybe ever.”

Dulcie cupped the uninjured side of his face and pulled him down for another kiss.

* * * * *